BECOMING
Mia

Wendy Teller

a novel of self-discovery
in the turbulent 1960s

WENDY TELLER

WENDY TELLER

Copyright 2018 by Wendy Teller
All Rights Reserved

ISBN 978-1-7321280-0-2
Printed in the United States of America

Credits
Cover Design: Richard F. Weyand.
Cover Photo: SrdjanPav; rights purchased through iStock.
"For Anne Gregory" by W. B. Yeats; public domain.
"Bill Grogan's Goat," author unknown; public domain.
"On Walden Pond" by Henry David Thoreau; public domain.
"Dover Beach" by Matthew Arnold; public domain.

WA

Published by Weyand Associates, Inc.
Bloomington, Indiana, USA
May, 2018

www.weyandassociates.com

This is a work of fiction. Names, characters, businesses, places, events, locales, and incidents are either the products of the author's imagination or used in a fictitious manner. Any resemblance to actual persons, living or dead, or actual events is purely coincidental.

WENDY TELLER

"It is easier to live through someone else than to complete yourself. The freedom to lead and plan your own life is frightening if you have never faced it before. It is frightening when a woman finally realizes that there is no answer to the question 'who am I' except the voice inside herself."
— Betty Friedan

". . . the self is not something one finds, it is something one creates."
— Thomas Szasz

WENDY TELLER

Freshman Year
September 1964 to June 1965

Chapter One

Mia paused on the porch and took a deep breath before opening the door.

Gina had insisted she come to this party, the last hurrah before their high school gang dispersed for college. She'd said the music would be great. Gina would be singing duets with her dad, always a treat, and there would be other singers, maybe even Pete Seeger.

When Mia peered in the front door, Gina ran over to her. She wanted Mia to meet someone special. She took Mia's arm, leading her through the crowded room, thick with acrid cigarette smoke. The woman stood in the far corner of the living room, straight-backed, surveying the crowd. She was 50ish and stylish in a bohemian kind of way: flowing muted batiks, sturdy leather sandals, jangling bracelets on both wrists, graying Afro.

Gina started the introduction. "This is Mia, Daniel Brower's daughter."

The haughty woman's flinty eyes widened, her lips compressed into a deep frown. "A man like that shouldn't be allowed to have children."

Mia gritted her teeth and stared at Gina.

Gina's attempt to suppress a grin failed. Her eyes glinted. Mia swallowed, turned, and walked away, slowly, precisely, with her head high, her back straight.

She had thought Gina was her friend, but Gina had changed since she started seeing Harry. Harry was older, at least 20, always wearing red suspenders, carrying his copy of *Das*

Kapital, reading from it in his native German and rendering translations.

As Mia stepped into the chilly night, she collided with Nick.

"Hey, you leaving?" Nick looked confused.

"Seems Brower's daughter is not wanted at this gathering."

"What?"

"Nick, never mind. I don't feel welcome here, so I think I'll go elsewhere."

"Want company?"

"No, Nick." Nick had been paying her more attention ever since Harry had arrived. "You go and have a good time."

Nick hesitated for a moment, but then headed into the party.

Mia slid into the car and drove across the Berkeley flatlands, the poorer section of town.

Only two weeks until she left for Harvard. She couldn't wait. Harvard would have people who understood her. She hadn't fit in at Berkeley High. There were the social clubbers, the girls wearing Capezio flats and Lanz dresses, gossiping about who was dating whom, having parties every weekend, parties that provided subjects worthy of hushed whispers and tittering laughter the next Monday. She had been to one such party. That was enough.

She steered the car up Rose Street, the hills gently rising, turned onto Eunice, gaining more altitude, and then onto Euclid. She parked in front of the Rose Garden. The cold night air made her shiver as she sat on the terrace overlooking the gardens, staring at the glimmering lights of San Francisco.

The kids she spent time with — the Band of Outsiders as they called themselves — at least liked to do things she enjoyed: hike in the hills, play recorders and guitars, sing duets, write bad poems. They even tolerated her hexaflexagons and soma cubes. But. They took great joy in taunting her about her controversial father. Tonight was as bad as it had ever gotten. She wasn't angry or sad or ashamed. She was numb. She was tired of waiting for the next jab, tired of trying to defend herself, tired of the get-Mia game.

She was ready for serious people. People who excelled. People who would make a difference in the world.

Chapter Two

Mia stepped into Bertram Hall, telling herself her nausea was just from lack of sleep. The charter plane from San Francisco, filled with noisy excited students, did not make for a good night's rest.

Bertram Hall's huge entry buzzed with the chatter of the new arrivals and their moms, dads, and siblings. Mia's parents were three thousand miles away. It was expensive enough to send her to Harvard without paying for extra trips to settle her into college life.

She had overheard her parents discussing her college plans. Her father, always the worry wart, thought Mia was too young to go to a college on the other end of the country. Her mom knew she would be fine, confident her daughter was a mature and reasonable 16-year-old.

Her mom was right. Mia squared her shoulders. Of course, she was smart enough for Harvard. Of course, she would do well in her courses. Of course, she would become an architect.

She took in the room, a large space dominated by a grand staircase, a yellow and blue runner covering the gleaming wood steps. The carpet matched the runner; the curtains at the windows echoed its colors. But it was the grandfather clock, its ornate wooden case and the fat moon face half visible in a window above the dial, that drew Mia's attention. As she walked up to it, a voice called "Mia? Mia Brower?"

"Yes?" Mia turned toward the sound.

"Mia, I'm Jamie!"

Jamie? Yes, of course! Mia had stared at Jamie's face in the

Freshman Register, the book containing pictures of each member of the class of '68. She dropped her things and hugged her new roommate. Jamie only came up to her chin, making Mia feel gawky. She released the embrace and studied Jamie. Her oval eyes sparkled, giving her the aura of a child ready to play the ultimate prank.

"You're supposed to sign in with the house mother, but let's look at the room first. It's on the top floor."

Jamie headed for the staircase. Mia followed.

"It's so big! And there's a fire escape at the window, which might be useful for sunbathing or summer sleeping or...." Jamie turned, smiling impishly. "Oh, I can carry something." She took Mia's guitar. "You play this?"

"A little. Just some folk songs."

"I bet you're good."

Jamie climbed the staircase to the top floor and led the way down a narrow hallway. Mia got a glimpse of the bathroom, the floor tiled in tiny white hexagons and a bathtub sitting on lion's feet, a room installed in the 1920s and not touched since.

The hall ended at their room, the door set at an angle.

The room was clearly a repurposed space, with indirect light filtering in from the only window and making it feel like twilight. It smelled musty. But the room was large, with ample space for two beds, bureaus, desks and a large closet along the wall opposite the door. The slanted ceiling over each of the beds made the room cozier.

"What do you think?"

Mia stepped into the room and tapped on a post that stood in the center. "Good thing I don't sleep walk."

"It adds charm. I could see a snake climbing up it."

Mia wasn't sure why a snake would be appropriate and didn't want to know. She ignored the idea. Looking around the room, she noticed her trunk, which her mom had sent ahead, was placed at the foot of one bed. Another sat at the foot of the bed closer to the window.

"Oh, I took the bed over there. Hope that's OK."

"Sure." Mia wouldn't have taken whichever bed she wanted, but it didn't matter that much. She could hear her mother saying, "Pick your battles."

"And I'll take this half of the closet." Jamie opened the large door. "This desk and this dresser." Jamie looked at Mia.

"Sounds good."

Jamie talked nonstop as she placed items in the closet and drawers: the quad was nice, a good place to picnic; the Radcliffe library was right next door, very convenient; a bike would make it easier to get to classes, which were about a mile from the dorm. It was a pity they weren't closer to Harvard Yard, but since they were officially at Radcliffe, mere women, they had to put up with the inconvenience. It was harder to get into Radcliffe than Harvard, and the poor boys had to have all the advantages to keep up. But that was OK. Cliffies, as the Radcliffe girls were known, had all their classes with the guys and they received a Harvard degree. That's what counted.

Mia tried to keep up with the rapidly shifting topics as she put her things away.

"So what're you going to major in?"

"Design." The words felt funny on Mia's tongue. "I want to be an architect." That, too, felt strange, presumptuous. "What about you?"

"I'll major in French Literature. I want to become a wife."

Mia dropped the sweater she was holding and looked at Jamie. "A wife?"

"Sure. I have brains, but I wasn't so lucky with looks."

Mia picked up her sweater and looked at her roommate. She wasn't a beauty, but she was lively, friendly. "But Jamie, you're so bubbly."

"Right, bubbly, but not pretty. Chubby, too. Anyhow, there're lots of men here, smart men who will make a lot of money. This is my chance to find my dreamboat. So that's my goal."

"Oh," was all Mia could manage and went back to placing things in her drawers.

"What? You don't approve?" Jamie's grin had faded.

This sounded like social clubber talk from high school. Mia had thought she would escape from such people. She tried to smile. "No, it's just not what I'm worried about."

"Well, maybe you don't need to worry about getting a man. You're beautiful."

"I don't know about that." Mia thought of her unruly frizzy hair, a boring brown, her eyes too close together, her thin lips. "But really, I just haven't thought about marriage. It seems like there are so many other things to worry about."

"Like?"

"Doing well in school, starting a career. I don't know."

"Sure." Jamie answered quickly with an impatient edge in her voice. "Of course, I'll have a career. But I need a husband, too."

"I guess I just feel a little young to be worrying about marriage." Mia had just turned 16, probably two years younger than Jamie, but she wasn't going to tell Jamie that.

The gleam returned to Jamie's eyes. "Never too early to start. Anyhow, I'm looking, so if you see any eligibles let me know."

"OK." Had Mia offended her new roommate? She wasn't sure, but she needed a new topic. "You're from Illinois?"

Jamie, having emptied her suitcase, clicked it shut and placed it against the wall. "Winnetka, on Lake Michigan."

"Must be beautiful."

"It's pretty in the summer, lots of trees and the lake. It's nice when it first snows, but the winters are long and dreary."

"I've never lived where it snowed." She was looking forward to the change of seasons, something one of her school friends had raved about.

Jamie opened her foot locker and was sorting through its contents. "You're from Berkeley? That's near San Francisco, isn't it?"

"Right across the bay."

Jamie looked up. "I went to San Francisco when I was eleven. It was great. We went to Chinatown and Fisherman's Wharf. We saw the redwoods. There was a tree so big we drove our car through it."

"You were north of San Francisco then?"

"Yup. We drove up the coast. Beautiful. Cliffs plunging to the sea. Beyond words. Just gorgeous."

Mia felt a little closer to Jamie. She knew something about California.

Mia held up her guitar. "Where can I stow this?"

"Hang it on the wall?" Jamie pointed at a spot away from the window. "Would you play me a song?"

"Sure, but I'm not very good." Mia removed her guitar from its case, tuned it, strummed a few chords, and sang the first verse of Pete Seeger's "Where have all the flowers gone?"

"The voice of an angel."

Mia looked up. Two young men stood in the doorway. One was tall and thin. He had a chalky complexion and hair so fair it almost seemed white. His eyes were the color of ice shadows. The other, a handsome fellow, was slightly shorter, but robust, with a ruddy complexion and straight black hair.

"And the face of an angel," the dark-haired fellow said.

Mia felt her cheeks warm. "What are you guys doing up here?"

"We're just helping all you lovely ladies move in," the taller one said. "I'm Sam." He bowed his head slightly. "And this is

Chip." Sam smiled. "At your service."

"We're pretty well set," Mia said. Men weren't allowed upstairs, and she didn't want to get in trouble before she even checked in. She looked toward Jamie for support, but saw a quick shake of her head.

Jamie smiled broadly. "I'm Jamie, and this is Mia. You fellows at Harvard?"

"Sure enough," Chip said. He caught Mia's gaze, and smiled.

"We've come to help you ladies learn the ropes." Sam seemed to loom over the room, his eyes glinting. "Not the official stuff. The important stuff. Like where to party."

"Speaking of official stuff, I haven't checked in yet." Mia started for the door.

"Don't go, Angel Face." Chip's lower lip protruded in a pout. He was cute playing the disappointed little boy.

Mia sat back down on the bed.

"We're having a little party Saturday night," Sam said. "Would you like to come?"

"Sure!" Jamie said.

Mia hesitated. "Isn't Saturday the night for the freshman mixer?" She felt three sets of eyes glare at her. She ran her hand across the bare mattress.

"See," Sam said, an uneven grin spreading across his lips. "That's what we mean about teaching you ladies the ropes. The mixer will be dull, dull, dull. Lemonade, sugar cookies and fox trots. But our party will have real things to eat and drink, with real music and real people." He paused and added in a half whisper, "And other real things."

"It'll be fun," Chip said. "You'll see. We'll have a good time."

"Neat room." Sam walked to the window and glanced out. "And it has its own entrance." He turned back to look at Mia.

"That could come in handy."

Jamie giggled.

Mia stood and wrapped her arms around herself. "You really aren't supposed to be up here."

Sam glared at her. "You really know how to ruin a good time, don't you?"

"You fellows need to go downstairs."

Sam's lips curled; his ice blue eyes were hard. "Say, why do you sing protest songs?"

"Because I like them." Mia headed toward the door.

Sam strode to the door, blocking her way. His hands were on his hips, his legs slightly apart. He looked down at Mia. "You a peacenik?"

"It's easy to not like war. Anyhow, I need to check in."

"Let's go find some fun company." Sam turned abruptly and walked out.

Chip's eyes met Mia's, and he held her gaze, smiling gently. "You're right about war." He followed Sam.

"Damn." Jamie grabbed a pillow and threw it against the wall. "Damn, damn, damn."

Mia had enough of this high school nonsense. "I'm glad they're gone. They think they own the world."

Jamie looked at Mia and laughed, but her eyes were hard. "They do own the world. Clearly preppies, Exeter I bet. Or maybe Andover."

Mia pictured them: crisp shorts, alligator shirts, boat shoes worn without socks, gleaming thin watches — so preppy they were clichés.

"Perfect husband material." Jamie stood up and paced. "Slipped right out of my grasp." She walked out.

Mia sighed.

Less than a day ago, she was leaning over the railing of the Berkeley pier, watching the water lap against the pilings, singing a gentle tune. She had imagined going out with friends to a foreign flick, sipping coffee after the show, talking about it, what it meant, about what life meant. Talking deep into the night. She had inhaled the scent of the ocean, tangy and invigorating, not like the draining odor of stirred-up dust in this too hot — this *sticky* room.

She found the sheets the linen service provided and flung them open, releasing the faint smell of bleach, which cut through the air and revived her. The dark fellow, Chip, had a sweet smile.

As Mia smoothed the blanket on her bed, Jamie walked back into the room. "You and I have a date tonight." Her eyes sparkled. "Sam and Chip are taking us to the Blue Angel."

Chapter Three

The Blue Angel was what Mia's Berkeley friends would call a prom-night restaurant, with linen table cloths and napkins, heavy silver, china service, and crystal glasses.

"If you ladies don't mind, I'll just order for us," Sam said, "I know the staff here and always get the evening's best."

"Sounds great," Jamie said.

Mia agreed, just as she had earlier when Jamie had argued for the date: it's just dinner; Chip really likes you; it's important to make friends; do it for me.

Sam called the waiter over and, while they conferred, Chip asked, "So what are you planning to study Mia?"

"Design." Mia looked at Chip. His eyes were deep blue. "I want to be an architect."

"Why an architect?"

"I grew up in a beautiful house. Berkeley is full of them. I'd like to design houses as beautiful as those." She had spoken these words so often they were automatic and by now they felt fake.

The waiter returned and placed a dish on the table. "Brioche Rounds with Crème Fraiche and Caviar."

The waiter was back a moment later with another dish. "Foie Gras on toast."

The next time the waiter appeared he held a bucket of ice, which he placed on a stand next to Sam. He introduced the wine as Crémant d'Alsace and poured a small portion for Sam, who solemnly tasted it and nodded. The waiter poured wine for the others. Mia wondered about the rules for serving alcohol to minors, but the waiter seemed at ease. She'd been served while with her parents, and generally waiters looked the other way on prom night. So it made sense: a prom-night restaurant with prom-night rules.

Chip raised his glass. "To our beautiful ladies."

Jamie smiled and raised her glass. "To our handsome hosts."

They touched glasses and sipped the wine. It might be called Crémant d'Alsace, but to Mia it seemed like champagne. The bubbles were creamy in her mouth, and the alcohol calmed her nerves.

"Chip?" Mia asked. "Is that a nickname?"

"Sure. The trouble is I have so many names because I have so many relatives who needed stroking. My mother couldn't remember them all, so she called me Chip, short for chip off the old block, which pleased my father."

"But that's not what his friends call him. We call him...." Sam hesitated, and Mia saw Chip direct a fierce look at Sam. "Well, we have other names for him."

"Yeah, we call Mia 'Biter', because she bites her nails," Jamie said.

Where did that comment come from? She did not bite her nails! What could she say? She blushed and looked down at her hands, wishing she could disappear.

The conversation slipped by. She heard Jamie ask, "Sam, what are you taking?"

"All the guts I can find. I'm looking for gentleman's Cs. Probably English Literature, because you can bullshit your way through. Too many fun things to do to waste time on courses."

Jamie and Sam chattered on. Mia receded into herself. She felt Chip looking at her. She gazed back at him and returned his smile, grateful that he seemed to like her.

As they walked out of the restaurant after dinner, Chip said,

"I've got something I'd like to show Mia. We'll see you later."

Mia looked up in surprise. He was... she didn't care about the preppy part... but he was cute. And he seemed to be on her side, with his remark about war this afternoon and his kind smile after Jamie's nasty remark. Maybe Harvard would work out after all.

He took her hand and led her off into the warm night air.

"Where're we going?"

"You'll see." Chip slipped his arm around her waist. "I want to show you my favorite place in Cambridge, Angel Face."

Mia stopped. Maybe Harvard would not work. Maybe she was just another pretty face. "Please don't call me that. I'm Mia. Just Mia."

"Mia." Chip searched her face. "I like Mia."

He took her hand, and they walked again, the moonlight playing in the branches, a breeze cooling the air.

"Would you like to go sailing tomorrow?"

This Harvard man didn't waste time. "I don't know much about sailing."

"All the better. I can show you the ropes."

Mia studied him. "Show you the ropes" ominously echoed this afternoon's conversation. But sailing! Sailing sounded so romantic. "I'd like that."

They crossed the street and walked up a winding path into a park. The white of a sphinx-like statue shone in the dim light, and, beyond that, up a short rise, Mia saw shadowy stone slabs.

"Chip, this is a cemetery!"

"Mount Auburn Cemetery, my favorite Cambridge place." He pulled her close, swept her hair back, and ran his thumb along her cheek.

She pushed him away. "Don't you think it's disrespectful? Here of all places?"

"Not at all! The dead like company." He took her hand

again. "Come. Let me introduce you to my great-great-grandfather."

Chapter Four

Mia nudged the door to her dorm room open, thinking about Chip and the sailing excursion tomorrow. Jamie was lying on her bed reading.

Jamie put her book down. "Chip must've had something very special to show you."

Mia took off her shoes. "Mount Auburn Cemetery. It seems to be his family's burial place."

"See." Jamie stretched. "Perfect husband material."

"Maybe." Mia sank down on her bed. "Anyhow, what was that about me biting my nails?"

"Oh, that. Nothing really."

"Nothing?" Mia looked at Jamie. "You insist I come out to dinner and then you put me down in front of 'perfect husband material?'"

"No harm meant." Jamie smiled.

"No?" Mia pursed her lips. "Then what did you mean?"

"You don't get it, do you?" Jamie sat up and smoothed her nightgown. "The guys were both looking at you. I needed them to pay attention to me." She stood and stretched again. "And it worked."

"You said I bite my nails because they were looking at me?"

"Sure. In case you don't know, you are lovely and guys want you. They were salivating. I needed to level the field, so I pointed out you're not perfect."

"You!" Mia voice had risen an octave. "You liar!" She clenched her fists. "I don't bite my nails."

"Well, you must have some other distressing habit, and I

needed the guys to understand there's always a bad side." She reached for her foot locker. "I don't know what it is, so I guessed. I just guessed wrong."

Mia struggled to control her voice. "You are something else, Jamie. I can't believe you'd play such a dirty trick."

Mia took several slow breaths, trying to calm herself. Jamie seemed unashamed, not repentant or irritated or angry. If roles had been reversed, Mia would have had all kinds of excuses, but Jamie seemed to think her behavior was OK. "What kind of weirdo are you, playing tricks and then admitting them?"

Jamie shrugged. "Someone who believes in the truth. 'Ye shall know the truth and the truth shall set you free.'"

Jamie believed in the truth but lied. It didn't make sense. Mia shook her head and headed to the door. Maybe the housemother could find her another roommate, even if it was past 10 p.m.

Jamie ran around and blocked her way. "Look, Mia, I like you. You're nice. You're considerate. I want to be your friend. So I tell you the truth." She held up her hands, as if they could help explain her misdeed. "I'm sorry for making you feel bad, but I had to turn the conversation around."

Mia turned on her heel and scooped up a package of stationery from Jamie's desk. "As long as we're having an honest conversation — " she held up the papers decorated with the Harvard seal in bright red " — why did you buy this?"

Jamie tilted her head and squinted. "To send to my friends, of course."

"To make your friends feel bad? Like saying, 'I got into Radcliffe, and you didn't. I'm smarter than you are. Nan-nan-a-nan-nan.'"

"Oh, that's what you mean." Jamie face relaxed into a smile. "My friends got into good schools, too. Besides, they know I'm smart. No. They know I'm brilliant. And if they can't take the truth, if their feelings will be hurt because I admit I am who I am, then they aren't my friends."

Mia locked her eyes on Jamie's. "I am not sure I can take all this truth."

"How about a truce then?" Jamie walked back to her bed and pulled a quilt from her trunk. "I've got matching quilts. Would you like to use one?"

Chapter Five

Mia let the dorm door swing closed and took the steps two at a time to the street. "Is it a roadster?"

Chip took her tote and opened the door for her. "Sure, that sounds good. A roadster."

Mia saw Chip's eyes glimmer as she slipped into the low seat. "Did I say something funny?"

"No." Chip closed the door. "I just never thought of a Karmann Ghia as a roadster. It sounds so Hardy Boys."

"Sorry. I didn't mean to offend it!"

"It's proud, but it'll survive."

Chip drove the tree-lined streets of Cambridge and managed a tangle of on ramps and overpasses. Finally they were headed north through leafy country. The cool wind whipped Mia's curly hair.

"We're going to Beverly, which competes with Marblehead for being THE boating harbor. Of course, Beverly is the secret winner."

"I've heard of Marblehead, but I've never heard of Beverly."

He glanced over at her, nodding. "See. It's the best kept sailing secret."

"So you've been sailing from Beverly for some time?"

"Me. My father. His father. His father's father. Probably a Walsh built the first dock at Beverly."

"Did you grow up here, Chip Walsh?"

"Yes and no. I grew up in New Jersey. But all my great-grandparents were Bostonians. So between that and the fact that Walshes have been going to Harvard forever, I've spent a lot of time here."

Mia looked at him. The wind ruffled his hair, his eyes were on the road, but there was a slight smile on his lips. His arm draped on the door frame. "It must be nice to be so comfortable here."

"I guess I am comfortable. I have a lot of friends from Exeter. Sam, of course, and my other roommates and some others. There's also friends of the family, other alum kids."

"You're lucky. There's a couple of kids at Harvard from my high school, nice enough I suppose, but we just moved in different circles. So I feel pretty much alone."

"Jamie seems nice."

"She's interesting."

"That's a dubious thing to say about your roommate."

Mia didn't want to whine, so she tried to soften her statement. "I'm still getting to know her."

Chip pulled into a parking place at the harbor and unloaded a duffel, a cooler, and Mia's tote. They headed for the dock.

"Here she is, the Melinda." Chip stopped at a slip, halfway down the dock. The boat's gleaming white hull bobbed gently. The mast top, thirty feet above, swayed slowly back and forth.

"The Melinda?"

"Yeah. I don't know. It's one of my parents closely held secrets, how the boat got that name." Chip helped Mia into the boat and passed her the gear. He hopped aboard.

He reached in his duffel and pulled out a tube of tanning lotion. "Better put some on before we start. The sun can be pretty fierce out here."

Mia applied the lotion while Chip rearranged things on the boat. He started the engine, untied the lines, and backed away from the dock. They glided out of the harbor.

When they were well out of the harbor, Chip pointed the boat into the wind. "There's one thing you must know before we start. See this?" He pointed to a horizontal beam attached to the mast. "This is the boom, and it swings across the boat when the boat turns. You need to be seated when it swings."

Mia nodded.

Chip unfurled the sails, first the main sail and then the jib. Mia held the tiller, pointing it straight ahead as Chip instructed.

"OK, we're ready to sail." Chip pushed the tiller to the right. The main sail billowed and then stretched in a graceful arc, full of wind. The water split away from the hull as the Melinda slipped through the bay. The boat heeled at a gentle angle and the salt air cooled Mia.

"I'm going to tack, so the boom will come over the boat." Mia looked at him and nodded. "You can help by holding the main sheet."

Mia looked in the direction Chip was pointing. "Looks like a rope to me, not a sheet."

"You need to learn the jargon." Chip pushed on the tiller, and the sails fluttered a moment as the boat turned through the breeze and the sails filled again.

Mia looked across the bay. The harbor seemed peaceful now, its busyness hidden by distance. "It's beautiful here. Peaceful."

"It's like being in another world. All problems float away." Chip slid over on his seat. "But you're getting too peaceful." Chip patted the space between himself and the tiller. "You do the driving for a while."

Mia squeezed into the space, and Chip held her hand on the tiller, pointing the boat toward the far shore. She nudged the tiller. The boat headed in just the right direction to keep the sails full. She relaxed, savoring the tangy ocean, the wind against her cheeks, the warmth of Chip's body close to hers.

The sun was high when Chip took the tiller from Mia. "You'll make a great sailor. Let's head into this cove and settle down for lunch."

Chip lowered the sails, motored into the cove and dropped the anchor. The Melinda tugged at the anchor line. Chip pulled sandwiches and lemonade from the cooler.

The sun shone down from a cloudless sky.

"So why did you come to Radcliffe?" Chip leaned back, closed his eyes and let the sun warm his face.

"Best school I got into." Mia looked toward the shore, wooded, silent, deserted. The water was blue, clear, and smooth.

"You're from California, right?"

"Yup."

"The land of Hollywood and beach parties."

Mia laughed. "That's Southern California. We Northern Californians are better than that."

"How's that?"

Mia thought how commercial Southern California was, but this might not be the right thing to say. "They're frivolous, we're serious. They listen to surfing songs; we listen to English ballads. They watch *Beach Party*; we watch *The Seventh Seal*."

Chip nodded. "Anyway, you're a long way from home."

"Yes." Mia pushed away a wave of sadness. "I wanted to get away from home." Mia looked at Chip. "Didn't you want to get away from home?"

"Not really. Though I guess I've been away from home since I was 14, being at Exeter, so maybe that makes a difference."

"So why did you come to Harvard?"

Chip laughed. "I didn't know there were any other options!"

"No options?"

"My Harvard attendance was planned before I was born."

"Doesn't that make you angry?"

"Not really. I like Harvard. I've been coming here for reunions since before I can remember. It's home."

Mia fell silent. Chip's world was so different from hers, a world she could not imagine.

"We could probably use another dose of lotion." Chip riffled through his duffel and pulled out the tube. He smeared his face, neck, arms, and legs with lotion. "Your turn," he squeezed a dab of the white goo on his fingers and spread it on Mia's cheeks, her forehead, her nose. He spread another dab on her chin, her neck, her collar bone. He stared into her eyes as his fingers slipped down her T-shirt.

She sat back, feeling heat rising in her cheeks. She grabbed the tube from Chip. "We won't get home by curfew if you . . . ." She didn't know what else to say so she busied herself applying lotion.

Chip lowered a ladder at the back of the boat. "It's hot. How about a swim?"

Mia looked down at the blue green water, so clear she could see a fish finning across the cove. "Sounds wonderful, but I didn't bring a suit."

Chip grinned. "I didn't either. No problem. We'll go skinny dipping."

"Oh." She looked up into his penetrating eyes, then shifted her gaze. "No, thanks."

"As you like, but I'm going." He grabbed the bottom of his polo shirt and stretched the material as he pulled it over his head. His sun-goldened torso was smooth, muscled. He unbuttoned his shorts.

Mia looked down at her sodden tennis shoes.

"Off I go."

Mia heard the splash and the Melinda rocked gently.

Mia felt a spray of water on her back. She turned around to see Chip treading water and shoving another wavelet of water in her direction.

"Hey Mia! Come on in. The water's great."

Mia shook her head.

Chapter Six

Mia flung herself on her bed and sobbed. Exhausted by her crying, but not feeling any better, she called Nick. No answer. Gina. No answer. She longed for someone to talk to. Anyone.

Jamie came in a minute before 10, bubbling. "What a neat guy Sam is, handsome, and, well, makes a girl's heart flutter." Putting down her purse she looked at Mia. "What's wrong with you?"

"I hate Chip." The day's events came tumbling out.

Jamie kicked off her high heels and rubbed her feet. "So what happened when he got back in the boat?"

Mia sat up. "I told him I had a headache."

Jamie laughed.

Mia knew she shouldn't have confided in Jamie. Here she was, miserable, and her roommate was laughing at her. "What's so funny?"

"Nothing." Jamie's eyes softened and Mia wondered whether she really might be sympathetic. "But what did Chip do?"

Mia remembered the scene so well: Chip riffling through the duffel, pulling out a first aid kit, and then riffling through that. "He gave me some aspirin and we came home."

"Yes." Jamie pulled off her stockings. "But was he angry or mad or what?"

"He said I might have gotten too much sun. He found a hat for me. He said next time I should drink lots of water, wear a hat, use more lotion, and try to cover up more."

"Ha!" Jamie ducked out of her dress and slipped into her

nightgown. "Next time! That's good."

Mia was hot and sticky from sweat and tears. She was still wearing the T-shirt and shorts from the day's excursion. She wanted to take a shower, but she needed to talk. "Do you think he is some kind of pervert?"

"No! He could have raped you, you know."

Mia gaped at Jamie.

"He was a gentleman, bringing you home when you felt ill." Jamie looked in the mirror as she brushed her hair, black, shiny, straight. It was Jamie's best feature. How Mia wished her hair were straight.

"But he stripped, right in front of me." She sank down on the bed. No point in even trying to brush her hair in this humid weather. "Who does that?"

"Some people think swimming in the nude is OK. In Europe, they do it all the time. Maybe, in his family, that's just not considered a big deal."

"Really? Even when it is just the two of you?"

"I don't know." Jamie stopped brushing her hair and turned toward Mia. "If I were you, I'd ask him."

"You're joking!"

"No. Really. VERITAS. He should understand that, being a Harvard man."

***

Jamie burst into the room. "Mia, there're roses downstairs. For you!"

Mia looked up. After her talk with Jamie last night, she'd pushed Chip and skinny dipping to the back of her mind. Talking to Chip about it was out of the question. Besides, she had to get organized for the school year. What courses was she going to take? The course list, marked with stars and cross outs, slipped from her hand. "Roses? For me?"

Jamie grabbed Mia's arm and pulled her out of the room and down the stairs.

There they were, a dozen roses. Bright red roses. Who could be sending her red roses?

She read the card:

Beautiful Mia,
Hope your headache is better. I'll be by at 6 tonight, to take you out to dinner, if you are well, and to tend to you, if you are ill.
Love,
C

She dropped it on the table, raced up the stairs to her room, and grabbed her purse.

As she turned to leave, she collided with Jamie, who was carrying the flowers and the note. "Where're you going?"

"Out." Mia tried to dodge around Jamie.

"Where?" Jamie took another step to block Mia, who stepped back.

"I don't know, just out."

Jamie took another step and Mia gave up and retreated into their room. "Why?"

"So I won't be here when he comes."

Jamie frowned. "Huh?"

"I won't be here at his lordship's beck and call when he comes at 6."

"What's the matter with you?" Jamie set the roses on Mia's desk.

"What's the matter with you?" Mia spat the words back. "Would you date a fellow who thinks you are available whenever he calls?"

"Depends on the fellow."

Mia sighed. That was such a Jamie response. "A fellow who strips in front of you on your first date?"

Jamie straightened a rose here and a baby breath there and turned toward Mia, hands on hips. "Mia, Mia, you are being so unfair to him. He seems nice. Sam thinks the world of him. Give him a chance."

"Why?" Mia started heading toward the door.

"Because I can tell you like him."

Mia stopped and swung around to protest. "Well, I . . . ."

"Look at me and say you don't like him."

"How can I like someone . . . ?"

"C'mon Mia. Look at me, tell me you don't like him."

Mia stared at Jamie.

"OK, then. What are you going to wear?" Jamie opened the closet door and surveyed Mia's dresses.

***

"You feeling better?" Chip asked as he met her at the bottom of the stairs that evening.

Mia's stomach was whirling. Could she really ask him? She certainly was not going to ask him here in the dorm entry, where her dorm mates could overhear. She settled for deception. She nodded.

"There's an Italian restaurant on Brattle Street. D'Angelo's. OK?"

She nodded again.

It was another prom-night restaurant.

As they sat down at a little table in the back of the restaurant, Chip asked, "How about a little wine to help us consider the menu?"

"Is it legal for us to have wine here?"

"They know me here. It's OK." Chip signaled to a waiter.

Same old, same old, Mia thought. The rules just don't apply to Chip.

"You must feel better, because you are even more beautiful tonight than you were yesterday. And yesterday you were the most beautiful girl I have ever seen."

"Oh Chip, do you use that line on all the girls you date?"

Chip looked hurt but didn't answer.

"Chip, I came out tonight against my better judgment." Mia stopped. "That didn't sound right. I came out tonight because Jamie badgered me."

"Well, if you don't want to be here, I can call a cab...." His eyes were hard, his mouth tight.

"Look, Chip, this is really hard for me. It's an exercise in truth."

His eyes softened, his eyebrows lifted. "OK."

"OK." Mia paused and looked down. "I didn't really have a headache. I was just so, so taken aback by your swimming in the...."

His mouth relaxed into a little smile. "Oh, that."

"Yes. Not something a poor little girl from the back water of the West Coast is used to."

"Well, I'm sorry...."

Mia interrupted, not wanting to let Chip weaken her resolve to get it all out. "It made me think you were trying to, well, you know...."

Mia's stomach tightened as she watched Chip, but he just returned her stare. He asked, "Are we speaking the truth tonight?"

Mia nodded.

Chip's smile broadened and his eyes glinted. "Well, then I was trying to you know...."

Mia had expected anger or denial or something else, but not

pleasant acceptance. "Well," she said, "I don't believe in recreational sex."

"But this is not about recreational sex," Chip said. "I love you, Mia."

"Chip, how can you love me? You don't know me."

"I'm an excellent judge of people, and I know you, and I love you."

"Well, I am not an excellent judge of people, and I don't know you."

"See." Chip's eyes danced merrily. "You have an answer for everything. You're not just beautiful, you're clever." He reached across the table to take her hand. "You are gorgeous."

"Truthfully, I feel like you would say anything to flatter me." Mia hoped for some kind of response, but Chip said nothing as he caressed her hand. "Would you love me if I were ugly?"

"That's an unfair question."

"Seems perfectly fair to me."

"Yeats doesn't agree."

"Yeats?"

Chip's eyes glinted with mischief as he recited:

"NEVER shall a young man,
Thrown into despair
By those great honey-coloured
Ramparts at your ear,
Love you for yourself alone
And not your yellow hair.

"But I can get a hair-dye
And set such colour there,
Brown, or black, or carrot,
That young men in despair
May love me for myself alone
And not my yellow hair.

"I heard an old religious man
But yesternight declare
That he had found a text to prove
That only God, my dear,
Could love you for yourself alone
And not your yellow hair."

"Ah, Chip, you are either a horrible Don Juan or an incurable romantic."

"Yes, at least one of those."

Mia laughed. "Well, I do not know you, and I do not love you."

"But you like me well enough to have dinner?"

"It must be so. But not enough . . . ." Mia's voice trailed off.

"That's OK. I can wait. For you, I can wait." Chip's gaze dissolved her reticence. He took a sip of wine. "We need to order dinner, if I'm to get you back to the dorm by 10. Would you trust me with tonight's menu?"

She nodded, and Chip beckoned the waiter.

After Chip ordered, he turned his gaze back to Mia. "Have you chosen your courses yet?"

She was startled. Confronting his behavior was as easy as that? She asked the question, got the answer, and set the rules, and now Chip wanted to talk about courses? She forced herself to think about school. "Some are obvious: a design course because I want to major in design, an English course, basic composition, because the college forces me to take it. I'm really bad at English. And second year calculus, both because I can use it for my architecture credentials and because, well, math has always been easy for me. I guess that's part of being my father's daughter."

"Your father's daughter?"

"Yeah. He's a physicist."

"And that automatically makes you good at math?"

"Well, he loves math. He's taught me forever. Sang me lullabies about Pythagoras's theorem." Mia heart warmed as she thought about those lullabies.

"You're kidding!"

It made her happy to tell Chip about this crevice of her life, important only to her, but he seemed intrigued. "No, not kidding. I'll sing it for you sometimes if you'd like."

The aroma of chicken, garlic and bay leaf wafted from the dishes the waiter placed on the table. He poured wine, red and translucent. Chip raised his glass. "To Mia's successful Harvard year."

Mia nodded. "Thank you." They clinked glasses and sipped the wine.

"So it sounds like your course schedule is settled."

"Not quite. My problem is my last course. I want to take some core subject, just to get the requirement out of the way."

"How about a history course?" Chip twirled spaghetti on his fork. "How about Rice Paddies?"

Mia wished she was as competent a spaghetti twirler as Chip. She always cut her spaghetti at home, but that seemed so gauche here. "Rice Paddies?"

"That's what it's called. It's popular. A course on East Asia."

She wondered what this purebred preppy would call her if he knew her background: Jewish with a dash of Catholic and a twist of Protestant. Pound Puppy?

"It's taught by Reischauer. He wrote the book on East Asian history. Literally."

"Sounds interesting. Sounds intimidating. Like a course on the entire Western Hemisphere, only more exotic."

"Besides, with the Cold War, it might be good to understand what's going on in the Orient."

"Yeah." Mia thought about communism, her friends in high school, her dad.

"A penny for your thoughts?"

Mia focused back on Chip. "Oh, sorry. I was just thinking about my dad."

"Your dad?" Chip shook his head. "Rice Paddies makes you think of your dad?"

She could not use the words Rice Paddies. "Let's call it East Asian history, OK?"

"OK. But why your dad?"

"The Cold War. My dad is anti-communist. It's a long story. He's from Hungary and still has family there."

"Oh."

"It's hard to explain." Mia thought about how her dad talked about the communists, but she could not reproduce his arguments, let alone the emotion he conveyed. "Anyhow he's vocally anti-communist. He works on nuclear weapons, says a strong defense is necessary, was against the test ban treaty. He's testified in congress, been on Larry King and on Buckley's show."

"Daniel Brower? The physicist who was on the cover of Time a while back?"

"Oh, you know of him."

"Not much. Just what I read in the news."

Mia nodded. Mia thought of her Berkeley friends, mostly anti-nuclear. She usually avoided talking about politics. People got so nasty. But Chip seemed safe. "Anyway, East Asia makes me think of the Cold War and that makes me think...." Mia trailed off.

Chip sighed. "The Cold War. It's confusing."

"That's the perfect word. Confusing."

"That's part of the reason I'm taking Rice Paddies."

Mia cringed. "East Asian History."

"Yeah."

Mia changed the subject. "What are you majoring in?"

"History. I'm good at it, and it works well for getting into law school."

"Law school?"

"You don't seem to like law school."

"My grandfather was a lawyer," Mia said, trying to mollify her blunt response.

"I guess my going to law school is preordained, just like my going to Harvard. My father is a lawyer, his father was, and...." Chip looked up with a wry smile. "You get the picture."

"Are you comfortable having your life mapped out for you?"

Chip gazed past Mia and then looked back at her. "Sure. I like my life."

Mia considered Chip, so self assured, maybe because he knew where his life was going. But if her life was dictated, she wouldn't be self assured. She'd rebel.

Chip set his fork and knife side by side on the plate. "How was the chicken?"

"Wonderful."

"Black Forest trifle for desert?"

"Sounds good, but what is it?

"Black Forest cake without the cake."

"Yum!"

Chip ordered desert, which the waiter brought along with

an amber liquor served in tulip shaped glasses.

Chip lifted his glass. "To East Asian history."

Mia clinked his glass. "To East Asian history."

Chip took a sip of the liquor. "By the way, there's a party at our dorm rooms next weekend. Would you come? You could bring Jamie. And if there are other Bertram ladies, you could bring them, too."

"I don't know what Jamie's up to. Will Sam be there?"

"Sure. Sam will be there and some other fellows from Exeter. Hank. You'll like Hank. We call him Lanky Hank, because he is tall and skinny. And George, known as Geode, because he's spherical, but a math and science wiz."

"Speaking of nicknames, what is it Sam likes to call you?"

Chip set his fork down, his eyes focused in the distance. "Oh, that. I don't want to talk about that."

"That's OK." She grinned and patted the back of his hand "I can wait. For you, I can wait."

Chip returned his focus to Mia and frowned, but his eyes twinkled and a smile spread across his face. "I love you more each moment, Mia."

***

Lucy Luther sat down at Mia's table the next morning at breakfast. Lucy was one of the first upper class women to move back to the dorm. She had quite a reputation, painting her room black, writing strange poems, just weird stuff. Her nose was sharp and too big, her lips unpleasant lines across her face.

"You're a looker," Lucy said, staring at Mia. "You nose is a little crooked, but you are a thing to behold."

Mia concentrated on her scrambled eggs.

"Nice roses you got yesterday. One of those boarding school boys?"

Mia looked up at Lucy. Mia had thought Jamie a bit off, but Lucy was scary. "You're observant."

"Well, take some advice from me," Lucy bit into a slice of bacon. "Go slow. He's going to want to go all the way. Today. And then he'll drop you. They're all alike."

Jamie set down her fork. "You have some experience with that, Lucy?"

Lucy's smile was icy. "Just take some advice. Matter of fact, the best thing is to lead them on. Let them get excited. Then you control them. Just get them panting. It's so much fun." Her eyes drilled into Mia.

Mia hadn't finished her breakfast, but she had to get away. She pushed back from the table and ran up the stairs. In her room, in part to calm herself, she started making a list of supplies and books to buy.

Jamie came in and picked up her toiletry bag and towel. "What a piece of work."

Mia looked up. "Huh?"

"Lucy Luther." Jamie turned to the closet and pulled a sleeveless shift, a bold orange and crisp white, colors which brought out the apricot blush of her cheeks.

"Lucy does make one's skin crawl," Mia said. "And that comment about my nose."

"Same as my comment about your nail biting," Jamie said. "She's jealous, of your looks and of the roses, too."

"Oh. Maybe. By the way, when are you going to registration?"

"Right after I shower."

"Let's go now," Mia said. "Chip said it will be a zoo. We can shower after the melee."

"OK. Let me get my things." Jamie started to rummage through the papers on her desk. "I bet Lucy has no experience with boarding school boys."

Mia gathered the papers she needed for registration, checking she had the proper course number of East Asian history. "And those comments about leading them on."

"Pretty disgusting." Jamie placed several sheets of papers in her purse. "But I wouldn't go all the way."

Neither would I, thought Mia. "By the way, there's that party at Chip and Sam's on Saturday. You going?"

"Yes!"

Chapter Seven

Chip escorted Mia and Jamie up to his suite in Grays. Sam opened the door to a dimly lit and smoky room. In the background, the sound of a flute fluttered over piano chords and a persistent drum.

"Hey, Jamie. Hey, Mia," Sam said, "This is Gloria." Sam bowed slightly to a girl, a little taller than Mia with straight golden hair, hair that shimmered as she moved her head. She wore a filmy red dress secured with a broad band of red silk at the waist, allowing the fabric to cling at her braless breasts and swing freely at her mid thigh.

Gloria gave Mia and Jamie a quick nod, threaded her arm though Sam's, and held up a mug. "Hey, guy,' she said, pouting at him, "the well's dry!" Sam scooped her up and carried her to the other end of the room, where a table stood covered with bottles, glasses, and an ice bucket.

Jamie stiffened.

"Let's meet the other folks," Chip said, an arm around each girl's waist. "This is Hank."

Mia wondered whether Exeter accepted only tall men, or whether they fed them something to make them tower. Hank was even taller than Sam. His hair was a sandy brown. He wore a navy blue jacket, khakis, and a white button down shirt.

"He almost didn't come to the party, wanted to escape to the library. But we made him stay."

Hank extended a hand first to Mia and then to Jamie. "Hi, there," he said. "Nice to meet you."

"What's happening at the library?" Jamie gave Hank a big

smile.

"Not much." Hank looked down.

"I love libraries," Jamie said as Chip guided Mia farther into the room.

"This is Cindy," Chip said, pointing to a petite girl, dressed in jeans and a faded pink man's dress shirt, sitting on a leather couch.

"Hi." Cindy smiled and then flicked her cigarette ashes into a large plate on the coffee table in front of her.

"And Geode," Chip said.

Apparently, Exeter's plan to produce only tall graduates had failed with Geode. Mia could see, even though he was also sitting on the couch, that Geode was short. His features peeked out from his frizzled black hair and beard. His eyes loomed large behind his glasses' thick lenses.

"Hey, there," he said, reaching for potato chips that spilled out from a bag on the coffee table. "I hear you're Dr. Brower's daughter."

"Yes." Mia felt her heart plunge.

"Brilliant! He gave a talk in my summer seminar. He can explain anything and make it seem like kinder spiel."

"Now Geode, let me get my girl a drink before you talk her ear off," Chip said, guiding Mia toward the drinks table. "What would you like?"

"Wine," Mia said, seeing a wine bottle and not knowing what else to say.

Chip poured her wine into a stained Harvard mug. He poured a dark amber liquid into another mug and took a sip. He closed his eyes, apparently letting the liquid sit on his tongue. He swallowed, then studied her.

"You want a taste?"

Mia shrugged. "Sure." He passed her his mug, and she took a tentative sip. The liquid was thick, sweet and burned her tongue.

"Well?"

"Truthfully?"

"Truthfully."

"Reminds me of cough medicine."

"My father's best scotch is hurt, but you're a cheap date." Chip put his arm around her waist and guided her back to the sofa. He pulled up a chair and sat down, pulling her into his lap.

"Everyone's ga-ga over systems with transistors," Geode said, slurping from his mug and stuffing chips into his mouth. Mia wondered why he would eat potato chips instead of the other things on the table: shrimp, caviar, chocolate truffles, petit fours. "But it's just a fad. I mean all you have to do is listen." He looked around the room. "I mean if you listen, really listen, you can hear the difference. These transistor nuts don't listen."

Chip whispered in Mia's ear. "Geode's off on one of his lectures."

Mia surveyed the room, letting Geode's words drone in the background, since apparently he expected no response. Lanky and Jamie were sitting on hassocks at the far corner of the room. Jamie seemed to be doing most of the talking, Lanky nodding and smiling. Sam sat on the floor in front of the coffee table, Gloria leaned across his lap, arms wrapped around his torso. She nibbled his ear. His hands massaged here and stroked there. Mia looked away, not wanting to see more. Cindy was smoking another cigarette, flicking the ashes and sipping from her mug. Her eyes met Mia's for a moment, then looked down at her smoke, stubbing it out in the dish overflowing with ashes.

Chip's lips brushed Mia's neck.

"And these pre-packaged systems — " Geode had really

gotten into his subject by now, his voice louder and more emphatic " — they suck."

Mia stiffened. Suck was outside her verbal limits.

"KLH thinks it can sell you everything for $300, but they are selling you short."

"Interesting, Geode," Sam said, shifting Gloria and standing up. "I think the ladies have had all the stereo education they need for one night."

Geode smiled. "Yes, I suppose there are other things to do at a party."

"How about a little parlor game?" Sam asked, pushing the food on the coffee table to one side and plunking down what looked like a monopoly board. "Everyone needs to freshen their drinks before we start."

Geode got up, taking Cindy's mug and his own. Chip peered into Mia's mug, and, although it was almost full, took it to the drinks table. Sam refilled Gloria's mug.

Lanky stood up. "I think I'll walk Jamie back to the dorm. She needs to get up early tomorrow." Mia wondered what Jamie was up to as she saw the pair leave.

Geode returned from the drinks table with Cindy's drink and a hand-rolled cigarette.

Chip handed Mia her mug. It was filled to the top, so Mia took a deep gulp, hoping to prevent a spill.

"Why are you drinking wine, Mia?" Sam asked. "Don't you want something more substantial?" Sam's icy eyes were hard, as if his question was really a command.

"Back off, Sam!" Chip's tone, loud and hard, startled Mia.

"OK, OK." Sam raised his hand and backed away. "I just want Mia to have a good time."

They sat around the coffee table, Geode and Cindy on the couch, Sam and Gloria on the floor at one end of the table, Chip and Mia in front of the table.

"We need a little toke before we start," Geode said, placing the hand-rolled cigarette between his lips and flipping open a gold lighter. He inhaled deeply as he lit the cigarette. He held his breath for a long time, and, when he exhaled, a sweet, burnt smell wafted toward Mia.

Pot! She had heard about it but had never been around it, much less partaken.

Geode passed the joint to Cindy, who took a deep pull and, holding her breath, held it toward Mia.

"No, thanks," Mia said, leaning back trying to avoid the smell.

"Oh, Mia, you really need to try this stuff. It's the best." Sam's eyes glinted.

"I don't smoke."

Sam's laugh was humorless. "Ah, people who don't smoke like this stuff most of all."

"Sam." Chip took the joint from Cindy and shoved it into Sam's hand.

"Suit yourself." Sam took it and drew in a deep drag. His eyes watered as he held the smoke in his lungs. He passed it to Gloria. "OK, let's play." He passed out tokens. "Let's see, red for Gloria, pink for Cindy, and blue," Sam's stare made Mia scoot a little away from the table, "frigid blue for Mia." He passed out other tokens to Chip and Geode. "We all know the rules, except Mia. It's just like any board game. You roll the dice, move the number of places on the board and follow the instructions of the space you land on. Let's start with Mia, to make sure she understands."

Sam handed the dice to Mia. She tossed a seven and landed on a space that commanded "Drink."

Sam said, "OK, Mia, take a drink."

Mia sipped her wine.

"C'mon, Mia, that's not a drink."

Mia set her mug down with a thud. This was not what she had in mind when Chip had invited her to a "party."

Chip took the dice from her and he threw an eleven. The board commanded "Kiss your favorite girl." Chip put his mug next to Mia's. He drew her head toward his, his lips brushing hers, his thumb stroking her cheek.

Gloria snatched the dice from Chip and threw. Snake eyes. "Discard something you are wearing." Gloria locked her stare on Sam, inching her hem up her thigh. "Slip?" She grinned. "Panties?" She shook her head. "Not yet." She threw her head back giggling, her golden hair shimmering in the dim light. She pulled the band from around her waist and swung it in front of Sam.

Mia whispered in Chip's ear. "I want to leave."

"It'll be OK," he whispered.

Sam threw an eleven and placed his token next to Chip's: "Kiss your favorite girl." To Mia's surprise, Sam shoved Gloria aside, unfolded his long legs, and strode over to Mia. He pulled her to her feet. She tried to push him away, but his left arm held her tight, while his right hand pushed her chin up. His lips crushed hers, his tongue forcing its way deep into her mouth. She gagged on his sour taste, squirmed, and tried to shove him from her, but his hold was too strong.

She bit down.

He flung her away. "You bitch!"

She turned and ran to the door.

Chip was one step behind her. "I'm sorry."

"For what?"

"Sam."

Mia stomped down the stairs and into the clean night air. She took long strides, her shoes striking the concrete, her breathing heavy.

Chip walked beside her, but she ignored him. "Sam gets out

of control sometimes."

Mia stopped and turned toward Chip. "Let's review the party. You served alcohol, which is against the law and against university rules. You had pot, ditto. You had some kind of kinky game."

"Look, I said I'm sorry."

"That's nice." Mia started walking again.

Chip walked beside her.

"You don't need to walk with me. Matter of fact, I'd be happier to be alone right now."

"I can't have you walk back to the dorm at this hour alone."

"What hour?"

"It's midnight."

"What?" Mia was supposed to be back by 11. Her mind raced. Would she be grounded? In her befuddled state, she couldn't remember the rules, but she knew the dorm would be locked. She started to run. Chip ran next to her.

When she got to Bertram both front and back doors were locked. She went around to the side of the building. There was Jamie, sitting on the fire escape. She waved to Mia, motioning her to come up. Chip helped her up the first step, and she climbed unsteadily up the metal stairs.

Jamie helped Mia into the room and shut the window.

"I was worried about you!" Jamie said. "When you weren't here just before 11, I signed you in."

Mia stared at Jamie. She was something else. What would have happened if Mia hadn't come back? She had risked what? Expulsion? Mia wasn't sure, but Jamie had done her a favor worth a thousand nail-biting comments. "Thanks."

"So how was the party?" Jamie asked.

"Yuck." Mia needed to sort things out before she talked to Jamie about it. "You left early, so you know what I mean."

"It didn't seem that bad to me, but Hank suggested we go

for coffee." Jamie's eyes gleamed.

"I thought you liked Sam."

"So did I, but Hank — " Jamie seemed to be choosing her words carefully. "He's more my type."

"At least someone had a good evening."

The next afternoon a dozen red roses arrived for Mia. The attached note read:

Beautiful Mia,
I'm sorry you didn't like our party. I'll be by at 6 tonight. We can do anything you'd like.
Love,
C

At 6 that evening, the roses were in the trash and Mia was at the library.

Chapter Eight

Mia's first lecture on Monday was East Asian history. She had sat with Chip last week, but today she planned on arriving just before class started to avoid him. She headed to Memorial Church, or Mem Chu as the initiated called it. There was a room in the basement reserved for Cliffies, a refuge on Harvard Yard since the women's dorms were a mile away. The large room was furnished with mismatched tables, chairs, and sofas. Mia thought Harvard sent its furniture there to die.

She settled in a chair and thumbed through her history book, but her mind skittered this way and that. She arrived at the lecture hall just after 9. To her dismay the only empty seats were at the front.

"There's plenty of space up here," Professor Reischauer said. Mia felt he was talking directly to her, so she obediently walked to the front and took a seat in the first row. She tried to concentrate on the lecture, scribbling down what seemed like unrelated facts.

At last the lecture ended, and, being in front, Mia waited while the room emptied.

"Great lecture." Chip's voice was just behind her, and she felt his hand on her back. She turned to look directly at him.

"Sorry you were out yesterday," he said.

"I was busy," she said, "and I've got to get something read before my design class." She shoved through the crowd at the door and ran toward the Cliffie refuge, grateful men were not allowed in that basement room.

At 10:45 Mia headed to the Carpenter Center, the building

housing the visual arts department where her design class was held. It had just been completed the year before and was designed by the famous architect Le Corbusier. It was a strange combination of concrete and glass. She walked up the curving path to the front entrance. A steel handrail with a metal mesh fence below bordered the way. It made Mia think of an enclosure for rabid dogs. She looked at the windows set back in what looked like gigantic cubby holes. The building was stark and cold. She shivered and it was only September. How would it feel in January?

The classroom had high ceilings supported by large concrete columns and made her feel like an ant crawling around in a shoe box. Students sat on stools at ten large tables, and Professor Guillaume, an older man with longish wavy white hair, wandered from table to table. Mia sat on one of the stools next to a tall thin girl wearing a black beret, a long scarf wrapped around her neck, and a long skirt printed in beige, browns and black. She stared at Mia, who nodded in greeting and then looked down, not knowing what to say. The professor stopped at the table.

"Ah, Gertrud." He smiled at the girl. "Nice to see you." He marked something on a paper.

"Mia Brower," he said, looking at the paper, and then smiled at Mia.

"Yes," Mia mumbled. The room might be cold, but the professor, a famous artist, was warm.

Professor Guillaume went to the front of the room and pointed to stacks of magazines in boxes, explaining the next assignment, a collage. After the explanation, the students each took several magazines and started cutting pictures from them, arranging the scraps on sketch paper.

Mia felt panicked. How does one make a collage?

"So," Professor Guillaume asked, looking over her shoulder,

"considering the possibilities?"

Mia looked at him and nodded.

"Be brave," he said. "Jump in with both feet."

***

It was a perfect October day, the leaves in full flame, the air cool. For once, the gritty wind seemed clean, the sky a perfect blue, the sun shining, warming the earth just enough. Mia sat on the fire escape, a blank drawing page in front of her, a few black felt pens in a cup beside her.

Jamie stuck her head out the window. "Hank and I are going for a drive. Want to come?"

Mia looked up. "Thanks. I've got to get this design project done."

"You've been staring at the page for an hour, Mia. Come play. It will be obvious when you get back."

"Nah. You go ahead. Have a good time."

"It's Sunday. A day of rest. Seriously, I think you need a little break."

Mia shook her head. "It's funny, the clean white page seems perfect as it is, and I don't want to mar it."

"You're nuts. Just do it. If you don't like what you get, there's another perfect clean white page just below the one you're staring at." Jamie looked out over the oak tree, brilliant red. "Or better yet, come out with us and do it later."

"No, thanks. Have a good time."

By the time dusk was closing in, Mia had moved back into the room. Several pages were covered in dots, as the design project had required. And, as Jamie had promised, there were still several perfect white pages in the sketch pad.

Jamie came in, her cheeks red, clutching a bag of apples and a gallon of cider.

Mia looked up. "Looks like you had a wonderful time."

"It was pretty. And fun. And you would have loved it." Setting down her things, she came over to look at Mia's projects.

Mia stared at her, hoping to see a glimmer of approval. "This one here, looks like a dragon ready to spring," Jamie said.

Mia wagged her finger. "Veritas, remember?"

"Well, what do you think, Mia?"

"I hate them all. It's like there's a secret, a formula to make it work, and everyone but me knows it."

"You seem to hate design. The truth is you should be doing something you like."

"But I love architecture. At least architecture that I love."

"Circular thinking." Jamie chuckled. "C'mon. You've done your assignment. Let's go to the diner on Mass Ave."

As they walked, Mia buttoned her coat. The wind, which had caressed her earlier in the day, was now cold and oppressive. "So how's Hank?"

"Seems all's not well in the Gray dorm rooms," Jamie said. "Remember Gloria?"

"Sam's girl, the Night of the Drinking Game?"

"It seems she's become the fifth roommate."

"You're kidding!"

"Unfortunately not."

"How does that work?"

"She sleeps with Sam. Stays in most of the time. It's kind of an open secret, but the dorm proctor either doesn't know or is turning a blind eye. And there are all sorts of problems with it."

"Is she a Cliffie?"

"No. She's a townie. And she's not even 16."

"Not even 16?" Mia felt naive. She would have guessed Gloria was past 20.

"Yup, won't be 16 for several more months. Can you say

statutory rape? And all the roommates may be in legal jeopardy." Jamie looked at Mia. "On top of that, she's noisy, drunk, and Hank thinks she is into drugs. I mean, not just pot, but the scary stuff."

"Oh."

"He's talked to Sam about it, but Sam says he doesn't have the heart to turn her out. Geode agrees with Hank. And there are other issues. Liquor is the least of their sins. Geode says if the situation is revealed, they will all be in all kinds of trouble."

Mia waited for Jamie to say something about Chip's opinion, but Jamie walked in silence. Finally, Mia asked, "What does Chip think about all this?"

"Chip doesn't want to turn Sam in. Says Sam will find his way out."

"What's with Chip? I mean Sam is putting all of them at risk."

"Yeah. I don't know."

"What does Hank think?"

"He wanted my opinion. I told him, go now, do not delay."

The girls settled in one of the diner's booths, which was a little grimy. "Well, ladies, what'll it be?" the waitress asked in a thick Boston accent. They ordered sandwiches and cokes.

"You know, Chip always asks about you."

"Does he now?"

"He's a good sort, Mia. Hank says he's a really good guy."

"And you trust Hank's opinion."

"Yes."

"So Hank isn't one of those playboys who just wants to get a girl in bed?"

"Oh, no. Hank's — " Jamie's eyes were soft as she looked in the distance. "He's quiet." She sipped her coke. "He may be The One."

"Boy, you accomplish your goals quickly." Mia wondered

what Jamie would do next now that she had "The One."

"Maybe." She looked back at Mia. "I know that Chip upset you, but you've got to give him another chance. He's a good guy, and I can see, when he asks about you, that he cares."

"Good. Let him roast in hell."

Chapter Nine

On Wednesday nights the girls were required to wear skirts to dinner. The house parents invited guests, professors from various departments. It was supposed to be an opportunity for the girls to get to know some of the faculty.

According to Jamie, it was a nod to finishing school. Mia agreed. She hated to take the time to change out of her regular wear — jeans and a top — just to eat dinner, but she conformed.

Jamie conformed, too, but, as usual, on her own terms. She fashioned a full length skirt from a bed sheet and a loop of elastic. The material was draped over the elastic. It slipped easily over whatever Jamie was wearing. Tonight was the trial run of her Wednesday Night Solution, as she called it. "How does it look?"

"A little lopsided, but maybe that's the point?"

As they went down to dinner — they had missed the pre-dinner sherry in the living room — they managed to get a table without the guest and without a house parent. It was their preferred location. It gave them time to talk and allowed them to get back to whatever they wanted as soon as possible. Mia had a ton of reading for history, and she was having a terrible time keeping all the Oriental names straight. They didn't make sense to her. They all sounded the same.

"Hank and I are going to symphony this Sunday? Want to come?" Jamie asked.

"Oh. I always have so much work. How do you manage to have time to play so much?"

"First things first. The MRS degree, remember? Anyhow, a

little time away won't hurt you. Might even do you good."

"What are they playing?"

"I don't know, but it's bound to be good. It's the BSO, after all. And how can you claim to go to Harvard, if you don't attend the Boston Symphony Orchestra?" There were ironic quotes around the Boston Symphony Orchestra. "Really, Mia, it'll be fun and the hall is architecturally interesting."

Mia was sure this last bit came from Jamie's imagination. It might be true, but that would be pure coincidence.

"OK, OK."

Jamie looked up, and Mia followed her gaze to see Mrs. Staunton, the housemother, standing by their table. "Jamie, I'd like to talk to you for a minute after dinner."

When Mrs. Staunton moved on, Jamie said, "I bet it's my Wednesday Night Solution." Mia would have been mortified, but Jamie was gleeful. "Time to think up my next getup."

***

On Sunday, Hank ushered Jamie and Mia to their seats on the main floor of Orchestra Hall. The best seats, Mia thought. They must have been expensive. She gazed toward the stage, set up with chairs for the orchestra. The pipes for the organ shone at the rear of the stage. The hall was magnificent in an overbearing way, long and narrow, with very high coffered ceilings and statues in niches along the upper level's walls. She didn't like it.

But Mia loved classical music. In high school she had gone to concerts at U.C., where tickets were cheap and people wore everyday clothes: jeans, shorts, an occasional business suit or nice dress. Here the audience was dressed up in furs, jewels, expensive silks and wools. She was glad Jamie had advised her to wear her "parents' clothes," as Jamie called them: something to wear when visiting with your parents, or, more important, with your boyfriend's parents. She wore a cream blouse — not silk, but something that draped well — and a dark brown skirt. Jamie had lent Mia a beautiful string of amber, which set off her outfit. Mia amused herself watching people.

She sensed someone sit down beside her, and, when she looked, her pulse quickened. He was so attractive, his dark hair swept across his forehead, his blue eyes, his dark navy suit, and crisp white shirt, complete with a discreet blue handkerchief tucked in his pocket. She suppressed her desire to be touched.
"Hi, Chip."

"Hi, Mia." He settled in his chair. "Hi, Jamie," he said with a nod, "Hank."

Mia felt her heart pounding. Jamie knew Chip was coming. She pursed her lips. She mustn't make a fuss. She was a guest.

"Have you looked at the program?" Chip asked, taking the pamphlet from Mia's lap.

She blushed. "Er, no. I've been so engrossed in the hall and the people...."

"The Beethoven will be tremendous, of course, and the Hayden will be light, but I'm looking forward to the Mahler." Chip opened the program to the page that listed the pieces.

"Mahler?" Mia asked. "I don't think I've ever heard Mahler."

"Lucky you! You've got a real treat ahead of you!"

The house lights dimmed, and the conversational buzz quieted.

The orchestra played the opening notes of Beethoven's Seventh. Mia closed her eyes and let her ear follow the music she knew so well, and then her mind wandered, as it usually did. It kept returning to the fact that Chip sat beside her. She opened her eyes and looked at him. He had his eyes closed, but he must have felt her look, because he opened them. She looked down, hoping he had not noticed her stare. She focused on the music again. She knew each melody and anticipated each new theme. Her ear raced ahead, waiting for the next phrase and the next, until the final note of the final movement. It was a marvelous performance. The applause exploded, and the conductor came back for several curtain calls.

"What did you think?" Chip asked as the conductor left after another bow.

"I loved it. And you?"

Chip just nodded.

The conductor strode back to the platform, ready to start the next piece. The audience quieted immediately.

Mia didn't know the Hayden piece, but it was, as Chip had said, light, easy to follow, enjoyable. When it ended the house lights came on.

"A little something?" Hank asked.

"Sure!" Jamie said.

They went to the refreshment stand, and Chip asked Mia what she would like.

"Some sparkling water would be nice."

Chip ordered two sparkling waters and ushered her over to a table.

Hank and Jamie had disappeared, Mia noticed. Oh, well. Nothing could happen in this crowd.

"So how's life?"

"A little distressing," Mia admitted, wondering at herself. She had meant to keep her distance and here she was complaining.

"Oh?" Chip gazed into her eyes.

"Well." She paused, hoping to make light of her complaint. "I don't know how to keep all those Oriental names straight. So many seem to be exactly the same, and, even if they really are all different, they're so foreign to me."

Chip's face lightened. "If that's the problem, I have a method."

"Really?"

"Sure." He patted his pocket. "But I need pen and paper to show you."

The lights blinked, and Chip and Mia made their way back to their seats.

The Mahler was different. It was in many ways traditional, but there was also a smear to the music, as if everything was slightly out of kilter, a little dizzy, a little drunk. She was not sure she liked it. She was not sure she didn't.

When the music ended, the audience applauded enthusiastically. After several curtain calls, the audience began to collect their things and leave.

Hank stood. "How about an after-concert snack?"

"Sounds great," Jamie said.

"Chip, can you join us?"

"I'd love to. But I've a maiden aunt I promised to visit this evening."

His little smile made Mia wonder whether it was a maiden aunt or a hot townie. Her heart twinged with jealousy. How quickly her resolve had melted away.

Chapter Ten

Monday morning, Mia got to history early and set some notebooks on the desk next to hers. Chip appeared a moment latter. "This seat taken?"

"It's for you." Mia moved her things off the desk.

Chip slid into the chair. "So how did you like Mahler?"

"I'm not sure. I'll have to listen to it a couple of times before I know."

"Sounds like you're a serious music buff."

"I don't think so. But I do like some music." Music didn't interest her at the moment. "Chip, I'm curious about your method for keeping all these names straight. It'd be nice to know before the hourly next week."

"I'll show you."

That afternoon Chip stopped by Bertram, and he and Mia settled at a table in the dining room. Soon he had covered several pages with diagrams and time lines. He did have a system, and, as he drew, Mia began to understand it.

"How did you figure all this out?"

"At Exeter we studied lots of history, and I found if I could visualize it as a diagram I could remember it."

At 4:30 the cook chased them out of the dining room. She had to set up for dinner.

"Would you like to stay for dinner?" It seemed only fair after all the help Chip had given her.

"I'd love to, but I have a hot date tonight." He gave her an impish smile. "My father's mechanic is in town. Dad's considering buying a 1930 Benz."

"Too bad." Mia pushed aside the jealous pang. "Thanks for all the help!" She watched Chip walk down Shepard Street, swinging his book bag and humming a Mahler theme.

On Wednesday morning, Mia got to class early and saved a seat for Chip.

When he arrived, she said, "I'm confused about something." She pulled out the diagrams Chip had drawn. "See here and here." She pointed. "I think these should be interchanged, because..." she flipped open the textbook to a marked page, and read a highlighted passage.

Chip looked at the diagram, reread the passage, then looked at the diagram again. "I think you're right."

That afternoon, Chip stopped by the dorm, and again they studied in the dining room. The diagram did have some errors. At 4:30 the cook shooed them out.

"I'd ask you to stay for dinner, but it's Wednesday, which means it's formal."

"I know. How about we go to the deli on Mass Ave? We can eat and study."

"Let me get my coat." She raced upstairs.

Chip and Mia settled into a booth at the deli and ordered sandwiches. They spread the papers out and pointed and drew as they ate their food. Finally, Chip sat back with a sigh. "Look OK to you?" he asked.

Mia nodded. "How do you study for the test?"

"I have the questions, of course."

Mia's mouth fell open and she hurriedly covered it with her hand. "You have the questions?"

"Sure. Gray has a list of questions from previous exams. Doesn't Bertram?"

"No." She folded her arms across her chest. The guys had a system the women didn't even know about.

"Well, no problem. I made a Xerox of them. It's somewhere

here." Chip flipped through his papers, pulled out a thin folder and handed it to Mia. "Of course, there's no guarantee the same questions will be on the exam, but it's a good way to study. If you can answer these questions, you will probably do OK on the exam."

She opened the folder and scanned through the sheets. "Can I borrow these?"

"Sure. Just keep them. I'll get another copy." Chip took a bite of his sandwich. "Tell you what, you do your best to answer them, and I'll do the same. Then we can get together this weekend, and go over the answers."

***

On Sunday, Chip came over, and they settled in the dining room. No one asked them to leave, since on Sunday dinners were not served. By 4:30, twilight settled on the street, and Mia turned on more lights. At 6:00 Chip pushed the papers aside and stretched. "We've covered all the questions. I'm feeling pretty good about the material. How about you?"

"Not too sure." She rubbed her cheek. "I'll probably never be sure."

Chip gathered his papers. "We worked hard. How about dinner at the Blue Angel?"

"That'd be nice!" Mia wondered about her immediate enthusiasm. Chip the dangerous seemed to have faded into the distance, and Chip the eligible had taken his place. Was she sure this was a good idea? No. But she heard herself saying, "Let me get my coat."

She didn't object when Chip took her hand as they walked into the chilly evening.

They settled at a table in the back of the restaurant. After Chip ordered, he leaned forward. "Mia, I need your advice."

His eyes, usually so delighted, were sad.

"Sure."

"It's about Sam."

Mia felt her stomach tighten.

"I know, I know. You don't like Sam."

Mia had to smile, thinking how transparent she was. "You're right. I don't."

Chip's voice was low. "But he's not a bad guy."

Mia closed her eyes and shook her head. "That's not my opinion."

Chip looked down and ran his finger along a fork. "He was good to me at Exeter."

"OK."

"Boarding school can be tough. I mean with the other kids." Chip looked up, his eyes seeming to plead for an understanding response.

Mia considered being away from home. "I was at summer camp, and there were minor spats with the other kids, but the counselors always seemed to keep things happy."

"Maybe it's different at a school. It's longer. It's serious. Kids are older, less compliant." He stopped, looking at Mia, hoping, she supposed, for some support. She said nothing. He spoke again, a little louder. "Anyhow Sam made things work for me at school." He shook his head. "I owe him."

"So what's the problem?"

Chip looked around and then whispered, "Sam's dealing drugs."

Mia inhaled sharply. She had expected something else. Gloria. The presence of drugs. "Dealing?"

Without taking his eyes off her, he nodded.

"This is unreal." A torrent of words rushed out of Mia's mouth. "Gloria is living in the dorm room. But you don't do anything about that. Gloria is into drugs, the hard stuff. But you don't do anything about that. Now you find out Sam is dealing drugs. Why should you do anything about that?"

Chip looked around the room. "Not so loud, please."

She also looked around, hoping no one had heard. "Sorry."

"You know about Gloria?"

"Sure."

"Hank? Jamie?"

"Of course." Mia closed her eyes. "I would have gone to the proctor after one night of Gloria, after one puff of pot. I don't work on the same set of rules as you Exeter guys." Mia shook her head. She wanted to leave.

Chip covered her hand with his own. "Mia, please."

Mia searched his face, usually so confident, which now looked like a little boy's about to cry. She leaned back in her chair. "You asked for my advice. My advice is go to the proctor now."

"But I may be in trouble...."

"Yes, but you'll be in more trouble if you don't."

Chip resumed running his finger back and forth over the edge of the fork.

"What about Hank and Geode?" Mia asked. "What do they want to do?"

"They have been pressing me to come with them, but I have refused."

"They won't go without you?"

"They say I must come, otherwise it'll look like I'm complicit."

Mia took in a breath, holding back the next explosion of words trying to escape.

"Mia, I owe him."

Mia's thoughts swam. "What did he do for you that you owe him your education and your future?"

Chapter Eleven

As the days got colder, the Carpenter Center grew more frigid. This was a building for the desert, Mia thought, not the frozen north. The cold grabbed her heart every time she entered.

With each assignment her mind grew stiffer, making it hard to think. She had dutifully carried out each project, following all the rules and requirements exactly, and each project seemed to result in an unorganized mass of lines or dots or shapes or ads from magazines. Nothing came together. Nothing was pleasing to her eye.

That is not to say the other students' projects were not successful. With each project, she could see that others' work made sense, moved her. But not hers.

As she entered the classroom and pinned her newest assignment on the cork board, she took the stool toward the back of the room. Other students were chatting, but she said nothing. She did not belong here. How she envied those others, so comfortable, pointing at the images, laughing and talking.

Professor Guillaume came in, a little late, dropping his coat and hat on an empty stool, and started the discussion about the projects pinned on the wall. Mia tried to make herself invisible, hoping he would not call on her. Thankfully, he passed over her, but she still had to endure the one-on-one with the professor.

At last, it was time for her interview. He looked at her kindly. "Have you had a great misfortune?" That was enough, Mia's tears flowed and he looked even more worried. "There,

there." He handed her a tissue. "Whatever it is, maybe we should talk another day?"

Mia wiped her tears, blew her nose. "I'm sorry." She felt another wave of tears threaten, but she willed them away. "It's just that I can't seem to do the projects."

The professor laughed. "Oh, is that all?" His eyes softened, his smile slipping into a line of concern. "I mean, I'm glad you wish to do well, but I thought maybe your mother had died."

Mia gave him a feeble smile. "No, no, you must understand, this is just a little course, not so important."

"It's very important to me."

"Well," the professor said, "maybe that's part of the problem!"

Mia frowned.

"Look. You've followed all the requirements exactly. See, none of the lines cross, or even touch."

"That is what you said to do."

"Yes, and you were very obedient to my commands." He smiled again. "But you must also follow your soul. You must let yourself feel."

Mia looked at him. His words, although she knew they were meant in the kindest way, made her panicky.

"This is not a bad project," he said, "But it is stiff. I'd like you to do the assignment again, say tonight, and think of the rules not as requirements, but as suggestions. Let yourself go." He studied her. "Maybe have a little wine? Some nice music? A good friend?"

Mia nodded.

"Bring it to me Wednesday at 1? Can you do that?"

Mia nodded again.

"And be happy! This should be love not war."

***

It was not so easy to get wine in the dorm, even though they served sherry on Wednesdays. She wasn't sure how they managed that, given that almost without exception the girls were under drinking age. Wine was out of the question, and the good friend — well, she didn't think that was a good idea. Besides, she couldn't have Chip in her room after 10, and it was almost 9 already. She settled for her favorite record, little pieces with mellow guitar, sweet soprano, and flighty flute.

She stared at the blank page, so perfect. She liked blank pages better than works in progress. She guessed she might like a truly wonderful finished product, but she had never produced one. She sighed and drew her first line.

Fifteen minutes later, she stopped. It was insipid, stupid, ugly. She tore off the sheet, and now she had another beautiful blank page. A new first line. A second one. She stopped and considered. A third. Oh, it was worse than the previous attempt. She tore that sheet off. Beautiful blank page. How could she mar it? But she did, one pen stroke after another. Again and again her pen stabbed the paper, and she felt hot tears streaming down her cheeks, dripping onto the paper, pooling in the ink. She didn't even look at the paper when she had finished, but the tears, released at last, exhausted her, and she fell into a deep sleep.

She awoke to knocking, but it was not coming from the door. The luminous dial of her clock read 2:10. The knocking, insistent, urgent, came from the window. She crept over to look out, recognized the silhouette, and opened the window.

"Chip?"

"I need to talk to you." His voice was uneven, husky and low.

"Come in then." Mia stepped back and looked over at Jamie's bed.

Jamie stirred. "Something wrong?" Jamie asked, her voice

deep and drowsy.

Mia turned on the light. "What happened?"

Chip paced, his hands in his pockets, his shoulders slumped.

Jamie sat up in bed. "Chip!" Her voice was strong and commanding. "Chip, sit down."

Chip stopped and turned toward her. Mia noticed his eyes were red, perhaps from the cold walk to Bertram. Perhaps he had been crying. He sank into one of the desk chairs.

"What is wrong?" Jamie's voice was firm, but not unkind.

"Sam's been arrested."

"Arrested?" Jamie asked.

Mia sat on her bed, studying Chip. His coat, usually so neat, was askew, stains on its hem.

Chip stared at the floor.

"Because, because...." His hair was mussed. He leaned forward, his elbows on his knees, his head in his hands, his voice muffled. "We went to the proctor."

Jamie blurted out, "Good! At last!"

Chip looked up, his lips pressed together, his brows gathered in a stormy look. "Good? You say good?"

"Shhh," Mia cautioned. "We don't want to wake the authorities."

Chip closed his eyes and nodded. "Yes. Sorry."

"So," Jamie prompted, "you went to the proctor and ... ?"

"Hank, Geode, and I went and told him everything. Gloria, drugs, dealing...."

"And ... ?" Jamie asked.

"And he said he would talk to Sam. That we would need to talk with him again, with Sam present. That we should be available. So we went to the room to tell Sam the proctor wanted to see him." Chip's words were quiet and even. "About 8 we were called, and, well ... it was ... I don't know ... three against one. But...." Chip's voice drifted off.

"But what?" Jamie insisted.

"Sam said we were responsible for everything. I couldn't reproduce what he said. It made no sense." Chip stood again and paced. "When it was clear his story was ... flawed, he bolted, ran out of the room. We went looking for him, in our room, the common areas, everywhere. We gave up and went out to Cronin's for something to eat. We'd missed dinner. We left Cronin's and started to walk back to Gray when we saw Sam on the square. He didn't look too steady, so I started toward him, but Hank held me back. Sam stumbled across the street. I could see he was carrying something. Something heavy." Chip stopped, looking at Mia, as if she could somehow rewind time and stop what had happened. "He hurled it — a rock — at the Coop's window. I was trying to cross the street to ... I don't know to do what ... help somehow ... when a siren howled ... a police car ... then another ... they handcuffed him ... loaded him into a car."

"So this is good," Jamie said. "I mean, he was a real danger. It's good it is over."

"I can understand this is difficult." Mia lied. She didn't understand. She was trying to understand. "But why are you so upset?"

Chip rubbed his eyes and his temples.

"I mean he was going to get you in trouble."

"It's worse. Geode called Sam's father. He'll kill Sam."

"Yes," Jamie said. "I'd be upset if my child . . . ."

"No, I mean it. Sam's father is out of control."

"But, Chip," Mia said, "he'd find out anyhow."

"Yes, maybe it's better to have him know now, while Sam is under police protection," Jamie said.

Mia winced. Sometimes Jamie could be so mean.

Chip sat back into the chair.

"You OK?" Mia asked.

"I . . . suppose so. I mean, if we hadn't gone . . . ."

"Oh, for God's sake," Jamie broke in. "Don't you go feeling guilty. He's bad news."

"I suppose."

"But you need to get out of here. Before it's light," Jamie said. "Should I call Hank?"

Mia looked at the clock. 4:25. She didn't know when the sun rose, but Jamie was right. They had to get Chip out of the dorm soon. Chip looked crumpled. Mia wondered aloud whether they might hide him for the day.

"No!" Chip stood up, straightening his coat. "No. I'm OK." He headed toward the window, looking back into the room. "Thank you for . . . ." His words were jumbled. He shook his head and climbed out onto the fire escape.

***

Mia overslept. She was troubled by Chip's visit. She still did not understand the depth of Chip's upset, but she had to get to classes, had to think about the day ahead. She was not happy with any of her design pieces, but she had an appointment with the professor. She slammed all her sheets into the portfolio, shoved it into her book bag and headed off to Harvard Yard.

Chip was late to history class, bleary-eyed, but he seemed together. Reischauer handed the graded hourly exams to the TAs. Mia dreaded looking at her exam, particularly the essay questions. When the TA handed her the blue book, she peeked into the first page. Much better than she had thought. She sighed. Chip, sitting beside her, whispered, "How'd you do?"

"B+, and you?"

"I did OK."

As they walked out of the building after class, Mia asked, "Feeling better?"

Chip ran his fingers though his hair. "I'm OK."

"Any news of Sam?"

"No. All quiet. The quiet before the storm?" Chip flashed a sad smile and headed toward the library.

At 1, Mia knocked softly on the door to Guillaume's office. "Come in, come in!" He indicated a chair for Mia. "What have you got for me?" Mia pulled sheets from her folio and gave them to him. Her heart thumped as he looked at the first sheet. He paused. He turned to the second sheet. Then he turned to the third sheet. Oh my god, did she bring that third sheet? She wanted to grab it from him.

But he was smiling. "Now this has soul!" He said holding up the tear-streaked paper. "This says I am angry. I am impatient. I have troubles!" He looked at her seriously. "Here, you have allowed yourself to speak."

Chapter Twelve

There were flurries in the air as Mia entered the history lecture hall. Chip was sitting in his usual seat, saving the seat next to him. Mia walked over, pulling off her coat, mittens, and hat. It seemed so hot and stuffy in these halls, as if the college were making up for the miserable weather by overheating the rooms. She sank down into her chair.

It was the last lecture of the term, winter break started on Monday, and Mia had a seat on a chartered plane for San Francisco.

"You free tonight?" Chip asked.

"I guess so." It was as much a question as an answer. It was strange, his asking her before saying what he had in mind, but she guessed he felt comfortable enough with their romance, felt like he owned her, that he could box her in. She was annoyed, but it was the last day of classes. She was looking forward to going home. It was no time to try to prove a point.

"Great. My folks are in town, and...." He looked at her a little nervously. "Well, might you come out to dinner with us tonight?"

Mia inhaled sharply. Introduction to his parents. What did that mean? They had only been going out for a short time, and, well, she was putting the brakes on. It was a mess. She wanted him. But the evil Chip of before the concert still lived in her mind.

She wanted him. Oh, how she wanted him. But if they consummated their relationship, she felt it would end the relationship. She felt cornered into a position of "yes, yes, NO."

You may go this far, but no further. And each time, she wanted to go further. Chip had taken each of her restrictions in stride. She hated herself. She was a tease, just like Lucy Luther had recommended. If Chip had ever told her that, she'd have slapped him, but it was true.

Introduction to his parents was different. It'd be interesting to meet his parents. She supposed she wouldn't like them, being old Harvard types, probably upper crust and snobby. They would find her socially lacking, and that would be the end of the Chip-Mia show. So be it. She didn't need Chip. Though she didn't know how she'd get through history without his help.

"Mia?" Chip bit his lower lip.

"Oh, sorry." Mia swallowed and cleared her throat. "That would be wonderful. Meeting your parents would be a real treat."

***

That evening, as Chip held the door of the Yard of Ale restaurant, Mia rubbed her clammy hands against her coat. Why had she agreed to come? Jamie had helped her choose appropriate parent apparel and had lent her a string of pearls and matching earrings. Sweet Jamie! Mia exhaled, trying to calm herself.

Chip scanned the restaurant and headed to a table in the back. He hugged his father and kissed his mother on the cheek.

Mia wondered what the appropriate greeting would be.

Chip turned towards her and sputtered, "How rude of me. Mia, this is my father."

Mia offered her hand, and his father shook it with a gentle touch.

"And my mother." Chip stepped aside.

Mia offered her hand, which Chip's mother took.

"Sit, sit," Chip's father said. "It's so nice to meet you, Mia."

Mia murmured agreement. He was a handsome man, graying slightly at the temples, black straight hair, those beautiful blue eyes. And so elegant, the dark suit of a fine material, the thin watch, the silk tie, the crisp white shirt, the gold cuff links.

"Yes, Mia," Chip's mother chimed in. "So good to meet you. So glad you could squeeze us in before you fly back to California."

Chip's mother was as elegant as her husband. Thin, black hair, dark eyes. Gold earrings, just-right scarf at her neck, woolen suit, hands long, fingers slender. Mia felt her stomach tighten. What should she talk about with such put-together people?

"Yes." Mia smiled, her words tumbling out without her thinking. "So happy to meet you. Do you get to Cambridge often?" Where did that come from? It must have been her mother's etiquette training.

"I do come up quite often," Mrs. Walsh said. "My sister, Beverly, lives in Boston, and, now that Chip's here, it makes Boston that much more inviting."

So, Mia thought, Chip's excuse about visiting his maiden aunt might have been true.

"That, and the fact we are going to take possession of a real heap of junk," Chip's father added, giving Chip a little nod.

"He doesn't mean me," Chip said.

"Mia! Did you think I meant my handsome son?" Chip's father turned his gaze to her, his eyes glimmering.

Mia decided she liked Mr. Walsh. "No, no, of course not." Mia tried to put on a serious and slightly offended face.

"That's good." He said, forcing his lips into a frown. "I meant that piece of junk Bob and Chip bought."

"It's not junk, Dad. You'll see. Once I'm finished, she'll be a gem. You'll be envious. But I won't give her up."

"Gentlemen," Chip's mom interrupted, "maybe you should explain what you're talking about. Mia looks a little confused."

"Well, Mia, my son has a strange fondness for cars. . . ."

"Chip got this 'strange fondness' from his father." Chip's mom emphasized the strange fondness.

Mr. Walsh nodded to his wife and continued. "And for his last birthday I promised to buy him a car. I set a price limit, mind you, which was generous enough so he could get a fine, new, off-the-showroom-floor vehicle." Here Mr. Walsh looked at Chip and slowly shook his head. "But no. He spent the money on a perfectly undrivable 1958 Karmann Ghia, which he will now have to somehow make serviceable."

"I have all of Christmas break to work on it," Chip said, "And Bob and I can probably get most of it done."

"Bob's our handy man and sometime mechanic," Mrs. Walsh said.

The affection among these three was so thick Mia felt left out.

"Now, Chip," Mr. Walsh said. "I have a couple of things I want Bob to do, and, of course, your mother will need him to help get ready for the holidays."

"Right, dear," Mrs. Walsh said, "I need help with getting the house ready for the New Year's Party. And poor Bob might like a little time off for his own Christmas."

Mr. Walsh turned his gaze toward Mia. "Well, enough of our family's dirty linen! I am so glad to meet you, Mia, because we have heard about you from Chip."

"Oh." Mia felt a blush coming on. "I hope . . . ."

"Only wonderful things." Mr. Walsh grinned. "It's the parents' duty to find fault, not the boyfriend's."

"James!" For the first time Mia could see a look of annoyance on Mrs. Walsh's face.

"Oh, Mia will forgive me, I'm sure." Mr. Walsh turned toward Mia. "Will you, Mia?"

"Yes," Mia blurted and felt her cheeks warm.

Mrs. Walsh stared at her husband. Mia supposed she was willing him onto a different topic. He cleared his throat and changed the subject. "I hear you're Dr. Brower's daughter. He is, well, brilliant, of course, but also brave, I think."

"Brave?" Mia thought of her dad as smart and having a clear view of where he thought the world should go, but she hadn't considered him brave.

"Yes, brave. He's willing to say things many people don't agree with. He believes the way to peace is through a strong United States. He is willing to say that again and again."

"He does say it again and again," Mia said.

Mr. Walsh laughed. "I find it encouraging to have someone willing to speak his mind in the face of such strong and sometimes downright nasty criticism. Calling him Dr. Strangelove. Really!"

The conversation lulled, and Mia felt uncomfortable. She felt like she was expected to say something, to agree, to do something. Mrs. Walsh saved her by asking, "So, dear, what are you studying?"

Mia started in on her spiel about design and architecture. Her insides roiled, knowing she was having trouble with design. Mrs. Walsh said she really loved the colonial style of architecture, and Mia agreed she liked it, though, being in New England for the first time, she was just now getting to know it.

"I hear you are taking the East Asian history course," Mr. Walsh said. "What does that have to do with architecture?"

"It's one of my core courses. It meets the history requirement and it covers materials left out of a California public education."

"Good thing she's taking it, too," Chip said. "It makes studying so much better. She found a fatal flaw in my notes for the hourly exam."

And so the conversation continued from appetizer to dessert. It was focused on the young people. Mia wondered whether she should be asking about the adults but felt that would be rude. She knew she was under inspection, and the feeling of being an outsider grew. She was looking in at a close family comfortable with themselves and their position. They did not understand how hard it was to keep up, with Harvard, with design, with wearing parent apparel, with saying the right thing at the right time. She would like to be one of them, but it felt out of her reach.

At last the meal ended, arrangements for picking Chip up for the ride back to New Jersey were made, thank-yous said, and good-nights exchanged.

Chip walked Mia back to the dorm, his arm around her waist.

"Might I come up?" he asked.

Mia felt exhausted. She just wanted to sleep.

"It'll be three weeks before I see you again." He swept a strand of hair on her forehead.

"Sure, Chip."

So they sat on the porch, waited for the security guard to walk past Bertram, and, when they could see his flash light at the far end of the quad, they walked around to the side of the building. Chip jumped for the fire escape stair and pulled it down, and Mia and Chip climbed the fire escape, waving to Joan and Betty as they stepped past the second floor. They climbed into the window on the third floor and sat on Mia's bed.

Chip stroked her cheek. "They liked you." He looked into her eyes. "They really liked you."

"Did they?"

"Oh yes. I can tell." He smiled. "If they didn't, you'd have known." He kissed her and then held her at arm's length, his eyes solemn. "Did you like them?"

Mia considered the question. "Chip, I can see that you and your parents are so close. That makes me like them." She could see her answer disappointed Chip, but it was the best she could do.

He kissed her again, a deep soulful kiss. "I love you, Mia."

"Oh, Chip." Mia pushed him away. "The L-word again."

Chip looked like he had been slapped and rose, probably planning to leave.

Mia pulled him back down. "I'm sorry, Chip. It's just that I don't know what it means, 'love'."

"Isn't it clear?"

"No. Love sounds like a cop out to me. A word filled with sound and fury, signifying what? Lust? Need? Something else?"

Again Chip started to stand, but Mia held him.

"Chip, I'm not trying to be mean. I enjoy being with you. I lust for you."

"Good, let's . . . ?"

Mia smiled weakly. "But I don't know what it all means. It makes me wonder about myself."

"Mia! Mia! I've said it before. Maybe you didn't hear. I can wait."

"Yes. I heard you. But when you say you love me, it feels like a demand."

"I can love you and still wait."

"It feels like a demand, because I don't know what love means."

"I get that." Mia heard impatience in his tone. "But I can love you and still be content to wait."

"Chip, you aren't a virgin are you?"

Chip laughed.

"So, with the girls you bedded, how many did you say you loved?"

"Mia, I can't remember that."

"But you see what I mean, don't you?"

Chip stood, pushing off Mia's attempts to hold him. "I do love you Mia, but I can see you don't trust me. I suppose trust is a part of love, so I guess you don't love me. I hope that will change. Maybe we can talk about it after break."

Then he was gone.

Chapter Thirteen

The windshield wipers slapped, the fat rain drops thud-thud-thudded, and the lights of the cars splintered into rays through the wet glass. Mia's mom had been talking non-stop since they met at the airport gate. Her mom didn't like driving across the Bay Bridge, so Mia drove. Now she was navigating the various twists and turns of getting onto the bridge.

"Three students are coming for our Christmas Eve," her mom said. "Jorge is from Argentina and Monica is from Berlin." Her mom helped foreign university students settle in. She did this, she said, to repay Mrs. Blandings, the widow who shepherded her when she was a foreign student at Berkeley. "Jorge asked whether he might bring a friend. It'll be a party, so please save Christmas Eve for us."

"Sure."

"Your dad will be coming in from D.C. that morning. Could you pick him up?"

"OK."

"I made an appointment with Judy to have your hair cut. You look like you could use a trim. That's the 30th at 10. OK?"

"Sure."

"And we can go to the after-Christmas sales in San Francisco on the 26th, if you'd like."

"Thanks."

"Nick called, said you should call him."

"OK."

"So did several others. I kept a list."

"Thanks, Mom."

"You seem monosyllabic. Is everything OK?"
"Sure, Mom. Just concentrating on the traffic."

***

The next morning was bright and clear, but chilly. The California aroma — eucalyptus, camellia, and jasmine, spicy and sweet — and the familiar walk to campus — the flowered path with the pergola, the circular stone bench at the bus stop, the palms along the street — made her homesick. How could she be homesick when she was home?

When she got to Sproul Hall, Nick was sitting on the steps overlooking the wide-open plaza, normally full of students rushing between classes, but now deserted. Nick waved at her and stood. His curly brown hair was longer than the last time she saw him. He was wearing a navy blue sweatshirt with a large white peace symbol, rumpled frayed jeans, and tennis shoes. He held a battered briefcase.

They hugged.

"How's your love life?" he asked.

"Better than yours."

It was their customary greeting, developed since they met in junior high. They were friends, but there was a time when they had been more than that.

"The Forum?" he asked. The Forum was the Telegraph Avenue coffee shop they frequented in high school.

"Sure."

The headed down Telegraph, past the newsstand, the Sather Gate Dress Shop, where her mother shopped for her formal clothes, past Sather Gate Bookstore, where her dad bought his Christmas presents on Christmas Eve, past Larry Blake's, the restaurant her family went to on special occasions, noted for its perfect steak and Caesar salad, dressed and tossed at your table.

"Mind if we stop at the IFS?" Nick asked. It was his abbreviation for Intellectual Furniture Store, his name for Frazer's. Frazer's carried Scandinavian furniture, rugs, and other design necessities for Berkeley's faculty. "I need to get my mom's Christmas present."

"Great." Mia enjoyed browsing in the store.

Nick found a candle in the form of a light bulb that had a light socket as its base.

"So how IS your love life?" Nick asked as they resumed their walk down Telegraph.

"Better than yours and I don't think you'd like him."

"Why's that?"

"He's a preppy."

"Why'd you like him?"

"Sexy."

"That's all, just sexy?"

"No. He's smart. He's interesting. He likes me."

"Ah, well." Nick chuckled. "So much for being an architect."

"Nick!" Mia socked him, not too gently, in the arm. "So how about you?"

"Nice girl. You'd like her. From Stockton. A farmer's daughter. Has cows. Has horses."

"Doesn't sound like your type."

"She's also got rebellion."

They got their espressos and settled at a table in the almost empty shop.

"I saved something for you." Nick pulled a worn front page of the *Daily Californian*, the student newspaper, from his brief case.

The headlines read, "Police Arrest 800 Demonstrators; Faculty Support for FSM Protest." In smaller type was, "Strike to Protest Arrests." One picture showed Sproul Plaza filled with people, not the usual busy-between-classes full, but packed full. Another shot showed two policemen pulling a limp student through the hall.

"What's this about?"

"Don't you follow the news?"

"I guess not. I had other things to do. Like study."

Nick shook his head. "So there's been a little disturbance in quiet old Berkeley."

"I can see. What's FSM?"

"The Free Speech Movement."

"Free Speech? We don't have free speech?"

"Nope. Not when it comes to things like equal rights for blacks."

Mia considered Nick's statement. "I know the South is pretty medieval, but I thought blacks were treated fairly here."

"Think again, girlie."

"What? We have integrated schools, theaters, restaurants."

"Schools? Really?"

"Sure. Think about Mrs. Wyatt and her son, Craig." Mrs. Wyatt was a black English teacher at Berkeley High and her son was in their class. "And what about Clara and Jeremy?"

"That's the point, Mia. Those are all the blacks you knew in Berkeley High. But Berkeley is twenty percent black. All the others are in the shop track and you don't see them."

Nick was right.

"Anyhow, the university won't let us organize, so we had demonstrations, and then a sit-in and a strike. But this is just the beginning."

"Us?" She searched his face, which was calm but serious. "Are you demonstrating?"

"Of course. We can't claim to be free unless we are free."

"What about med school? What about your grades?"

"First things first."

Mia changed the subject. "What's new with the band?"

"Gina's still in St Helena." Nick had written that Gina had tried to kill herself and had been placed in a hospital north of Berkeley.

"Have you seen her?"

"Nope. And I can't seem to get in touch with her family."

"You know what happened?"

"Rumor is she had an abortion and her mom found out. Not good."

"Harry's baby?"

"I guess." Nick shrugged. "You know Harry left without a word?"

"That's what you wrote." The party scene from last August, the haughty woman, and Gina's grin flashed through Mia's mind. She hadn't talked with Gina since. "Did Harry know she was pregnant?"

"Don't know. Didn't keep up with all the dirt." He shook his head. "Maybe someone else would know? There's a party at the twins' house this evening. Stop by for the latest gossip."

"I'll stop by." Mia wanted to sock Nick. He could be so condescending. "By the way, what is the latest gossip?"

"Other than Gina nothing new. The twins are around, good diligent students." Nick's voice was tinged with disdain. Julie, one of the identical twins, was one of his ex-girlfriends. "Dennis is around, too, especially for the demonstrations. I think he has a job at a pizza joint. Mike is at school, too, but he's kind of loopy. Grace is, well, Grace."

Mia pushed back from the table. "Mind if we stop at Cody's on the way home?" Cody's specialized in paperbacks, books not carried at Sather Gate Bookstore: Alinski, Marcuse and Fritz Perls, books in French, German, Spanish and Russian.

After cruising Cody's, they stopped by Eclair's, the bakery, and bought some Florentines. Mia managed to save some for her mom.

"I've got to pick up Dad at the airport Christmas Eve morning. What to come along for the ride?"

"Sure!" Nick grinned "Back from making the world safe for nuclear weapons?"

Mia cringed. She was homesick.

Homesick for Chip.

***

When Mia got home, she rushed upstairs to the spare bedroom, which had an extension phone. Her mother called it her study. Floor to ceiling bookcases covered one wall. They were filled with so many heavy books that the floor sagged.

She closed the door. Here she could call Chip undisturbed and away from prying ears. She dialed information first to get his number, hoping it was listed. Fortunately, it was. She took a deep breath and dialed.

"Walsh Residence," an unfamiliar voice said.

"May I speak with Chip, please?"

"May I ask who's calling?" Mia didn't recognize the voice. She imagined it was the maid.

"Mia." Maybe Chip knew several Mias, so she added. "Mia Brower."

"Just a moment, please."

After a wait and some rustling, Chip said, "Hello." It was not a warm hello, but a standard I-am-a-well-mannered-preppy hello.

The scene in Mia's room, night before last, ran through her mind. "Hi, Chip." Was he still angry? "How's being home?"

"Fine."

"I just was out to coffee with a high school friend, Nick. He can be, well, difficult." Mia waited for some response, but Chip was silent. "It made me wish you were here." Again, there was silence. "Chip, is something wrong?" Maybe someone was listening and he couldn't talk?

"Mia, long distance is expensive. We'll talk in Cambridge."

"OK." He must still be angry.

"Goodbye." The line went dead.

What was going on? He wouldn't worry about how much long distance cost, would he? He certainly didn't worry about the cost of a dinner at the Blue Angel. It was an excuse. If someone was listening, he could have said now is not a good time to talk, I'll call back later. But he didn't. He said they'd talk in Cambridge. That was like saying, don't call again.

He was as difficult as Nick, just in a different way. She was right to put the brakes on. If she wasn't right there with him, he had other things to interest him. Maybe another girl? Just like Harry, who left without a word? She was just an amusement on his way to leading the successful preppy life. He was right, she didn't trust him. It was time to break up.

**

Mia smiled to herself as Nick slid into the front seat beside her. He wore a neat navy sweater over a white shirt, crisp chinos and loafers. He knew how to dress for parents. She smiled again when they greeted her father at the gate. "Hello, Dr. Brower." He used her father's preferred form of address. Nick knew how to annoy her and how to butter up her dear ones.

Her dad gave her a hearty hug and then held her at arm's length. "Well," he said, pronouncing the W as a V, as he always did, "my daughter seems to have survived so far."

He focused on Nick. "How's Berkeley? Have you convinced Mia she should have stayed here?"

They walked to the parking garage. Her dad placed his hand on her shoulder, an affectionate gesture, but it also helped him balance, made his limp less noticeable.

As they were driving back to Berkeley, her dad at the wheel, Nick asked, "What do you think of the Free Speech Movement?" Mia noticed Nick used the full name, rather than the initials, trying, no doubt, to appear neutral.

"I believe in free speech."

"So you think the demands are appropriate?"

"Well, I don't know. There is a difference between speech and advocacy. Being allowed to talk is different from being allowed to recruit. If people are asked to act, that may get in the way of open discussion. Open discussion is a fragile thing."

"It seems members of the Democratic and Republican parties are allowed to recruit and collect donations."

"Is that so?" her father's eyes widened. "Well, well. It's an imperfect institution, which should not surprise us." His smile was broad. "It was devised by mere humans."

"True, but it can be changed, improved."

"Yes, yes," Her dad smiled even wider. "We should make it equally unfair."

Chapter Fourteen

Mia felt nauseous after the red eye flight from the West Coast. When they landed at Logan, the ground was covered with grimy snow. A cold, wet wind blew through the coat that had kept her warm in Berkeley. On the taxi ride from the airport to the dorm, her spirits sank deeper as she stared out at the gray snow punctuated with yellow urine stains and puddles of black slush.

Jamie had not gotten back yet, so the dorm room felt empty and cold. Mia unpacked and sat at her desk reviewing the things she had to do before exams. She had an English theme to write, a portfolio to put together for design, and a problem set to complete for math. Thankfully, there was no project required for East Asian history. She also had to study for finals.

She was not worried about English. She would do her best and hope for a gentleman's — or was it a gentlewoman's — C. She did not think she could do better than that, so she might as well not spend time worrying about it.

Math would be no problem. She would complete the problem set and might also call the fellow who needed help before and see whether he wanted to study with her. She would be providing most of the help, but it would be a good way to review the material. And it would build up her cosmic brownie points.

East Asian history was a problem. She remembered her call with Chip, and a dark mood flowed through her. She was determined not to call him. She was on her own. She would make her own diagram. She'd ask around about the list of questions. Hopefully, she could get it from someone.

And then there was design. The portfolio was to contain 5 pieces, all of them based on the assignments from class. She did not like any of hers. She didn't know what to do. Panic set in.

Better start working instead of mooning about.

She started to redo the first design assignment. What was it the professor had said? She couldn't really remember, but it was something about letting her soul out. She didn't know what that meant. She put on her favorite music, the same record, which was getting so well-loved it buzzed with scratches.

Her design was awful. What else did the professor say, good music, wine, good friend. Remembering just made her sadder. She felt she was out of 'good friends.' She made another attempt at the design, letting her mind wander as she placed dots on the page. Where was Chip now? Would she hear from him? She was hitting the paper with the pen, dot after dot, when Jamie came in, huffing with the effort of carrying her overlarge suitcase.

"Hey, Mia. How was break?"

Mia shrugged. "How about yours?"

"Oh, it was fun. Lots of parties. Nice to see my high school friends." She maneuvered her suitcase onto the bed. As she clicked the latches it sprung open and she started unpacking. "Sure missed Hank though. We talked every day." She stopped to survey her heap of dirty clothes. "My parents were a little upset about the phone bill." She looked over to Mia. "Hard at work already?"

"Finals are not that far off, and I have design projects to complete." For the thousandth time Mia wished she could be as carefree as Jamie.

"You're a regular grind. Hank and I are going to the movies tonight. They play all the Bogart movies during reading period.

It's a rite of passage. There's a certain amount of — " Jamie stopped for emphasis " — 'audience participation.'"

"Like?" Mia said.

"Oohing and aahing. Hissing and throwing of popcorn." Jamie stuffed clothes in her laundry bag. "Should have done these at home, but I was having way too much fun." She got her detergent box and looked at Mia. "Maybe you and Chip can come with us."

"I don't think so."

"Why, what's wrong?"

"Nothing. Just pre-finals jitters, I guess."

"No, Mia, this looks like more than worry about finals."

Mia looked at her design project. She really didn't want to tell Jamie about Chip. She would tell Hank, so whatever she said would probably get back to Chip.

"How's Chip?"

How could Jamie know the problem was Chip? Mia felt tears spill down her cheeks. Between sobs Mia told Jamie everything.

"Well, Mia, I think you're right, not to go to bed with him. I, myself, plan on being a virgin on my wedding night. I mean, all this talk about free love, that's bunk. Ladies of the night don't believe in free love!"

Mia had to laugh. "But what about Hank?"

"Oh, Hank knows exactly what the score is, and if he doesn't like it, that's too bad."

"You don't feel pressured?"

"No. Nobody pressures me!"

"And you aren't tempted. I mean, well, one thing leads to another."

"Sure. I'm tempted. But I have my principles. If I require Hank to wait, I have to wait, too."

"And you don't feel like a tease?"

"Nope."

Mia was beginning to feel a little better.

"But," Jamie added, "you're wrong."

"Huh?"

"I'm sure that when Chip says he can wait, he means it."

"But he . . . I mean, I know he wants . . . ."

"Sure. But Chip is a good guy. And if he says he can wait . . . ."

"Well. OK. Anyhow, I think I really angered him, and I haven't heard from him. I don't want to appear too anxious."

"OK. Be like that. But you're missing a good time." Jamie picked up the stuffed laundry bag and the box of detergent and started toward the door. "See you when my clothes are clean."

Ten minutes later the phone rang.

"Mia!" Mia's heart raced as she recognized Chip's voice. "Did you know the Royal plays all the Bogart films during reading period?"

"Jamie told me." Mia wondered whether Jamie had arranged this call.

"Great. So Hank and Jamie are going tonight, and I thought it would be fun. Want to come with me?"

***

That night Chip and Hank arrived together, and all four walked down to the Royal, smothered in hats, coats, mittens, and scarves.

"So how were your holidays?" Chip asked.

"Nice. Too bad we have finals hanging over our heads, though," Mia said.

"Ah, well."

"How about your vacation?"

"It was great," Chip said. "I saw friends, and there was my

mother's famous New Year's Day party, so I saw all my relatives. Good times! But you know what I enjoyed the most?"

"What?"

"Working on my car. Bob and I made a list of all the things that need to be done. If I'm lucky, I might get everything done by graduation."

"You like working on the car that much?"

"Mia, I like that more than anything else I can think of."

They settled in their seats just before the movie, *Casablanca*, started. It was everything Jamie had promised: Oohs in the mushy parts, aahs at the silly scenery, hisses at the corny lines accompanied by the throwing of popcorn. The theater provided unlimited popcorn to eat and to throw. Mia loved it. She whistled and hissed. When the credits scrolled across the screen, she felt calmer.

As they walked back to Bertram, Chip asked, "Would you like to study for the history final together?"

"Yes, of course. When would be good?"

"I haven't done the diagram yet. How about day after tomorrow?"

"Sure," Mia said.

When they reached the front door, Chip held it open for her. "Thanks for coming, Mia. I enjoyed it."

Mia was startled. Chip had not touched her all evening. And here he was saying goodnight without so much as a peck on the cheek. "Goodnight," she said, as cheerily as she could.

Jamie came bustling in an hour later. "Have a good time?"

"Yes. It was fun," Mia said.

"And everything OK with Chip?"

Mia was silent, contemplating the gossip route back to Chip. She couldn't help herself, she needed to talk. "I guess, but Chip didn't touch me all evening." Mia looked at Jamie. "Do you think he doesn't like me anymore?"

Jamie shook her head. "Oh, I bet he would still say he loves you. I've no idea what's going on. But you know what I think, right?"

"Ugh! Veritas!" Mia let out a tremulous breath. "But I'm not sure how to even start."

The next afternoon, Chip called. "Want to go the Royal tonight? It's the *African Queen*."

"Sure."

"Great. I'll pick you up about 7:00."

And there he was, waiting as she came downstairs at 7:00. The walk to the theater was colder than the previous night. Mia shivered even with an extra sweater under her winter coat. She could see Chip was cold, too, as he wrapped his arms around his body. But he did not touch her. Not during the walk to the theater, not during the movie, not when they went out for hot chocolate afterward. Mia knew she should ask him what was going on, but she avoided the topic, talking instead about finals, his work on the car, anything. The scene at the dorm at the end of the evening was a repeat of the previous evening.

When she got to her room, Jamie was waiting for her. "Well, did you ask him?"

"No."

"Why not?"

"I just can't."

"Mia, nonsense. Ask him!"

"I can't."

"Then this relationship is doomed, my dear." On that cheery note Jamie left the room. Mia cried herself to sleep.

Chip and Mia had agreed to study for the history final the next day. Chip came over in the early afternoon, and they spread out in the living room, comparing diagrams and notes. Chip had brought an extra copy of previous years' finals questions. They studied well together, and Mia felt confident about that exam. Chip suggested they go to the Bogart film again that evening, stopping for dinner at the deli.

At dinner, Mia was on the verge of asking about his apparent lack of interest in her but stopped herself again and again. As they left the deli and walked down Mass Ave toward the theater, Chip walked next to her. She took a breath and quietly slid her hand into his. He took her hand, gave it a little squeeze, and they continued to walk, hand in hand.

"Chip, would you mind if we went for a coffee or something, instead of going to the movie?"

"Sure, Mia."

They stopped at a diner, a grubby place, but quiet, and Chip ordered two coffees.

"Here you go, Mia."

Mia looked down at her coffee and poured sugar into it, stirring it for a long time. She never took sugar in her coffee. Finally she looked up at him. "Chip, I don't know what to think."

He looked at her, waiting.

"Since break, you've been, well — " and she blurted it out " — you haven't touched me. Don't you find me attractive anymore?"

Chip smiled gently. "Mia, it just seemed that we had gotten off on the wrong foot. That you were feeling pressured."

Mia nodded. That was certainly true.

"So I thought maybe we should start all over."

"Start all over?"

"Yes. We will start again. We will do only what you want to do."

Mia felt her face flush.

"That's all. Just go at your own speed."

"Oh." Mia gulped. "But that puts me . . . I mean, well, it puts me in a strange place."

"You mean, you might not want me to know how much you enjoy the...."

Mia nodded. She could feel the heat in her cheeks.

"I can't help that, Mia. I'm just looking for a way to make us work."

***

Mia had done each of her five design assignments several times. She still had two days before she had to submit her portfolio. She sat on the bed considering the pieces. There was one, the first assignment, that had possibilities, but it wasn't there yet. The others felt hopeless.

"Go talk to your professor," Jamie said, assembling her books as she got ready for a study date with Hank.

"I don't even know what to say to him." Mia didn't want to show these poor re-tries to him.

"Say that! Say you don't know what to say, but that you're stuck."

"And what good will that do?" Mia felt her stomach tighten.

"I'm not sure, Mia." Jamie slung her book bag over her shoulder. "But it seems like you should give it a try." She buttoned her coat and left.

Mia didn't like the suggestion, but liked the solitude of her room even less. She flipped through the works once again and picked up the phone to call the professor.

She was amazed the professor was willing to see her on such short notice. She assembled her work in the folio, placed it carefully in the book bag, put on her coat, hat, and mittens, and headed out.

It was an icy walk to the Carpenter Center, the wind blowing a fine sleet that seemed to penetrate her coat, her sweater, her skin, so that, by the time she reached that severe building, she was shaking. She was not sure it was just the cold that made her shiver.

She raced up the two flights to the professor's office. He was sitting at his desk, leaning back in his chair, studying a design. He turned his head when she knocked.

"My dear, you look like a frozen Mona Lisa. Come in, come in." He indicated a chair. "Hang that coat of yours over there by the heater, so it can dry out a little."

"Thank you for seeing me."

"Of course. Maybe a cup of tea?" He nodded towards a hot plate with a kettle. There were a variety of mugs and cups there, in different colors and styles. He got up without a reply, and chose a large mug in calming tones of blues and greens. "This is my special cup for frozen students." He held it up for her to see the indented middle. "It is both a vessel for hot liquid to warm the insides and a hot bottle to warm the outsides."

He made the tea, handed it to her and settled back in his chair. "So what have you brought me?"

Mia pulled out her folio and handed it to him. He carefully took out the pieces and placed them on his desk. "So which of these do you like the best?" Mia pointed to the first assignment. "And you like it because?"

"Because I can see things in it. Because it seems to have character, but — "

"Yes."

"I can't tell you what's wrong with it, but it's just not right." She looked at him, hoping to see an answer. "I don't know how to make it right."

"That, my child, is the great mystery."

"I've tried a number of times." Mia shuddered thinking of the pile of rejected attempts on her floor.

"Of course. But doing design is not like scrubbing a floor. It's not something you can accomplish by trying harder. You have to allow your soul to work."

"How?"

"Oh, if I could answer that, there would be no need for design courses or design professors. I'd make one poster with the answer, and my work would be done."

Mia sighed.

"My child, I can see you are working hard, probably too hard. Now, I suggest you simply submit these as your portfolio. And if you really want to, but only if you truly desire it, you might try one or two of these again. Your soul will wake up when it is ready. All we can do is give it space, nourish it. Fretting will not help."

Chapter Fifteen

Jamie walked into the room carrying the mail. "Grades are in." She handed Mia a few letters, the top one from Harvard College.

Mia's hand trembled as she opened the envelope and pulled out the single sheet. A in math. Good. C+ in English, as expected. B+ in history. Wow! That was good.

Then her eyes settled on the design grade. C. Oh. C. Oh, no.

Jamie was looking at her. "Well?"

"C in design." Mia let the page fall to her desk.

"Well, that's not so bad."

"Oh, yes it is. How can I be an architect if I get a C in design?"

"Mia, it's just one course. And that is such a subjective thing. One person's art is another person's trash."

"And the professor was so nice. It feels like he stabbed me in the back."

"What about your other grades?"

Jamie took the grades from Mia's desk.

As Jamie scanned the sheet, Mia realized she hadn't asked Jamie about her grades. How selfish! "How'd you do?"

"Fine." She looked at Mia. "These aren't bad. A B+ in history is great. That course is supposed to be a real grind. And an A, not an A-, but a full A in math. That's outstanding. I mean, Susan is taking first-year calculus and she's having an awful time."

That afternoon Chip and Mia went to downtown Boston. They had planned to go to the Museum of Fine Arts, but decided to go to Filene's bargain basement instead. They walked through the crowded aisles, clothing squeezed together on racks, various garments on the floor. Mia threatened to buy a pink and lavender man's shirt for Chip. Chip retaliated with a black floor length dress, with a high collar and long sleeves.

"It's perfect for you."

"It'll go well with my great-grandmother's button-up boots."

When they tired of wandering the store, they went to a diner and settled into red vinyl chairs at a matching Formica table. They ordered coffee and strudel.

Mia bit into the flaky pastry, its fruit sweet and tart. "Maybe I should quit school and learn how to make perfect strudel." The sun shone through the windows, making the little shop warm. Mia slipped out of her heavy coat.

"Really, you get so down, just because of one grade in one course." Chip sipped his coffee.

"A C! In the required course for my major!" Mia fiddled with the pastry on her plate. "Oh, Chip, what am I going to do?"

"Live, breathe! Don't worry so much! According to Bugs Bunny, you shouldn't take life so seriously because no one gets out alive."

"That's supposed to cheer me up?"

"No?" Chip wiggled out of his coat. "Well, if you could make strudel like these guys, I'd open a shop for you."

A departing customer opened the outside door, allowing a frigid blast of wintry cold to sweep in. Mia cradled the hot coffee mug in her hands.

"Mia, remind me. Why do you want to become an architect?"

"Because I love the house I grew up in. Because it makes me feel safe and happy. Because I would like to create such extraordinary spaces."

"Hmm." Chip looked at her. "I hope this doesn't make you angry, but — Why don't you major in math?"

"Math?"

"Yes. Math. You seem to take to it like a duck to water. I mean, that course you took is notorious. People say it's so hard. And you didn't break a sweat."

"But — " she shook her head " — I know what a real mathematician can do."

"Hey, I know your father is brilliant, that he's a genius. But you don't have to be a genius to be a math major."

"But what do I do with a math major if I don't become a mathematician?" She had a vision of herself ten year later, in front of a room of pimply teens passing notes and giggling. "A high school teacher?"

"You're arrogant, you know." All trace of good cheer had faded from his face. "It's not all about what you do as a career. And you don't have to be a world famous whatever to be OK."

"Easy for you to say." Sometimes he made her so mad. "You have your life and your success all mapped out for you." He was majoring in history. He would get a law degree and join his father's firm. He just had to make reasonable grades and he was managing that fine.

Chip nodded. "But, Mia, career is not that important."

"You mean, career is not that important for a woman." Her raw tone embarrassed her.

"Or for a man. It is a way to make a living. But it's family that's important, and friends and community. You have those and all else will fall into place."

She shook her head. He just didn't get it.

They sat in silence, finishing their treats and sipping the coffee. Mia looked out at the street. The sun shone brightly and people no longer hurried against the cold. The wind must have died down.

"OK. Let's look at it from another angle," Chip said. "Maybe the problem is the professor."

"I feel betrayed. Professor Guillaume was so kind when I went to see him and then he gave me a C."

"Maybe you should take your next course from another professor."

"It's either Guillaume or Professor MacDougal, who has a bad, bad reputation."

"How so?"

"Mean!"

"Well, maybe not, then."

Mia studied Chip's face. His blue eyes were kind, in spite of her childish behavior. "Chip, thanks. I'm sorry."

They pushed back from the table, Chip paid at the register and they walked into the street. The sun had warmed the chill air. Chip stopped and pointed to a low slung car. "See that Avanti? The blue one?"

Mia studied the car's too long nose. It looked slightly cross-eyed from the way the fenders jutted out beside the headlights.

"It's got such a nice look."

Oh, well, Mia thought. She didn't get cars.

"Smooth, aerodynamic. And it has a lot of oomph." He stared at the car. "Not a lot of those made. We're lucky to see it."

"So, Chip, what do you like more, looking at the exterior of the car or working on the guts of the car?"

"Why? Do I have to choose?"

"No. I was just curious."

"To be honest, I've never really thought about how to design the exterior. I do like looking at them, though. It makes me happy. Maybe like looking at 'interior spaces' makes you happy. And I love fixing cars, getting greasy, figuring out how things work, what is wrong. It fascinates me."

"So, if that makes you so happy, why don't you become a car mechanic rather than a lawyer?" She should be ashamed, poking him like this, but it was just too tempting.

Chip stopped and turned toward her, his eyes sparkling, "Oh, Mia, you witch. You won't let me get away with anything, will you!" He wrapped his arm around her waist and pulled her to him.

Chapter Sixteen

Mia slid into the chair next to Chip, dumping her book bag and wet coat on the chair on the other side. She was early to history class and was surprised Chip was already there. He looked up at her, closed his notebook hastily, and nodded.

"What you doing?" she asked.

"Just doodling."

"Let me see!" She reached for the notebook. He pulled it out of her reach. "What, drawing naked women again?" He was hiding something! "Come on." She wagged her finger, indicating he should give it to her. Chip hesitated. Mia could tell he really wanted to show her. "Give it here!"

He handed it to her. There were sketches of cars and fenders, hoods and wheels. She turned back a page. There were side views, each little drawing a slight variation. "I like this one," she said, pointing to a drawing at the bottom of the page.

The professor cleared his throat loudly, and she realized the class was waiting for her and Chip to pay attention. Mia blushed, closed the book and scrabbled for her own notebook. This was the last lecture before the hourly exam, so it was review. She listened, took notes, and thought about the diagram she and Chip were working on. She sighed. If only design had a secret formula for success like the diagrams for history.

Changing to Professor MacDougal's section of design had been traumatic. At each class, the professor would go to the works pinned to the wall and, using a red marker, would slash a thick mark here and another one there. His favorite words were "makes no sense," "ugly," and "kindergarten stuff." She was not the only student who had left the room in tears. Even the pieces she thought were good he destroyed with his red felt weapon.

On a cold, wet March afternoon, Mia had an appointment to see Professor MacDougal. He had demanded she make the appointment. There was no invitation to sit, no hot cup of tea, no talk of nourishing her soul.

Mia stood in front of the professor's desk. He looked up. "You have no talent." His voice was businesslike, cold. "If you withdraw your design major, I will give you a C in this course. But you must never take another design course at this university. If you do, I will see to it that you fail. Is this clear?"

Mia stood, not moving, reviewing each word in her mind. Never. Take. Another. Design. Course. Fail. Fail. Fail.

"Clear?" His voice was louder, penetrating.

Mia focused on him.

"Is that clear?"

He was getting up from his desk. Mia, actually afraid he might hit her, nodded.

"That is all then. You may go." He settled back in his chair and started sorting through papers on his desk.

And go she did, out of the office, down the cold corridors, out of the chilly steel and glass front door, back to the dorm, tears running down her cheeks. Mrs. Staunton, the house mother, saw her as she ran in the front door and up the stairs to her room. A moment later, as Mia sobbed into her pillow, Mrs. Staunton knocked gently on the door.

"Are you sick, Mia?"

Between sobs, nose-blowing, and eye-dabbing, she told Mrs. Staunton about her interview with Professor MacDougal. Mrs. Staunton sent Mia to the dean that afternoon.

The interview with the dean was short. She was a middle-aged woman, dressed in what Mia thought of as intellectual clothes, a top with primitive designs of animals in browns and blacks, a longish black skirt and sensible shoes. Dean Michel told Mia there was plenty of time to change majors. For the moment, she should do something fun and not worry too much. They made an appointment to have another conversation in a week.

When Mia returned to the room, Jamie was at her typewriter, banging away. She stopped typing. "Rough day?"

And, of course, the whole story tumbled out, for the third time that afternoon.

"Well, he sounds like a real bastard!"

Mia nodded.

"But maybe he did you a favor."

"Veritas," Mia said, anticipating Jamie's thoughts.

Jamie smiled. "You're working way too hard and you don't seem to enjoy it."

Mia nodded.

"Take something easy. Or easy for you. Like math?" Jamie beamed. "Take something easy. Then marry Chip."

"Really, Jamie." She picked up the phone to call Chip.

Twenty minutes later he was downstairs. He must have run the entire way.

They walked around the quad, Mia telling her story again. When she had finished, Chip held both her arms and studied her face. "Thank goodness. I thought your mother had died."

Mia recalled that Professor Guillaume had said the same thing. "But this is important. This is my life!"

"Yes, yes, but this storm has been brewing."

***

After a week thinking about her major, Mia still didn't know what to do. Her mother said she should do what she enjoyed.

But she didn't enjoy anything. Her father, typical father, said children should be allowed to make their own mistakes. Jamie insisted her major didn't matter, just as long as she married Chip. And Chip, sweet, patient Chip, just listened.

The dean was friendly, but got down to work immediately.

"Mia, you can talk to a counselor, who can give you some interest tests and based on those results, we can help you choose courses for next year. Or we can plan courses based on work you have already done."

"I took those interest tests in high school. I think I know what they will say." The results had advised her to become a forest ranger. She wasn't interested.

"What about history then? You've done very well in the History of East Asia course, a known difficult course."

Mia thought about all the help she had gotten from Chip. "What about math?"

The dean frowned. "I couldn't recommend math. Women do not do well in math."

Mia shook her head. "Excuse me?"

The dean smiled weakly, her eyes warm but dismissive. "Women don't do well in math. History is much better."

What kind of deans did they have at Radcliffe? "But I got an A in Calc II."

The dean looked down at the sheet in front of her. "My goodness, you did. That's good." She looked back at Mia, the warmth in her eyes replaced with a steely sharpness. "Still, women don't do well in math."

Mia closed her eyes. This woman made Chip look like a raving women's liberationist.

After her appointment with the dean, Mia headed for Divinity Street, where the math department shared a building with the Yenching Library. It was early April, and the forsythia buds showed tiny yellow lines where their flower petals were pushing out, promising that spring had not skipped over Cambridge. Mia felt lighter, happier than she had been since she came to Harvard. She patted one of the stone lions that guarded the walk to the building's door, jogged down the path, and ran up the steps to the math department office. Nan, the math department secretary, was at her desk sorting through a manuscript. She looked up with a smile.

"Hi. What do I need to do to become a math major?"

"You need to make an appointment with an adviser. Do you know who you'd like to talk to?"

"No idea." Mia shook her head. "But I'm taking second year calculus from Professor Griffin. I like him. Might that work?"

"Sure." Nan paged through a calendar at the side of her desk and arranged for Mia to meet with Professor Griffin. "Here's a little information for math majors." She pulled a booklet from the shelf behind her. She smiled at Mia again. "It'll be nice to have another lady around here. We are few and far between!"

Mia put the booklet in her book bag, thanked Nan, and walked to Gray. She picked up the house phone and dialed Chip's number. Please be there, she thought. The phone rang and rang. She hung up. As she turned to go, she felt a hand on her shoulder.

"Slumming, are you?"

She looked up into Chip's face. "Hmm."

He scanned her face. "My, you look happy! Don't tell me you murdered Professor MacDougal and came here to confess."

"Not quite that. But you're close."

"So?"

"Invite me up and I'll tell you all the gory details."

"Fair enough." Chip signed her in.

"So who have you murdered, with which implement, and in what room?" Chip pushed a pile of books on the sofa to one side, so they had room to sit.

"The dean seemed to think women should not be math majors."

Chip's right eyebrow arched up. "You're kidding me, aren't you?"

"No. Absolutely not kidding you. She said she couldn't recommend math as a major because women don't do well in math." Mia relished Chip's annoyed look. "So I decided that was what I needed to do. No stupid dean can say I can't be a math major."

"OK. But that seems a little thin for choosing your major, doesn't it?"

"I suppose." Mia chuckled. "I went over to the math building, a nice friendly place, much nicer than the Carpenter Center. I have an appointment with Professor Griffin to talk about the major."

"Sounds good."

"And Nan, the secretary, acted like I was actually welcome, like I was not an imposition on her."

"That's good." Chip smiled. He chuckled. He laughed.

"What?"

"Now I know how to get you to do something." His eyes twinkled. "Just say girls can't do it."

Mia grew red in the face. She grabbed a cushion from the couch and slammed it into his shoulder as hard as she could. He pushed it aside and drew her to him.

Quite a while later Chip looked at his watch. "Oh, damn, we missed dinner. Well, I think the Blue Angel's calling."

A hint of spring warmed the air as they walked to the restaurant. They talked of courses and midterms and Hank and Jamie.

"Do you think it will last?" Chip asked.

"Sure." Mia wondered why Chip would question that

relationship.

After they had settled at a table and ordered, Chip said, "I have something I wanted to talk with you about. My cousin Julia is getting married."

"Oh."

"The wedding will be at Martha's Vineyard, a few days after the end of exams."

"Sounds nice." Mia knew that Martha's Vineyard was posh.

"So." Chip cleared his throat. "I was wondering whether you would come with me to the wedding?"

"Why, Chip, that sounds so nice."

"That isn't a yes."

Mia didn't want to make him sad. Not today. "Well, then, yes."

"Wait, I should tell you, it'll be the whole weekend."

"Sure!" She razzed him, too happy to hold her tongue. "Ask me for a date, and then, like a true lawyer, we get to the fine print."

He ignored her. "There will be a rehearsal dinner the night before, on Friday. I'm not in the wedding party, but apparently I'm supposed to show up at the dinner. The wedding and the reception are on Saturday. And a family brunch on Sunday. So I will be monopolizing you the entire weekend."

"I'm exhausted already." She tried to think about the weekend. "Do we drive down for each of these events?"

"No, no. My parents are renting a house for the summer. They have plenty of room. Mom would love to have you. Matter of fact, I think you'll get a note from her in the next couple of days, asking you."

"Oh, Chip." Mia's silliness receded and her stomach took a nervous flip. "I know how to be on good behavior for dinner, but an entire weekend?"

"Don't worry. We'll be able to get away from the folks now

and again."

Mia could see how much he wanted her to come. Should she give him a real yes? There would be no backing out. Or no? Or maybe?

"The house they rented is supposed to be nice, right on the water, with a private beach."

"OK," she heard herself say. What was she doing? She pinched herself, thinking how rude she must sound. "It sounds wonderful. Thank you."

"That's a yes, then?"

"Yes."

Chip beamed.

As they walked back to the Radcliffe quad, she felt a glow. Perhaps this was happiness.

When Mia opened the door to her room, Jamie was cutting the pages of a book. It was one of those books, printed in Europe, where the pages were not pre-cut.

"What're you doing?" Mia asked.

"Hank and I stayed out a little later than planned, so I haven't read my assignment. But I can't appear in class without having the pages cut."

"You're disgusting, Jamie." Mia shook her head. "I work like the devil, to mediocre results, and you, you just slide right through."

Jamie slit another page. "You could help. I need the pages of this book cut, too, and I'm running out of time." She held up a second volume and a knife.

Mia settled in to the chore. "But listen, I have all kinds of news!"

Mia started telling Jamie about her day, the interview with the dean and going to the math department.

"It's about time! The design department sounds like a bunch of sadists. And being a math major, that was a no brainer. This way you'll slide right through, too." Jamie slit another page.

"How many pages were you supposed to read?"

"Oh, the usual, about two hundred, I suppose." The sound of the knife through the pages made a satisfying whoosh.

"Anyhow, then I went over to Chip's and told him all the news, and we went out to dinner to celebrate."

Jamie nodded. Whoosh. Whoosh.

"And he's asked me to come with him to his cousin's wedding."

Jamie put down the book and knife and looked at Mia. "My god, Mia, he really must love you!"

Mia looked quizzical. "Love me?"

"Yes! Introducing you to his parents, that's a good sign, but inviting you to a family wedding? That's a whole different level."

"It is?"

"Sure. It's an announcement. It says, 'Here's my girl.'" Jamie looked at Mia with raised eyebrows.

"I didn't think of it quite like that." Mia wondered whether she liked being announced as Chip's girl.

"So tell me all about it." Jamie settled back in the chair, ready to relish the whole story.

"It's going to be over a whole weekend on Martha's Vineyard. Chip's parents have rented a house down there, and they have invited me to stay with them."

"Wait!" Jamie held up her hand.

"What? That it will be a whole weekend?"

"No, you goose! That his parents have invited you to stay with them."

"So?"

"Oh, Mia, you are hopeless." Jamie shook her head. "Don't you see? It's not just that Chip is serious. No. He's asked his parents to invite you!"

"Yes."

"And his parents are serious. Because otherwise they wouldn't have invited you."

"Oh." Mia frowned. "You're making me nervous."

"Good! I might not have trouble with my courses, but you slide right into a SERIOUS relationship with a handsome, eligible man who adores you."

"What about Hank?"

Jamie looked away. "He likes me, I know that. But, well, just look at it this way. I haven't met his parents."

"Oh," Mia thought about Chip's question. Maybe Jamie and Hank weren't a done deal.

Jamie turned her gaze back to Mia. "Anyway, you lucky bum. What are you going to wear?"

"I," Mia swallowed, "I haven't even thought of that." She looked at Jamie. "Oh, Jamie, I'm scared. I mean, I don't want to be on display. I'll put my foot in my mouth for sure."

"Cool it, kid." Jamie's eyes had taken on their usual mischief. "The bride will be the center of attention. You'll just be a side show."

Chapter Seventeen

Mia went to her meeting with Professor Griffin the following week. He was a tall fellow, mid-fifties, graying hair, and handsome. He greeted her with, "Glad to have you join the gang."

"Thanks." Mia tried to relax.

"I think I met your father at a conference. It was a while ago. Daniel Brower?"

Mia nodded.

"Not a bad mathematician for a physicist." Mia understood this was a compliment, but she felt uneasy. She did not want to be compared to her father.

Perhaps Professor Griffin sensed her unease because he changed the subject. "So why math?"

Mia wished she had some sensational reason: I've loved math since I was born; I dream in equations. But she couldn't think of anything. "To be honest, I seem to do better in math than in any other subject."

"Excellent." The professor had a soft smile that reassured Mia. Maybe Veritas worked even with professors. He cleared his throat. "Have you considered what branch of math you might want to pursue?"

Mia frowned. Just deciding to change into math had been so difficult. "No."

"Good! That means you have lots of interesting exploring to do." And with that, Professor Griffin discussed possible courses. They laid out a plan. "But Mia, if you think you want to alter this, just let me know. I suggest you look into the texts of each course, they are all in the math library."

Again he flashed an encouraging smile. "Stop by anytime. If my door is open, visitors are welcome."

Instead of going back to the dorm, Mia walked across campus toward the Coop to buy a new notebook for her mathematical exploring. As she passed by Mem Chu, she noticed Chip's tall figure. He was talking to a fellow who seemed out of place, his olive green jacket, too large for his shoulders, hung unevenly, his crumbled gray slacks' frayed edges fell over tan boots, worn and mud spattered. There was something familiar about the man's stance, slouching and uneven, but Mia saw only his back and could not place him.

Chip looked up, saw Mia, and waved her over.

"Hey, Mia, you remember Sam."

Mia looked at the man. Sam! Of course. The white-blond hair, the ice blue eyes, still hard, and the crooked smile. But he was thinner. And dingy.

"Hi, Sam."

"Hey, Mia" Sam's smile vanished. "I owe you an apology."

Mia could think of a number of things Sam should apologize for. "Oh?"

"Yeah, you were right about war."

That was not on her list.

"Don't you remember? That first time we met? You were singing that protest song, and I gave you trouble about it?"

Mia riffled through her memory.

"You know." Sam began to sing in a deep voice, pure and clear, "Where have all the flowers gone?"

"Oh yes. I remember." Mia had to smile. That seemed so long ago.

"You were right. The U.S. is waging war against the Vietnamese people." Sam face was solemn now. "Here." As he looked through a satchel that hung across his body, Sam's watch glimmered from under the frayed cuffs of his jacket. He pulled out a sheet and handed it to Mia.

It was a black and white flyer. To the left was a crude line drawing, of a woman carrying a child in a sling on her back and a little boy standing beside her. To the right, block letters read:

**END THE WAR
IN
VIETNAM
MARCH ON
WASHINGTON
APRIL 17, 1965**

In the lower right hand corner were the words, in block letters, Students for a Democratic Society. The words Vietnam and Washington were in a larger font, clearly hand written. It was rough and cheap.

"You and Chip should come to the march. It's important."

"Maybe we will." Chip looked at the sheet.

Sam adjusted the satchel strap across his shoulder. "Gotta get to a meeting."

Sam started across the Yard.

"Stay in touch!" Chip shouted.

Sam turned his head. "Sure!" He placed his fingers to his temple and gave a friendly salute.

Chip stared as Sam strode behind Mem Chu, his gait fast, but uneven. "Maybe he has found his way. Maybe it was best he left school."

Sam was thrown out of school, he had not left, but Mia didn't want to quibble.

"He's not a bad guy."

Mia didn't agree, but she nodded.

Chip took the flyer from Mia. "Maybe Sam has found a way for himself."

"But what do you know about Vietnam?"

"Nothing really. But it's good the subject be brought up." Chip gazed to where Sam had disappeared behind Mem Chu. "And it's good for Sam. He says he's off the booze and drugs."

"That's good." And, Mia thought to herself, it's good he is out of my life.

Chapter Eighteen

The forsythia burst open a sunny yellow, as Mia had never noticed in Berkeley. The daffodils bloomed, and the tulips and the apple trees and the pears. The sweet warm air, carrying the scents of spring flowers, caressed her. Mia walked along the Charles River, to see the kids with kites and the dogs running. The perfect days nourished her feelings for Chip. He was handsome and kind. She was the luckiest girl alive, at least as far as romance was concerned.

Her studies were not excellent, but at least she did not feel she was heading for calamity. And she was in a department that seemed to want her.

There were two clouds in this sunny picture.

The first was the summer. Chip would intern at his father's firm. But she had no summer plans. She had been so busy worrying about school and Chip and Martha's Vineyard that she had forgotten to plan the summer. Her parents said she should come home. Maybe she could get a job, they said, or perhaps just have a relaxing summer. It seemed like limbo to her, but she had no alternative.

The other problem, the one that bothered her more, was Martha's Vineyard. What would she wear? Who would she meet? Would she know what to do? She had been to just one wedding. That sounded strange to Jamie, whose typical summer included half a dozen weddings. But Jamie had a large family with aunts, uncles, cousins, and every other type of relation known to man. There were just five other people in Mia's family: her mother and father, her grandmother, her aunt and a cousin. She did have other family, but they were still in Europe, people Mia had never met. Mia's parents talked about them, but for Mia they were like characters in a fairy tale, people who only existed in stories.

The wedding ceremony itself didn't bother her. Mia knew the basic etiquette of church going. It was the parties. Three of them in three days.

Jamie offered to help with the wardrobe and encouraged Mia, saying everything else was a matter of being herself. Chip and his parents seemed to like her the way she was, so just keep doing what she always did, saying what she always said. Besides, Jamie had reminded her, remember Veritas. Be yourself. If they don't like that, so be it.

Jamie went through Mia's closet, choosing outfits. They looked through Jamie's jewelry — Mia didn't have jewelry — and found some pieces. Then they went to Filenes' and found just the right dress for the reception. Mia would look, Jamie assured her, prettier than the bride. "But you mustn't look better dressed," she added with a giggle.

***

Reading period came. Mia studied for her finals. Exams came. She took them. It was as exhausting as last time, but not quite as terrifying. The day after her last final, she did her ritual cleaning and laundry. And she packed for the weekend at Martha's Vineyard.

As she packed, she thought about Chip. Did she love him? What did it mean to love someone?

There was one thing for sure. She lusted for him. They hadn't gone to bed. They had made out, and each time they had gone a little further. And each time, when Mia said enough, Chip had stopped, without a whimper or a curse. Now

Mia wanted to go all the way. She wanted it, right now, more than she wanted a career, or to be married, or anything else.

But what would Chip think of her then? Or Jamie? Or her parents?

She wasn't worried about her parents. Her mom had written a 'To Whom It May Concern' letter before she departed for Radcliffe, giving permission for her minor daughter to receive birth control. She had said perhaps it was better to have lost one's virginity before marriage. "So one is not driven to marriage just to go to bed with someone. Marriage is about sex, but also a lot of other things. Better to have the sex part settled, so one can consider the other aspects: children, finances, who does the dishes."

Mia snorted, thinking about her mother's logic. Jamie's logic was just the opposite. "I will not give sex for free. The price of my virginity is a marriage certificate." Maybe that made sense for Jamie. She would have ascertained her potential mate's opinion about the other things, particularly the dishes, before she agreed to marriage.

Mia was different. She didn't think that far ahead. She tended to focus on one problem, and all other things faded into the background. Maybe her mother was right. Maybe it was better to get the sex question out of the way.

And Mia didn't think Jamie would care, from a moral point of view. She would advise against it, but she would not condemn Mia.

So that left Chip. Funny. Chip's opinion was most important, and about that she was most uncertain.

What would Jamie say? Veritas! Ask him! And so, Mia decided, as she closed her suitcase, she would ask him.

The thought excited her.

And terrified her.

Chapter Nineteen

Chip picked Mia up the next day. He was driving a black Karmann Ghia, borrowed from one of Bob's friends. It was just like his car, which sat in pieces in his father's garage. Chip was so excited about the car, and the progress he and Bob had made, and what still needed to be done, that he talked and talked and talked about it. Mia let him go on. The time for The Conversation was not while he was driving.

The day was bright, the top of the Karmann Ghia was down, the sun was hot, and by the time they had taken the ferry to Martha's Vineyard and driven up to the house, Mia felt wilted.

Chip's mom greeted them at the door, telling Chip to take the suitcases up to Mia's room and his own. She led Mia into a comfortable cool room overlooking the water.

"This is stunning." Mia looked out the floor to ceiling window at a perfect picture: blue sky, a sandy path leading through tall grass, variegated in shades of green, and beyond the deep aqua water with a lacy white edge where the waves spilled against the beige beach.

"Yes, we love it." Mrs. Walsh brought in two lemonades and set them on the table. "I hope you like lemonade. I also have water, if you prefer."

"Lemonade is perfect."

"I don't know how much Chip has told you about the proceedings." Chip's mom apparently believed Chip had said very little. "My niece, Julia, is getting married. She's a dear, almost my own daughter, really. You know she is my twin sister's child."

"That's neat."

Chip came into the room, sat at the table, and took a sip of lemonade. "I assume this is for me." He smiled as he lifted the glass toward his mother.

His mother shook her head but smiled. "Now as far as plans, Chip, tonight we will go to the dinner. It will be at George's parents' house, just a little ways away. I've got the address and the directions, in case you want to go separately." Mrs. Walsh handed Chip a paper. "We need to be ready by about 4:00. Then tomorrow the wedding is at Grace Episcopal Church. You know where that is, right?"

"Sure, Mom." Chip listened while his mother rattled off all the logistics, like a military operations officer, making sure everything was in place before the battle.

"It's a 1 o'clock wedding, so I would like to leave here at noon. The reception is at 4:30, at the Fisher House. The brunch on Sunday is at your aunt's summer home. Since she's in Woods Hole, we will need to take the ferry. But that's more relaxed. Brunch starts about 12. I'm not sure whether you would want to leave from Woods Hole or whether you want to come back here. We'd love to have you as long as you'd like."

"Mom, that's sweet, but I think we better head back to Cambridge from the brunch. Mia has a plane to catch on Monday."

"Of course, dear, but please be timely." Mrs. Walsh turned to Mia. "Sorry, but I thought we should get this all figured out."

***

Mia and Chip lay on the sand warming up from their frolic in the sea. The water was cold, and the waves, according to Mia, were wimpy, not like California waves, not waves you could surf in. But she had to admit, it was lovely, the blue sky, the gray-green of the salt water, the tangy smell of fish and salt and distant places.

Mia still hadn't asked her question. The longer she waited the easier it was to avoid. But she had to ask. Just not quite yet. So she thought of another question to ask. She rolled toward Chip and drew a gritty heart on his sandy chest.

"So what is Sam's nickname for you that made you so mad?"

"Grease Monkey." Chip sat up and leaned on his arm.

"Because you love working on cars?"

"Yeah. One time he came to stay with my family. I took him out to the garage and showed him the cars, one of my dad's in particular. I opened the hood, and started showing him this and that, and pretty soon I was covered in grease." Chip looked at Mia, his lips smiling, but his eyes troubled.

Why would that make him so mad? "That's not all, is it?"

Chip looked off toward the ocean. "No. That's not all. Of course, that's not all."

"And?"

Chip looked back towards Mia, looked deep into her eyes. "Mia, this is a very sordid thing. It's hard to talk about it."

Mia waited.

"Sam was a sad, mixed-up character, and I was under his thrall." Chip's eyes widened, his face glistened with sweat. The waves whispered on the shore and the gulls called. "We were intimate." His voice was ragged and low.

Mia swallowed. She tried to imagine their embrace, but her mind blocked it.

"I complained the first time...not that I didn't like it...but...he told me I was responsible to bring...."

The words came in spurts even as Mia tried to blot them out.

"He made me bring...." Tears mingled with the sweat on

Chip's cheeks. "the lubricant." Chip's eyes darted past Mia, shifting far out to sea. "He reminded me by calling me Grease Monkey."

Chip's silent tears dripped from his face, clearing rivulets on his sandy chest.

Mia swallowed again even though her mouth was dry. "Are you still under his thrall?"

"No." He took in a tremulous breath. "That ended years ago." Chip wiped tears with the back of his hand. "In boarding school." Chip looked at Mia. "Can you still . . . ."

"And that's why the whole thing with Gloria was so hard?"

"No. That was something else. Not wanting to get him in trouble." His voice was stronger, more confident.

"But he seemed to be the — " Mia rejected the word dominant " — strong one."

"He was once, but — " Chip paused. "He got crazier and crazier, like he wanted to be in trouble. Senior year, I got him out of a mess."

"So that was why you were so happy he had found a cause?"

"Yes."

"Have you seen him since we saw him in the Yard?"

"No. Haven't heard anything, either." Chip brushed sand from his chest. "Mia, I've never told anyone about this."

Mia rubbed her hands across the sand. She wanted to say I understand or it's OK, but that wasn't true. She did not understand, and it was not OK. She just nodded.

Chip sighed. "I must really love you."

Mia looked out at the infinite water, wishing she were at some distant place.

Chapter Twenty

Mia let the hot water beat against her back as her mind raced. Was Chip gay? What did this all mean? Was it time to bolt? Should she go to the party tonight? Maybe she could say she was sick. When everyone was out, she could call a cab and somehow get back to Cambridge.

She stepped out of the shower, taking a thick towel from the rack. She took several deep breaths, trying to relax.

She was in no danger. Chip would not hurt her, so the downside of staying was negligible.

She ran her fingers through her hair, feeling the sand. No time to wash it.

She decided she was staying.

She brushed her hair, hoping to get most of the sand out. Her hair was throwing a curly tantrum, ringlets heading in all directions.

Yes. She was staying. It would be rude to leave, overly dramatic.

She slipped on her panties. Better to just go through the weekend. She fastened her bra. She and Chip would be apart for the summer. She pulled on one stocking. She wouldn't call or answer the phone. She wouldn't write. She pulled on the other stocking.

She took the red silky dress from the hanger and shimmied into it.

By the fall Chip would have found someone else.

She zipped the side zipper and looked at herself in the mirror. Not beautiful. Her eyes were too close together, her lips too thin. But the dress, a simple sleeveless bodice with a full skirt, showed her sleek body, her slightly muscled arms, her long legs.

She wondered how she would manage the party tonight.

She found her white flats. Jamie had insisted she could not wear black shoes to a summer wedding and wanted her to buy red shoes to go with the dress. They had compromised on white.

Jamie had given her lipstick, too, but she didn't know how to use it and had no patience for it. She took the golden tube from her purse, pulled the cover off and screwed the lipstick up. The color did match her dress. But if she tried to put it on and messed up . . . .

There was a knock at her door. "You ready?" Chip asked.

"Just a moment." She lowered the lipstick back into its case and left it on the dresser.

She opened the door.

Chip inhaled. "Oh, you are beautiful."

"Thank you." She hoped the formality would keep Chip at a distance.

"Look Mia, I probably shouldn't have told you about me and Sam."

"It's OK," Mia said, turning back into the room to get her purse.

"But I don't want this to . . . ." Chip sighed and started again. "I love you, Mia. I hope you can understand this and not let it get in the way."

Mia forced herself to smile. "We'd better be off to the party."

Chapter Twenty-One

The groom's parents' house looked like a little Cape Cod Cottage from the road, but that was deceptive. The party was held in the back yard, a vast expanse of green sloping down to the sandy brown shore, the blue water beyond. Sturdy tables sat on the lawn covered with crisp white linen. Eight sets of translucent china, gleaming silver, and sparkling crystal marked the places at each table, and bouquets of wild flowers in purples, yellows and pinks decorated each center.

The party was already humming when Mia and Chip walked along the path to the drinks table. Chip introduced her to George, the red-headed groom, and Julia, the bride, dark and tall like Chip. Then there were the groom's parents and the bride's parents, the best man, the maid of honor, and on and on. Chip wandered the lawn, always smiling, always saying the right thing, and always an arm around her waist or clasping her hand. Even though she wanted to keep her distance, she was grateful for his protective presence in the sea of people.

Finally the introductions were completed, and Mia stood, trying to seem occupied looking out to sea, when a little red-headed boy of seven or eight came running up, almost colliding with her.

"Is your dad really Dr. Brower?" The youngster looked up at Mia, his expression demanding an answer. "Chip says your dad is Dr. Brower."

Mia smiled at the boy's impatient face. "Yes."

"Wow. I saw him on Disney's show about the atom."

Mia laughed, remembering the show. "Did you like it?"

"Oh yes! I want to grow up to be just like him. I want to be a scientist and build a rocket that goes to outer space."

"Oh, Justin!" A slender woman with the same red hair walked up, taking the youngster's hand. "I hope you aren't disturbing Mia!"

"Not at all." Mia smiled at Justin. "Such enthusiasm!"

"Could I meet Dr. Brower?" Justin's stare required a positive response.

"Justin, please!"

"Really, that's fine," Mia answered the woman's unspoken apology. "Justin, maybe if you are in California you could meet him."

The boy beamed. "Thanks." He darted off.

"I hope you don't mind...."

"Not at all." Mia smiled again. "It's nice. My dad would be so pleased to have inspired Justin."

"I'm Joan," she said, "George's older sister."

"So many people...."

"Sure." Joan's straight red hair shone. "I hear you are at Radcliffe. I'm a Cliffie, too. '52."

"Really?"

"I bet things have changed a little since my time." Joan glanced at the man who had just walked up. "This is my husband, Jeff."

"Hi, there." Jeff nodded his head. "Chip tells me you're a mathematician."

"Hardly. I'm just a math major."

"Good choice. I majored in math. Had a great time. Then became a lawyer. Not nearly as much fun, but it pays the bills."

The sun was sinking when the company finally sat down to dinner. Chip sat on her left, Jeff on her right. The meal was a sequence of delicacies, shrimp and caviar with white wine, steak and lobster with red wine, crème brûlée with sweet port, coffee and cognac.

During the courses Jeff and Chip exchanged stories about Harvard, and Justin explained the idea of a chain reaction as it had been demonstrated on the Disney show. Mia marveled that the young boy had understood exponential growth. She thought of her father and smiled to herself. He had explained exponential growth so simply a child could understand.

***

"You had a good time?" Chip held the car door for her.

He wore his party attire so easily, such a handsome man. She tried to recall her distance, but she didn't feel distant. He had been the perfect escort, always there when she needed him. Then she realized it. "Chip, you set me up!"

Chip took a step back, concern clouding his eyes. "Set you up?"

"Telling Justin about my dad and Jeff about my majoring in math"

"Oh, that," He cast his eyes down, but there was a smile on his lips. "Sorry."

She laughed at his apology, put her hand on his shoulder and kissed him. "Thank you." She slid into the car. What had she done? Just hours ago she was ready to bolt. And now it didn't matter. Now she was in love again.

"A penny for your thoughts." Chip turned the ignition off. They had driven all the way home in silence.

"Oh, Chip."

Mia could see his head turn toward her in the dark car.

"I'm so confused. I don't know what to think. I mean about Sam."

"I don't know what to think either." Chip resettled in his

seat, his body toward her. "I can't believe I told you."

"You told me because I insisted."

"I guess so."

"Chip, you were so kind to me this evening. It was a perfect evening."

"I'm glad."

"I love you, Chip."

"From the girl who doesn't know what love is?"

Mia heard herself speak, like it was someone else talking. "Do you remember when I said I could wait for you to tell me about your nickname?"

"Of course."

"And you said you could wait...." She swallowed. "Chip, I want to make love to you." An eerie 'it's-not-really-me-talking' thrummed through Mia's being.

Chip gaze was steady and sober. "Are you sure?"

Mia was sure if she stopped she would never again get the nerve to have this conversation. "But I'm afraid you will think less of me."

"No. No, I won't." Chip's eyes wide, holding her gaze.

"That you will be bored with me."

At this he laughed. "I haven't gotten bored yet."

She had asked the question, and she had gotten her answer. She wasn't satisfied, but she knew she could never be sure. She knew what she wanted and this answer had to be enough. "So let's...."

"Mia, are you sure?"

She rubbed her thumb against the silky material of her dress. "I think so."

"That doesn't sound sure to me."

She cleared her throat and said firmly, "I am sure."

"Let's see if you're sure tomorrow night." He leaned over and placed a chaste little peck on her lips. "I love you, Mia. I want you to love making love."

Desire surged through her body. She could not sleep.

***

There was a gentle knock on her door.

"Mia?" Chip's mother crooned, "Mia, sorry to wake you, but it's getting late. I think you'd be better off with some breakfast before the ceremony."

"Oh, sorry." Mia sat up in bed and blinked. "What time is it?"

"It's 11:00, dear." The way Mrs. Walsh said dear made Mia feel she belonged.

"I'm so sorry to have slept so late! I'll be ready in a jiffy."

The breakfast, getting ready for the wedding, the ride to the church were a blur. At the church, Chip was always by her side, holding her hand, his hand on her back, his arm around her waist.

There were a couple of hours between the ceremony and the reception. Chip and Mia drove around the island. Each turn in the road, each sand hill, each little bay had a story. Here his dad took him sailing in a dingy when he was four. That was his favorite candy store, where Aunt Beverly would buy him sweets. He stopped at the store and bought her a white plastic medallion on a cord. It had a red rose painted on it, a child's party favor. He placed it around her neck and tucked it under her blouse, so it didn't show. "Our secret," he said, with a kiss on her cheek.

When they arrived at the reception, the party had already started. There must have been three hundred people there, and Mia froze. Chip held her hand and the introductions started again. So many people!

They approached a birdlike lady with a long thin nose and

frizzy gray hair. "Aunt Beverly, I'd like you to meet my friend Mia." His arm around her waist comforted her. "Mia, this is my mother's sister, my Aunt Beverly.

Aunt Beverly peered through her glasses, which had been fashionable a decade earlier. She looked Mia up and down, until Mia felt she was a specimen being examined for possible infestation. "Not bad, my boy, not bad."

"Oh, Beverly, you are perfectly impossible."

"Ah, so that's where you get your defects." Beverly flipped her hands scooting Chip away. "Now off you go, dear, so I can instruct Mia in the proper handling of my nephew." Beverly started in on a stream of family stories: how the twins loved to deceive parents and teachers since they were identical; that Chip was quite premature, even though he weighed over ten pounds when he was born; how Chip's father was really not a Boston Brahmin, his forebears arriving just before the revolution. They were interrupted by the call to be seated for dinner.

Dinner was another gourmet extravaganza: food and wine and conversation. There were toasts and jokes. The orchestra was twenty strong. They played old favorites and new hits. But what Mia liked most were the waltzes. She and Chip danced, and she felt like she was floating.

A little after nine, Chip leaned over to her. "Ready to escape?" She nodded, Chip took her on his arm and they said their goodbyes. At last they were in the car. "I have a special place I want to take you, the most beautiful place in the world." He stopped the car at a little inlet where the waves caressed the shore, the moon, just a sliver short of full, hung above the ocean, its light shimmering on the water.

They walked barefoot on the sand. Chip stopped and turned Mia toward him. He touched her cheek. "Have you decided? Do you want...."

"Yes." She held his gaze. "Yes."

Chapter Twenty-Two

Mia packed her bags for the summer, remembering. Remembering each small detail.

She trembled at the thought of his touch.

She put her sweaters and long johns in the footlocker.

His lips against hers. Their embrace.

She placed her swim suits and sun dresses in her suit case.

She remembered the long walk they took when they returned from Cape Cod. They walked, their fingers intertwined. They talked of nothing and everything.

She sighed and took up a pen to write a thank-you note to Mrs. Walsh. The words flowed on the page by themselves as she thought of him. His musky scent. His hair blown by the wind. The way he touched her cheek.

Pull yourself together, she thought, otherwise you will land in Kansas City instead of San Francisco. She checked the time, enough to run out to the mail box a few blocks away and be ready when Chip arrived to take her to the airport.

The early summer air was warm, but not yet hot, so she enjoyed the walk, smelling the sweet lindens in bloom. The mail box door creaked as she opened it and dropped the letter in, creaking again as she let it slam shut.

"So he won the bet, did he?" Mia pivoted around at the raw voice. A tall man, leering, stinking of tobacco and alcohol, looked down at her. Sam.

"What?"

"I can always tell when a girl has been laid." His cruel smile was lopsided.

Mia started walking back to the dorm.

"Remember me?" He matched her strides. "Sam." He placed his hand on her shoulder and jerked her around to face him.

He looked ten years older, his hair longer, greasy. "Oh, yes, Sam. I have someone waiting to take me to the airport." She turned and started walking.

She felt the heavy hand on her shoulder again, stopping her. "Oh, but you will want to hear what I have to say." His eyes shone in the sun, hard and cold. "I said he won the bet."

"What bet?"

He pulled her closer, his sour breath gagging her. "The bet that he could seduce you."

"What are you talking about?"

"We made a bet that he could get you in bed, and I see he has succeeded. He'll be wanting to collect from me, I expect."

Mia searched Sam's face. Was he mad? "Who is 'he?'"

Sam laughed, a narrow nasal guffaw. "Your lover boy, of course." The laugh stopped abruptly, and he moved his head close to hers, his fingers digging into her shoulder. "Chip, you little whore." He released her with a shove.

Chapter Twenty-Three

Mia ran back to the dorm, panting as her feet pounded the sidewalk. She would get a cab before Chip came to take her to the airport.

She raced up the stairs, tossed her last things in her suitcase, slammed the lid, and leaned on it with all her weight, but a three-inch gap sneered up at her. Her hands trembled. She pulled out her toiletries and stuffed them in her already bulging purse. Sitting on the lid, the case's clasps almost met. She pulled out a bulky sweater. She'd wear it, even in the 80 degree heat. The lid shut, she fastened the clasps and locked the case, hoping it would not spring open.

The suitcase banged against her legs as she lugged it down the stairs, her purse flopping against her side. She dropped her things and sat at the reception desk, scanning the phone list for the number of the cab company.

"Mia?"

Mia looked up into Chip's expectant face. How dare he smile at her. The arrogant bastard.

"Mia, what's wrong?"

At least his smile was gone. Mia steadied her voice. "Nothing." She looked down at the list again. "I'll take a cab to the airport. No need to bother you, now that you won your bet."

"My bet?"

"I ran into Sam this morning and he was lamenting he lost that bet."

"Sam?"

"Oh, come on. Don't pretend you don't know about the bet." Mia's hands shook as she reached for the receiver.

The kitchen door slammed and Mrs. Staunton, the house mother, walked into the hall carrying two jugs of water. "Is Chip giving you a ride to the airport this morning?"

"I'm just calling a cab. It seems Chip may have other things that need to be done today."

"Well, if you need help getting to the airport, just let me know." Mrs. Staunton wandered toward the family's rooms at the other end of the living room.

"Mia, the bet...I remember now." Chip's whisper was husky.

"Remember?" Mia wanted to scream.

"Please, Mia," Chip looked over his shoulder toward the family residence, "Not so loud."

"Yes. I can be very quiet," Mia whispered, "since there is nothing to discuss."

"Mia. Mia."

"Please leave."

"Not until you understand." He stood straight now. "That bet was made the first time I met you."

"Whenever. I can't believe you would make such a bet."

"I was different then."

"Why should I believe you have changed?"

The grandfather clock chimed the quarter hour. Mia looked at her watch realizing she was running out of time. She reached for the receiver again and started to dial a number. Chip grabbed her hand and pulled it away from the receiver, which clattered on the desk.

"Everything OK?" Mrs. Staunton was peering from the living room doorway.

"Everything is fine, Mrs. Staunton," Chip said as he picked up Mia's suitcase. "I can take Mia to the airport." He headed for the front door, carrying the suitcase.

Mia sat at the desk. Should she tell Mrs. Staunton she didn't want to go with Chip? She couldn't do it. She didn't cause scenes. It was not what she did.

"Have a good summer, Mrs. Staunton." She tried for cheery and followed Chip out.

Chapter Twenty-Four

Mia's head swam. Chip maneuvered the labyrinth of roads, traffic circles, and ramps. He talked, but his words did not penetrate her thoughts. Just get me to the airport, she thought. Cars skittered here and there. Horns honked. Chip talked. Just get me to the airport, she silently urged. Finally, they pulled into a space at the parking garage. She opened the door before Chip had turned off the ignition. She would have run for the terminal, but she had to wait until Chip pulled her suitcase out of the trunk. As he set it on the ground, she grabbed it and started towards the terminal. It was heavy and slowed her progress, banging against her legs. Perspiration ran down her chest; her arm pits were soaked under the heavy sweater.

"I can carry that for you." Chip tried to clasp the suitcase, but she turned away, keeping the handle out of his reach.

When they got to the terminal, a long line waited to check in. Damn. After she was checked in, she could go to the ladies room and wait for the flight there, but she had to wait in line.

Chip continued to talk. "Really. The very first time. In Bertram. I didn't know you."

The man ahead of them in line, in a dark suit, all crisp, an older man, lined face, turned and leered at them. Mia could see the pores of the man's nose.

"Sure, Chip. I understand." Maybe that would shut Chip up.

"Good." The leering spectator turned away, losing interest in the scene. Chip took the suitcase from her and put his free arm around her waist.

She needed to get checked in. Then the ladies room. Then

run for the flight.

Chip talked, but the words didn't make sense. "Write." Only three people ahead of them in line. "Maybe I'll visit." The next two people went to the counter together. "You can show me the sights." The leerer went up to the counter. "Would July work?" What was taking so long? The leerer wanted to change flights. "Mia?" The leerer was angry with the attendant. Oh, please. Just finish. Mia felt Chip stroke her cheek. "Mia? Would July work."

"July?" She looked at him. He was a stranger. Just get through this. "Sure, Chip."

"Good. I'll see when I can get away from the law firm."

The woman at the counter called out, "Next."

Chip put the suitcase on the scale and Mia checked in quickly.

She stuffed her boarding pass in her purse, pushing down deep, so it wouldn't fall out. They walked to the gate. "I need to stop at the restroom."

Chip nodded and she ran into the restroom across from her gate. Wetting paper towels, she went into a stall. She wiped her face, trying to calm down, to cool down. Twenty minutes until she could board. She passed the wet towels across her brow, down her cheek, her neck, her chest. She felt the plastic charm Chip had given her. It was only two days ago. It was a long, long time ago. A different planet. She tugged at the charm angrily until the string broke and the charm slid along the floor. Reflexively she grabbed it, squeezing it tightly in her hand. She checked her watch. Time to board. Almost. She could not stand this stall. She had to leave. Swinging the stall door open, she burst from the ladies room. There was Chip, his eyes on the door.

"You OK?"

"Yes, Chip." She tried to whisper, but the words came out

loud and raspy. "I'm fine. Without you." She held the plastic medallion in one hand, her purse in the other. "Don't call." She felt like swinging the purse to hit him as hard as she could. "Don't write." She was afraid something would fall out. "Don't visit." She threw the medallion down and ground it into the floor.

The plastic crunched.

Summer 1965

Chapter Twenty-Five

"So what's bothering you?" Mia's mom leaned against the door jamb of Mia's room.

Mia had made it through her arrival at the airport, where Nick picked her up. She had survived dinner with Nick and her parents, and even an after dinner conversation. She hadn't said a word about Chip. It was as if the whole Chip affair were a bad dream that hadn't happened. But her mom, being her mom, knew something was wrong.

"It's nothing, Mom." Mia seldom talked about her friends with her parents. Sometimes she'd pass on a silly bit of gossip, but she avoided the important issues about her friends, especially boyfriends.

"Does it have anything to do with your trip to Martha's Vineyard?" Her parents had already asked about that trip. Mia had talked about everything but Chip: the beauty of the ocean, all the people she had met, and the elaborate parties.

Mia's throat tightened. She did her best to keep her voice even and her face calm. "Mom, I'm fine. Just a little tired."

"You didn't say much about your host. Was it Chip Welch?"

"Walsh." Mia cleared her throat. "Chip Walsh." Saying his name made it all real again. A sob escaped, and her mom was hugging her, which only made more sobs erupt, followed by a flood of tears. Her mom reached for the tissues, handing her one after the other, until Mia finally was sated. She gulped and hiccupped. She blew her nose and tried to avoid her mother's eyes, but there was no going back.

***

Mia searched her mother's face. "What kind of person would make that kind of bet?"

Her mom, sitting on Mia's desk chair, took a long drag on her cigarette. "Kids do all kinds of silly things." She gazed at Mia and smiled wryly. "I could name a few of your own shenanigans."

Mia ran her hand along the flowered chintz bedspread. "But, Mom, this is different." Mia looked down and pursed her lips. "Chip is as waspy as they get. He has sailboats, went to Exeter, summers on Martha's Vineyard. And he saw me as an object to conquer, like a little peasant girl."

Her mom flicked ashes into the ashtray. "At one point in time."

"But doesn't that say something about his arrogance?"

"It says something about it at one point in time."

Mia didn't really like the bedspread and the curtains, which she had chosen when she was 10. "But does that change?"

"Why not?"

"How do I know it has changed?"

"You don't. Not for certain."

Mia gazed at the huge stuffed dog, an Easter gift from years ago, taking up the corner of her bed.

Her Mom stubbed out her cigarette. "I don't really know this man."

Mia looked up in surprise. Her mother called one of her friends a man. Given what had happened, she supposed Chip should be called a man. And she was a woman. A grown woman.

Her mom stood and smoothed her skirt. "You know him, as best one human can know another. You need to decide what you will do. But, being a mother, I'm selfish. I don't really care about this Mr. Walsh. I care about you. I have confidence you will work this out, with integrity." She hugged Mia. "It hurts like hell right now, I'm sure. But you'll work it out."

Chapter Twenty-Six

"Your mom tells me you are suffering from a broken heart." Mia and her father sat in her mom's study. They were playing solitaire, or patience, as her father liked to call it.

Mia wondered how much her mother had said, but she didn't worry about it. Her dad was always careful not to embarrass her, or anyone, really. "Yes."

He shuffled two decks and carefully placed eight cards at the top of the card table, each one making a satisfying slap as it hit the table. He began rearranging the cards, lower cards of one color on higher cards of the other color.

"Did I ever tell you about my broken heart?"

"Never." Mia was relieved not to be talking about Chip. And she was curious about her father's broken heart.

"Your mom graduated from university. We knew we were going to get married, but I was still a student, so we couldn't marry yet."

Mia knew the story well, her mom's version anyhow. Her mom was not going to sit in Budapest with nothing to do. There was a world to explore. But she did wonder why they didn't get married right away. "Why not?"

Her dad looked up from the cards, an amused look on his face. "You sound like your mother!"

"Well? Why not?"

Her father went back to arranging cards on the table. "In those days a man did not marry until he could support his wife."

"She could work, couldn't she?"

"Don't they teach you history at Harvard?" He shook his head, but his eyes were merry. "There was a depression. There was no work in Germany, not for a foreign woman, even one as talented as your mother."

Of course. Mia should have remembered.

Her father focused on the cards, placing a red 5 on a black 6. "Can I do anything else?"

Mia looked at the columns of cards. "I don't think so."

Her dad placed another set of cards, one on each column from the deck in his hand. "Your mom didn't want to stay home and she couldn't find work in Budapest, either, so she applied for a fellowship."

Mia knew about the fellowship, how she had come to Berkeley to study organizational psychology.

"She would be gone two years." Again he arranged cards on the table according to the game's rules. "I was sure she would never come home."

"But she did. I can see that you would miss her, but she came home. So why was your heart broken?"

He looked up from the table. "I did a terrible thing." Her father rolled the Rs. "I told her if she left I would not marry her."

Mia thought about this. "Maybe that wasn't so terrible. After all, who knew what would happen. Maybe you would meet someone else. Maybe she would meet someone else."

"No. We had said we would marry. We were going to marry. I was trying to make her stay in Budapest until we could marry."

Mia didn't understand, but she didn't want to press the point. She felt she should understand, and she didn't want her father to know she didn't, as if he had moral standards she didn't share.

Her father sighed. "But she went anyhow."

"So did you think you really wouldn't marry her."
"I didn't know I could think, my heart hurt so."
"So what did you do?"
"I worked."
"So you could get your degree and get a job and marry her?"
"No. I just worked, because then I did not think."

Mia was amused by the "did not think" phrase. She knew what her father meant. He couldn't think rationally about her mother. But his work was all about thinking, just thinking about something else.

"You might try that. It worked for me. It still works for me when I'm upset."

He got upset a lot. About politics. About the testing ban. And there were other things he was upset about, both of her parents were upset about, that they didn't talk about. She didn't know exactly what they were, but she could guess. She was not the only one who was harassed about his opinions.

Her dad concentrated on the card game, placing cards here and there. "Your mother tells me you want to work on math this summer."

"Yes. Professor Griffin gave me a list of topics I might look at."

"That is splendid. Ah!" He saw he could close a set of cards. "I hope you get stuck so you'll have to come to your old father for help."

Chapter Twenty-Seven

"I hear you and Chip had a little soap opera." The connection was crackly, but Jamie's style came through loud and clear.

"True." Mia wondered how much Jamie knew and how she knew it, but she was not going to give her more information.

"What happened?"

"Jamie, I really don't want to talk about it." There was fuzzy white noise on the line, but Jamie was silent. "I thought you'd be in France by now. You're not calling from France, are you?"

"No." Jamie's chuckle pierced the static. "Lord knows it's expensive enough to call from Chicago."

That zinged Mia's heart. She was ungrateful for Jamie's concern. "I'm sorry, Jamie." Mia was in the study. Her dad was at work, and her mom already knew, but that left Bertha, the maid. Mia didn't want Bertha to hear this. She sidled over to the door, pulling the phone cord to its full extent and shut the door with her outstretched foot. Only then did she whisper into the receiver. "The short story is I went to bed with Chip, and the next day I ran into Sam, who told me Chip won the bet. What bet I asked, and he said he and Chip had a bet that Chip could get me to go to bed with him."

There was a Jamie whistle on the line. "Is that all?"

Mia had to laugh. "Yeah. That's all. But wouldn't you be mad?"

"But, from what I heard, there was a bit of a scene at the airport."

Mia remembered the crunch of the plastic heart. "Yeah."

"That was after the love scene and the disclosure scene, I take it?"

"Yeah."

"So if all Chip was interested in was the bet, there would be no reason for him to take you to the airport, right?"

"Look, Jamie, I can see you have all the information already, so why don't you tell me how you know all this?"

"Chip called me."

"Oh."

"He is heartbroken."

"Well, that makes two of us."

The static on the line dipped, which made the break in the conversation more uncomfortable. "How could I love someone who would make such a bet? I mean, it's as if women are just animals."

"Mia, people can change."

"Sure." That was a Chip line. She should have known Jamie had heard this from Chip. At least Hank didn't know about it. Maybe. Or maybe Hank was the one who suggested Chip call Jamie. "But tell me this, how did Sam know if Chip didn't tell him?"

"I don't know. It's not a secret you and Chip are serious. The trip to Martha's Vineyard was front page news among the guys."

"But that didn't mean we were lovers."

"No. Maybe Sam guessed."

"Or maybe Chip told him?"

"Oh, Mia. I don't think so. I think Chip loves you."

"Maybe. But how did Sam know?"

"Sometimes it's obvious."

"Oh, come on."

"Really. I bet there was a dreamy faraway look in your eyes."

It was true. Mia had been in another world, but was it that obvious? "Jamie, why do you care about all of this?"

"Because I like you." There was a little lift at the end of that sentence and Mia wasn't sure whether it was a statement or a question. "Because I like Chip. Because I think you were made for each other. Because I like happy endings."

Mia didn't want to soften, but she felt herself, for a moment, transported back to the second just before she ran into Sam. "Thanks, Jamie."

"You should call Chip."

"Maybe."

"Call him. Make up. It'll be good."

"Maybe." She wanted to get off the phone, wanted space to think. "Thanks, Jamie. Thanks for caring." That sounded lame.

"Sure. Anyway, I'm off to France tonight, so no more calls from me, though I might send a postcard, reminding you to call Chip."

Mia was relieved. "Have a good time in France. See you in the fall."

"Call Chip!" The connection clicked as Jamie hung up.

Chapter Twenty-Eight

Why did all math books start with set theory? Well, maybe not all, but this one did. Mia knew she should read it, to make sure she had all the information for the rest of the book. She flipped through the first chapter. She wondered what Chip was doing right now. Probably at his father's law office. Probably wearing a suit and tie. So handsome.

No. She would not think about Chip. She made herself look at the definitions. She knew that one, and the next one, and the first proposition. She wondered whether Chip was really heartbroken. He must be at least a little, otherwise he wouldn't have called Jamie. So he must really love her. She should call him.

No. She would not think about Chip. She knew the next definition and the next one. Really, give her something new. Ah, a little proposition to prove. She pulled out paper and proved it in two lines. She stretched and looked out the large window to see lofty trees. It was a beautiful day today, a warm summer afternoon, but she liked being in the library. It was safe somehow, surrounded by strangers, so she wasn't alone, but she also was alone. She didn't have to pretend to be happy. Of course, she couldn't cry, and why would she cry, for that arrogant preppy?

No. She would not think about Chip. She glanced down at the book. The definition of Cartesian Products of sets. She flipped to the next page. There was a definition she had never seen before. She read it over twice. She closed the book. Would the integers modulo a prime fit the definition? But was she sorry? No. She closed her eyes. Should she call Chip? Wouldn't that show she needed him more than he needed her? After all, he could call her. Why did she have to make the first move? But she knew the answer. She was the one who cut off the relationship, so she would have to be the one to say she was sorry. But was she sorry?

No. She would not think about Chip. She opened the book again and looked at the examples. Of course, she could see the first example worked. The second example was just a generalization of the first example. The next one was interesting, and she worked out why it was true. She worked out the next example, too. Then came a theorem, which she had to read three times. She closed the book and tried to prove the theorem. It took a little while, but she felt she had a good proof. She opened the book and followed the explanation, which was essentially her proof.

She started working on the problems. They weren't too hard. Except the last one. She didn't know how to approach this. She closed her eyes and thought. She had it! She wrote her proof down. She thought it was right, but there were no answers in the book. She'd have to think about it.

She stretched. The once-crowded room was almost empty. She looked up at the clock. She'd better get going. She didn't want to be late for dinner.

Chapter Twenty-Nine

Nick had stopped by now and again, asking how she was, telling her that her high school friends thought she was a snob, not associating with them. Sometimes they had gone out for coffee. He had talked about his summer job and about Vietnam. She had nodded, not really listening, her latest math concerns bubbling in her mind.

He had insisted Mia join him for an "outing" on August 6th. Mia was leery. It was the 20th anniversary of the Hiroshima bombing, and Nick, being Nick, might be dragging her off to a peace demonstration. She had nothing against peace, but she hated these rallies. The speakers always said nuclear weapons caused war. They implied that her father, who had worked on them, who spoke publicly, spoke publicly every chance he got, about the need for a nuclear arsenal, was responsible. Sometimes they mentioned her father explicitly.

Nick had promised this outing had nothing to do with The Bomb and she really must come. So she agreed.

He was at her front door at 10. The morning fog had not burnt off yet, so Mia grabbed a sweater as she headed out the door.

"Glad you consented to come on this expedition." They walked toward Cedar Street.

"You haven't told me where we're going."

"Down to the Santa Fe Station."

"We going for a ride?"

"Nope, we're going to stop a train."

Mia stopped. "What?"

Nick, a step ahead of Mia, turned toward her. "There's a train of troops going through Berkeley sometime this morning, and we plan to stop it."

"Just like Bill Grogan's Goat?" She started singing:

Bill Grogan's goat, was feeling fine.
Ate three red shirts, right off the line.

Bill took a stick, gave him three whacks,
And tied him to, the railroad tracks.

The whistle blew, the train grew nigh;
Bill Grogan's goat, was doomed to die.

He gave three moans, of mortal pain,
Barfed up those shirts, and flagged that train.

"Very funny." Nick pursed his lips. "This is serious, Mia."

"Planning on getting arrested?"

Nick placed his hands on his hips and stared at her.

"Or getting run down?"

Nick stared.

"Why should I come to this?" Nick had bragged that more than 15,000 people had shown up for the Vietnam Protest in May. It seemed every warm body counted.

"Because you will learn something."

Mia said nothing.

"You can't say you don't agree if you don't know what we're talking about." He smiled.

Mia did not smile back. "How will my attending a train hijacking help me understand?"

"When we stop the train, we'll talk to the troops. We'll explain why the war is wrong."

"Why can't you just tell me?"

"There'll be people there who are much more persuasive than I. They'll convince you."

Mia wrapped her arms around herself. The breeze was cool, but in truth she was hugging herself as she considered the demonstration. She should go home. But she was curious. Who were these people who protested? Were they all just like Nick? College kids? And there was a tug, a desire to be one of those protesting. War was a bad thing, something you should be against.

"You can leave anytime you want."

"OK."

They started down the hill and turned onto University Avenue. They walked in silence, the traffic getting heavier as they approached downtown and then lighter as they walked farther down the main east-west street between campus and the bay. The shops were shabbier as they headed toward the wrong side of the tracks.

When they were a block away from the Santa Fe Station Nick picked up his pace. Mia could see a group of people, maybe 100 or so milling in front of the building. By the time Mia caught up, Nick was talking to a short man with curly brown hair. Mia guessed he was in his mid-thirties. He talked fast.

"No trains yet. Not sure when they'll come through. Half the people here are police or FBI or something. See that guy over there?" Here the man gave a slight nod to the right. "He's got a microphone. Just so you know, he's recording everything. FBI for sure."

Nick nodded. "Steve, this is my friend Mia."

The short man gazed at Mia and smiled. She was grateful Nick had not used her last name.

"The gang is working on signs and such, over there." Steve

pointed to the arches of the railway station. Mia could see several people working on a long banner and others painting smaller signs on sticks.

The morning fog had burnt off, and Mia was too warm. She took her sweater off and tied it around her waist.

Nick pointed north, toward the El Cerrito hills. The tracks were straight for three blocks before they curved to the right. Little bungalows, built in the '30s, lined the tracks on either side. Mia saw a large sign by one of the houses spelling out the words "God Bless Our Soldiers." The hills in the distance were brown, houses peeking out here and there.

Nick turned back to the sign makers and began to help, beckoning Mia to join in. She shook her head. She was here as an observer, not a participant. She sat on a bench under the portico. Apart from the sign makers, there were quite a number of men talking among themselves, most in suits or sports jackets, probably police, railroad personnel, and even, as Steve had warned, FBI. There were several with camera equipment, reporters and their photographers perhaps.

A low rumble and a forlorn wail sounded in the distance. The sign makers looked toward Steve, who shook his head and pointed to a train schedule attached to his clipboard. Mia guessed this was a scheduled train. The protesters went back to the business of making signs.

The red engine, a yellow sun painted across its nose, slowed to a stop. The doors of one of the sleek passenger cars opened. Two men in business suits stepped down, followed by a lady in a tailored dress, wearing a hat and gloves. She looked at the protesters and hurried into the terminal.

Nick and his fellows started putting away their materials, having done all they could on the signs. They milled around, talking quietly.

Just as Mia began to wonder whether the troop train would

come, there was a distant roar and a train horn sounded. Steve gave a trilling whistle and the sign makers rushed for the tracks. They arranged themselves so the banner, which Mia could now see read "Stop The War Machine," was in the middle and the signs were at either side.

She looked toward the hills. A red and yellow engine came into view, its horn blaring. It wasn't going terribly fast, faster than she could walk, but she could have outrun it. The horn sounded again, quite loud.

Mia located Nick on the far side of the banner. He was holding a picket and staring in the direction of the train. The horn blared again, so loud now that Mia put her fingers in her ears.

She looked at the train, two blocks away. Great clouds of steam issued from the diesel engine's nose. Mia's heart raced. She looked back at the protesters who stood their ground. The train, a block away, ran steadily along. It was not slowing down!

The banner holders ran to either side of the tracks, ripping the sign. Mia willed Nick to leave the tracks, but he stood there, his sign held high.

The horn blasted again, so loud it hurt Mia's plugged ears. Now it was half a block away. Now it was just across the street. Like a lumbering voracious carnivore, it bore down steadily, rumbling, steam now obscuring the lower half of the engine.

Nick's figure disappeared in the white vapor.

Mia heard a scream.

Then silence.

Chapter Thirty

"Everyone was impressed with your volume!" Nick grinned at Mia two days later as they had coffee at the Forum. "They say I should marry you right away, since you can shriek so loud when you think I'm dead. And you were beautiful when you fainted."

"Not funny, Nick." Mia sipped her espresso. "I suppose I should be happy you're not too depressed. The demonstration was a disaster."

Nick raised an eye brow. "A disaster?"

"You didn't stop the train, you didn't convince any soldiers to desert."

"Sure, but that's not the point. . . ."

Mia looked up at Nick. "Not the point? I thought you told me that was the point."

"Yes. It was the point. And we didn't accomplish that goal, but we got press coverage."

"So I saw. The Gazette covered it, and KPIX had a not very complimentary editorial . . . ."

"Not just the Berkeley Gazette or a San Francisco TV station. It was in the New York Times!" Nick stared at Mia, tapping the table with each paper he mentioned. "And the Chicago Tribune. And the L.A. Times."

"So that's the point? Getting publicity?" Mia was staring back. What an ass Nick was. "Too bad you didn't get killed then. Just imagine what kind of publicity you could have gotten if there was a mangled body on the tracks."

"Oh, come on, Mia. Let's be reasonable."

"I am being reasonable." Mia fumbled in her purse and withdrew a rumpled piece of paper. "Look here." Mia smoothed the mimeographed sheet on the table and read from the end of the page:

"If the government won't stop a train, but is willing to kill citizens protesting this unjustified war, then the United States is doomed."

Nick grabbed the paper from the table and scanned it, his face darkening as he read.

"Where did you get this?"

"Someone was handing them out at North Gate this morning. You can have it."

"I don't have a problem with the description of what happened, but this last piece, 'willing to kill citizens'...." Nick looked off, his eyes squinting, as if he were trying to find an answer.

***

"He's a red diaper," Mia's mother said as she finished reading the flyer.

"Red diaper?" Mia had never heard that term.

"His parents were communists."

Her dad took the flyer. "At a time, Libácska, when we all thought the communists might have some answers. Remember how you got in trouble with your stepfather for visiting Tisca in jail." He started reading.

"That was before the Moscow Trials. Anyhow, I don't think the Stones changed. And I think Steve Stone follows the same pattern."

Daniel Brower looked up from the flyer. "Don't be so quick to condemn."

"Just turn to the end. Accusing the U.S. government of

killing its citizens is beyond the pale."

Daniel cast his eyes down the page, read quickly and looked up. "Those are angry words. But just because whoever wrote this is beyond the pale, does not necessarily justify the Vietnam War."

"Right." Her mom stubbed out her cigarette. "The point is these people want to make the government villains so it will be impossible to have a reasonable debate."

Mia's dad nodded.

"Does that remind you of something?"

"All of human history?" Her dad smiled at his own joke. Her mother sighed and lit another cigarette. After a brief silence, Mia's dad looked at Mia. "What do you think?"

"Math is easier to understand."

Her dad laughed. "You're a quick study."

Mia could have hugged her dad. He understood. She was ready to get away from this political nonsense. She was ready to go back to Cambridge and study math.

Sophomore Year
September 1965 to June 1966

Chapter Thirty-One

Mia looked around the room she and Jamie would share this year, smaller than last year's room, but situated on a corner with two large windows. Off to the left was her room, meant to be a closet, but big enough to hold a bed, which had already been placed there. She dumped her suitcase on the bare mattress and surveyed her domain. This was perfect, a tight womb, a place where she could work undisturbed.

"There you are!" Jamie bundled into the room, her arms full of linens. She deposited her load on her bed and gave Mia a bear hug. "How are you? How was your summer?"

"I'm fine," Mia said. "I did a lot of math." Jamie was tanned and smiling with the usual mischief in her eyes. "How about you? How was France?"

"Great, beautiful." Jamie beamed. "So nice I only missed Hank every five minutes or so."

These words stung.

Jamie's face morphed into a scolding teacher look. "I heard you haven't called Chip."

"Who's Chip." Mia stiffened for Jamie's assault.

"You still can call him." Jamie picked up the receiver of the phone in the room. "Dial tone. All ready for your call."

"I can't trust him." Mia looked out the window, doing her best to suppress her tears. Chip had not been a dream, it had happened, and now that she was back in Cambridge, back with Jamie, she was confronted with the reality. All the math in the world could not protect her from this moment.

"Hank says he is very sad, very much in love with you."

Mia's laugh was bitter. "The much overused L-word." Mia forced a smile and looked at Jamie. "It's a new year, a new major, and I've sworn off men."

Jamie continued to stare at Mia for a moment and then turned to the pile on her bed. "If you'd like to use the quilt again this year, here it is. And here are some curtains, courtesy of my mom. We have two windows in here and one in your little room. Can you believe it, three windows! So I was thinking these in here." She held up material with a cheerful red and white folk pattern. "And — " she held up a piece of white material edged in buttercups " — this for your little window."

Her room did have a window, strange for a closet, but perhaps before it was a closet it was something else.

"Thanks, Jamie."

"Sure." Jamie said. "Have you gotten your books yet?"

"I've gotten my math books." She had gotten them in Berkeley and wished she could stick her nose in them right now. "I still need to get my music and biology books though."

"Great. I'm going to the Coop right now. Want to come? I was thinking a throw rug would cheer the room up, and I think the Coop has some."

They walked down Garden Street. It was hot and muggy and grit blew in the wind, just as it had last year. Berkeley would be sunny, cheerful, and a refreshing 65 right now. But Jamie was her friend, and math would be her support.

***

Professor Petran, who taught linear algebra, was pudgy and had glasses with thick black frames, short brown hair with a sprinkling of gray, a friendly smile, and a passion for his subject. As he talked, the ideas, which Mia had visited this summer, were even clearer. The way he presented the material, there were mysteries to be solved and magic to be discovered. Mia was entranced. The lecture flew by.

"That's it for today." Professor Petran collected his papers. "I'm afraid I have to run. I have a class to get to, so I won't have time for questions now. But come visit during office hours, or any other time for that matter."

Mia looked at her watch and realized she had to get to her music class and it was on the other side of campus. She gathered her notes, stuffed them in her book bag and ran to Mem Hall. When she got to the large auditorium there were only a few empty chairs in the back. Mia made her way through and settled in a seat.

"Hi!" Mia looked at Professor Petran as he sat next to her. "Is this the class you had to get to?"

"Yes." Professor Petran grinned. "And what a gem this will be."

"That good?" Mia had signed up for this class because it met a core requirement and it got good reviews.

"Yes!" Professor Petran nodded. "I've been meaning to take this class for years. Something always got in the way, and I said next year. But there is no next year. This is the last year Woody will teach."

"Woody?" Mia said.

"That's what we students call Professor Wood."

"We students?" Professor Petran was a well known mathematician.

"Sure." Professor Petran chuckled. "The glorious thing about academia is you can be a student your entire life."

Mia nodded and smiled.

The crowd quieted as Professor Wood, a fragile man with thinning white hair, walked to the podium. Mia scanned the large room. She froze when she noticed Chip several rows in front of her.

Professor Wood started going through housekeeping details and then began his discussion about Gregorian Chants. Mia had never considered this music, but she was fascinated. Professor Wood would play a bit of music on the sound system, speak about it, and then play the music again. Mia heard the music in a different way the second time. At the end of the lecture, the students clapped. Mia clapped, too, spontaneously. This class was a gem, just as Professor Petran had promised.

Mia took her time gathering her things. She wanted to be sure Chip was gone before she left. As she walked into the sunshine, Chip's voice called her name. She inhaled and clenched her teeth.

"Hi," he said.

He was so handsome, the deep blue eyes, the lock of black hair that swept across his forehead, ruddy cheeks, even a smile on his face. She wanted to hold him. She had to be firm. No going back. "Chip, it's over."

"But you don't understand." His smile faded. His eyes were penetrating, as if he could capture her with them.

She did not trust herself to look into those eyes. She looked past him. "I understand that I don't trust you." She looked at him quickly and then away again, adding before he could say something, "and I think you said trust is a requirement for a relationship. So it's over."

"Mia, please." His voice quavered. "Just come for a cup of coffee."

Could a cup of coffee hurt? She wanted to say yes. But this was not a little game. This was her future. She had to protect herself. "You know my mom is from Budapest?"

"Yes."

"On special occasions when she was a child, she would be

taken to visit the castle in Budapest." Mia saw Chip's curiosity. "The king who owned the castle had many beautiful things. One room was devoted to pictures of all the horses he loved best." Mia paused and stared directly at Chip. "Another room was devoted to pictures of all the women...."

She trailed off, letting Chip's imagination finish the thought. His face was ashen, his eyes glistened.

A slap would have been less effective.

Chapter Thirty-Two

The next day Mia skipped up the stairs of Sever Hall, the steps worn by years of students. She was early. She took a seat in the back, watching the students as they came in. In last year's history class, the kids tended to be clean, crisp, had good posture and friendly smiles. This was a math class. Math students were not dirty, but rumpled. They did not meet your gaze, as if they were looking inward.

One fellow was wearing hiking boots and carried a backpack rather than the ever-present book bag. He, too, was rumpled, but with a certain "I'll be out in the forest as soon as possible" style.

A woman sat beside her and offered her hand. "Hi. I'm Alice."

"Hi, Alice. I'm Mia."

Alice's honey hair was cut short. "We'll probably be the only women in the class."

Mia shrugged. "Is that a problem?"

"No." She pulled out a notebook and placed a pencil beside it. "Just nice to have another woman here." Alice wasn't rumpled. Her white shirt was neatly pressed, maybe even starched. A bobby pin held her hair in place. She could have walked out of Mia's first-grade reader.

Mia smiled. "It'll be good to have a buddy to study with. I'm in Bertram. Where are you?"

"Elliot, right next door. You a math major?"

Mia nodded.

"Me, too."

Professor Wise walked into the room, placing his materials on the podium, his slender fingers arranging the pages.

The buzz in the room quieted immediately and the professor began to speak. He had a nasal voice, not unpleasant, but it was distinctive. He covered the usual housekeeping topics quickly and then started his lecture, turning to the board, scribbling things so quickly Mia had a hard time keeping up. When he had covered the whole chalkboard, he started erasing equations to make room for more.

Mia's hand cramped as she tried to write everything down. A shard of panic grew in her throat. How was she ever going to master all this? She kept copying and writing and pushing the panic aside. She peeked at the clock above the board. Only half past the hour. Keep writing, she told herself. Keep writing.

Finally the hour was over. Professor Wise stopped writing, it seemed, in mid-equation. He packed his things and walked out. Only when he was gone did the usual buzz of student conversations start up again.

"Phew," Alice said. "That was a cyclone."

"Sure was." Mia massaged her cramped hand.

Alice placed her notebook and pencil in her book bag and stood. "I've got to run to another class. I'll try to phone tonight." Her skirt came to well below her knee and she wore sturdy lace up oxfords. "OK?"

"That'd be great." Mia exhaled and tried to relax. Maybe she could figure some of this out with Alice's help.

Mia paged through her notes. There were eight pages, and she didn't understand a thing.

"You'd think he was running for a train." The fellow with the hiking boots was standing beside her.

"Yeah." Mia looked up. He had black hair, chocolate brown eyes, and a cheerful smile. "Never have I taken more notes or understood less."

"Ah," the fellow said, "Don't let Wiseberg scare you."

"Wiseberg? I thought it was Professor Wise."

Hiking boots chuckled. "That's my name for him. I guess, given how fast he goes and how much ground he covers, Wise seems too short."

"I can see that." She sighed. "I think I might drop this course. It's only the first class, and I'm totally lost."

"It's not that bad." He leaned his backpack against the desk. "I've got to get over to the math building. I'm the librarian for the next two hours. If you'd like, come with me and we can go over the lecture."

"That'd be so helpful." Mia's shoulders relaxed. Maybe, with enough help she could survive this class. "I'm Mia, by the way."

"Jacob." He shook her hand and slung his backpack over his shoulder.

"Are you majoring in math?" Mia asked as they walked to the math building.

"I've been majoring in math since grade school." He looked at her, his eyes shining. "Math is my best friend."

"Boy, I wish I felt that way about it."

"Are you majoring in Math, too?"

"Yup." Mia's shoulders tightened. "But I hope that isn't a mistake." She grimaced. "Given Professor Wise's lecture."

"Ah, don't worry about that."

"But he doesn't motivate the subject, he doesn't give you time to think, he just — " Mia considered using the word regurgitate, but decided that was crude. "He just writes."

"I know. It's almost like regurgitation."

Mia laughed. "Exactly."

"But you have to feel for the fellow."

Mia blinked. "Why should I feel for him?"

"I suspect he is so into this subject it's obvious to him."

They climbed the stairs to the math department, and Jacob, having retrieved the key from the office, opened the library door.

The library was the size of a large classroom, lined in bookcases. There were several tables where people could work.

Jacob settled at one of the tables and Mia sat beside him. They bent over the notes Mia had taken, Jacob explaining each equation and answering Mia's questions.

After an hour, Mia looked at her watch. "Jacob, I'm afraid I have to go to biology. You've been so helpful!" She stood.

Jacob looked up at her, his brows arched. "We're not done." He pursed his lips. "Would you like to meet after your class and go over the rest?"

Of course, she wanted to. "Do you have the time?"

"Sure. Stop by my co-op. It's on your way back to the quad."

Chapter Thirty-Three

Biology was taught by the famous Professor Creek, but the famous professor was a disappointment. The first lecture was anatomy of cells. But what was a cell? It seemed everyone knew, like everyone knew what an egg was. But Mia didn't know. It was her day to be muddled.

After class, she walked to Jacob's co-op, a two-story older house several blocks from the quad. Muddy footprints ascended the steps to the porch, which needed a new coat of paint, and the lawn needed a trimming. She was searching for a doorbell, when Jacob appeared at the door.

"Hey, there." He pushed open the screen door. "We can work in the dining room." He led her through the living room furnished with a couch and overstuffed chairs. The dining room had several tables, seating for about twenty people, Mia guessed.

"Cup of tea?"

Mia sighed. "What luxury. Tea with math help."

Jacob chuckled and led the way into the kitchen. An eight-burner stovetop and three large ovens dominated the kitchen.

"This is quite a food factory."

Jacob explained the workings of the co-op. The men who lived there were responsible for all the work at the house, including cooking the meals, cleaning and lawn mowing. "That's why this place looks well-loved." Jacob found two mugs in a cabinet. "We aren't that good at the chores." He poured hot water into a tea pot. "But it's a lot cheaper than living in a Harvard house." He smiled at Mia. "Sugar? Honey?"

"Honey. Thanks."

"Is your dad really Dr. Brower?" Jacob asked, as they settled at the table

Mia nodded.

"Nan told me." Jacob poured tea from the pot. "Too bad he didn't stay in math rather than going into physics."

Mia laughed.

"What's so funny?"

"I've heard a lot of people say a lot of things about my father," she said, "but that's a new one."

"No. Really." Jacob passed a mug to Mia. "He won the Eötvös Prize when he was in high school and he was as good as von Neumann." He looked at her, seeming to want her to agree.

Mia ran her thumb over the warm mug. She wondered how Jacob knew all this about her father. "He wouldn't say that."

Jacob shrugged. "Anyhow, he'd have been a good mathematician."

Mia pulled out her notebook, and they soon were deep into complex analysis. When they finished the last page of Mia's notes, she stretched and looked at her watch, "I've got to get going." She organized her papers and put them back in her book bag. "Thank you so much!"

"No problem," Jacob said. "See you Thursday."

As she walked home, Mia wondered what she would do without Jacob's help. It would make her a little uncomfortable, asking for his help. Maybe the next lecture wouldn't be so hard. She did have another week before she had to finalize her class schedule, though it would be hard to find something else she wanted to take that still had room.

After dinner, Alice came over and they went over the lecture together. "Boy, you have this material down!"

Mia did feel more confident of the material. "To be honest, a fellow, Jacob, went over the material with me, otherwise I'd be lost."

"That explains it." Alice gathered her things. "Jacob is a genius." She nodded, as if she were giving herself support. "He's a genius."

"Really?"

"Yup. He's young for a sophomore. Maybe 18."

"He doesn't look it." Mia pictured her study sessions with Jacob, trying to guess his age. "Or act it."

"No." Alice nodded again. "But he's a genius. He takes math in like it was the Sunday comics."

"True."

Alice stood and picked up her book bag. "He's going to Boston Hebrew Teacher's College."

Mia blinked. "You mean he went to Boston. . . ."

"No!" Alice shook her head. "No. He's going now. He does that, and he goes to Harvard."

"How can he go to two colleges at once?"

"Got me. I dropped out of BHTC when I started college."

"I should think," Mia said. "So you knew him at BHTC?"

"Yup." Alice's gaze shifted past Mia. "He seemed like a pretty closed sort to me. Stuck to his studies, didn't seem to have friends." Alice looked back at Mia. "Polite enough, if you talked to him, but never went out of his way to start a conversation."

"Lucky he's willing to help then."

Chapter Thirty-Four

The next Wiseberg lecture was as incomprehensible as the first. Mia sat in the classroom at the end of class considering her options. She wanted to drop the class, but, having looked at other possible open classes, she didn't see a good alternative.

"So?" It was Jacob, looking down at her.

"Oh." She closed her eyes and shook her head. "Just as bad as the first one. Maybe even worse."

His brown eyes were deep, soft. "Let's go to the library." He smiled. "C'mon. We'll figure it out."

Mia pulled her things together. "It seems like such an imposition on you."

"Nonsense. It's my way of reviewing the material. You're helping me study." He waited for her to get up and then followed her out of the building.

The leaves were still a dark, dusty green, but the air was crisp. Mia wished she could go hiking. She looked at Jacob, with his backpack and boots. "You do a lot of hiking?"

"Hiking?" Jacob lifted an eyebrow.

"Sure." She cringed. Had she offended him? "You look ready for a hike with your boots and backpack."

He laughed. "I do like to hike, and given that boots are expensive and back packs can hold books, why not use them for school and outings?"

Mia exhaled. She hadn't put her foot in her mouth. "Makes sense."

"Do you hike?"

"Oh, yes." She stopped and looked in the distance.

"Cambridge is a little urban." She gazed back at him. "No place to escape for an outdoors fix. Unless you go to the cemetery." The cemetery made her think of Chip. She looked down.

"You ought to come to the Outing Club." He started walking again. "We have trips almost every weekend. To New Hampshire, Vermont, Upstate New York." He smiled at her. "There's a meeting Monday, to plan the next excursion. You ought to come."

They arrived at the library and settled into a review of the lecture, Jacob explaining, Mia asking questions and taking notes. "You're a great teacher." She packed up her things. "Thanks."

After a review with Alice that evening, Mia felt confident of the first two lectures. She decided she would stick with Wiseberg after all.

***

The Outing Club meeting was held in a classroom in Sever. When Mia arrived, six men stood in a circle talking, but Jacob was not there. She settled in a chair feeling awkward. She had assumed Jacob would attend. She wanted to leave, but that felt awkward, too.

The fellows continued their conversation, apparently not noticing her. To her surprise, Glen, her English session leader from last year, walked in. She was so relieved to see a face she recognized, she smiled at him, even though she didn't really know him.

He sat beside her. "I didn't know you were an outing type."

"I am. I just heard about this club."

"Great way to get out of Cambridge." Glen placed a binder on his desk. "Lots of nice people, too."

As she was chatting with Glen, Jacob came in and sat on her

other side. She nodded a greeting to him.

Glen got up and started the meeting. Apparently he was the president of the club. They talked about the arrangements for an upcoming square dance. Having completed that item, Glen described the trip next weekend. They would leave Friday night and get back Sunday afternoon. They would hike on Saturday and they would stay at the Outing Club cabin.

Glen asked who would be going. Several people raised their hands, including Jacob and Glen. Mia realized everybody was looking at her. She felt her face grow warm.

"Mia," Glen said, "want to come?"

Mia didn't know what she wanted. She fumbled for a response. "Sounds like fun, but I don't have equipment." She looked around the room. Everyone was still looking at her. "What would I need?"

"Sleeping bag, warm parka, hiking boots, backpack, rain gear." Glen rattled off. "But I have a bunch of spare stuff, if you need to borrow something."

"You'll like it," Jacob said. "And if Glen doesn't have everything you need, I can probably lend you some things."

It seemed she would be the only woman. How would that feel? She had to say something. If only she had said she was busy this weekend. "OK," she heard herself say, "if you can lend me equipment, that'd be great."

Glen nodded. He counted up the hands, seven in all. "Barb will be coming, too. That makes eight."

Another woman! Thank goodness.

Glen asked for a volunteer to drive. He'd take his car, but they needed two. One of the fellows said he'd drive. Assignments were made for getting supplies. Glen estimated the cost of the trip, which Mia thought was inexpensive.

Jacob walked with Mia after the meeting. It was a cloudy night, the only light coming from the lamps in Harvard Yard.

"New Hampshire is beautiful this time of year."

"What's the cabin like?"

"It's hardly the Hilton." Jacob laughed. "Just a one-room cabin. No indoor plumbing. We do have the luxury of a well. Outside, of course. Lord keep the well going, because the Outing Club doesn't have the money to replace it!" He looked at her. "I hope I'm not scaring you."

"No." Having shelter was more than Mia had had on some of her camping trips. "I love camping."

"Then you'll like this. It has a big fireplace, which doubles as our stove. And we pay one of the farmers to deliver wood. Not split, mind you, but at least we don't have to chop down our own trees."

"I'm happy another women is coming on the trip."

"Barb comes on most of our trips. She and Glen are a couple. She's nice, kind of a Joan Baez look-alike. Maybe I think that because she plays guitar and sings. Anyhow, she's our house mother."

Chapter Thirty-Five

Mia borrowed a sleeping bag and knapsack from Glen, but he couldn't find boots that fit her. She could wear her tennis shoes, but Glen advised against it. Her feet might get wet and cold. The boots might be the excuse she needed to cancel the trip. She had lots of work. It would be hard to get everything done if she took two days off. Besides, even with this unknown Barb on the trip, she was uncomfortable on a trip with so many men.

Professor Wise's lecture was another mystery. Jacob volunteered to help again. As they walked to the math library, Jacob asked, "Are you all ready for the trip this weekend?"

"Actually, I don't think I'm coming." A flicker of regret raced through her mind. "I don't have boots."

Jacob shook his head. "That shouldn't be a problem. Stop by the co-op this afternoon and we'll find you boots."

Jacob was waiting for her on the co-op porch when she arrived after her biology class. "I've got quite a collection here."

In the middle of the living room floor were at least ten pairs of boots. She measured her foot against one pair Jacob held up. She looked at him. "I know I don't have Cinderella feet, but I'm not one of the stepsisters."

Jacob's face flushed. Mia put her hand over her mouth as she realized how unkind she'd been.

"This pair looks like it might work," she said, hoping to smooth over her gaff. She tried them and they were comfortable. "These are perfect." She looked up at him. "Are you sure it's OK?"

"It's OK." Jacob's voice was soft, and his face was still pink.

Seeing Jacob so miserable deepened her regret of her stinging remark. "Thanks so much for going to all this trouble." She leaned forward and gave him a kiss on the cheek and turned toward the door.

All the way back to Bertram, she relived that moment. Why had she done that? As a thank you? Did she even like him? She squirmed with embarrassment.

Chapter Thirty-Six

Friday night the beige VW Beetle pulled up in front of Bertram, and Barb got out. Barb was tall, slender, with straight black hair long enough to sway at her waist. Jacob's description, a Joan Baez look-alike, was perfect.

Mia, who was sitting on the step, got up. "Barb?"

"You must be Mia." They went into the dorm, where Barb said hello to the house mother and signed Mia out.

Mia deposited her knapsack in the trunk and slid into the rear seat, next to Jacob. She said hi to Glen, who was driving.

"It'll be about a two hour trip," Glen said. "We'll stop for gas and a snack after we get out of this cement jungle."

Mia settled back in her seat.

The little car slid easily through the highways of Boston and out into the moonless night. Glen described the hike they were planning tomorrow, about nine miles round trip and more than 3,000 feet in elevation gain.

"But the summit is only at 4,500 feet," Barb said. "The mountains here are frost heaves."

Mia laughed. "Where're you from, Barb?"

"Denver. Colorado knows how to build mountains."

"I'm from California," Mia said. "We have some pretty nice mountains, too." She felt Jacob's hand on hers. She didn't move.

It was close to midnight by the time they arrived. Mia shivered as she got out of the car. She looked up to stars puncturing the inky blackness, a sight that made her heart sing, a sight she'd not seen for too long. The four picked up their gear and climbed a hill to the cabin, Glen's flashlight lighting the way.

The cabin, lit by two kerosene lanterns, was a large single room with a huge stone fireplace along one wall and a ladder leading up to a loft. There were several chairs, a bench, and mattresses on the floor. It seemed even colder in the cabin than outside, so getting the fire started was the first order of business. The other four — Bob a physics major, Bill a chemist, and Bart and Bret, two biologists — had already arrived and were working on the fire. Glen helped and soon a lick of flame rose from the pile of wood.

"Better hit the sack," Glen said, heading up the ladder with his gear. "We don't want to waste our hiking day sleeping."

Barb followed him up the ladder.

"You married folks have a good rest," Bob said with a chuckle.

Mia looked at Jacob.

"No," he said, "they aren't married."

The others had put their things on mattresses, claiming their sleeping space. Mia looked around and placed her things on a mattress in the far corner, away from the others. She unrolled her bag and climbed in, fully dressed. It was so chilly she even kept her parka on.

***

She felt a tickle on her cheek and opened her eyes. The sun streamed in through a grimy window, and she looked up to see Jacob, brushing her face with a peacock feather.

"Outing Club alarm clock," he said. "Time to rise and shine."

She sat up and looked around. Everyone else was up, some eating cereal, others getting their knapsacks together. Jacob handed her a mug of hot coffee. She looked past him and saw the percolator sitting at the edge of a large grate over the fire.

She sipped her coffee gratefully. It was cold in the cabin despite the fire and the sun. She had a quick breakfast and then helped Barb assemble peanut butter and jelly sandwiches for their trail lunch.

Soon they were at the trailhead, starting their climb. As they went, they walked in pairs, talking about school and hiking, about hobbies and what they did during the summer. The pace was perfect for Mia, and she felt her school tension melt. The crisp clean air, the leaves just starting their autumn finery, the physical activity made her giddy. The sun filtered through the trees. Conversation was easy.

They stopped now and again for water and trail mix.

By noon they had arrived at the summit. A cloud hung over the top of the mountain and they walked the last ten feet in a snow storm.

"This is kind of crazy," Mia said to Barb.

"It's often like this," Barb said. "But this is perfect. Ten feet in snow and the rest beautiful and warm." She snapped a picture of Glen, bundled in his parka, holding the ragged flag that stood at the summit. "How about a picture of you two," she said, indicating Mia and Jacob. She arranged them in front of the tattered flag, arm in arm, and snapped several more shots. Then they descended the ten feet to a sun warmed spot and sat on rocks to eat lunch.

"Better than fillet mignon," Bill said, biting into his sandwich.

"It's funny how a little exercise and a beautiful spot make food taste better," Bob said.

They started down the trail, Mia talking with Bart about her troubles with biology.

"Creek is a brilliant scientist, but he's a sourpuss and can't teach worth a damn." Bart's comments made Mia feel a little better. "If you need help, just give me a holler. I'm sure between us, Bret and I can get you on the right path."

They reached the trailhead about 2:30 and drove into the village to buy what Bill said was the best cornbread ever made. By 5:00 they were supping on canned stew and cornbread.

It was dark by the time they had cleaned up. Glen piled more logs on the fire and told a scary story. Bob started on his scary story but was convinced by the cat calls that it had been told once too often. Barb pulled out a guitar, a well-loved thing that was part of the furniture in the cabin. She had a beautiful voice, which made her seem all the more like Joan Baez. She sang ballads and protest songs.

"May I sing a song?" Mia asked.

"Oh, sure," Barb handed her the guitar.

Mia sang a song Gina had written, using the words of a Houseman poem. It was about the beauty of nature, and even though it was a song about spring, it captured the happiness Mia felt. Then she sang Pete Seeger's "If I Had A Hammer."

"You have a nice voice, Mia," Barb said, "though I find it strange Dr. Brower's daughter would sing a protest song."

Mia's heart raced and her face flushed. "You liberals think you have a monopoly on wishing for peace!" She placed the guitar on the floor and fled the cabin. Her tears were hot.

The cabin door slammed. "Don't mind Barb," Jacob said, "she's self-righteous."

Mia shivered. Jacob had brought her parka, which he placed around her shoulders.

He pointed up at the stars. "How many constellations can you name?"

She looked up at the sky and pointed to the Big Dipper and the Little Dipper, to Perseus and Cassiopeia. "But," she said, "it's even more fun to make up your own constellations." She surveyed the sky. "There,' she said, pointing to this star and that. "It's a motorcycle."

"A motorcycle? Not a bicycle?" he asked.

"No, a motorcycle. I'm sure."

"Well, I see an integral sign, see there and there, and a summation sign...."

"And an alpha and a gamma and...."

Jacob pulled Mia toward him and kissed her. He looked into her eyes. "Cold nose, warm heart." He kissed her again.

By the time they returned to the cabin everyone else was asleep. Jacob pulled his sleeping bag next to Mia's.

She unzipped her bag. She held his gaze. "Two can sleep warmer than one."

***

Mia woke before the others. She looked at Jacob, his breathing even, his face peaceful. Dread swept over her as she remembered Barb's remarks and Jacob's embraces. She wanted to be home.

The ride back to Cambridge was quiet, but civilized. Jacob held her hand. She felt too injured, too vulnerable, to object, but it reminded her of the truth of last night. Things had happened so quickly. It wasn't that she minded last night. She'd encouraged Jacob. But that was last night. Last night, she'd wanted the solace, but now she was not sure it was good. She felt numb.

The next day, Mia found an envelope in her mailbox. The loopy handwriting read:

Dear Mia,
I apologize for that comment. Totally out of order. I've enclosed a peace offering and I hope you will come on many more outings.
Sincerely,
Barb

A color photo fell from the envelope and Mia picked it up. Mia and Jacob, arm in arm, bundled in parkas, faces pink with the cold, smiled at her.

How elusive happiness was.

The next day, Tuesday, was one of the bad days, as she thought of complex analysis and biology days. Jacob flashed her a smile and brushed her hand with his as he settled next to her. The equations whizzed past as they always did, without the slightest chance of their sense entering her brain. Wiseberg finally collected his things and walked out.

Jacob smiled at her. "Ready for review?"

She nodded. As they headed out the door, he took her hand. He beamed. His step was happy.

She had meant to tell him she was not so sure about their affair, but she couldn't say anything right then, as they walked to the math building. And she couldn't say anything in the math library. She would talk it over with him this evening.

"How about having dinner at Bertram tonight?" she asked as she got her things together to go to biology class.

"Sure!" He radiated happiness.

He looked so happy that evening, as they walked back to the co-op and up to his room. So she said nothing.

They settled into a routine, a comfortable routine. Reviews after class, dinners together, evenings in his room.

Maybe this was love.

…
Junior Year
September 1966 to June 1967

Chapter Thirty-Seven

"What did Thoreau see in this puddle?"

"C'mon, Mia." Jacob put his arm around her. "Just look at those colors."

The trees across the lake still sported some green, but mostly they blazed red, yellow, and orange. "OK. You're right. That's one thing California lacks. Autumn colors."

"And this is so close to Cambridge."

They had left in early morning first light. By now it was sunny but chill, and mist rose from the water. The lake was, Mia thought, like a geisha girl, revealing just so much of herself.

"Yup." She inhaled the smell of autumn on the air. "It is nice." They locked their bikes at a rack at the edge of the parking lot and stood on the sandy beach looking across the lake. "Still, I had expected something more dramatic. This is, after all, the famous Walden Pond."

Jacob laughed. "Maybe it's like the integers." They crossed the beach and found a wide leaf-covered path into the woods. "You know. Integers are boring: 1, 2, 3."

"Yeah. I know. But then you look further. There are the primes, and the numbers modulo a prime, and before you know it, you're face to face with Fermat's Last Theorem."

Jacob stopped and pulled her to him. "You can finish my sentences. No wonder I love you." His kiss was soulful.

He took her hand and they walked farther in the woods. The leaves crackled under their feet. They stopped at a mound of stones at the side of the path. A large sign, letters carved in wood, stood beside the stone heap.

> *"I went to the woods because I wished to live deliberately, to front only the essential facts of life, and see if I could not learn what it had to teach, and not, when I came to die, discover that I had not lived." — Thoreau*

Mia sighed. "That's a scary thought — 'discover that I had not lived.'"

Jacob grinned and shook his head. "You have thought much more about life than I." He started down the path again.

It was true. Jacob did not think about his life plan. He knew what he was going to do. Mia had floundered, but things were clearer now. She felt pretty good about her math classes this year. Jacob wasn't in either of them, but Alice was. She and Alice studied together, and if they got stuck, which wasn't that often, they asked Jacob.

They turned off the path onto a barely traveled trail. It ended abruptly at a promontory, maybe 50 feet above the water. Jacob pointed down at the water. Mia made out a blue heron, barely visible in the gray mist. Here was Walden's Last Theorem; this was what drew Thoreau.

They returned to the path and continued walking, side by side. A squirrel skittered through the leaves and up a tree, chattering a distress call. Mia looked overhead and spotted a bird of prey looping above.

Jacob looked in the direction she was pointing. He looked back at her and flashed a quick smile. "I need to talk to you about something." His face grew somber, his hands pushed deep in his pockets, his shoulders slumped. It was Jacob's distress call.

"What's wrong?"

His voice was low and the words, half mumbled, came quickly. "My mom wants me to invite you for Thanksgiving."

Mia was startled. They had been going together for a year now. He hardly ever spoke about his family, so the invitation seemed not only awkward but odd. Was it that Jacob was getting serious? Was it time for him to introduce her to his family? She wasn't sure how she felt about that. But she and Jacob were together all the time. Her world was built around him. She studied him. He was a good sort. Maybe she was in love with him. "Thanks."

He squinted. "Was that yes?"

"I guess it depends whether you want me to come to your house." She loved teasing him. It was so easy. "I mean, I'm sure your mom is a very nice lady, but I'm more interested in pleasing you."

His eyes relaxed and his lips curved in a happier smile. "I love you, Mia." He took her hand and started walking again. "I must admit my parent's house is not my favorite place and holiday dinners are, at best, trying." He stopped and gazed into her eyes. "Having you there would make it almost bearable. At least I think it would."

She searched his face. "Not real positive, are you?"

They walked again.

"I'm just being honest." He sighed. "My mom scurries around and tries to stuff you like a liver goose. My father is quiet and, well, we don't get along. And my sister quarrels with my mom. It's slow torture."

"Hmm." Mia closed her eyes and shook her head. "Sounds great."

"OK! OK!" He stopped and held up his hands. "I'd like it if you'd come for Thanksgiving."

She took his hands and gave him a peck on the cheek. "I'd love to."

They had reached a little beach and sat in the sand, soaking in the sun that had burned off the mist. Looking over the water, Mia saw a turtle sunning himself on a log. She pointed the creature out to Jacob.

He nodded and smiled wryly. "Ah, to be a turtle and carry one's house on one's back. A house of one's own. No relatives to annoy you."

Chapter Thirty-Eight

Wind blew the ever-present grit in grimy whirlwinds past the bare trees. Jacob and Mia walked to the subway, bundled in parkas, hats, mittens, scarves, their heads bent down to avoid the worst of the wind. As they descended into the station, the air, laced with the stench of oil, smoke, and urine, grew hot and humid.

"A little like descending into the first level of hell," Jacob said. "Not so bad, but just wait to see what's on the next level."

The trip to Jacob's family home in Milton involved several transfers, which Jacob pointed out on the subway map.

"It takes over an hour," he said. "My parents wanted me to live at home, to save money."

"That would have taken a huge chunk of time." Mia wondered how he managed as it was, with BHTC.

"That's what I told them. But really, it wasn't the time so much. Just couldn't have done it. If I stayed home either I'd suffocate or I would have killed them."

It was a long dirty trip. When they finally got to Milton, Mia was happy to be out in the fresh air, even if it was cold. Milton reminded Mia of the town in her first grade reader: streets where Dick and Jane lived, with picket fences, sidewalks and trees. It was less congested than Cambridge, more homey, more cheerful.

"I have tickets to a Pete Seeger concert Saturday," Jacob said, "if you'd like to go."

"Oh, yes!" Mia wondered that Jacob would spend the money for a concert. "Such a treat!"

"Yes, well." Jacob's smile was sheepish, as if he knew what she was thinking. "I needed something to get me through dinner tonight." Then he put his arm around Mia. "Even you are not enough to cheer me through a family dinner."

They reached Jacob's house and walked up the stairs.

"It's a duplex. My grandfather lives downstairs."

Jacob pushed the door open after unlocking it. Aromas of beef and gravy mingled with spice scents Mia didn't know.

"Hello!" Jacob's voice was loud and formal.

Mrs. Frenkel came scurrying, her slight frame vibrating. Her graying hair was short, and she wore a dull yellow apron over a loose fitting house dress covered with red roses and green leaves. Her cloth slippers slapped against her heels as she walked.

"Oh, oh," she said, pulling Jacob down to deliver a wet kiss on his cheek. "My darling," she said looking at him, her eyes moist.

Mrs. Frenkel turned to Mia. "You must be Mia!" she said. "My Jacob says you will be great mathematician." She pulled Mia down and delivered a wet kiss on her cheek.

"So nice to meet you," Mia said.

"Take off coats." Mrs. Frenkel hung their parkas in the small over-stuffed closet.

"Come, come. Sit!" Mrs. Frenkel commanded, leading them through a small living room and into the dining area. "What will you have? Coffee? Tea? Soda? And maybe a little something to nosh? A little cake?"

"Nothing for me," Jacob said. Mia stared at him. Not even a thank you for his poor mother?

"Some coffee would be nice." Mia wanted to make up for Jacob's rude behavior more than she wanted coffee. Mrs. Frenkel disappeared into the kitchen, just off the dining area.

Mia looked into the living room. A white shag rug covered

the floor. Plastic runners protected the path from the front door to the eating area. An upholstered couch, covered in an off white sateen, stood along one wall, with two matching chairs on either side. These were also protected by plastic. A dark wooden table, heavy, with carved vines, sat in front of the couch. A TV faced the couch. In the corner closest to the eating area, a chair, unprotected by plastic, stood by itself. It was covered with a heavy floral patterned material, so worn in places that the once red flowers were faded to a sad dark pink. An upright piano was crammed beside the TV.

A heavy set man, perhaps an inch taller than Mrs. Frenkel, emerged from the hall. But for a fringe of hair at the back of his head, he was bald. His face was creased, his skin blotched with black spots. He walked slowly, seeming to have difficulty getting his heavy belly from one place to another.

"Hello," Jacob said. Then, turning towards Mia, "This is my father."

Mia stood and shook hands with Mr. Frenkel. "Pleased to meet you."

Mr. Frenkel nodded and mumbled something Mia didn't understand.

Mrs. Frenkel appeared from the kitchen carrying a tray with an ornate coffee pot and matching cups and saucers, a silver cup with sugar cubes and a silver creamer with a yellowish thick liquid, which must have been concentrated milk. A stack of dessert dishes and a coffee cake crowded the tray. She placed the tray on the table and started serving cake to her husband.

"No," he said, pushing her hand aside.

"Oh," she frowned. "How about you, Mia?"

"That looks lovely." Mia smiled at her. Mia didn't want cake, but somehow, she hoped, by accepting the food, she would soothe the poor woman. "Thank you."

Jacob flashed Mia a look. Mia didn't know what it meant, so she ignored it. Mrs. Frenkel didn't offer her son cake.

"Uncle Misha and Aunt Myra are coming," Mrs. Frenkel said, looking at Jacob. "Can you get two chairs from Saba's?"

Jacob disappeared out the front door and Mrs. Frenkel went back into the kitchen. That left Mia alone with Mr. Frenkel, the man who had yet to say a comprehensible word. Under the table, Mia dug her fingernails into her palm.

"Your father." Mr. Frenkel spoke slowly, with an accent similar to her father's. "Your father is a great man."

"Thank you." Mia flushed. She'd heard this often, but had never found a comfortable response.

"No." Mr. Frenkel's voice rang harsh, as if Mia had contradicted him. "He is great man. He will save this country from the communists."

"He does what he can." Mia bit her lip.

"Yes, he will save this country from the communists. And he will save Israel, too."

Jacob pushed through the front door, carrying two chairs. Mia exhaled slowly.

There was a knock on the door. Jacob set the chairs at the dining table and returned to the door, giving dutiful hugs to Misha and Myra, and what looked like a sincere hug to a bent, skinny man, clearly his grandfather. Jacob helped the old man to the chair in the corner. Mia stood to greet the newcomers.

"You must be Mia." Myra looked so like Jacob's mom Mia was grateful they wore different clothing. Myra pulled Mia into a hug and a not so delicate kiss on both cheeks.

"Mia," Misha said, edging his wife away, "what a privilege, the daughter of the great man." Misha seemed satisfied to just shake hands.

Jacob's mom bustled out of the kitchen and hugged her sister and brother-in-law. "Myra," she said, "I just got pictures from

Joey's Bar Mitzvah. We look after dinner."

Just then Becky, Jacob's sister, appeared in the hall doorway, dressed in jeans, a man's shirt, which hung on her like a tent, and bare feet. Her long hair, wavy and raven black, hung loose and disheveled around her shoulders. She hugged her uncle.

He held her at arm's length. "Out partying last night?"

"Ach," Jacob's mom said, "over at her friend's. I bet they got no sleep."

Becky ignored her mother, hugged her aunt and grandfather, and came over to Mia. She shook Mia's hand. "Nice to meet you."

"Sit," Jacob's mom said and placed people at the table. "Becky, help with food. Jacob, get plate for Saba."

Mia sat uncomfortably between Misha and Jacob's father, while Becky and her mother transported dish after dish onto the table. There was a beef brisket, and rolls, and potatoes, and gravy. The foods, placed on fine china, were shades of browns and creams and tans, except for the beans, which were a dusky olive green. There were pickles of all sorts, kinds Mia had never seen before.

Little wine glasses sat at each place. Jacob's dad opened a bottle of Manischewitz, poured himself a glass full, and passed the bottle to Mia. She poured a little into her glass and passed the bottle on. This seemed to be the signal to start passing dishes and soon plates were being passed in both directions.

Jacob's mom and Myra did most of the talking. Mrs. Feldman this, Keller's son that. The names of people came and went so fast Mia didn't try to keep up. She amused herself by looking around the table. Jacob and Becky were making signs to each other, while Misha and Jacob's father ate in silence. Grandpa dozed, his plate on a little table by his chair.

The food was salty and heavy, and Mia was thirsty. She took a sip of the wine, but the sweet syrup caused her to gag. She swallowed and coughed. She wanted water, but didn't want to ask for it. She did her best to eat everything on her plate, grateful she had taken small portions.

There was a break in the ladies' conversation and Jacob's mom looked around the table. "Mia, you have nothing on plate, you must have more."

Mia already had eaten more than her fill. "I've eaten so much already."

"No, no. Have more." Mrs. Frenkel passed the platter of brisket.

Mia dutifully took another small helping.

"Jacob?" His mother's look was almost a plea.

"No."

Mia stared at him.

"Becky?" his mother looked at her daughter. Becky just shook her head.

At least the men took second helpings. Someone appreciated all of Mrs. Frenkel's work. The ladies took up their conversation again and Mia happily faded into the background.

It seemed to take forever to finish the meal, but at last Jacob's mom pushed her chair back. "Everyone full?" She looked around the table.

"Becky," her mom said, "help with dishes."

Mia pushed her chair back to get up and help, too, but Mrs. Frenkel shook her head.

"No, Mia, you are guest. Guests do not help in my house."

Mia meekly pulled her chair up to the table.

Myra, Becky and Mrs. Frenkel were busy clearing the table and washing the dishes, which left Mia with Jacob's father, Misha and Jacob. Mr. Frenkel poured himself another glass of wine. He passed the bottle to Mia, who passed it on. Mia noticed Jacob's glass was clean.

Mr. Frenkel looked at his son and cleared his throat. "So, you going to help in the shop this weekend?"

Jacob grimaced. "Dad, I've got work to do."

"Well, so do I and I could use some help."

"Dad, I've got work for Harvard and for BHTC. If you want me to help, let me quit BHTC."

Mr. Frenkel's nostrils flared. "You know your mother would never allow that." He took out a cigar and offered one to Misha. "But you must help during winter break. I absolutely need help."

Jacob said nothing.

The room filled with smoke.

Becky appeared from the kitchen and wrinkled her nose. "Hey, Jay, let's go for a walk."

"Sure." Jacob looked at Mia. "Walk?"

Mia nodded.

The young people, after dressing for the cold, left.

"The Tavern's open. Want to go there?" Becky asked.

"Open on Thanksgiving?" Jacob asked.

"Give thanks, Jay."

They walked into the wind. Mia shivered. It seemed even colder outside after the heat of the house. Mia wished Jacob would take her hand or put his arm around her shoulders, anything that would give her comfort in a world that was not hers. But he walked between his sister and Mia, his hands in his pockets.

"So how're you surviving?" Jacob's question was directed to his sister.

"Not too bad," Becky said. "I spend most of my time over at Nina's. It's OK, since she's Jewish and Mom likes her mother. But it means I'm not practicing." Becky gave a hollow chuckle. "Might be a good thing. Maybe it'll convince them I have no musical talent."

They reached the tavern. It was gloomy inside, the walls paneled in dark wood. They ordered coffee, and Mia also got a large glass of water, which she drained, and asked for another.

"Thirsty?" Becky asked. "You should have asked for water back at the house. I could've gotten you some."

"Thanks," Mia said.

"Also," Becky said without the slightest hint of a smile, "if you're going to be around the house at all, you need to learn to say no."

"Oh?"

"Mom will stuff you like a liver goose, if you let her."

"A liver goose?" Mia had heard Jacob use that term, too, but she didn't know what it meant.

"A goose that is force fed, so the liver becomes enlarged." Jacob sneered. "Makes great pate."

"Ugh." Mia looked from Becky to Jacob and back again. "Aren't you a little hard on your mom?"

Becky's dark eyes glinted. "Empathizing is a luxury reserved for people who don't have to live with her." She turned to her brother. "How's things with you?"

"Not bad," he said. "I finish BHTC this spring. I might finish Harvard this spring, too. I have enough credits."

Mia exhaled. "Why finish early?"

Jacob focused on Mia, as if he hadn't realized she was there. He sighed. "First, I want to get my PhD. Mathematicians do their best work before they are 25. That leaves me less than six years. I need to stop piddling around. I need to make some real mathematical progress."

Becky shook her head. "But that's not the only reason."

Jacob nodded, not taking his eyes off Mia. "I want to be out from under my father's thumb. As soon as I get a graduate fellowship, as soon as I can support myself, I won't have to work in my father's shop, I won't have to go to BHTC, I won't even have to come home for Thanksgiving."

Mia bit her lower lip and looked down. This was why Jacob had not talked about his family before. But this — she hated to think of it this way — vehement loathing of his parents was scary. "Is it that bad?" She felt both siblings stare at her.

Becky sighed. "They aren't cruel or mean. They don't beat us. They feed us and give us material things. They love us. There's no doubt they love us. Maybe they love us too much."

"I know my parents love me, and I've had some tough times with my mom, but the way you two talk...."

"It's not like that for me," Jacob said. "I know Mom loves me. She hasn't a clue about me, but she loves me. I'll give her that. Dad is something else. I'm a great disappointment to him."

"Going to Harvard? A summa cum laude to be? A disappointment?"

"My dad wants me to take over his tool and die business."

"You're kidding!"

"I wish I were. I've been a disappointment to him since I was little. I can't draw. I can't measure worth a damn. I'm clumsy with tools. He makes jokes about having to package a first aid kit with a hammer for me."

Becky nodded. "He really is a piece of work."

"He makes fun of me in front of his friends. I'm surprised he hasn't said something in front of you."

"He wants to make a good impression because of Mia's dad," Becky said.

"So does your mom feel the same way?" Mia asked.

Jacob's lips pressed to a thin line and his brows lowered, but it was Becky who answered. "She's so angry they hardly speak."

Mia gulped. "I'm sorry."

"Yeah," Jacob said, throwing some bills on the table. "We

probably need to get back to the zoo."

They walked in silence. Mia wished she were in the dorm.

Jacob's mom met them at the door. "Oh, there you are," she said in a cheery voice. "Just in time for coffee and cake." They settled back at the table, mom pressing food on them, and the ladies chatting.

Misha turned to Mia. "Did you know your friend Jacob was born in Warsaw?" The buzz at the table stopped and all eyes turned to Misha.

Mia shook her head. "Really?"

"Just after the war. I told Herman and Ruth it was crazy for Jews to bring a child into this sad world. Two miserable little Jews who lived through war in Poland, and they wanted to have child. Stupid!" Misha said. "But I was wrong! Look at him. Handsome fellow, don't you think? And smart? Going to Harvard!" Misha shook his head. "I was sure wrong."

Jacob stared down, his face beet red.

***

"I shouldn't have brought you."

They walked toward the Milton MTA stop.

"What family doesn't have its ups and downs?" Mia asked, half to herself.

"What?"

"Just a quote from 'A Lion in Winter,' when the king and queen are, well, I don't remember the details, just say there's plenty of fireworks." She wanted to comfort Jacob. "Anyhow, I'm glad you brought me. I got to know you a little better by meeting your family."

"I hope not." Jacob frowned. "I'm not like my family."

Mia wondered whether this was true.

"They consider themselves Jews. For my mother, it's all

about her friends, all supposed Jews like her."

"But aren't they Jews?"

"No!" Jacob shook his head. "They go to synagogue on High Holy Days, they go to all the Bar Mitzvahs and Bat Mitzvahs, but they don't have any idea what the Torah says, what it means to be a Jew. My mother requires me to go to BHTC so she can brag to her friends, but she has no idea what I learn there. It's all appearances."

"Aren't you being a little hard on them?" He was so mean! "They survived the war. Haven't they suffered enough?"

Jacob stopped walking and gripped her arm so hard it hurt. His eyes glinted. "Don't pull that bullshit on me. Suffering does not give one license for anything."

"OK." She looked away. "I didn't mean to...." Her voice trailed off. "I guess I just don't understand."

"Thank you!" he released her arm and started walking again. "Saying you don't understand is honest." He stopped and turned toward her, his eyes kinder. "I'm sorry. I always have trouble at home, and I'm taking it out on you."

"Apology accepted." She gave him a quick kiss on the cheek and searched for a more pleasant topic. "You were born in Warsaw?"

"Oh, that." Jacob's eyes glowed. "You might not realize it, but Misha was jabbing me, reminding me of my parents suffering, while jabbing my father, reminding him how proud he should be. They're all crazy. I wish I could divorce them. I will divorce them as soon as I can support myself."

It seemed all topics were filled with fury. "Why did you bring me?"

"I don't know. Maybe hoping they would be better behaved in front of you." They had reached the station and were waiting for the train to come, huddling against a wall to shelter from the wind. "No. To be honest, I brought you because my mother kept nagging me about you."

"Your mother? You told your mother about me?"

Jacob snorted. "No, I didn't say a word. It was the Jewish Ladies Intelligence Network."

"Huh?" Mia stared at Jacob.

"I don't know how she found out, but someone at Harvard told her."

"I see." Mia considered for a moment. "I hope I haven't been indiscreet."

Jacob laughed a good honest laugh. "Mia, are you Jewish? I mean you're really good at feeling guilty."

Mia smiled. "Jewish blood."

"Explains a lot," Jacob said. "No, I don't think you've been indiscreet, other than studying with me at the math library and hanging around the co-op." Jacob looked at Mia. "I mean it's kind of obvious, isn't it?"

"OK, so people at the math department know. And your mother has a secret line into the math department?"

"Oh, she has several." Jacob's face was more relaxed. "But I think it was Alice."

"Alice?"

"Sure. You study with her and she must at least know we're a couple."

"You blame Alice?"

Jacob thought a moment. "No. Not at all. But I envy her."

"Envy?"

"She's a real Jew. She gets solace from the religion. And she is straight and honest and works hard."

"But she gossiped about you."

"Probably." Jacob shrugged. "She probably told one of her friends, in passing, not thinking much of it. Then it spread like a virus. She probably said very little and the tidbit grew and grew before it reached my mother. But it's not Alice who's impossible. It's my parents."

Chapter Thirty-Nine

Jacob had borrowed Glen's VW for spring break and the little beast was huffing and puffing up the highway towards the Outing Club cabin. Mia had her socked feet shoved into the vent at the floor, hoping to get a smidgen of warmth from the air that blew off the engine. They had three glorious days ahead of them, three days to themselves at the cabin. No one else was interested in three days in an unheated, no plumbing cabin. Everyone else headed south to thaw their bones. But Jacob didn't have the time or the money and he wanted to get away. And if Jacob was going away, Mia would come, too.

They lit the fire and heated hot chocolate. Jacob added another log. "Well, my princess, where would you like to sleep? We could retire to the royal bedroom." He said, indicating the ladder to the loft. "Or, like mere peasants, we could sleep in front of the fire."

"I'm feeling rather peasantlike tonight. I'd be happier a warm peasant than a frozen princess."

Jacob laughed and started arranging mattresses and sleeping bags near the fire.

Mia unloaded her backpack. "I'm looking at classes for next year. Would you take a look?"

Jacob wiped his hands on his jeans, found some mugs on the mantelpiece, rinsed them with water from a jug, and poured hot chocolate. "Sure." He handed Mia a mug and sat on the bench. "So what're you thinking?"

She sat next to him and sipped her cocoa as she ran down her list of courses. Jacob suggested some alternatives.

She set her mug on the floor and lay her head on his shoulder. "What about you?"

He wrapped his arm around her shoulder and pulled her closer. "I've got it planned." He rattled off a list. "Or maybe I'll just graduate early."

Jacob had mentioned graduating early several times. Mia had ignored those comments, hoping he would not do it. Besides, if he wanted to go to grad school, he would have had to apply by now. As far as she knew, he hadn't. This thought of leaving Harvard early was just a dream. So again, she ignored it.

Mia pushed these thoughts aside. "So we won't be in any of the same classes again."

He looked at her, his brows raised, his lips pursed. "That's the way it looks."

She shivered. "Hope I don't run into a Wiseberg course."

He rubbed her back. "We'll see about professors, make sure you don't sign up for a Wiseberg." He kissed her gently. "I can help you if you get stuck." Reaching for her hand, he pulled her up. "And you're better at math than you know." He swept a strand of hair from her cheek, his eyes glimmering. "And you have other talents."

They tumbled onto the sleeping bags.

***

In the morning, they ate a quick breakfast, packed up their gear, and drove to the Mount Washington trailhead. The trail was covered with snow and was difficult to follow, so Jacob suggested they walk on the cog railway. They strapped crampons to their boots and started. The crampons sank into the snow over the rail ties and gave them a secure footing. Mia savored the cold clean air against her cheeks and the crunch of each footfall.

"I talked to Professor Petran about my plans about graduating."

She grit her teeth, but was silent. If Jacob left, what would that mean for their relationship?

"He said I shouldn't."

Mia responded too quickly. "Why not?"

"He talked a lot." Jacob stopped, looking across the shimmering landscape. "I don't know whether I remember all his arguments. There are lots of good mathematicians here. I should work with as many as possible." He paused and looked down. "Having a degree, whether a BS or a PhD is not necessary to do new work, to getting papers published, so I shouldn't be in such a hurry. If I establish my credentials before I graduate, I will have a better chance to get into any graduate program I want. And a better chance to get a generous fellowship." Jacob looked at Mia. "I think that was about it."

"And you think?" She tried to keep impatience out of her voice.

"They all make sense," Jacob said, "except...."

"Except?" Mia asked, though she knew what was coming.

"Except staying means I would still be on my father's dime."

"Did you tell Professor Petran that?"

Jacob chuckled. "He pulled it out of me. He'd offer an argument, and I'd say, but I still want to leave early. After a while, he said there must be something else going on."

"Professor Petran is such a good sort." She thought of his lectures and the music course they had shared. He was so down to earth, so approachable. "I wish he were my adviser."

"I'm sure he'd accept you. Just ask him."

"Maybe."

They started walking again. She looked down at her boots, one in front of the other. The rails were about five feet above the ground. "Hey, Jacob. We're getting a little high. Is this safe?"

Jacob stopped for a moment and looked down. "Sure. The crampons will keep us secure."

Mia looked down again. She was just being a sissy.

Mia thought about Jacob's conversation with the professor. "Did the good professor have a solution?"

"Not exactly. He asked if I had financial aid."

"Do you?"

"No." She heard his bitter snort. "My dad said I wouldn't get aid, because he made too much money."

Mia tried to imagine the conversation.

"And then he went into a tirade about snotty colleges putting their noses into other people's business."

It must have been a nasty conversation. Mia was sure Jacob did not share this with the professor. "You told Professor Petran you didn't have aid?"

"I didn't go into the details. Just said I didn't have aid and thought I would not qualify for it. That's where we left it."

They entered a clearing where the sun shone. The ice had melted on the tracks leaving the wood bare. The tracks were about 8 feet above the ground now and the crampons did not dig into the wood, leaving Mia balanced on the tips of the crampon spikes. She considered saying something.

Her steps made a clomp, clomp, clomp sound. Then her boot hit something smooth and hard, something that did not give way and she felt her foot slide from under her and she was tumbling.

Over. Over. Over. She saw the leafless trees, the sun glinting off their icy bare branches, the blue of the sky, the white of the snow, the brown mud where the sun had melted the ice.

Thud.

Pain shot through her arm.

Jacob looked down at her. "You OK?"

"I think so." She pressed down with her right hand. Pain zinged through her arm. She switched to her left hand and scrambled up. "Maybe we'd better go back to the cabin."

Jacob nodded.

"On the ground this time."

It wasn't a question, it was a command. Perhaps Jacob took it as a criticism because he looked down with a frown. They walked down the hill, using the tracks as a guide.

The pain, which hadn't seemed that bad when she fell, was growing. Her arm throbbed.

At last they got to the car.

"Do you have any aspirin?"

"Of course." Jacob slid his backpack off and searched. He handed her two aspirin. She took the pills, using only her left hand. She sipped from the canteen.

"You're going to have to help me with my crampons. My right arm isn't working."

***

They parked at the bottom of the hill leading up to the cabin. "We need to get back to Cambridge. And I don't want to walk to the cabin."

He pocketed the keys. "I'll pack up and be down, soon as I can."

Her arm pulsed with every heartbeat. It was getting colder in the car and she shivered. It felt like forever before Jacob came down the hill carrying their gear.

"How bad is it?" They pulled onto the road, going back to Cambridge.

"It's pretty uncomfortable." She squirmed, trying to settle her arm so it would hurt less. "I just want to be back in my room."

"Oh, no. It's health services for you!"

She felt beads of perspiration on her forehead. An acid taste rose to her throat and her stomach spasmed. She swallowed and hoped she wouldn't vomit. The smallest movement set off flares of hot pain, so she sat as still as she could.

"You OK?"

"Yes." Talking sent another spiky jolt down her arm.

"It'll be about another hour, I'm afraid." He glanced over at her. "Or we might stop earlier, if you want." No answer from her. "But I think it would be fastest if we just went to Cambridge."

"Yeah."

She submerged her thoughts in Jordan Normal Forms.

***

"Nothing serious." The fellow wore blue-gray scrubs, a pen neatly clipped in his pocket. "Just a cracked ulna. I'm going to put a cast on it and give you something for the pain."

Mia nodded. She didn't care what he did.

They had chased Jacob away, he not being a relative.

"You live at Bertram?" Scrubs looked at his clipboard.

She nodded.

"We'll keep you overnight," he said. "The dorms are pretty deserted right now, so it's better if you stay here. We can make sure you are comfortable and on the mend."

She took the pill he was offering.

When she woke, sun was streaming in the window and the sky was a deep blue.

"Deceptive," Jamie said, nodding towards the window. "It's colder than a . . . ." Her sparkling eyes finished the sentence for her. "You'd think it would be warmer in April."

"Hi." Mia's stomach churned. "You been here long?"

"Oh, just a fifth of a century," Jamie said. "So what happened to you?"

Mia shook her head and noted that, though the world seemed fuzzy, at least her arm was comfortable. "Little fall."

"And?" Jamie's eyebrow rose in a question.

Mia told her the whole story.

Jamie shook her head, her fists on her hips. "You'd think old-what's-his-name would be here."

Chapter Forty

Old-what's-his-name didn't show up that day. Or the next. Or even the day after that. Mia had called the co-op, but nobody answered. She had called several more times. Finally, on Sunday evening, someone answered. She left a message he should call. But he didn't. After she had left a message, she didn't call again.

She worked in the math library on Mondays. Jacob usually stopped by to talk, but not that day. And there were no messages from him at the dorm and no calls.

On Tuesday, she walked to the math department, even though she didn't need to. She saw Jacob in the hall talking to Professor Petran. He nodded to her absently and continued his conversation. She dodged into the library and took out her geometry, paging through her notes and the book, but no information got past the turmoil of her emotions. She looked at the clock. She should go if she wanted to get back for dinner. As she was gathering her things, Jacob came in and sat in the chair next to her.

"How're you doing?" He smiled at her.

Fury bubbled up. "Fine." She stood and grabbed her book bag with her right hand. She winced in pain and dropped her things on the table.

He picked them up. "I'll walk you home."

"Don't bother." She snatched the bag from him, turned on her heel, and raced out the door and down the steps.

Alice came over that evening to study geometry with her. She raised her brows when she saw the cast on Mia's arm.

"What happened to you?"

Mia didn't want to go into details, particularly because whatever she said might get back to Jacob. "A little too much fun hiking."

"You OK to study tonight?" Alice's gaze scanned Mia's face. "We could do it another day, if you want."

Mia hoped the distraction of working with her friend might take her mind off Jacob. "I'm fine."

The studying went well, and Mia did feel more relaxed when they had finished going over the notes from the last class.

Alice closed her notebook and straightened her papers. "I saw Jacob this weekend." She carefully placed her things in her book bag. "We were both at a Bar Mitzvah, my cousin's."

"Oh." So that's where he'd been.

"He was there with a girl we know from BHTC." Alice continued talking, but Mia didn't hear a word of it. She felt ill.

"Alice," Mia said, interrupting her in mid-sentence. "I'm sorry, but I don't feel well."

She raced to her room, flung herself on her bed, and wept. She buried her face in her pillow so she didn't make a sound.

How could he? He had broken one girl, so he threw her out and found another. No. That's crazy. Maybe he didn't like her because she was not brave enough? Or because she had blamed him for walking on the rails?

***

Wednesday Mia had library duty again. As she was contemplating whether she hoped Jacob would join her, as he usually did on her library days, or whether she'd be happier if he didn't stop by, he stepped into the library. She immediately took some books that needed to be shelved and went to the far corner of the room.

He followed her. "What?" Jacob's voice was abrupt, his eyes were wide. "What's going on?"

She looked at him and melted into sobs. Jacob put his arm around her shoulder and guided her to a chair.

"What's wrong?" he asked.

How could she explain? How could she tell him how much she hurt? She didn't want him to know how much she needed him. "I guess it's just the pain killers. I guess they, well...."

He hugged her. "I'm sorry you're having problems. I thought, well...." He didn't finish his sentence. "Anyway, I have all kinds of news I can't wait to tell you."

"Oh," she said, not wanting to let him into her heart. She wanted to hate him. But she was curious about his news.

"Yes." His eyes sparkled, his smile widened. "Professor Petran has gotten me a full scholarship for next year."

"Oh."

He nodded. "It's on merit, not need, so my Dad didn't have to fill anything out. And he can't veto it."

"That's impressive."

He released her and stood. "We talked about me living in Dudley house. That would mean no more co-op. No cooking and cleaning and shopping."

She nodded.

"Yes! So much more time for math!" He looked at her.

She laughed inwardly, a nasty laugh. What about time for her, she wondered.

"What do you think?"

She didn't want to be drawn into this conversation, but the words came anyway. "I have trouble seeing you at Dudley." She winced. Why did she care. "I mean, moving in your senior year. It'd just seem strange."

He nodded. "You know, I was having second thoughts about that." He leaned against the table. "I think you're right.

Better to stay at the co-op."

He looked out the window. Mia could see his thoughts churning. He looked back at her. "But that's not all." He spoke so quickly she thought he might choke on his words. "I'll be helping Professor Petran with his textbook."

She was impressed. "My."

"And he's invited me to stay with him this summer!" Jacob smiled. "That means no Milton, no Dad's shop."

"You've hit the jackpot." She could see he didn't hear the sarcasm.

"So how about we celebrate this evening?"

She wanted to say she was busy. She wanted to be with him. She nodded, even as she said no inwardly.

"Clara's?" He beamed.

"Oh, Jacob! That's so expensive." Jacob had never taken her there.

"This is special. And there's no one I'd like to celebrate with more than my special girl."

She felt the tears welling up again. She closed her eyes, willing them away, willing her unease away. He did care for her.

She fell back into her comfortable routine, studying with Alice, getting help from Jacob as necessary. The semester quickly came to an end.

During the summer, Mia worked on a project at MIT to computerize a library's card catalog. The work was interesting, challenging even, but not overwhelming like some of her courses. And, at the end of the day, her time was her own. No worries about exams. The same went for weekends. They were gloriously all her own.

She rented an apartment with Jamie, not far from Professor Petran's house. Jacob stopped by almost every night. They saw movies and went to concerts. Some evenings they just walked.

215

The summer sped by.

Spring of Senior Year
April 1968 to June 1968

Chapter Forty-One

Something was wrong. When Mia stepped into the apartment, Jamie hadn't greeted her with her usual "What's new?" Instead, she was sitting motionless in her chair, her eyes fixed out the window, her hands in her lap.

"Hi, Jamie."

Jamie turned her head and looked at Mia. "Oh. Hi."

"You OK?"

"Yeah."

"You seem a little — " Mia searched for the right word " — distracted. Did something happen?"

"I don't know."

"Jamie, that doesn't sound like you. You always know."

Mia had hoped for at least a little smile, but Jamie just stared. Was she in shock? What could possibly be wrong? Certainly not academics. She was on the path to a Magna in History and Lit.

"How's Hank?"

"He's OK."

That was the problem. The usual response was a long list of Hank's amazing qualities or adventures they were planning.

"Only OK?"

Jamie had turned her attention out the window again. The silence was so long Mia wondered whether Jamie had heard her question.

At last Jamie sighed. "He says we shouldn't get married."

Mia inhaled sharply. She knew Jamie and Hank had been discussing marriage. First it was just hypotheticals, like how many kids do you want. Then it got more serious, things like how important was religion, how do you handle money, who does the dishes.

"Does he want to break up?"

"He says no." Jamie reached for a tissue and blew her nose. "He just doesn't want to get married."

"Did you have a fight?" Jamie had never admitted to fighting with Hank, always painting their relationship as perfect.

"No."

It must be something else. "Did he say why he doesn't want to get married?"

"Yeah. He says we should wait until he gets out of the army."

"That'll be at least four years!"

Hank was going to volunteer for the army, going into a program for officers. He had planned to go directly to law school, but, with the Vietnam War going on, he felt it was his duty to serve.

Jamie looked at Mia, her eyes welling with tears. "Yup."

"Did he say why you should wait?"

"I don't know." Jamie took another tissue from a box and wiped her eyes. "I didn't hear much after he said we should wait."

"I bet he had some good reasons."

"Maybe."

Mia really didn't know Hank. He was reserved. And proper. Did he want to date other women? That didn't seem likely; the army was not the best place to meet women. So what could it be?

"Maybe he doesn't think it's fair to you."

Jamie looked up, her eyes wider. "How's that?"

"If you get married and he's in the army — in Vietnam —

then you'll be married, but you'll be alone."

Jamie's body sagged again, as if that wasn't the answer she wanted. "I don't care."

"But does he know that?"

Jamie closed her eyes. "I don't know."

Mia was feeling more confident about her theory. "I bet he doesn't want to tie you down, given that he will be gone for long periods."

Jamie nodded. Mia could see her gears working.

"I bet he wants to be sure you know how hard it will be. He wants to give you a choice."

Jamie was sitting up now, her eyes brighter.

"Tell him you don't care if he's gone. Tell him you want to get married now. Tell him. . . ." Mia's voice drifted off.

Jamie stood, pulled her coat on, and disappeared out the door.

That evening, as Mia was working on her senior thesis, Jamie burst into the apartment, eyes dancing.

Mia could feel her excitement. "What?"

Without a word, Jamie thrust her left hand forward. On her finger was a diamond, dazzling in the light of the lamp.

Mia hugged Jamie. "Wow!"

"Will you be my maid of honor?"

"Of course."

Mia smiled, but sadness swept through her. Everyone had a plan, everyone was moving forward. Jamie was getting married. Alice was going to Brandeis.

Jacob had gotten into every program he applied for, with full support. No wonder, given that he would graduate Summa, that he had already published two papers. But Jacob, who had shared all the good news with Mia, hadn't asked her what she thought, where she might like to go, hadn't even hinted he might be sorry to not be with her.

Mia was on her own. She'd gotten into Madison, a good school. Going to a new department, where she didn't know the faculty or the students, seemed forbidding. And, without Jacob, she was not sure she could manage.

She felt her world was coming to an end.

It was not just that students in Berkeley were rioting and students at Columbia had occupied buildings, or that students in Paris, even though they were not being drafted, were going on strike.

It was not just that President Johnson had stunned the world by announcing he would not seek another term. Mia and Jamie had watched the speech as it was broadcast live. They watched it on their little black and white TV, the picture grainy, the president looking worn. They ate pizza and watched.

It was not even that Martin Luther King had been assassinated. Mia and Jamie watched that on TV, too, the same grainy picture, the same pizza. It was an event they didn't digest, something to think about after they had turned in their senior theses.

Their male classmates might be drafted. If they went to graduate school, or were medically unfit, they were exempt, but all others were subject to the draft. Jacob would go to graduate school, so he was safe. Hank would enlist.

***

One pleasant spring evening, the breath of warmth soothing on the air, Mia and Jacob sat on the quad. She told him about Hank's plans.

"Jamie's upset, of course, because," and she plucked a blade of grass, "well, there is the danger."

Jacob leaned back on his elbows. "The probability is extremely high that he will be OK."

"True." Mia smoothed the grass blade with her fingers. Most people didn't think in probabilities when a loved one was in harm's way. "And it means they will be apart, of course."

"Sure."

"And it puts their lives on hold." Mia searched Jacob's face, willing him to be concerned. She looked away. "Anyhow, I really respect him for enlisting."

Jacob stood and stretched. "In my case, I cannot afford to take four years and do something other than math. These four years will be the most productive of my career."

How many times had she heard Jacob talk about mathematicians doing their best work before they were 25? But there was a nagging feeling on Mia's part that somehow Jacob was going to graduate school to get out of the draft. That wasn't fair, because Vietnam or no Vietnam, Jacob would go to graduate school. Maybe the ugliness was he felt no regret that he was not doing his part.

But she should not judge him. She was not subject to the draft because she was a woman. And she was doing nothing about the war.

Jacob brushed off the grass clinging to his pants. "I feel that doing math is my destiny, that I was put here at this time to do math. I feel that to delay doing math would be to tempt the gods, to go against what is fated to be."

Mia stood, too. "Jacob, those are strange words, full of pride, with religion mixed in."

"Yes. They are. I've never said this to anyone else. There is no one but you who I trust enough to tell. But it's the way I feel."

Those words warmed Mia.

"Math is my home. Math is where I live. It is where I go when I go to sleep. It is what I think about when I wake up. I did not will this or decide this. It has been this way since before

I can remember."

"How I envy you." She looked in the distance. "You know where you're going. I don't."

"Cheer up," Jacob said. "You'll find your way. You'll make a fine mathematician."

"But I don't live in it the way you do."

"True," he said, "but there is more than one way to be a mathematician."

Mia replayed that conversation over and over. She wished she had a plan. Up until now she had done what she was expected to do. But, now that she could do anything she wanted, she didn't know what she wanted. She wanted a destiny, a firm desire with the talent to go with it. But she didn't have a desire, and, despite Jacob's encouragement, she wasn't sure about the talent.

Mia applied to graduate schools because it was expected.

Professor Petran said Madison was a good school, a very good school. They had offered her a full fellowship, no teaching required, just do math. "Perfect!" Professor Petran said.

Jacob got into Princeton, with a full fellowship, and University of Chicago, with a full fellowship, and Berkeley, with a full fellowship. Oh, and Harvard, too, with a full fellowship. He told her about how he weighed his options. Berkeley wasn't rated as highly as the others, but Jacob had met a professor who taught there, John Sitar. He liked Sitar's work. And Sitar liked Jacob's work. He could get his degree quickly, maybe even in two years. Certainly in three.

Mia had applied to Berkeley, but she hadn't heard from them.

Chapter Forty-Two

Mia should love her senior thesis, should, like Jacob, think about it as she ate her dinner, as she brushed her teeth, while she slept. And she did. She thought about how she might not be able to finish it.

There was no doubt she would not produce an original result, but she must at least explain others' results. When she thought she understood something and began writing, she would find a hole. Then she panicked. That's when she started thinking she should just chuck the whole thing. Not write the thesis. It would mean graduating without a cum laude.

If she didn't finish her thesis, what would she do with herself? She couldn't go to graduate school without the thesis. And that brought her back to what she was going to do with her life. So she went back and tried to fill the hole. She would fill that hole and feel a little better. Until she found the next hole, and the process would start again.

Her daytime traumas were nothing compared to her nightmares. Her thesis had to do with mappings. She would dream of the mappings as if they were transforming her. She would toss and turn, imagining herself morphed again and again. Her right hand became her left foot, her head turned backward. With each change she became more and more distorted, until she woke.

Jacob was using one of his published papers for his senior thesis, and he had managed his classes and exams so he could leave school a month early. He was giving a paper at a math conference in Italy. The closer the date of his departure came, the more heartsick Mia felt.

The night before he was to leave, they planned to go out to dinner. Mia had just hit another hole and wasn't ready when Jacob arrived.

She greeted him in the lobby of her apartment building. "I'm sorry Jacob. I've run into another hole."

"No problem."

"But I still have to shower and dress. Look at me!" She looked down at her dirty jeans, her not so clean T-shirt.

"Tell you what," Jacob said. "Why don't you show me the issue and I'll think about it while you get ready."

Mia nodded and brought down some papers and books. "So, you see, this implies that is all wrong." She looked up at Jacob, who was looking off in space.

He turned to her with a smile. "This is interesting. Very interesting. Have you thought about this?" He started scribbling on the paper.

"Yes, but that won't work because of this." She took the pencil and wrote an equation.

"Why, yes. You're right." He rubbed his chin. "You go get ready. Let me ponder."

She went upstairs, showered and put on Jacob's favorite dress. She didn't have time to wash her hair. She combed it, tied it back with a silk scarf and looked in the mirror. Not too good, she thought, looking at the dark circles under her eyes.

When she came downstairs, Jacob was waiting, a huge grin on his face.

"Look, Mia," he said, patting the chair next to him. She sat and he walked her through some equations and showed her some diagrams.

"These diagrams make things so much clearer." She looked at him, hoping for an explanation. "I've never seen them before."

"I'm not surprised." Jacob grinned. "I just invented them."

Mia stared at him. "You just invented them?"

"Yes." Jacob beamed. "But they do show what you are trying to explain, right?"

She nodded.

"And they get you out of the difficulty you were having, don't they?" he asked.

"I think so."

"So if you write this up as your thesis — I mean with the diagrams — I'll bet you get a magna." He scratched his head and then stared at her. "No! I have a better idea." His eyes danced. "Write it up as a paper and as your thesis. The paper will be a joint paper."

"But I couldn't write the paper. I didn't invent those diagrams."

"Mia, you asked the question. Asking the right question is the first step in solving a problem. You certainly deserve to co-author the paper."

She squinted. "You sure?"

"I know it." He stacked the books and papers in a pile. "Now take these upstairs and let's go get dinner. You know how grumpy I get when I'm hungry." He growled.

They went to Clara's, their celebration restaurant. Mia was quiet, while Jacob bubbled. Professor Sitar would be at the conference, and he had promised to introduce Jacob to this famous mathematician and that other one. The names cascaded out, Mia barely able to follow who was who. She didn't care really. It was clear he was thinking about the future and the future did not include her. Her throat tightened. She gulped wine, the buzz mellowing the pain.

They walked back to Mia's apartment.

"Write up what we talked about tonight and send it to me as soon as possible." He looked in his coat pocket for a scrap of paper and wrote his address in Italy on it. "If you get it out in the next couple of days, I should be able to get comments back to you before you have to turn in your thesis."

"OK." This was the last she would see of him in — she didn't know when she would see him again. "Would you like to come in?"

He shook his head. "Mia, I've still got some things I've got to get done, and I have an early call."

"OK." She turned to the door, afraid the lump in her throat would explode into tears.

"Mia." He took her shoulder and turned her around. "Don't be sad." He wiped tears from her cheek. "Life is long. We'll see each other."

He kissed her chastely.

Chapter Forty-Three

"Mia, this is beautiful." Professor Petran took off his reading glasses and looked at her. "How did you discover this?"

"I didn't." She stared at the professor, looking for a reaction. "Jacob did."

Professor Petran chuckled. "I should have known." He put on his reading glasses again and skimmed the pages Mia had written. "It has his fingerprints all over it."

"Fingerprints?"

"Yes, fingerprints. Jacob thinks in a certain way, and you can see him thinking." He read a little more, turning the page.

"Jacob said I could turn this in as my senior thesis and submit it as a joint paper with him."

"Of course."

"But it's really Jacob's work." She searched Professor Petran's face for a hint of rejection, but it wasn't there.

"If Jacob is offering to make you a co-author, I think you should accept."

"Really?"

"Sure. He's a mature mathematician. He knows whether you deserve to be a co-author."

She ran her hand along her jeans. This all felt strange, but, given Professor Petran's reaction, it must be OK.

He paged through the papers. "Is this your final version?"

"Oh, no." She sighed. "I have problems." She pulled out several sheets of questions.

Professor Petran scanned the list and then looked up at Mia over the top of his glasses. "This is very good, Mia, these questions. They can be included as a list of topics for future research."

"Really?" Her eyes widened. "I'm afraid some of them will make the whole thing fall apart." She took the sheets from him and scanned down the list until she found an item. "Like this one." She pointed out the problem that worried her the most.

"Well, I've not read the paper. Why don't you leave me a copy, and we'll talk about it in a couple of days." He handed the papers to Mia and leaned back in his chair. "Take these to Nan. She can make a copy for me and a copy to give to Professor Vector, who is going to the conference this evening. That way your co-author — " Professor Petran smiled at her " — will have a copy of the draft tomorrow."

"And stop by day after tomorrow. We can talk about what you have and your questions."

**

Mia reread her draft several times the next day. Her discomfort with her future rattled unchecked in her mind. She still had not heard from Berkeley, so she assumed she would be going to Madison.

She had talked to a math postdoc from Madison, to find out what she could: where to live, whether to get a car, and so on. He was helpful and encouraging. He loved Madison, thought the department was good, and said there was plenty for a graduate student to do, especially one who liked to hike. The environment was much more rural than Cambridge, and it was pretty.

That evening Jamie was getting ready for a party given by one of her professors. "What're you doing tonight?" Jamie searched through her jewelry box.

"Probably I'll curl up with a mystery."

Jamie pulled a string of pearls from the box and looked at Mia. "Why don't you come to the party? Hank will be there, too, so you'll know someone else."

"Oh, I couldn't do that. I mean, I don't know anything about history. I'll stand out like a sore thumb."

"Au contraire, ma chérie!" Jamie fastened the necklace. "These history types are so tired of seeing each other. A math major will be an exotic personage."

Mia shook her head and shoved her hands in her pockets.

"Come on," Jamie urged as she went to Mia's closet. She sorted through the dresses and pulled out a red dress. "This will be perfect." Jamie laid the dress on the bed. "Now go. Shower. We don't want to be late."

Mia got up. Perhaps it would be good to have a diversion for the evening.

The party was in a little Victorian house, much too small for all the people there. People were on the porch, on the front steps, on the lawn.

Jamie pushed her way through the crowd to the refreshment table, got two glasses of wine, and introduced Mia to several of her fellow students.

Mia chatted with a woman who was going to graduate school at Yale. She was interested in medieval art, and they talked about the Gregorian Chants Mia had learned to love in her music class.

After several minutes the woman excused herself, leaving Mia alone in the crowd of people. She hated this feeling, a wallflower among interesting people. It was hot in the house. She made her way to the front porch.

She walked down the stairs and onto the front yard. The moon was full, lighting the evening so shadows fell on the lawn. The air outside was warm and filled with the sweet smell of spring flowers.

"Beautiful evening."

She turned to look up into Chip's face.

"Oh, hi," she said. "Yes, it is." Chip was not the person Mia wanted to see. "I was just going home."

"So soon?"

"It was nice of Jamie to invite me, but I really don't know anyone here."

"You know me."

"Yes." Mia let the rest of the sentiment hang in the air.

"Oh, come on, Mia." He smiled and his eyes were easy. "I won't bite." Mia stared at him. "Besides, I hear you are practically engaged to the next Nobel Prize winner in math."

"They don't give Nobels in math." Mia poured her sour mood into this little historical tidbit. "It seems Nobel didn't like Mittag-Leffler, who would certainly have gotten it if a math prize were given, so he didn't create a Nobel in math." She said it in an arrogant way, hoping to shoo Chip away.

"Interesting!" Chip didn't seem at all deterred. "So your friend will not get a Nobel, but he'll get some other prize in math?"

"Jacob's good." She left off the part of his going off to the conference and her feelings of being rejected.

"So why has Jacob left you alone on such a beautiful spring evening?"

Damn Chip! "He's giving a paper at the Lake Como Math Conference in Italy."

"Impressive." Chip pressed his lips together and nodded. "I hear you're going to Madison for grad school."

"It seems so."

"Well, good luck, Mia." Chip looked directly into her eyes. "I remember when you were having so much trouble figuring out what to major in, and look at you. You were meant to be a mathematician."

"Thanks." She wasn't going to tell him about her doubts.

"Look, Mia. I know it didn't work out between us." His eyes were soft, he held his palms up. "But I'd really like to be friends."

"Sure." Mia wasn't going to be rude.

"Could we shake on it?" Chip offered his hand.

Mia shook his hand. "Now I really must go home. I just need to find Jamie and let her know."

Mia found Jamie after a short search and made an excuse of not feeling well, then headed out the door, only to find Chip waiting for her.

"I'll walk you home." It was a statement, not a question. Mia didn't feel like making a scene so she accepted.

They walked in silence, an uncomfortable silence. Finally he spoke, so quietly Mia barely made out his words. "I'm going to enlist."

Mia inhaled sharply. It didn't make sense, she didn't trust him, told herself she didn't like him, but she didn't like the idea of his enlisting. She wanted him to be safe. "You don't have to. You could get a law school deferment."

"I know. But it doesn't seem right to wiggle out of my duty."

She liked him for this.

"It's a four-year commitment. Going to OCS."

"OCS?"

"Officer Candidate School. When I get out, I can go to law school." They had reached Mia's apartment building. "It was good to see you, Mia." He held the door for her. "Goodnight."

She slipped in the door and turned to look into Chip's eyes. "Good luck, Chip." She meant it. She watched him walk down the street.

Don't even go there, she told herself. He always was a charmer, and then, when you least expected it, the unsavory underside showed itself.

Chapter Forty-Four

Mia's meeting with Professor Petran the next day went well. He had a few minor corrections and saw the way out of one of her questions. "But," he said, "all in all, this is very good, certainly sufficient for a senior thesis. So write it up and submit it."

He sat back in his chair. "Have you heard from Berkeley yet?"

"Not yet."

"Well, you'll probably hear soon." He leaned forward, folding his hands. "I don't mean to pry, but I think you might consider something when you make your choice of graduate school." He paused, looking at Mia. "You might want to go to Madison precisely because Jacob is not there."

Mia straightened up. "Why?"

Professor Petran's gaze shifted to some point beyond Mia. "I think you have the potential to be an excellent mathematician. Being around Jacob — " he looked back at her " — it might be too easy for you to rely on him for answers. It might be better for you to have to work harder."

"Oh." She looked down. "Sometimes I'm not sure I can do math without Jacob." That was not true. It wasn't sometimes. It was all the time.

"That is damned nonsense!"

Mia stared at the professor. She'd never heard him use profanity. She'd never heard him use that tone.

"Mia, the work you are doing on your thesis is very good. And if you keep at it and enjoy it, you will be a fine mathematician." The professor's tone had returned to its normal mellow self. "Anyhow, I don't know that I should have said anything. It's just something I thought you might consider."

Mia tucked his words away for later. Right now she would enjoy finally, finally, finally seeing the end of her thesis. She skipped down the steps and turned toward home. She bought herself a celebratory ice cream at Brigham's. The ice cream dripped on her papers. She didn't care.

When she got to the dorm, there was a fat envelope from Berkeley sitting on her desk. Jamie must have gotten the mail. Mia tore the envelope open, pulled out the contents, and scanned it.

"Well?" Jamie tried to look over her shoulder.

"They accepted me." She smoothed the letter. "And they're giving me a TA-ship."

"A TA-ship?"

"I'll teach a section of first year calculus and they will pay tuition and give me a stipend."

"So it's not as generous as Madison's offer?"

"No. But it's Berkeley." Mia looked at Jamie, who was shaking her head. "You don't seem to approve."

"It's fine." Jamie sat down. "It's just not as good as Madison."

"True." Mia considered whether to be truthful. Jamie would ferret out the truth. She might as well get the discussion out of the way. "But Jacob is there."

"Old-what's-his-name?" Jamie laughed. "The way he left, I don't know why you would care where he is."

"I know, but at least I'll know someone there."

"Pshaw," Jamie said, "You'll meet people. You don't need old-what's-his-name."

"Oh, Jamie." Mia pursed her lips. "You don't get it, because you've never had trouble academically. But graduate school. I mean, do you know that you have to pass prelims, oral exams, where you are supposed to know everything about everything."

"I know, Mia, but — Oh, you know what I think." She shook her head again. "But there was something else I wanted to talk to you about."

"Sounds ominous."

"When I asked you to be my maid of honor, I should have realized Hank was going to ask Chip to be his best man."

Mia tried to visualize the wedding with her partnered with Chip. Her shoulders tightened.

"I want you to be my maid of honor, but . . . ." She trailed off. "I mean, I don't want it to be torture for you."

"No." It wouldn't be that hard. They had managed the other night just fine. "That's OK. It'll work."

"Thank goodness." Jamie exhaled.

"It's OK." Mia felt she was trying to reassure herself as much as she was trying to reassure Jamie. She looked at Jamie. "Did you know he is going to enlist, like Hank?"

"Sure. Those two are close. They've been talking about the war for a long time."

Chapter Forty-Five

Mia sipped her wine and looked around the room. The light was low. The candles on the table glowed. It was a large dinner party with Jamie and Hank, their parents, several other brides maids and groomsmen, the flower girl, and the little ring bearer. There were aunts and uncles from both sides of the couple and miscellaneous kids ranging in age from just walking to just entering Harvard.

She was feeling mellow and kept looking at Jamie, who, despite her far from statuesque figure, glowed happiness. Hank seemed so relaxed, so perfect a groom, so blissful.

Chip joined Mia. "They look happy together, don't they?"

"They do." Mia laughed as she remembered how dismissive she had been when Jamie said she wanted to be a wife. "It was her goal, from the day I met her, to find the perfect someone. And I think she did."

"You sound a little sad."

Mia looked back at the couple as they talked to their guests. "Jamie and Hank have something special, something they want, something they worked hard for."

Chip turned to look at their friends. "They do."

She wished she had that, too, but she wasn't going to say that to Chip.

He turned back to Mia. "Off to Madison this summer?"

"No. I'm staying in Cambridge. I spent the summer after sophomore year working on a library project at MIT, and I worked there last summer. So I'll be working there again this summer."

Chip's eyebrow arched up. "What do you do for them?"

Mia felt her shoulders relax. "At first I was finding keywords for research papers. But last summer I worked on programming for them and I'll be doing similar stuff now."

"Sounds interesting."

"It's fun, especially when I've managed to get the computer to jump through hoops. Those computers are contrary beasts. You know, if you mispunch just one card, the thing refuses to talk to you. And woe is you if you drop your card deck."

"Card deck?" He looked confused.

"You communicate with the beast with decks of cards. One command per card."

"Hmmm." He nodded but didn't look like he really understood.

She chuckled. "I like it, even if sometimes the computers seem so dumb." She wondered whether she should just stay in Cambridge rather than go to graduate school. Working with computers seemed so much easier than doing math. "What about you?"

Chip's gaze wandered back to the wedding party. "Hank and I have agreed to enlist at the same time."

Mia looked at Chip. Was he frightened and wanted to have Hank's support? Or the other way around? Or maybe both frightened and wanting to give support? He didn't look frightened, but then men weren't supposed to.

"Anyhow, Hank won't be ready until September, what with the honeymoon and settling Jamie in an apartment." He sighed and looked back at her, his eyes sad. "I'm working at my dad's firm until we're ready to sign up." His eyes brightened. "If you're in Cambridge, maybe we could have dinner sometime when I come up to visit Aunt Beverly."

"That'd be nice." She had answered so quickly. It was the wine.

***

The wedding march started, and all eyes looked up the aisle for the bride, but Mia looked at Hank standing at the altar. He radiated serenity. A subtle smile played on his lips as he looked at Jamie walking slowly down the aisle. Mia followed his gaze. She couldn't see Jamie's face. Her veil hid her features. But Jamie's joy was evident in the way she held her head, the way she walked.

Mia wondered whether she would ever feel confident enough in a man — or in herself — to marry. That was such an unromantic way of thinking of it, but it was such a big step. She couldn't imagine making such a commitment. Maybe Jamie's goal, to get an MRS, wasn't so absurd. Maybe that should have been her goal.

No. For Jamie it was different. Jamie would have a career. It would come to her with ease.

Jamie and her father were at the altar, and Jamie's father lifted her veil. Jamie beamed. Her eyes sparkled. She was beautiful.

After the ceremony people lined up to congratulate the couple. Little girls and old grandpas, men in business suits, ladies wearing silk dresses, generals and first lieutenants, wearing their uniforms, hugged or shook hands, smiled and nodded. Finally, the last grandma gave her good wishes, and the bridal party walked down the steps to the waiting limos. Jamie's uncle, General Johnson, was directing everyone to the proper car.

As she walked down the church steps, Mia heard a chant coming from up the street. "Hell, no, we won't go, Ho Chi Minh is going to win."

Mia saw a procession of people, maybe a hundred or so, walking down the street. One fellow in front had a megaphone, leading the chanting. A man carrying a big bucket walked next to the leader.

The group stopped a block away. "Draft cards, we want your draft cards." A man carrying a sack dumped what looked like draft cards on the ground and the man with the bucket poured a red liquid on the cards. "Drown those cards in blood."

The crowd left the mess on the street and started walking down the street, approaching the bridal party. "Hell, no, we won't go, Ho Chi Minh is going to win."

When the group was within half a block, the leader stopped the crowd and pointed at General Johnson, whose medals gleamed on his uniform. "War criminal, war criminal," the leader shouted. "Drown him in blood."

The man with the bucket ran towards General Johnson, and, when he was within a few feet, he threw the bucket towards the general. Red liquid spattered over General Johnson, on Hank's suit, and across the front of Jamie's white gown.

The leader and bucket carrier looked at their work and grinned. The mob melted away.

Mia ran up to Jamie. "Oh, Jamie."

"It's OK, Mia." Jamie's eyes were steely. "It's OK."

Hank and Jamie talked quietly. Then Hank turned to the party. "Our guests are expecting us. Let's not disappoint them. We'll go directly to the reception."

The little flower girl was crying. Jamie leaned down and dried her tears. "Stiff upper lip, kiddo," Jamie said. "Come ride in the car with Hank and me." So the flower girl climbed in the car, followed by Jamie, Hank, and the ring bearer.

***

"A big hand for Mr. and Mrs. Henry Richardson," the DJ announced over the sound system, and the wedding guests applauded as Jamie and Hank walked arm in arm into the hall.

The applause died out as the guests saw the red stain across Jamie's gown. A worried buzz filled the hall.

Instead of sitting at the head table, Jamie walked to the DJ and took the microphone from him. "On our way from the church to the reception, we were waylaid by an anti-war demonstration. Fortunately, we are all OK, but my wedding gown did sustain cosmetic damage." Jamie displayed the red stain across the front of her dress.

"Hank and I know there are many patriotic people who do not believe we should be fighting in Vietnam, and we know many men are being drafted and being sent to war against their will. And we know it is not always possible to know when to fight and when not to fight."

Jamie shifted the microphone to her other hand and stood tall.

"But Hank and I believe this is an important war to fight. As many of you know, Hank is enlisting. And I am very proud of him for serving his country. I know many of our friends, like Chip, Hank's best man, are going to enlist. And many of our friends and family have served in the armed forces during World War II and the Korean War."

"So I have a favor to ask of each person in this room who has served in the armed forces, who is currently serving, or who plans to serve. Please, come sign my dress. It will make it that much more valuable to me and Hank."

The wedding crowd was silent. The sound of Hank's steps echoed as he walked to the DJ's podium and boldly wrote his name in black ink across his bride's bodice.

"Chip, come up here." Jamie stared directly at Chip, who joined them at the podium, took the pen from Hank and wrote his name on Jamie's sleeve.

"And my new dad." Jamie looked at Hank's father. "Served in the Pacific in World War II, and I am so proud of him."

Hank's dad got up and wrote his name on her other sleeve.

"Uncle Johnson, c'mon," Jamie said. "And Dad, I need your name."

"And what about the staff here?" Jamie asked. "If you have served the country, Hank and I would be honored to have your signature."

Slowly men and women formed a line, waiting to add their names to Jamie's dress.

Chapter Forty-Six

Mia sat down across from Chip. She regretted saying she'd meet him, feeling that she needed time to figure out what to do about graduate school. But it was easier to just have dinner and deal with her future later.

"Cabernet." Chip nodded to the glass at her place. "I hope you still like that."

"Yes, thank you."

"I hope that frown isn't for me."

"Oh." She exhaled and willed her shoulders to relax. "I'm sorry. Just a bit upset."

"Why?" Chip's eyes were soft.

"Oh, it's nothing, really." She didn't want to talk to Chip about Jacob. "I was surprised you decided to enlist so soon. I thought you were going to wait for the fall."

"Yeah, well, the wait was just . . . ." Chip shrugged. "Not fun. Somehow it seems better to jump in the pool." His face was paler than usual, his lips tense, his brows collected in a frown. "I called Hank." He looked down and rubbed his finger along his fork. "He understood." He sighed and looked up. "I think he might also start earlier than expected, just not yet. They are still . . . well . . . ." Chip blinked and looked away.

"Chip, you're blushing!" Mia grinned and shook her head. "I've never seen you blush."

Chip looked up at Mia, not a glimmer of amusement on his face. "You don't know do you?"

She gasped. "Know what?" Her pleasure melted. "No, I don't know. What is it?"

"One of your roommate's crazy plans."

"Which is?"

"She wants to get pregnant before he leaves, just in case...." Chip closed his eyes and shook his head.

"How like Jamie!" Mia laughed. "I can hear her now. 'Veritas, Hank, I want something of you forever, and in case you don't come back....'"

Chip stared at Mia, his blue eyes hard. "You seem to like it. I find it cold."

"It depends on the way you look at it. It's also a declaration of how much she wants to be around him, how much she loves him."

Again he looked past her, his lips pressed in a thin line.

Better change the topic. "You came up to say goodbye to Aunt Beverly?"

He returned his gaze to her, his shoulders slack. "Yes." His eyes were softer. "By the way, Aunt Beverly said to say hello."

"She's such a character."

He nodded and his lips broke into a gentle smile. "She is."

Mia picked up the menu. "So what's for dinner, Chip?"

"I'll have the filet. And you?"

Mia put down the menu. "Sounds just right."

Chip signaled the waiter and ordered. That duty taken care of, he looked back at Mia. "So, do tell me, Mia, why the frown when you came in? Is everything alright?"

"Everything is just fine," Mia said. "It's just that I have to make up my mind about whether to go to Madison or to Berkeley."

"It's a big decision, but I don't know why you'd be so upset."

Mia looked at Chip. She wanted to talk to someone. She needed to talk. Here he was. And he hadn't flirted, not really. He had said he wanted to be a friend, and right now she needed a friend. She exhaled and plunged in. "I just got a letter from Jacob. He says he has a friend in the math department looking for a roommate, Liz, her name is, and it is a pretty little house not far from campus." Mia looked at him. He was staring at her, drinking in every word. "He has sent a list of the courses I should take first year. And he has reserved an office for me, close to his."

"I don't understand." Chip squinted and scratched his chin. "He's trying to make you comfortable. Seems nice to me."

"No. He assumes I will go to Berkeley. He assumes I'll follow him like a puppy dog." Her angry tone surprised her.

"But wasn't Berkeley your first choice?" Chip leaned forward, still squinting.

"It was, but Jacob's attitude makes me just want to go anywhere else, Madison, or even just stay at MIT."

Chip shook his head. "You can't let Jacob's wanting you to be in Berkeley deter you. Besides. I still don't understand. It seems like he wants you close. Isn't that good?"

"He wants me close, if it is convenient."

Chip's blue eyes stared at her as he slowly shook his head.

She shouldn't say more. She knew she shouldn't say more. She should just let Chip think she and Jacob were a done deal. But she needed to talk. Jamie was off getting settled in Chicago and all her other friends had left Cambridge. "When he left for his math conference, he left with a see-you-sometime. I had hoped our relationship was more important to him than that."

"I see."

"I shouldn't have said anything. But I'm so upset about it. His leaving when it looked like I was going to Madison, implicitly cutting off the relationship, and now, when it looks like I'll be in Berkeley, starting it up again."

"Maybe he wasn't ready to make a commitment, but also didn't want to cut things off." Chip spoke softly, gently. "He's so happy you might come to Berkeley, that he's trying to make it as comfortable as possible."

Chip was defending Jacob. He really did want to be her friend. It didn't seem that telling him all this, spilling out her heart, made him try to seduce her again. It made her feel close to him.

It made her want him to seduce her.

Graduate School
September 1968 to May 1970

Chapter Forty-Seven

"You must be the famous Mia." The woman was thin, her hair straight and wispy, her features angular, which gave her a hard look.

"I'm Mia."

"Liz." She offered a weak smile.

Mia wondered whether she would get along with her new roommate. "Why famous?"

"You're Brower's daughter." Her face looked sour.

"My dad might be famous, but that doesn't make me famous."

"Well, there was your mother, who came to inspect at the beginning of the summer. She was quite particular, wanting to see your room and the bathroom, and whether we had proper cleaning implements, and goodness knows what else." Liz's smile was sour, just like her face.

"I'm sorry. I hope she wasn't too much of a pain."

"Hey, she paid more than two months rent just to reserve the room, so whatever trouble she was, was worth it." Liz's laugh was hollow. "And then there is your boyfriend."

Boyfriend? That was news. At this moment she wasn't sure what her relationship with Jacob was. They had exchanged letters over the summer, and there were a few phone calls about the paper.

"He talks about you all the time."

Mia tried to look past Liz into the house. "This is lovely."

"Yeah." Liz opened the door wider. "It's a sweet deal. I guess the landlord likes to rent to graduate women." Her smile was cold. "Makes sense, of course. We take care of property so much better than the undergrads or the men."

"Sure," Mia said. "Might I see my room?"

"Oh, right." Liz opened the door wider and let Mia come in. The entry way was tiny. The living room, two steps down, was dominated by a stone fireplace kitty corner from the door.

Liz led the way up several steps, into a hall with three doors. The first door led to a small room, with enough space for a bed and desk. "Your room is here." There was also a little closet and a window looking out over the backyard, filled with budding roses, camellias, and mums, crowding to reach the sun.

"I love it."

"Yeah, it's nice."

The 1930s bathroom's floor was tiled in little white hexagons. There were utilitarian towel racks, a free standing sink, and a bath with a shower head.

"Not bad," Mia said.

"Let me show you the rest of the house." Liz went down the stairs. "I let this girl, Claire, stay in the garage, free of charge. I told Jacob about it."

"Yes. He wrote me."

"Instead of rent, she cleans the house. Does a pretty good job of it."

Mia looked around. There was dust on the woodwork, but otherwise it was OK.

The kitchen was off the living room. There was room for a two-person table, a sink, a fridge, and a stove the same vintage as the bathroom. The floor in the kitchen had the same white hexagonal tiles. The window over the sink looked out over the backyard. It was small, but clean and tidy.

"Claire takes special care of the kitchen. She likes to cook. You can store stuff in the fridge and on the shelves, but she wants you to date things and she purges perishables older than a week." Liz rattled off the rules. "She'll also cook you dinner or pack you lunch for a price. Prices seem to vary, depending on her mood, so I'll let you talk to her about that."

"She sounds like an interesting person."

"Yeah," Liz said. "From Iowa or Indiana or somewhere. Got into drugs. Dropped out. Got into EST."

"EST?"

"EST. Think extreme encounter group. I think it's just another drug, but I'd never say that to Claire. Anyhow, I'm sure she'll tell you all about it." Liz chuckled without humor.

"She works for a Mexican restaurant on Telegraph, El Toro. She wants to become a cook." Liz shrugged. "Claire's not a bad sort. Just a bit mixed up." Liz picked up her purse and rummaged in it. "Here's the key."

"Thanks."

"You can park on the street." Liz scanned Mia from head to foot, then stared at her. "Are you a serious student?"

Mia straightened up. "What?"

"I mean, what with not coming to Berkeley immediately after graduation and all, I wasn't sure you were serious about math."

"Most students come to campus the summer after graduation?" This Liz was nosy, opinionated, and pushy. Mia missed Jamie.

"Yes." Liz's voice was clipped. "And Jacob seems so set on you. It's just — " She twisted her thin hair with her fingers, staring at Mia. "It just seemed like you were coming here just to be with him."

At this Mia laughed. "My college roommate was after an MRS degree." Mia felt defensive, but she was not going to appear weak in front of this pushy woman. "No, Liz, I'm not like that. I do want to be a mathematician."

"So how come you took the summer off?" Liz's stare was unrelenting.

"I had a job at MIT, working on a database system for libraries." Mia hoped that sounded, at least the MIT part, important enough.

"Well, you couldn't have needed the money, given that your Mom paid for two months rent when you weren't here." Liz shook her head and grimaced. "I hope you don't plan on becoming a librarian." Liz said librarian in the same tone as one might say "someone who cleans latrines."

"Liz!" Mia tried to soften her voice, but it came out shrill and high. "I'm not sure where you're going with all this 'I hope you plan to be a mathematician stuff.'" She took a deep breath. "I'm here to get my PhD. Now can we move on?"

"Soorreee" Liz sneered. "It's important the department graduate women. I mean, too many women come and leave before they get their doctorates. It gives the department the feeling women aren't serious. That's not good. That makes me mad. So if you're not serious, I wish you'd just quit now."

Chapter Forty-Eight

Mia was pulling her last suitcase out of the car's trunk when she heard a familiar voice.

"Let me get that."

She looked up into Jacob's smiling eyes. She was silent.

"So how've you been, stranger?" Jacob lugged the suitcase up the walk. "What do you have in here?" he asked, not letting her answer his first question. "Bowling balls?"

"Math books."

"Should have known."

Mia led him to her bedroom, and he placed the suitcase next to the bed.

"This the last of your things?"

"Yes."

"Great. Let's go get some ice cream. There's a great little place just around the corner on College."

"I've got to return the car to my parents."

She wasn't sure how she felt about Jacob, after his cool farewell in the spring. No, the truth was, she knew exactly how she felt. She was mad, angry, livid, and there was nothing that would make her feel so good as to tell him off.

Except.

Except she never told people off.

"Then we'll return the car and walk back. There's a great pizzeria on Euclid, right on the way back."

She studied him. Veritas, as Jamie would say. A long walk back to the apartment might be a good time to have a talk. "OK."

***

"You certainly seem to have tamed my parents," Mia said, as they walked down the steep hill toward campus.

"Tame them?" Jacob asked. "Your parents don't need taming. They're wonderful. Your mom's interested in things I'm doing, so helpful getting me settled here. Of course, she doesn't understand what I'm doing."

Mia bristled. "My mom wrote her senior thesis on Cesaro Summations."

Jacob stopped walking. "Harvard?"

"University of Budapest. Fejér was her adviser." That should clobber Jacob's condescension.

Jacob stared at her, his faced clouded. "Mia, what's wrong?"

Mia erupted. "Let's see. You leave me in Cambridge with, what was it, almost a hand shake. See you around. Maybe. Sometime. I had no idea when I might see you again, whether you even cared for me."

"Mia, what're you talking about?"

"So I have no idea when I might see you again, no idea you even cared for me, thought maybe our affair was just — what? convenient? — but if I couldn't get into Berkeley, well, it was over." She didn't bother to wipe the tears as they streamed down her face. "And then when I did get in, you just assumed I would follow you here, like a puppy."

Jacob tried to put his arm around her shoulders, but she shrugged him off.

"I feel like I'm disposable." Her face was hot, sobs shaking her.

"Mia, what can I say?"

"You can explain why you were so cool towards me when you left Cambridge."

"But I wasn't cool, was I?" He searched her face, willing her, she supposed, to take back her statement. "Preoccupied, perhaps. Nervous about giving my paper. Excited about the diagrams I discovered. But — " Jacob stopped talking, looked off down the street, and then returned his gaze to her. "Mia, you're my girl. I don't sleep with women at the drop of a hat. You're important to me."

Mia stood there. These were the words she wanted to hear, but she didn't believe them. She let the silence hang in the air.

"If you weren't important to me, I wouldn't have spoken to Professor Sitar about you. I made sure he knew how good you are."

This set off a new torrent of tears. "So you got me into Berkeley? So I really am your little plaything?"

"Mia, Mia! No, of course not. You got in on your own merits." After checking several of his pockets he pulled out a bandanna and gave it to her. "I showed him our paper. It was the paper that did it. It's not every grad student that enters the program with a paper accepted."

"It's not accepted yet." Her sobs subsided, and she wiped her tears.

"Actually — " Jacob grinned " — it is. That's the welcome to Berkeley present I was going to give you." Jacob reached into the pocket of his jacket and pulled out an envelope, which he gave to Mia.

Mia scanned the letter and looked at Jacob. "It's really your paper, you know."

"No, Mia, it's ours." He put his arm around her waist, pulled her to him, and kissed her gently. She did not resist. "And that is why you are important to me. You are a mathematician. You will understand my work. You will understand me."

"I don't have a clue about your work," she said, pushing him away.

"You will."

Dread seeped through her. She saw herself as Jacob's appendage. Her role in the world would be to serve him dinner, read his papers, and catch his spelling errors. But she didn't know how to say this, or explain it. She had already made enough of a scene.

"I'm starving, and the pizza place is still blocks away."

Jacob took her hand and headed down the hill.

Val's, the pizzeria, was in a courtyard off the street. It was crowded and noisy. Jacob ordered beers for them both and a large pizza.

"After dinner we could stop by my apartment. It's a little out of the way, but it's a nice afternoon, and you always liked a long walk." He looked at her over his beer mug.

She was too tired to argue. "OK."

Jacob talked about the conference. Sitar had introduced him to several well-known mathematicians and he described each one. The words skimmed over Mia. Jacob talked on and on, oblivious to Mia's discomfort.

The pizza came. Jacob asked whether the courses he had recommended seemed reasonable. He explained she would have to take orals in three topics. He thought she was best off taking them in algebra, topology and analysis. If these assumptions were correct, then the courses he recommended would help prepare her for the exams, both because they covered much of the material that would be on the exams and because it would allow Mia to get to know the professors who were likely to give the exams.

"What are the exams like?" Mia fiddled with the pizza crust.

"Each is an hour long. They're oral exams. Three professors are in each exam and they ask you questions and you answer them."

"What questions do they ask?"

"There's the rub." Jacob reached for another slice of pizza.

"If you knew what they would ask, you'd be home free." He looked at Mia. "Oh, don't look so worried, Mia. There are lists of questions that are usually asked. Also, certain professors ask certain questions every time. So once you know who'll be on your committee, you'll know what to study."

"When do you find out who will be on your committee."

"About a month before the exam. That gives you plenty of time to prepare."

"Plenty of time for you, perhaps." Mia hated Jacob's confidence.

"Ah, Mia, you've got to start being more positive. You'll do fine. I'll help you."

"Thanks." Mia hated herself. She should be able to do this by herself.

"Anyhow, the exams are given in the fall and spring. I think I can take them this fall, so I will be able to help you, having been through them."

"This fall?" Mia asked. "So soon?"

Chapter Forty-Nine

They walked toward Jacob's apartment. Dusk was settling over Berkeley, and, one by one, the street lights turned on.

"First star I see tonight." Jacob put his arm around her waist.

Mia looked up in the clear night sky and wondered what she should wish for. Maybe to feel sure. Sure of Jacob. Sure of herself.

Jacob lived in an old apartment building — 1930s, probably — with tile floors in browns, reds, blues, yellows. His apartment was on the second floor, a one bedroom.

Jacob switched on a light to show a sparsely furnished room, a couch, a coffee table. A little kitchen was off the living room, with a tiny dining table in the corner. There were two doors off the living room, one to the bedroom, the other to the bathroom.

"What's that?" Mia pointed to a backpack piled in the corner of the living room. There were blankets and a pillow under the backpack, a notebook, a few pens. "Have you been camping?"

"No. Those are Sam's things."

"Sam?" Mia shuddered, thinking about the Sam she had known. Of course, this was a different Sam

"Yes, Sam. He sleeps on my couch sometimes. It's a long story. Too long for tonight." Jacob pulled Mia to him and kissed her, his hand drifting down her back.

Mia pushed him away. "You'll break my heart, Jacob. It's best I go."

"Mia, I've been dreaming of this moment."

"You'll have your degree in two years, Jacob. Then you'll leave, just like before, and my heart will break."

"Mia, Mia." Jacob pulled her to him again. "There won't be a next time." He kissed her. "Next time we'll leave together."

That was what she wanted to hear.

His brown eyes searched her face. "You are my destiny."

His gaze wandered past her. "You and math are my destiny."

**

Mia shivered. She pulled on her T-shirt, but was still cold. "Do you have a sweater or something I could borrow for the walk home?"

Jacob rummaged through his dresser and found a dark blue sweat shirt.

She pulled it on. "A little like a tent, but quite chic, don't you think?" Mia did a pirouette for him.

He didn't reply, but stroked her cheek.

"I better be getting home," Mia said. "Will you walk with me?"

A key unlocked the front door. Mia peered out the bedroom door.

A tall man with blond hair so light it was almost white pushed into the living room. He looked at Mia, startled. "Oh. Hi," he said, taking a step back. "I didn't mean to intrude."

"No problem, Sam. This is Mia," Jacob said, "Mia, Sam."

"We've met." Mia's heart raced. Sam was like a bad nickel.

"Hi, Mia." A crooked smile spread over Sam's face. "We meet again." His eyes glinted, like sunlight on ice.

Jacob looked from Mia to Sam and back again. "You know each other?"

"Yes." Mia grabbed her purse off the couch. "Let's go, Jacob. I need to get home."

"OK."

"What? You don't want to share your girl?" Sam asked.

"I need to get home."

Sam stared at Mia. "Just stay for a cup of tea." He shifted his gaze to Jacob. "One of the guys gave me some tea. He said it was very good."

"It's not special, is it?" Jacob asked.

"No, no. Just something imported from Taiwan. See." Sam pulled a little wooden box from his pocket. "All packaged up. Not special. Black tea. I don't know what kind it is, but the fellow was so grateful for my advice, he gave me this tea."

Jacob looked at Mia. "Do we have time for a cup of tea?"

Mia could see Jacob wanted her to stay. She had fussed enough. Better to stay.

Sam walked into the kitchen, a slight limp to his stride. He wore wrinkled and not very clean jeans, a gray T-shirt and a plaid flannel shirt. His boots were military surplus. His stringy hair hung to his shoulders.

He returned several minutes later with three mugs of tea, steam rising. He placed them on the coffee table and went to fetch sugar and spoons.

"So," Sam said, sitting cross legged on the floor, "you're going to study math here?"

"That's right."

"Why math?"

"It seems that I am good at math, and so I should study it."

Sam laughed. "You sound just like your lover here."

Mia looked at Jacob and felt the blood rising in her cheeks. "I'm not as good as Jacob," she blurted and then felt her face grow even warmer, realizing too late she had admitted Jacob was her lover.

"There're not many people as good as Jacob." Sam blew on his tea and took a tentative sip. "Hmm. This is good."

"So," Jacob asked, "what advice did you give to earn you

this splendid tea?"

"The usual. Medical deferment from a 'good' doctor, admitting you are gay, conscientious objection, refusing the draft, emigrating, the easiest being to Canada."

Mia's mind was racing. Sam must be counseling men on how to avoid going to Vietnam.

"And the tea giver, he chose...?" Jacob asked.

"He's going to try the medical deferment route. I gave him a list of sympathetic doctors and told him to come back if he needed more advice." Sam took a slurp of tea. "Another man saved from Nam. Maybe if we get enough men to refuse, we'll starve the army."

"You know that's not going to happen," Jacob said.

"Maybe not, but every guy who finds a way not to go makes it a little harder for the U.S. to continue this insane war. A good thing." Sam turned his intense gaze to Mia. "Don't you think?"

The silence was thick. Mia rubbed her thumb along the hot mug. "I have a good friend who just enlisted." She didn't bother to tell Sam this enlistee was also his good friend.

"Really?" Sam raised his right brow. "Why'd he do that?"

"He thought it was his duty." She shuddered as Jamie and Hank's reception flashed through her mind. "He didn't talk about it much."

"Poor deluded fucker!"

Mia flinched. But Sam's tone was not harsh.

Chapter Fifty

The evening was cool as Jacob and Mia left the apartment building.

"So you know Sam?"

"Yeah. We met a long time ago."

"Where?"

"He was at Harvard. Was kicked out for. . . ." Should she tell Jacob all about it? She couldn't tell him about the bet. That was too humiliating. But maybe some of the other stuff. "I think he was dealing drugs. Hard drugs."

"Really?"

"That's what I heard."

"Probably just a rumor." Jacob shrugged.

"No. I think it was true." Again, she wondered how much she should say.

"He seems to be clean now. Maybe he was just exploring."

"Maybe. But I'd be careful. He seemed a little . . . unstable." Mia didn't want to go any further. "How'd he come to stay with you?"

"He was at some rally. I started talking to him, and he seemed really committed to the movement. I liked that. We went to Val's. He asked if he could crash for the night. That was maybe a few weeks ago."

They walked south along Oxford, the campus on the left, downtown Berkeley across the busy street.

"He was a student at S.F. State, but he quit because he thought the war was wrong."

"I don't see the connection."

"When he quit he lost his deferment and got a draft notice."

They turned onto the campus, walking through a small grove of redwoods.

Mia stopped and turned to Jacob. "He wanted to be drafted?"

"He wanted to get a draft notice so he could refuse. He'll end up going to jail. That's what he wants."

"He wants to go to jail?"

"To make a statement against the war." Jacob started walking again, holding Mia's hand.

Mia remembered the paragraph in the train flier from years ago, something about the government murdering its citizens. Sam wanted to be a martyr.

"And in the meantime he's helping people find ways not to go to Nam, guys like the fellow who gave him the tea."

"So why does he sleep on your couch?"

Jacob stopped and looked up at the campanile. "I love this. I love to hear it strike the hour."

Mia would not allow Jacob to change the subject. "Why does he sleep on your couch?"

"He doesn't have a job. He doesn't have money. He needs a place to crash. So I let him sleep on my couch."

"So you must also be against the war, since you're helping Sam."

Jacob looked into the distance. He looked back at Mia. "I'm agnostic about the war. I don't know what is going on with the war. There are people who feel strongly about it, on both sides, but I couldn't take a position unless I studied the problem. And I don't want to take the time away from my math."

Mia wasn't going to let Jacob squirm out of the discussion. "But you are taking a position by helping Sam."

"I suppose so. The anti-war people are the underdogs, so they need help." He put his arm around Mia's waist. "So that the discussion about the war is balanced."

This sounded so logical, but it made Mia uncomfortable. It seemed Jacob was taking a side in the discussion and was weaseling out of the responsibility for taking a side. Then again, she really didn't know what was going on. She had heard some heated discussions. In truth, until now, most of the people she knew believed the war was necessary, and she hadn't questioned that.

They walked on in silence, through another little wood on campus, across Sproul plaza, and down Telegraph.

"Want to stop for coffee?"

Before she could answer, someone grabbed her from behind, spun her around, and hugged her. Nick pushed her to arm's length and studied her. "How's your love life?"

"Nick! You scared me."

Nick's slim figure was decked out in a gray suit, white shirt, tie, and black dress shoes.

"What're you doing in that Halloween costume?"

"Long story." Nick straightened his tie, as though it were uncomfortable. "Just here for the day. I had to check out the old haunts."

"Rumor has it you're interning for Senator McGovern in D.C."

"Rumor's right." Nick turned toward Jacob and extended a hand. "Your lady has no manners, I can see. I'm Nick. Old flame."

Jacob took a step back, as if an overly friendly puppy were trying to pee on his shoes. But he took Nick's hand and smiled weakly. "Jacob Frenkel."

"Yup. No manners. But she's all right. Known her since middle school. She's OK."

Mia had to smile. Nick was an ass. But he was a nice ass. Besides, she wanted to hear his news. "Could you join us for coffee? Or a drink?"

"Love to. But gotta run. Red eye to D.C. tonight. Gotta help the boss end the war." He gave her another hug and started walking toward campus.

Jacob looked after him and shook his head. "So? Coffee? Drink?"

They stopped at the next little cafe and ordered coffee and cake.

"Who is the McGovern man?"

Mia was pleased to see a glimmer of jealousy in Jacob's eyes. "Old friend from high school."

"Has he always been a whirlwind?"

Mia could see Jacob's smile was insincere. He was jealous.

"No. He used to be quite laid back." She took a bite of cake. "I haven't seen much of him lately, though I try to keep up." She sipped her coffee. "He was going to go to med school, but then the war heated up. That's why he's interning for McGovern. Working to end the war. Sort of like Sam." She set her coffee down. "But different."

"You don't seem to like Sam."

"I don't like him." Why did she feel so threatened by Sam? His past history was terrible, but Jacob had spent more time with him than she had, and he seemed to think he was safe. "He seems to know all about me. Like asking why I study math or talking about you as my lover."

"He was just being friendly." Jacob forked a bite of cake. "And talking about me as your lover, you should blame me for that."

"So you told him all about me, then?"

He looked up at her with a twinkle in his eye. "Yes. I bragged about you until he couldn't stand it."

Sam must have known who she was, but he didn't say anything to Jacob. That was strange. More than strange. It was creepy, as if he were stalking her.

Jacob's eyes grew serious. "Maybe you don't like him because he's against the war."

"No." How dare he say that? "I like Nick, and he's against the war." She did like Nick, even if he could be impossible. Sam was scary. "Besides, I don't know enough about the war to dislike someone because they're against it." She played with her spoon. "No. There's the past history. The drugs. And...." She took a breath. "It's like he can see through me and know what I'm thinking. Like he wants to control me."

Jacob shook his head and smiled. "I'm sure he's harmless."

Mia pushed her empty plate aside. "I want to ask you about something else." She stared at Jacob so she could see his response. "What did you mean when you asked Sam whether the tea was special?"

"Oh, that." Jacob's eye lid twitched ever so slightly. "One time he brought me some 'special' brownies and didn't tell me they had pot in them. I was really upset."

"You have to check he isn't putting drugs in your food?" Mia blurted.

"Mia, that's unfair!" Jacob shook his head, his lips pinched tight. "I was pulling his chain. A joke."

Chapter Fifty-One

Light streamed in Mia's window, waking her. It took a moment for her to remember where she was. Her new home was charming, so much cozier than her rooms in Cambridge. She stretched, got up, and searched her suitcase for fresh clothes and her toothbrush.

Fifteen minutes later, she headed toward the front door. She'd have to get some breakfast at a shop along College, since she hadn't gotten any groceries yet.

"Hey, there," a husky voice called from the kitchen, "you must be Mia"

Mia turned to see a tall women, long hair unkempt, a shirt in brilliant stripes of blues, greens, violets, and yellows, bell bottom jeans, creased and wrinkled, and heavy leather sandals.

"Yes," Mia said. "Claire?"

"That's me!" A friendly grin spread across Claire's face. "So glad you're here. Liz, well I owe her my life, literally, but she can be a bit of a downer." Claire's smile dropped to a mock grimace. "So serious."

"She does seem to be goal-oriented."

"Oh!" Claire held her hand up, as if she were holding a delicate tea cup, pinkie extended. "You're so polite!" She giggled. "Anyhow, how about a little breakfast, a welcome meal, on the house. I can make all kinds of things: eggs, bacon, oatmeal, fruit. I've got some yummy apples and pears, coffee — "

"That'd be great!" Mia interrupted, thinking Claire's menu would go on forever if she didn't.

"C'mon then." Claire turned toward the work space. "Coffee?"

"Oh, yes."

Claire poured steaming black coffee into a heavy pottery mug and placed it, with milk, sugar, and a spoon, on the little kitchen table. "Sit."

"Liz tells me you work at El Toro."

"Yeah. Just bussing right now. The pay sucks, but I eat there and I'm learning how to cook their dishes." She placed her finger on her lips. "That's a secret though." She broke into a wide grin. "What's for breakfast?"

"How about some scrambled eggs and an apple?"

"Coming up."

"So you're going to be a cook?"

"That's the plan. At least for right now. Gotta have a plan, you know."

Claire collected eggs and an apple from the fridge. "Of course, I had a plan when I got to Berkeley. I was going to become a vet. But, well, things didn't go as planned."

"What happened?"

"Turned on, dropped out, ended up wandering around Telegraph without a dime, looking for something to eat."

"Whoa." Mia wondered how Claire could say all this with such cheer.

"Panhandling. Not a pretty picture." Claire beat the eggs. "Lucky me! Liz walked by, stopped, and walked back to me. I'd been in her calculus section, you know. She was my TA. She took one look at me and brought me back here. Fed me, told me I could stay here as long as I kept the house clean and stayed off drugs."

The old sourpuss had a heart. "That's pretty special."

"Well, it doesn't come free," Claire poured the eggs into a skillet. "I get to hear about how women have to respect themselves, and all that. Have you heard any of that stuff yet?"

"I think I've had an introduction, but not the whole course."

Claire looked up with a wide grin. "You're OK, Mia." She placed the eggs and apple on the table. "Enjoy!"

Mia took a taste of egg. "Claire, what did you do to these eggs? They're wonderful."

"Like them?" Claire beamed.

"Yes! You're a great cook."

"Not yet. But I'm working on it." She poured herself a cup of coffee and sat opposite Mia. "Liz is a saint, even if she is high and mighty. Lent me the money to go to EST."

"EST?"

"Haven't heard about EST?" Claire looked surprised. "You should go. Like, it'll get you together. I mean, it changed my life. I am here now."

Mia listened to Claire talk and each word made sense, but together they were a jumble. Claire's face was earnest. Mia didn't know what to say next and she didn't feel comfortable talking about the here and now. She changed the subject. "I really like your sandals."

Claire stretched her legs to admire them. "You like my Jesus boots? They are pretty cool. Made them myself."

"You're kidding!"

"Yeah, I could make you a pair. I mean for $50."

"Whoa," Mia said. "I'm a student. Can't afford that."

"I'm offering a course then, just $25. Plus materials, of course."

"Sounds like fun," Mia said, "but I think I'll have my hands full with courses and my calculus section."

"I figured," Claire said. "Just trying to find ways to make a buck. I mean, as I said, the job at the El Toro doesn't pay much." Claire took a sip of her coffee, then stood up. "Oh, I almost forgot to tell you, I can cook for you." She pulled out some papers from a drawer. "Here's my current list of dishes. You can order specific dishes if you let me know a day or two ahead. Or if you just come in late and want dinner, it's whatever happens to be handy."

Mia looked over the list of dishes. "This is quite a selection. I'm sure I'll want you to cook for me."

"Yup, and I can make any of those dishes special, if you want."

"Does that mean what I think?"

"Yup."

"But I thought you said you weren't doing drugs."

"Oh, well." Claire shrugged. "Pot isn't a drug. Besides, I need it for my profession. It heightens your sense of taste, you know."

"I didn't." Mia voice had a prudish edge.

"Oh!" Claire's smile faded. "You aren't going to tell Liz, are you?"

"No." Mia tried to put a reassuring smile on her face. "No, I won't tell Liz."

Chapter Fifty-Two

Mia found her office in T-5, a long low building across the street from Le Conte Hall. The T stood for temporary, the buildings having been built just after World War II to help accommodate the influx of soldiers taking advantage of the GI bill. The office was a large room with windows along one side and a door to the hall on the opposite wall. There were four desks distributed along the wall space. She was wondering which desks were taken, when Jacob walked in.

"Office, sweet office!" He set a pile of books on one of the desks.

"Hey, there," Mia said. "Glad to see you. Which one of these desks is free?"

"That one's for you." Jacob pointed to a desk. "Liz uses this one, and here's mine. That one over there has been claimed by Ray. Though, if you like that one better, you can probably take it. Ray hardly ever comes in and he doesn't leave his stuff here."

"That's OK. This one's fine." She blew the dust off the desk.

"They don't provide custodial services."

"I should say."

"Have you looked over the courses I suggested?"

"Yes, but there are five of them." She set the books she brought on the desk. "Can I manage five courses?"

"Not to worry. Start with five. You can drop one if you want."

Annoyance grew in her chest. "But I don't think I could even keep up with four courses."

"It won't be as hard as you think." Jacob sat in his chair, leaning back. "You don't have to worry about grades."

"Don't have to worry about grades?" Mia wondered whether Jacob had forgotten she wasn't a genius.

"Don't have to worry about grades," Jacob repeated. "The professors give only As to grad students. They don't want anyone to get kicked out, don't want them to be drafted because they couldn't stay in school. So they give all the men As. And if they do it for the men, they feel they have to do it for the women."

Mia turned her chair so she would face Jacob and sat. "That's weird."

"May be weird, but it'll give you a chance to relax and just do math."

Mia leaned forward, her elbows resting on her knees. "But surely, if I don't do well in class, I'll make a bad impression. That'd be bad."

"Oh, Mia." Jacob exhaled a heavy sigh. "When will you learn? Just do math. Be yourself and do math. You'll be fine."

"You sound a little like my new roommate."

"Claire?" A glimmer of humor lit his eyes.

Mia smiled. She liked Claire, but she was also leery. "Have you ever talked to her?"

"A little," Jacob said, "though I try to avoid it. Once someone goes through EST, they become insufferable."

"What is EST?" Mia hoped to get a more coherent explanation than she had gotten so far.

"I'm not sure," Jacob said, "and I don't want to find out. Some self-help thing, which is probably a scam, but people pay hundreds of dollars for it, and after that they can't admit they made a mistake."

Mia's mind skittered over the last 24 hours: Claire, drugs, "special", draft dodging. "This world is so different than

Cambridge."

"Sure," Jacob said, "but you grew up here. I thought you'd be used to it."

"No, Jacob, it's a different town. Not the one I left four years ago."

"Well, don't let it get in your way." Jacob stood and pulled Mia toward him. "The math department is great. Don't worry about the craziness around it. Just concentrate on your work. The rest of the craziness will change and flow like an image in a kaleidoscope. It's strange and wonderful, but basically it's a toy, a distraction from what's important."

Chapter Fifty-Three

Mia had to get to her calculus class.

A chanting crowd gathered on her left. The police were on her right, with shields and face guards, gas masks and billy clubs, tear gas canisters hanging at their hips. They stood, observing, like malevolent cats.

Mia had to get to class. She had to get to Wheeler Hall, but the crowd — chanting "Hell, no, we won't go!" — stood between her and the building. She noticed a tall, ragged figure, wearing red suspenders, holding a megaphone, and leading the chant. Those red suspenders. Where had she seen them?

Harry!

She turned to her right, clutched her book bag, and started to run. She felt her toe dip into a missing brick on the plaza. She tried to catch herself with her other leg, but she couldn't extract her toe. She sprawled on the ground, the contents of her book bag spilling onto the damp bricks, all her students' problem sets spread over the plaza soaking up the morning dew.

She scrambled to her feet ignoring the wetness at her knee and her stinging palm. She was grabbing the papers when she noticed another hand, long and thin, picking up the papers. Her eyes swept from the hand, up the frayed shirt, to the face and the ice blue eyes. "What're you doing, Sam?"

"Just trying to make sure you don't get caught up in the little drama these people have planned."

Mia wanted to scream at him to stop, but she needed to get those problem sets and get to class. She nodded and continued picking up papers. She hated Sam more for helping her. She knew he was doing it because it helped his cause. She picked up the last set and walked the two steps over to Sam, who held out the things he had collected. She snatched the papers.

"What? Not even a thank you?" His blue eyes twinkled, but even ice can glint. She was sure he knew her discomfort.

Stuffing the papers in her book bag, she ran to the east end of the building. It was blocked by a dozen or so demonstrators. Not knowing what else to do, she raced toward her office, hoping to find Jacob there.

Not there. Her heart pounded. She gasped for air. She walked to Val's. Climbing the hill disciplined her breath and calmed her. She was going to meet Jacob there for lunch, but she was early.

By the time she cleaned her skinned knee and palm and settled at a table with a cup of tea, her heart had quieted. Why did that upset her so? Was it the potential for trouble, the nearness of an unpredictable mob, the fact Harry was leading the group, the presence of Sam?

She opened her book and took out her problem set. She tried to concentrate, but "Hell, no, we won't go" rang in her ears. She tried to block the sound and looked at the problem again, fiddling with equations, trying to find a trick to make things cancel.

"Hey, there." Jacob pulled out the chair opposite her. "You're early."

Mia consulted her watch. "So are you."

Jacob's eyes shone. "I have a thesis topic!" He sat and pulled out paper. "Look here, suppose you have two systems, one determined by this — " and he wrote an equation " — and the other determined by this." He looked at Mia briefly and returned to his paper. "We can look at the first system like this — " he drew a diagram " — and the second system like this." He looked up at Mia to see if she was following. "Don't you see that?" Jacob frowned.

"Jacob," Mia said. "I'm upset. I'm having trouble concentrating on my little analysis problem set. I don't think I can comprehend your thesis topic right now."

"Why?" Jacob's face betrayed more annoyance than concern.

"There was an anti-war demonstration in front of Wheeler."

"So?" Jacob's lips curled dismissively. "There's always a demonstration."

"I could've been swept up in it."

Jacob's expression softened. "Just stay out of their way."

"But it's not just that there was that demonstration." Mia searched his face. "It's that Sam was there."

The annoyed look returned to his face. "So?"

"So." Mia wasn't sure why she found this so upsetting, but she tried for an explanation. "I can respect someone who refuses the draft. He's making a statement about his belief. But someone who goes to demonstrations, that's different." Mia didn't mention Harry.

"Different?"

"Some demonstrations have turned violent." Mia thought back to the troop trains in '65. "People have gotten hurt. People have been arrested."

"Mia, we've discussed that. It'll blow over. Just concentrate on what you're about. Don't worry about the rest of it."

Mia was silent. She wanted to push all this war stuff out of her mind. She didn't want to think about it. But it was palpable. She could hear the chants. She could see the police with their masks and the demonstrators with their scowls. She felt her heart pulse and her hackles rise. She didn't want to think about the war, but the demonstration brought the problem to her doorstep.

The fact that it didn't concern Jacob made her feel distant from him. Again she felt he was secretly against the war, but they had already talked about that.

Jacob let out a sigh and put a smile on his face. "Anyhow, I do have a thesis topic, and I'd really like to tell you about it when you're ready."

"OK. Just not right now. Later." She studied his face. He was excited and pleased. "But Jacob, your orals are tomorrow. Most people would be worrying about them, not about a thesis topic."

"Maybe." Jacob shrugged. "I'm not worried about them though. Think they'll go just fine."

Chapter Fifty-Four

Jacob flew through his exams, getting As in all three. That evening they celebrated at an Italian restaurant in Oakland, complete with Chianti bottle candlesticks on the tables. Jacob explained his thesis topic. Mia asked questions, and was sure she didn't understand. They walked the five miles back to Jacob's apartment, holding hands, Mia feeling the warmth of the wine and the pleasure of his touch.

The next morning Mia wrapped herself in Jacob's robe and walked toward the kitchen, passing Sam, who was asleep on the couch. Her stomach churned, but she was determined to soldier through. She was tired of scenes.

She noticed a black kitten curled between Sam's arm and torso, its paw over its eyes, as if it was shielding itself from the morning light.

She put water on for coffee, and took a bowl and filled it with cereal. The sun shone through the kitchen window, cheering the little room. Sam sauntered into the room, raking his fingers through his hair. The little kitten followed him, his tail held straight up, his steps jaunty.

"Like my new little pal?" Sam asked, fixing himself some instant coffee.

Mia wanted to be cold to Sam, but the kitten was so cute.

"I'm trying to find a good name for him." Sam poured milk into a bowl and placed it on the floor. The kitten trotted up to the bowl and started scooping droplets of liquid with his tongue. "Schrödinger was quite good, I thought, but then I thought maybe Jacob might like to name him after a mathematician."

Mia stared at the cat, lapping the last drop from the bowl, then sitting, licking the side of its paw and scrubbing its face.

"Maybe after Jacob's thesis adviser. Or some other mathematician Jacob likes," Sam said.

"Trying to bribe Jacob into accepting the kitten?"

Sam looked up, his eyebrows arched. "You think he won't want the kitten?"

"I don't know. He seems to want to concentrate on his work. A cat would be a distraction."

"Maybe he needs some distractions," Sam said, lifting the little fellow up and cuddling him in his arms. The cat's contented purr filled the room.

"I suppose." Mia wanted Sam not to be there.

"So, Mia, you don't like thinking about the war," Sam said. "But how about your father?"

Mia felt like flinging her still-full cereal bowl at him. But she didn't. "I certainly can't speak for my father."

"But surely you know what he thinks." Sam's eyes drilled into her.

She looked away. "Sam, I'm not going to be drawn into a conversation about my father's views. You can figure them out for yourself by reading his articles. He's made no secret of his opinions."

"I have read some of them. He seems to hate the Russians."

The kitten began fussing, so Sam put him down. The kitten rubbed against Mia's leg, and she stroked him. He jumped up on the kitchen table, curled into a ball, and went to sleep.

"He distrusts the communists in Russia," Mia corrected, "not the Russian people." Immediately she regretted saying anything.

"OK. Why does he hate the communists then?"

"For starters, they wouldn't allow his elderly mother, his

widowed sister, and her child out of Hungary."

"Well, the U.S. treats its citizens just as badly. Don't forget Alger Hiss." There was a gotcha smile on Sam's lips.

"I don't know about Hiss. All I know is in this country my father, a Jew, is well treated and well respected. I know I can study what I want to study, say what I want to say, live where I want to live. I can say the Vietnam War is wrong, or I can say it is right. I'm even allowed to move to Russia if I don't like it here."

"You can do these things. But many other people can't. You're special, because of your father."

"Near as I can tell, the same is true of Jacob."

"Jacob is lucky, but there are lots of people in this country who are not so lucky."

"Maybe."

"So you see, this country is wrong. It's criminal what it is doing in Vietnam.

"Criminal is a strong word." Mia pursed her lips

"Strong, but appropriate."

"Who's this?"

Mia had been so engrossed in the conversation she hadn't noticed Jacob come into the kitchen. He stroked the little fellow sleeping on the table.

"He doesn't have a name yet," Sam said. "I was hoping you might name him."

"Hmm." Jacob picked the kitten up, "Einstein? Newton? Erdos? Euclid? That's it Euclid!"

"You mean you'll keep him?"

"I've always wanted a cat." Jacob stroked the fuzzy creature. "My mom would never hear of it."

Mia burned. Jacob could find time to care for a cat while he seemed so preoccupied with math that he didn't have much time for her.

Jacob scratched the kitten behind the ears. "Euclid. He's Euclid." Looking at Sam, he asked, "Do you have cat food? Or a litter box? Or — what else would a cat need?"

"I think food and litter pretty much covers it." Sam shot Mia a triumphant smile.

Chapter Fifty-Five

"Congratulations!" Mia held the receiver close to her ear. "A boy!"

"Yup!" Jamie's voice was distant, but it was Chicago. "Jackson Henry Richardson, seven pounds seven ounces, 21 inches long, hollers for dinner, looks just like Hank."

"He must be beautiful."

"He is gorgeous, beautiful, fabulous," Jamie said. "Honestly, he is perfect. Don't know how I'm going to leave him to go back to classes."

"When are you going back?"

"Soon as I can. Mom and Adele will look after him while I'm in class. Good thing they live so close to Northwestern."

Jamie had moved in with her parents when Hank left for Nam. She had gotten into Northwestern Law School, a good place for her, Hank had reportedly said, because she liked to argue so much.

"So when will Hank get to see the baby?"

"We're not sure yet. We'll have to figure that out."

"How's he doing?"

"OK, it seems," Jamie said. "Of course, we'll all be happy when he can come home." There was a muffled whimper in the background. "Hold on a moment, his lordship calls." After a few moments of rustling, Jamie was back on the line. "Latched on. All's quiet on the eastern front."

"Sounds so nice." That feeling flooded Mia: others had their lives in order while she, pretending she could be a mathematician, was going through some kind of charade. She pushed those thoughts aside.

"Anyhow, it seems having a newborn has great advantages."

"Like you're in love with your baby." Mia wondered what else Jamie could want.

"Of course, that. But it seems new mothers aren't eligible for jury duty."

"What?"

"Got a call to sit on a jury. Asked if I could bring my newborn. They said they didn't want me."

Mia chuckled. How Jamie. She didn't try to negotiate. She just threatened to bring her baby. "That's better, I suppose."

"Maybe. But I would have gone if Jackson could come, too. I've never been in a court. I thought it would be interesting."

Mia laughed. She could see Jamie with bundled baby, lugging infant supplies, and taking nursing breaks.

"Enough baby talk. How's life in Bzerkeley?"

"Not bad," Mia said. "Grades are no problem, straight As last quarter. The main thing is to pass prelims. I hope to take them in the fall. Jacob is helping me study and so is Liz, my roommate."

"Liz, the puritan feminist?"

"That's the one." Mia chuckled. "As my roommate Claire says, she's a saint. But she is a puritan. She's not crazy that some nights I don't come home." Mia put on a nagging mother tone. "You should at least tell me so I know you're OK."

Jamie laughed. "So you wrote that old-what's-his-name is coming out to Chicago for a conference in June. You should come with him."

"I can't," Mia said. "I've promised to take care of Euclid while Jacob's away."

"The great black cat?"

"Yup. Euclid and Jacob are buddies. I sometimes wish Jacob

loved me half as much as he loves that cat."

"The thing about cats is they don't talk, which makes them great companions for egoists."

Mia sighed. She should defend Jacob, should object to the old-what's-his-name line, but she was ambivalent. Jacob hadn't disappeared on her, at least not physically, but he seemed so consumed with his thesis. The only things they talked about were his thesis and her prelims.

Jamie's voice turned somber. "There's something I thought you needed to know." Jamie paused long enough that Mia wondered whether she was OK. "Chip was wounded in Nam."

"Oh, no!" Mia had assumed the service Hank and Chip were doing was an unpleasant task, like cleaning a latrine, but they would come out of it unharmed.

"I'm afraid so," Jamie said. "His right foot has been amputated."

"Oh, no."

"He's in a clinic in Walnut Creek."

"Walnut Creek?" Mia asked. "Why Walnut Creek?"

"I'm not sure," Jamie said. "Hank wrote that it is a good clinic and there were some kind of family ties to the people who run it."

"Oh." The information was swimming in Mia's head.

"Anyhow, I think Walnut Creek is pretty close to Berkeley, isn't it?"

"Yes." Mia imagined Chip in a hospital bed. "Maybe half an hour or so."

"Well, I've got his phone number, if you'd like to call him."

Mia said nothing.

"Would you like the number?"

"Yes, yes, of course. Just let me get a pen."

Chapter Fifty-Six

Mia stared at the paper for a full twenty minutes. Did she really want to call Chip? Liz would say she had better things to do: study for prelims, do class work, grade calculus papers. Why would she call him? He had been perfectly decent to her the last several times she saw him, but that had been at his request, or Jamie's, not because she wanted to see him. And if he were just passing through the Bay Area on his way to wherever, she would not have called him.

It wasn't that she wanted to see him or that she had nothing better to do. No. She felt like she owed it to him. She had to see him because he had been wounded. It seemed corny, but she felt that way.

She also wondered what he thought of the war. He had been there. He must know what it was about. He must have answers to all Sam's questions.

She dialed the number. An efficient voice answered, "Foster Residence."

That was weird, Mia thought, that a clinic would be a residence. She could still hang up or say I'm sorry, I've got the wrong number. But she said, "I'd like to speak to Chip Walsh, please."

The voice was cool and crisp. "Who's calling?"

"Mia Brower."

There was a moment's pause and muffled voices, and then "Mia."

"Hi, Chip." Mia didn't want to ask him how he was. That might be the wrong thing to say. "I was just talking to Jamie.

You've heard their little one was born yesterday?"

"No." His voice was light, cheerful.

"Yes, a boy, Jackson Henry Richardson. Jamie sounded so happy, so Jamie."

Chip laughed.

"So she told me you'd been wounded, that you're in Walnut Creek."

"Yes." Chip's voice was a little lower, a little clipped.

"And, well, I'm not that far away." Mia wondered at herself as the words tumbled out. "I thought if you'd like a visit, I could come see you."

"Oh, Mia, that would be...." His voice steady, but cool. "It would be good to see you." There was a pause. "Might you bring some licorice?"

***

As she drove through the long tunnel to Walnut Creek, she ran through the phone conversation with Chip. Odd somehow. He seemed tentative. Or distant? And licorice? Could he not get it himself? Maybe not. Maybe he wasn't able to leave the clinic.

This all seemed so confusing. One moment she was drawn to him, maybe a little too much. The next, he seemed like a stranger, someone who had been to war, someone she would not be able to understand, or even know how to talk to. Were there safe topics? You can't just say show me your foot that isn't there. Maybe she should not have suggested a visit. But it was too late to turn back now.

Walnut Creek was a small town just over the hills from the Bay Area. Mia found her way to a modest house in a middle class neighborhood, nothing that looked like a clinic. A handsome woman in her mid-forties answered the door.

"Mia?"

"Yes." Mia offered her hand. "Mia Brower."

"I'm Julie Foster." The woman's handshake was warm, comfortable. "So nice of you to visit Chip."

Music drifted in the hall, barely noticeable, like a light mist. It was familiar. Mia tried to place it. Mahler? Yes, it was Mahler. It jangled her nerves, those tones, almost lyrical, but just a little off.

Mrs. Foster ushered her into a sunny room, large and airy. There was Chip, his back to the room. Mia started at the sight of him, his black lustrous hair, his shirt sitting just so, gray slacks. Had he dressed up for her visit?

Chip turned and unfolded himself from the chair, slowly and with a stiffness that was foreign to his assured, fluid old self. "Mia." His voice reflected his stance, reserved, wooden.

Mia glanced down at his feet, his black leather shoes polished. Nothing seemed unusual, except, maybe, the right foot was at a slightly awkward angle. She looked back at his face, feeling guilty about her curiosity, hoping he hadn't noticed. He stood straight, almost rigid. She felt a tightness in her throat. She went to him and hugged him. She did not notice Mrs. Foster leave the room, closing the door behind her.

"Bring that chair over here and sit. I can't stand for very long." Chip sank back into the chair. When she was seated, he smiled, but it was a formal smile. "So tell me how you are, what you've been doing,"

Mia searched for a safe topic, something that would keep the distance. "Berkeley's a strange place. There're the hippies, the radicals, the townies, and the academics. They make a strange concoction." Her gaze wandered past him to a poster of a blue Avanti, like the one they had seen in Boston so long ago.

"But do you like it?"

Mia looked back at Chip in surprise. That was more like the

old Chip. Maybe this wouldn't be so difficult. "I don't know!" She laughed. Chip laughed, too, a warm laugh, a little more relaxed. She thought about Chip's question. "I guess I like it. But mostly I'm petrified of my prelims."

"Prelims?"

"Oral exams." Mia explained how the exams were run. "I've never been good on my feet, don't like talking in front of people. Oh, it's just — " She put her hand on her stomach and smiled. "I think I'll throw up every time I think about it."

"But do you like what you're doing?"

Mia was surprised at his persistence. He was staring at her, his blue eyes steady, requiring an honest answer.

"I don't know. I'm so bound up in worrying I have no idea whether I like what I'm doing."

His eyes softened, his shoulders relaxed. It was as if she had passed some kind of test and he was now ready to accept her.

"Maybe you'll just have to get past them to figure it out."

The conversation stalled. Mia looked about the room, searching for another topic. She noticed a bulletin board, with drawings of cars, rear views, side views, front views.

"What's that?" she pointed to the board.

"Oh." His gaze shifted to the drawings. "I've just been sketching a little."

She walked to the bulletin board to examine the pictures more closely.

"I don't know much about cars, but these look really good to me."

"Thanks." His smile was small, sad. "It seems that drawing, well, it's the one thing I seem to be able to do right now . . . ."

She had so many questions — what was he doing here in this non-clinic, why not back with his parents, what happened in the war. But those would have to wait.

Mia reached into her purse and pulled out a bag. "I've

brought you some licorice, but I didn't know what kind you liked, so I got a couple of kinds."

She spilled the bag's contents on the desk and half a dozen packages of candy fell out.

"Mia, you're an angel! These are my favorite," he said, setting one package aside, "and these are definitely no good — hard and flavorless — and these two, I've never tried."

He chose one of the unfamiliar packages. "Here, let's sample this one." He opened the package and offered her a piece. "What do you think?"

Mia bit into the candy and closed her eyes, letting the bold sweetness fill her mouth. She looked at him and nodded.

He bit into his piece, looking deep into her eyes. "It's great."

His smile melted. "Better than my favorite."

His eyes filled. "My new favorite."

Tears rolled silently down his cheeks. He snatched a handkerchief from his pocket and wiped his face. A fragile smile settled on his lips.

Mia instinctively went to him and hugged him. She did not want to look at him; she knew he needed his privacy. And she needed hers.

She was uncomfortable with this invalid Chip, unsure what she should do. She wanted to escape. A long moment passed. She held him until she felt his body relax. Then, with a gentle rub across his back, she withdrew.

"Chip, I'd better be off. I've got to get the car back," she lied.

"Sure." His smile was distorted so it almost looked like a sneer.

"I'll come again." She wanted to make it easier to leave. "Next week maybe?"

"Sure."

She felt guilty for lying, for wanting to escape.

"You have a scrap of paper? I'll write my phone number

down. You can call if you want. Just not after 10:00 at night. My roommate — Oh, my, I haven't told you about my roommate. She's a story all by herself. Well, next time."

Chapter Fifty-Seven

The week flew by with classes, students, and prelim preparations. As the day of her promised visit approached, she tried to think of ways to back out. Chip was like his music: almost Chip, but just a little off. She did not know how to act around him. But she felt indebted to him, for going to Vietnam, for doing what he thought was his duty, while she did nothing about the war. The least she could do was visit him.

Mrs. Foster greeted her at the door and led her down the hall to Chip's room. Mrs. Foster knocked gently on the door.

"Yes." The voice was muffled and distant.

"You've got a visitor, Chip."

The door opened a crack, and Chip peered out. He saw Mia and swung the door open. "Mia."

"Hi, Chip."

Mrs. Foster interrupted the silence that followed. "I'll be in the kitchen if you need anything."

"Thanks." Mia walked into the room, which seemed darker today, and close. "Chip, do you ever get outside? I mean, a little fresh air would do you good, I'd think."

"No, not much." He looked down at his foot. "Did you know I lost my foot?"

"Jamie told me." With this introduction, she felt she was allowed to look at his feet. She glanced down and then looked back at him. "Is that why you don't go out?"

"Maybe a little." He paused. "I walk kind of strangely. I mean I have physical therapy and I guess it's getting better, but I think people will look at me, like I'm a freak or something."

She smiled at him. "Maybe they'll look at you like you're a war hero."

He snorted. "No. They don't think of Nam vets as heroes."

Mia's heart dropped. There she went, making a bad situation worse. "I'm sorry." The room, which was depressing her, must not help his mood. They needed to get out. "Come, let's go for a walk or sit outside, even just on the front porch. A little fresh air would be good."

"OK." He hesitated. "I walk with a cane, you know."

"OK. Where's the cane?"

She scanned the room and, seeing a cane in the corner, she retrieved it.

"I walk slowly."

He was delaying.

"That's OK."

She suppressed her instinct to help him up. Instead she picked up her purse and headed towards the hall.

After letting Mrs. Foster know they were going out, they maneuvered through the door. Mia entertained Chip with stories of Liz and Claire and Jacob. She didn't mention Sam.

"So you like teaching?"

"More the older students than the kids," she said, "but yes, it's fun. It makes me feel like I know something. It's a relief not to always be facing stuff I don't really understand."

They found a bench near the town's downtown and sat down. Chip closed his eyes, and he seemed to be drinking up the sun.

"You know, Mia, I think you were right, getting out feels really good."

"Chip, can I ask a question?"

"Of course."

"Why are you staying with the Fosters?"

He opened his eyes and stared off in the distance. "That's

not a simple question."

"If it's too hard, pretend I didn't ask."

"No, no."

Mia followed his gaze across the street to a bulky brick building. Large letters on the roof spelled "creamery."

"I guess I'm happy you asked it."

He sat for a long moment, staring at the building.

"It's really mostly because I'm not ready to get back to the real world." He looked at his foot. "I mean, my foot is as good as it will get, the prosthesis is fitted and pretty comfortable. The physical therapy, well, I go, but really I can do everything they're doing by myself."

There was another long pause.

"It's that sometimes I feel...I don't know...I have trouble putting it all behind me."

He shifted on the bench, again focusing on the building across the street.

"I mean, I guess some fellows can store all that away and move on, but some of the things...things I saw, things I did...it just comes back when I don't expect. And sometimes, well, I can't help it. I just, well...."

The tears flowed down his face. He reached in his pocket and pulled out a handkerchief.

"You see, I can't really go to law school in this condition."

"Sure."

She put her hand on his shoulder.

"So I'm here." He recomposed his face. "Sort of in hiding, I guess, not really knowing what I will do or who I am."

"I know who you are, Chip."

But did she? This was not the self-assured Chip of freshman year, handsome and haughty. This was not the fine fellow of Jamie's wedding, solicitous and so proper. This was Chip without his polished outer shell, his soft vulnerability exposed.

Mia's heart flooded with warmth for him. His truth was naked, not dressed up with fancy words, bristling with confidence to keep her at a distance. His trust filled her with awe. She remembered, from years ago, his saying she did not trust him, so she could not love him.

She pushed these thoughts from her mind.

This was not where she wanted to go.

Chapter Fifty-Eight

"Chip, I've got some magazines for you." Mia handed him a bundle.

She had been visiting weekly, drawn to him. She felt it helped him, and that made her feel she was doing something positive in the world, maybe a little like Jacob helping Sam. They went out for walks and sometimes stopped for coffee or ice cream. His walking was getting better, steadier, so sometimes he didn't take his cane.

He flipped through the assortment: *Car and Driver*, *Car*, and *Motor Sport*. "These are great, Mia! Thanks."

They went for a walk and settled on the bench across from the Creamery. It was their favorite spot.

He seemed happier, more confident, today. Maybe she could ask him. She took a deep breath and plunged in. "Chip, do you think we should get out of Vietnam? I mean you were there, so what do you think?"

Chip was silent for a long time. "I don't know. I mean I hope I haven't wasted my time." He sighed and in a whisper he said, as if to himself,

"Ah, love, let us be true
To one another! for the world, which seems
To lie before us like a land of dreams,
So various, so beautiful, so new,
Hath really neither joy, nor love, nor light,
Nor certitude, nor peace, nor help for pain;
And we are here as on a darkling plain
Swept with confused alarms of struggle and flight,
Where ignorant armies clash by night."

Mia strained to hear. "What?"

"Just the end of a poem." He looked at her. "Dover Beach, written in the 1850s, I think. Matthew Arnold."

He repeated the lines to Mia. "The world hasn't changed since the 1850s, has it?" He resettled on the bench. "Still, the way this country works, the leaders decided to go to war, and we choose the leaders. We have elected new leaders. Will they do better? I don't know."

"Yeah." This did not make Mia feel better. She had wanted Chip to tell her that the war was justified, that it was necessary, that it was honorable.

They sat in silence, the sun warming them, a gentle breeze soothing them.

Chip sat up and took a deep breath, as if he were expelling the gloom, moving onto a better topic. "Can you keep a secret, Mia?"

"Depends what it is." She enjoyed teasing him.

"No. Really."

His solemn insistence surprised her. "Sure."

"I've been thinking." Chip shifted on the bench. "I've been thinking maybe I don't want to go to law school."

"That doesn't seem like such a terrible secret to me."

"Maybe not to you." As he exhaled he seemed to deflate. "But I think it would be, well, a terrible disappointment to my parents."

"To your parents?"

"Yes," he said. "They've planned on my taking over the firm. I mean from the time I was little. I used to go to the office as a kid and sit at a desk and pretend I was writing, just like my dad."

"But surely your parents only want you to be happy."

"Mia, that may be true for your parents." Chip looked at her. "But as I said, my parents, my dad, in particular, have planned for me to be a lawyer. Forever he has planned that."

"Yes," she said, "but your parents would understand. I know they would understand."

"Why do you say that?"

"Because they love you. I've only met them a couple of times, but I could see that they love you."

He was silent again.

"So if you didn't go into law, what would you do?"

"Dare I say it?" His eyes softened as he looked in the distance. "It seems like such a dream."

"So say it. I want to hear."

Mia did not interrupt the silence. Finally, after an intake of air, as if he were diving into deep water, Chip said, "I'd like to design cars." He looked at her apprehensively.

"Wow! I like that. I think you'd be good at that."

"Really?"

"Yes. Really."

Chapter Fifty-Nine

Mia had convinced Chip to come to Berkeley, to talk to her mom about what he might take at U.C. to start him on his way to designing cars. Her mom had scheduled appointments with some academic advisers.

As she drove to Walnut Creek to pick Chip up, Mia kept running through the arrangements, hoping everything would go smoothly. Chip was going without telling his parents, and he felt, Mia knew, this was a betrayal. Had she pushed too hard? Was this really her fight? Somehow she felt it was.

Mia calmed herself by thinking about her parents, always cordial to her friends, putting them at ease. She thought about her family home. The stone retaining walls would open their arms in welcome, the airy entry hall would draw Chip in, the cozy little nooks and comfy chairs would embrace him.

Finally, after the drive to Berkeley, they had settled in the living room, the spice of the redwood paneling wafting in the air. Her father's voice filled the large space.

"Mia tells me that you were wounded in Vietnam, that your foot was amputated."

Mia looked at her father in surprise. What was he saying? Didn't he understand how sensitive Chip was? Chip would hear this as, "Mia told me you are a freak." Mia fingered the smooth wood of her chair's arm.

Chip sat straight-backed at the edge of the sofa. "Yes, Dr. Brower, that's right."

"Please call me Daniel." Mia recognized that ploy. He'd used it on others, who had been honored to be on a first-name basis with the famous physicist. "So I will be comfortable calling you Chip."

"Of course, sir."

Mia smiled at Chip's non-agreement, proud of him, not allowing himself to be wooed so easily. She noticed her father's wry expression.

"You know, I lost my right foot when I was just a little younger than you."

Oh, her father was a crafty fellow! Mia never thought about her dad's amputation because he didn't seem to think about it. But now he was using that missing foot to good advantage. And why had she never told Chip? It might have been helpful. But she never thought of it.

Chip sat up even straighter, like a soldier at attention. "I didn't know."

"I did. Not in the midst of a battle or by an ambush. Not doing something heroic."

Mia was startled by the bitterness in her father's voice. Anger with himself, she supposed.

"No, I was a damned fool. I was running for a train so I wouldn't miss an excursion. I thought I could jump on, even though it was already moving. I slipped and fell. And...."

Chip's face was pale, his lips thin. "I'm sorry."

"Don't be. I manage well." Dad took a cookie from the plate on the coffee table and devoured it in one bite. "I was lucky. I was in Germany at the time and had an excellent surgeon."

He didn't add that the good doctor disappeared in the middle of her dad's recovery. The surgeon was wise enough to see bad times coming for Jews, something her father had missed. He managed to escape, too, but that was later.

"I was given prostheses that are comfortable, that work." Her father pulled up his right pant leg. "See. I am wearing one of those today. Forty years later."

Chip's polite mask melted, his eyes widened to stare at her father. "They last that long?"

"Not really. My wife has had it repaired an infinite number of times." Her dad pointed to stitching along the scarred leather that laced up, like the upper part of a boot, encasing his lower leg. "This wears out after time, but she has found a shoe maker who repairs it." He leaned forward to unlace his shoe.

Chip stood, coming around the coffee table to get a closer look as Mia's dad slid his shoe and sock off, revealing an ivory-colored foot form. "This is plastic, and it has held up better."

Chip knelt and ran his fingers over the smooth surface. He looked up at her dad. "Can't you have a new prosthesis made?"

"I've tried, but nothing works quite so well."

As her dad began unlacing the prosthesis, a wave of unease surged through Mia. She had seen the leg without the foot thousands of times, the knob at the end of the shin with its pink swirling scars. It was as normal to her as her own foot. But exposing this blemish to a new acquaintance, a young man, was an intimate act, like disrobing in front of a stranger.

She should not be here. She slipped from the room.

Sitting on the entry hall step, trying to calm her rapid breathing, she could hear the muffled duet of their voices, and then the sweet music of Chip's mellow laugh.

It was the sound of the pre-war Chip. Would it last? What magic did her father possess? When she mentioned Chip's disability, something she dared do few times, he was upset. Yet her father was allowed to do it. The single-footed men had bonded. What was she to do? Cut off her foot?

The French doors to the living room opened, and Chip emerged, a smile on his face, his step light. "Oh, Mia, what are you doing here? Why did you leave?" He looked down at her, the good humor slipping from his face.

"You and Dad seemed to be getting on, so I thought I'd let you get to know him a little better." At least part of this was true.

Chip's gaze shifted to the window. "He's something, your dad."

Mia murmured agreement.

"I'm glad we came." He sat down next to her. "He makes me feel like I can handle this... I guess because — " Again his gaze shifted to the window. "Because he doesn't pity me."

Was that it? Did she pity him?

Yes. She was petrified of saying the wrong thing, always dancing around the glaring realities.

She sighed, closed her eyes, and leaned back against the stair.

Never mind. Whatever her shortcomings, this had not been a mistake.

This was going to be all right.

Chapter Sixty

As she walked up Bancroft, Mia could see Chip leaning against the railing in front of the International House Cafe. The International House, or I-House as it was called, always seemed a little out of place to Mia, a white stucco behemoth on Piedmont Avenue, frat row. The founder had placed this extravagant building under the noses of the frat boys in 1930, to let them know what he thought of their exclusion rules.

I-House was her mom's favorite campus place, having lived there herself as a foreign student. It was her contact point for many of "her students," foreign students she helped as they made their way through the university. So it was natural for her to recommend Chip look at I-House for housing if he decided to come to Cal. It was the last stop on his tour of the campus.

"Hi, Chip." Mia climbed the several steps to the landing.

Chip smiled when he saw Mia.

"How was I-house?"

"Great. Friendly."

They walked north toward Mia's parents' house.

"A Japanese fellow showed me around. He's an engineer and says he could help me with my courses." Chip stopped a moment. "And Mia, I see what you mean about beautiful interior spaces. The building is magnificent."

They started walking again.

"So are you ready to start classes?" Mia asked.

Chip held up his sack of papers. "Just as soon as I go through these and figure out what I want to do."

"Who did you talk to?"

"I can't remember all the names. I have a list if you want to know."

"That's OK."

"I saw someone from mechanical engineering, and someone from a design group, and a general engineering group, and an adviser who said my bachelor's degree could get me in as a special student. He told me about the GI bill. It seems I can get tuition and books paid and some money for living expenses, too."

"No reason not to start, then." It would be nice to have Chip in Berkeley. No need to borrow the car, no drive out to Walnut Creek. She could see him any time.

Chips' voice was more somber. "There is at least one reason not to come."

"You didn't tell your parents you were coming to see U.C. today?"

"No."

"You haven't told them you might not go to law school?"

"No."

This seemed ridiculous, but her father's advice to let children make their own mistakes echoed in her head. It applied just as well to friends. She forced a cheery voice. "If we go a little out of our way, I can show you my grade school."

Chip was distracted, but mumbled, "Sure."

Mia hated grade school but she loved the building, another one of the 1930s masterpieces of the area's architects. They walked past the playground and the auditorium with its array of windows looking out toward the bay. Her narrative — there's where we played hop scotch, that's where the school fair was held — seemed to lighten Chip's mood.

"Let's sit for a moment here," Mia said, pointing to a low wall looking over the school yard.

"I met a friend of yours today." Chip was looking out over the playing field.

"Who? Jacob?" She was pretty sure Chip had met Jacob before. Other than him, she couldn't think who Chip would know in Berkeley.

"Sam."

As with everything having to do with Sam, dread soaked through her soul. She looked at Chip who continued to look away from her.

"Why didn't you tell me Sam was here?"

"I like to pretend he isn't here." That sounded mean, but it was true.

"He's not a bad sort."

"Maybe." She remembered how Sam pushed her into conversations about politics. "He's always trying to get me to — I don't know — trying to get me to say I'm against the war."

"Yeah. That's what he does." Chip finally looked at her, as if the momentary coldness had dissipated. "But he believes the war is wrong and thinks it's his duty to convince others. Is that so bad?"

"No. But it's more than that." Now it was Mia who looked across the field. "I feel as if he is trying to get me to say my father is wrong. More than wrong. Evil."

"Mia!" Chip shook his head. "That's a bit much. I mean, I know you don't like Sam, and I can understand that. But I don't think he'd do that."

Mia considered what she had said. It did sound paranoid. "Sorry. You're right." A breeze rustled the leaves. "Did he try to convince you the war was wrong?"

Chip laughed. "Of course. Wants me to become a vet against the war."

She searched Chip's face. "Are you going to do it?

"Probably not. It feels like it's unfair to the fellows who are still there." He stood and picked up his papers. "He gave me something to read. I'll think about it."

Chapter Sixty-One

Mia had hoped she could escape jury duty. Perhaps if she had a baby, like Jamie, she would have escaped. But apparently imminent prelims — only six weeks away — did not weigh on the court like a newborn did. Maybe, she thought, she had been chosen because she was a U.C. student, pleasing to the defense. But she was also relatively conservatively dressed and spoken, pleasing to the prosecutor.

At least the trial should be short. The defendant, in his 40s, with unconvincing credentials, was accused of blocking traffic. Several witnesses, a police officer, a shopkeeper, and a motorist had identified the defendant and said they saw him blocking traffic. The defense, while being mealy-mouthed about whether the fellow was actually blocking traffic, noted the man was demonstrating for an end to the Vietnam War. This was a duty, a sacred duty, for all who understood what was really going on, and if the fellow committed a misdemeanor in the execution of this sacred duty, that should be forgiven.

At least this was what she had gotten out of the almost three hours of testimony. She was hoping they would be out of the courthouse by 6 or maybe 7. Soon enough for a quick dinner and some studying.

***

The twelve jurors filed into the jury room and settled into the sturdy wood chairs. The room, lit from above and from a large window that looked down on the park in front of the courthouse, was cheerful, but Mia wished she were studying. The court clerk had placed the judge's instructions in the center of the table, along with legal pads and pens.

A slight man with wavy white hair broke the silence that had settled on the room. "Maybe we should introduce ourselves, before we get down to business. I am Karl Leopold. I teach history at the university." The man spoke with a slight accent. "I have lived in Berkeley, let's see, it's almost thirty years now." The professor looked to his right.

A black woman said, "I'm Julie Hudson. I work for the Whites. That's Professor White and his wife." Ms. Hudson smiled shyly and looked down.

"Jason Chang, manager of the Bank of America Branch on Shattuck." Mr. Chang's face was pleasant. Mia wondered at his apparent calm since his job must be difficult. At least it wasn't the branch on Telegraph.

Mia waited for Mr. Chang to say something else, but when the silence felt awkward, she introduced herself. "Mia Brower. I'm a student at U.C."

She looked at the fellow across the table. He reminded Mia of an evil genie, a bald head, a hulking figure, a dark sneer. "Jim Simon, retired longshoreman."

The next lady, grandmotherly, was dressed in a tailored dress and was made up just so. "I'm Molly McClure, army wife." She sighed. "Er, that is army widow. I lost my husband last spring. He'd just retired. Guess he didn't know what to do with himself, so he died."

The uncomfortable silence settled again. A young black fellow, wiry, with a pencil mustache finally spoke. "Charlie Whitsome."

The other five people introduced themselves quickly but Mia did not catch their names.

Again it was Professor Leopold who broke the silence.

"Maybe we should make name placards until we get to know each other." He reached for the legal pads and pens in the center of the table and passed them out. Mia made her name placard and looked up.

Professor Leopold was scanning the judge's instructions. "It says the first thing we need to do is elect a foreman."

An older man with graying hair spoke. "Professor Leopold, why don't you be foreman?" The speaker's placard identified him as Tom Blake.

That would speed up the process, so Mia nodded. "Yes, that would be good."

Everyone was silent.

"OK," Professor Leopold said. "If everyone agrees?" He surveyed the room, but no one spoke. "OK, then." He paused again, making sure, Mia assumed, no one had an objection. "There is one charge against the defendant, blocking the traffic." He paused and looked at the judge's instructions. "Indeed. Officially it says 'Obstructed the road and interfered with traffic.'" He looked around the room. "Maybe we could have a quick vote and see what people think."

Mia thought, maybe we could get this over with. What was there to think about?

The professor continued, "OK?" No one objected. "All in favor of a guilty vote?" Mia saw the professor, the colonel's wife, and the bank manager raised their hands, as did she. Julia Hudson looked around the room and slowly raised her hand. Five other people, one by one, after looking around the room, raised their hands. The longshoreman sat with his arms folded across his chest and a scowl on his face.

"Indeed. Mr. Simon, you seem to have some objection. Maybe you'd like to convince the rest of us?"

"What about free speech?" The longshoreman's words were loud and punctuated.

"Indeed. But as the judge instructed," the professor's words were distinct, as if he were in his lecture hall, "the right to free speech does not give someone the right to break other laws."

Mia looked back at Mr. Simon, who leaned forward in his chair.

"But if the defendant quietly stayed on the sidewalk with his picket, no one would pay attention."

Tom Blake, an older fellow wearing a sports shirt, spoke up, "Free speech rights do not guarantee that people will listen."

Good point, Mia thought.

"But they must listen." Mr. Simon's voice had an urgent edge. "This war is wrong. We are sending young men to die." He looked around the room, his eyes settling on the young black fellow. "What about you, Charlie, have they tried to nab you yet?"

The fellow stroked his mustache. "I'm at Merritt College."

"Ah!" Simon's voice boomed. "So you escaped?" A sneer crept across Mr. Simon's face.

The black fellow continued to stroke his mustache.

"What about your brothers?"

The young black man put both hands on the table and leaned forward. "Don't go pushing me."

Leopold sat straighter. "Please, gentleman. Let's keep this on topic." He cleared his throat. "And civil."

Simon spat back. "The war is not civil. This is about the war."

"Actually this is not about the war." The placard identified the speaker as Ben Hashimoto. He spoke quietly, seeming to hide behind his glasses. "This is about blocking traffic."

"That's right." The bank manager, Jason Chang, said. His salt and pepper hair made him seem wise and his calm voice was firm. "Maybe we should have a vote to see if we all agree the defendant was blocking traffic.

"That's not the point." It seemed Mr. Simon did not want to have such a vote. "What about you Ms. Hudson? They're drafting all the blacks they can get their hands on." Julia Hudson looked up at Simon. Her lips trembled. Mr. Simon leaned forward, saying slowly, "You want your folks to fight Whitey's war?"

"Sir." Jason Chang's voice was louder now and firm. "This is not about the war. It's about someone blocking traffic."

Simon glared at Mr. Chang. "Sometimes people have to be inconvenienced to hear the truth." Simon pushed back from the table and stood, his clenched fists on his hips, his menacing body leaning forward, his chin jutting out. Mia shrunk back in her chair.

Professor Leopold also stood. He looked fragile compared to the longshoreman staring across the table at him. Mia admired the professor's courage, literally standing up to Mr. Simon, but she would not bet on him in a fist fight.

"Let's take a break," the professor said.

"Yes, I need a break." Tom Blake stood, taller than the professor, but still not a physical match for the evil genie.

"Agreed." The juror named Gerry Hemple stood. Mia was grateful to see Mr. Hemple was as big as the genie. He put his fists at his waist and stared at the longshoreman.

Mia assumed the break was to calm things down. She saw the professor talking to Mr. Simon. Others avoided that conversation and talked quietly among themselves. She went up to Julie Hudson, who stood looking out at the park. She was wiping her eyes with a handkerchief.

"You OK?" Mia asked.

"Yes'm." Julie stuffed the handkerchief in her sleeve and looked at Mia.

"I think I met you when I was about ten. I was staying with Bertha. Bertha Ritter."

Julia searched Mia's face.

"My parents were away and I stayed with her for about a week."

Julia looked uncertain, but she said, "Why, haven't you grown up."

"Guess so." Mia laughed at herself. She hated those comments when she was little, but she realized Julia was trying to smooth the conversation along. "Bertha wanted to show me your parakeets."

"Oh, yes. I do remember." Julia's face relaxed. "You sure seemed to like those birds."

"Still do. Do you still raise them?"

"Sure do. Lovely little things." Julia smiled.

Mia knew Julia sold her birds to a local pet store to make extra money. It couldn't be much.

"Let's all come back together." It was the professor. Hopefully he had negotiated a resolution to the trial if not the war.

After everyone settled into their chairs, the professor spoke. "Let's have a vote on whether the defendant blocked traffic. Everyone who believes the defendant blocked traffic raise their hands."

Mia raised her hand and watched as the others raised theirs. There was a scowl on his face, but Mr. Simon raised his hand. The professor had found a way out of their dilemma. Thank you, professor!

"Indeed." The professor smiled, looking around the room. "It seems we all agree the defendant blocked traffic, so let's now vote whether we find him guilty of blocking traffic."

Mia again raised her hand and looked around the room. Everyone raised their hands. Except Mr. Simon. And Mr. Whitsome.

"Indeed." The professor's lips were compressed in a frown.

"Mr. Whitsome, would you explain how you can agree the defendant blocked traffic, but was not guilty of blocking traffic?"

The young black man stared at Mr. Simon as he said, "Jury nullification."

"Jury nullification?" The words slipped from Mia's mouth. "What is jury nullification?"

"Indeed." The professor shook his head wearily. "Jury nullification is when a jury decides not to find a defendant guilty even if he has committed an act the law says is illegal."

"How does that work?" Mr. Hemple leaned forward, his palms on the table.

"It has been working for a long time. Unfortunately." Mr. Blake shook his head. "If a jury doesn't believe the law is a good law, or if they think it is unconstitutional or inhumane." Mia wondered how Mr. Blake knew all this.

"But didn't we take an oath to — " Mrs. McClure paused, pursed her lips, and then continued. "Oh, I can't remember exactly what the oath was. But didn't we promise to listen to the facts and then find the fellow guilty or not guilty based on the facts?"

"Indeed!" The professor nodded.

"We agree on the facts," Mr. Simon said, nodding toward Mr. Whitsome, "but Charlie and me don't think the law is right. If we need to stop traffic to stop the war, so be it."

"Here, here!" A gaunt man at the far end of the table said. He had a pallid complexion and disheveled long brown hair. Alan Lightfoot. Mr. Lightfoot hadn't spoken a word until now. "Me, too. I think it's a bad law. I change my vote to not guilty."

"I don't get it," said the bleach blond who sat next to Mr. Lightfoot. "You mean we don't need to follow the law?"

"It sounds like that is what the gentlemen think." Mrs. McClure snorted. "Sounds like mob rule."

"Indeed!" The professor nodded.

Chapter Sixty-Two

The judge declared a mistrial at two in the morning.

Mia had promised to drive her parents to the airport the next day. Normally this would be a treat, a little time away from her normal loop: sleep, eat, teach, study, repeat. But today she was jumpy. She had not studied yesterday, and today was melting away.

Taking her father to the airport was relatively easy. He did forget things now and again, but he had an army of secretaries to get him out of difficulties. He was usually pretty relaxed.

Her mother was another story. She packed and repacked, making sure she had all the right clothing and accessories. It seemed strange for her mom, the original feminist, to be worried about such things, but she was. And, underneath her calm, she was nervous about traveling. She claimed she liked it, but she didn't behave that way.

Finally, everything was loaded into the car, including her parents, her mom in front and her dad in back. Mia started the car.

"Chip finally talked to his parents about U.C." Mia pointed the car down Cedar Street.

"How'd it go?" Her mom had heard all Mia's concerns about Chip and had counseled her to listen but not give advice.

"I guess they were pretty upset."

"It's a change they weren't expecting. Besides, since he can do this without their help, it's a declaration of independence." Her mom chuckled. "It's hard for us parents to accept that our children are grown up and want to do, as you youngsters would say, their own thing."

Her dad leaned forward between the front seats. "I'm all for doing your own thing. I always do my own thing."

Her mom's laugh was not altogether happy. "Yes, you do. You certainly do. But Mia, don't worry too much. They'll make their peace with it."

"They have no choice," her dad said. "Mia, you haven't told us about jury duty."

"Freedom isn't free."

Her mom pushed in the cigarette lighter. "Mia! Really!"

"Sorry, Mom. I know, I should be grateful to be an American. And I have nothing to complain about compared to people in the military."

The lighter popped. Her mother placed the glowing end to her cigarette and inhaled. "Like Chip!"

"Yes, like Chip. But the whole thing felt like a waste of time."

Her dad asked, "What was the trial about?"

"A man was charged with blocking traffic." Mia turned onto University. "Of course, it wasn't quite that simple. He was in an anti-war demonstration. The demonstrators blocked traffic. Police asked them to clear the road, and they refused."

"Do you think this man actually was guilty?"

"Dad, you seem more interested in this than I was. You should have been on the jury."

Her dad chuckled. "I don't think they'd ever select me for jury duty."

"They'd be right. You'd argue everybody out of everything." This brought a little laugh from her mother, which cheered Mia.

"So this was not a life or death trial," her mom said, "and it sounds pretty cut and dried. It must have been over quickly."

"Hardly." Mia merged onto the highway. "One of the jurors

said that because the defendant was exercising his right of free speech, he should not be found guilty."

"Interesting concept." Her dad's voice boomed cheerily. "What if the charge had been murder."

"We didn't go there." Mia was grateful no one had tried that argument.

After paying the toll for the bridge, she told her parents the details of the trial. "So after we told the judge there were jurors who were advocating jury nullification and after he talked to each one of us, alone, he finally declared a mistrial."

"Jury nullification?" her mom asked.

Mia had come to the concrete spaghetti on the San Francisco side of the bridge. She had to concentrate on getting in the correct lane to make the proper exits, so she wasn't listening.

"Mia, what is jury nullification?"

Having gotten on the freeway to the airport, she answered, "I don't understand it, but it sounded like a jury could decide not to find someone guilty of an act that was illegal, even if the defendant committed the act — " Mia steered into the middle lane " — if the jury thought the law was bad."

Mia could hear her father take in a breath. "So a jury could make up its own mind about what is legal."

"That's the way it sounded to me."

"What was the argument?" The cheer had drained out of her father's voice.

"The defendant was demonstrating against the war. The war was wrong. Therefore he should not be found guilty."

"I see." She could almost hear her father's mind churning. "Was there just one fellow who advocated this?"

"A longshoreman. And a black kid, a student at Merritt, joined him. And there was another fellow, who didn't say much, sort of a flaky street person. Once he got the idea of 'making our own laws,' he always voted with the longshoreman."

"A longshoreman?" her mom asked. "How old was he?"

"Not sure. Maybe your age. Maybe a little older." Mia pulled into the parking garage. She would help her parents check in and walk them to the gate. It seemed to make her mother less apprehensive.

"The Communist Party infiltrated the longshoremen's union in the 30's."

Mia wondered about her mother, always finding a communist connection. She expected her dad to object. He usually did when he thought her mom was not being fair. But he said nothing.

"You think the fellow was a communist?" Mia asked.

"Maybe not a communist, but if he was in the union in the 1930s he was probably exposed to lots of communist propaganda."

Mia thought about this. "So you think the whole jury nullification. . . ." Mia didn't finish the sentence.

"How did the other jurors react?" Her dad asked, as they waited in line to check in.

"Some of them were pretty quiet. There was one fellow there, a history professor — he was the foreman — who argued against the idea. And a lady, a colonel's wife, was outraged. There were some businessmen, too. They argued for a guilty verdict. The longshoreman stood his ground, and, once he had a little support, he became even more adamant."

They were at the front of the line. Her father checked in, passing the luggage to the attendant. Mia gazed at her mother, who looked more agitated than usual. She wanted to calm her. "Anyway, he wasn't acquitted, and now I can go back to studying."

Her mom nodded. "Yes. You've done your civic duty. And I'm glad the fellow was not let off."

Her dad shook his head. "If it was a mistrial and the charge was a misdemeanor, they may well not try him again. It's too costly. The longshoremen may have won the day."

"Oh." Her mom's eyes narrowed.

They walked to the gate and settled in chairs. Her mom fumbled in her purse and brought out a cigarette.

"But you can't expect the right outcome every time." Her dad lit her mom's cigarette. "Assuming guilty was the right outcome." Her dad stuffed the lighter back in his suit pocket. "Juries are made up of people, fallible people. Just like we cannot assume fighting this war is the proper thing to do just because our government says so. The government is made up of people. Fallible people."

"All true and neatly philosophical my dear." Her mom stubbed the just-lit cigarette in the ashtray at the chair arm. "But people, like the longshoreman, are causing real harm, whether they know it or not."

"It's the price we pay for a system that works pretty well."

"Sure, but the price is high." Her mom had a fresh cigarette between her fingers, which her dad lit.

"It's not as bad as you fear." He patted her hand.

"When I hear people saying 'The issue is not the issue,' I think I'm right to be worried." Her mother took a deep drag on her cigarette.

"The issue is not the issue?" Mia had never heard this slogan.

Her dad shifted his gaze to Mia. "The complete saying is 'The issue is not the issue, the revolution is the issue.'"

Mia was still digesting this when her mom added, "There are people in this country, communists or anarchists or whatever, who would like to have a revolution." Mia nodded. "They are happy to join any discontented group and help create chaos. They join in a peaceful rally and make sure it ends in violence. That's what happened at the Chicago convention riots." Mia nodded again. "The trouble with revolution, in addition to the people hurt or killed, is that you don't know what you will get. Think the Soviet Union."

Chapter Sixty-Three

The end of October was upon Mia. She had studied for prelims, had books scattered over her floor, papers sprinkled on top. It was the day before the prelims. Jacob said she knew the material well enough. Liz said she should not try to cram one more fact into her brain. She had done her work. It was time for a long walk in the Berkeley hills.

She walked in the shade of eucalyptus and bay trees, the spicy aroma mixing with the dust of the trail. The sun scattered through the trees, and in the distance she could see hills covered in waves of golden hip-high grass. It was a different world — no equations, no campanile, no books or professors. She felt the tension melt as she breathed, in, out, in, out, climbing the hills to a little summit. There she could see the bay, San Francisco, the sun drifting down towards the Golden Gate Bridge. She ate the peanut butter sandwich she had packed and peeled the orange. The sweetness of the pulp, a little acid but pleasant, reminded her the world was bigger than grad school or exams or getting a degree. Reluctantly, as the sun fell farther towards the ocean, she packed the remnants of her meal and started back.

It was dusk by the time she got home.

Claire met her at the door. "Your dad called." She handed Mia a piece of paper. "Said you should call his secretary, Mrs. Spalding."

Her dad would often use his secretary to deliver messages. Mia took the paper and went to take a shower. Then she called Mrs. Spalding.

"Oh, Mia," Mrs. Spalding said, "so glad you called. Your dad wanted me to call you." Her voice was friendly, efficient, a little breathless. "There is some kind of demonstration in Berkeley tonight," she said, "and the flyers for this demonstration say they plan to march on your parents' home." There was a pause on the line. "Mia, are you there?"

"Yes, I'm here."

"So your dad wanted me to make sure you did not go there tonight. Do not go to your parents' house."

"OK," Mia said. A demonstration was not that unusual. A march on her parents' house was something else.

"Where are my parents?"

"They're safe," Mrs. Spalding said. "Don't worry about them. They are safe."

"Can I call them?"

"Better not right now. If you have any questions or whatever, just call me."

"OK."

"I'll make sure they are in touch as soon as the coast is clear."

"OK." A lump grew in Mia's throat.

"Mia don't worry. Everything will be just fine."

The lump grew larger. "OK."

She was going to thank Mrs. Spalding, but the line went dead. That was not like her, to not sign off.

Mia ran the conversation through her head. Mrs. Spalding never said don't worry. She felt her throat tighten around the growing lump. She called Jacob. No answer. She'd go to his apartment. Maybe he would be there by the time she got there.

It was a long walk, almost three miles, and she ran most of the way. An endless loop of "Hell, no, we won't go" ran through her mind with images of men with masks, body armor, and gas canisters. By the time she got to Jacob's, she was panting.

She rang the bell. No answer. She knocked on his door. Pounded. No answer. She opened the door with her key. She would wait for him inside. She needed to see him. Needed to be held. Needed to be reassured everything would be fine, as Mrs. Spalding had promised.

She pushed the door open. Euclid greeted her, rubbing up against her leg. She switched on the light and tried to sit on the couch, but she couldn't sit. She paced back and forth, her panting quieting, the cat following her.

Her eyes settled on the heap of Sam's things in the corner. She noticed a bright yellow flyer, like other flyers Sam had produced. She picked it up. "Kill the War Monger" ran across the top of the page in black block letters. Below the header was a picture of a sinister man — brushy eyebrows, penetrating eyes, lips slightly parted to reveal teeth, as if the man were growling.

It was her father. But it wasn't her father.

Mia dropped the page. She riffled through the papers. Here were plans for the demonstration: who would distribute flyers, what was to be taken, people to notify, reporters for the radical newspapers. Sam must have organized this.

She flung the papers down and ran for the door. There was a pay phone at the drug store on Shattuck. She ran the few blocks to the phone, pushed a dime in the slot, and dialed the operator.

"Get me the Berkeley Police," she said when the operator came on.

There was a click, and then, "Berkeley Police Department. How may I help you?"

"There is a march on Dr. Brower's house this evening," Mia said.

"Yes."

321

"Go to," and Mia gave Jacob's address and apartment number. "The man who has planned this demonstration has information there." Then she slammed the receiver in the cradle.

She gulped. She imagined her house surrounded by goons in ragged jeans and frayed shirts. She could see them with torches, lighting the plants on the path to the house. She could see the orange yellow flames licking the porch, crackling as they climbed the pink stucco.

She turned toward the hill. Her feet pummeled the pavement, forcing her breath into an even beat. Her eyes focused on the sidewalk. Ahead, where Vine T-ed into her parents' street she saw four dark figures, blocking the intersection. Her feet pounded faster, her breath came in short gasps. The figures looked like giant cockroaches with their rounded hard helmets, black face masks, bug-eyed goggles.

"Stop!" A human insect stepped in front of her, his baton across her chest.

***

The red of the police car light swept across the street as an officer walked Mia to her front door. Claire, who had been peeping out the door, stepped out and hugged Mia.

"What happened?" Claire guided Mia into the house. "You mustn't get so alarmed about those stupid exams." She hugged her. "You should go to EST. It'll help you see what it's all about."

Liz came into the living room, wrapping herself in her robe, her hair untidy. "What's going on?" she asked. "Mia? You OK?"

Claire released Mia, who stood there, crying.

"Go get some whiskey," Liz said. "Come, Mia, sit down.

What's the matter?"

Mia sat as commanded, and Liz gave Mia a tumbler of whiskey. "What's wrong?" Liz looked at Mia. "Your exams?"

Mia shook her head no.

"Jacob?" Liz asked.

Another negative shake of the head.

"What then?"

"My father. My father's house," Mia said.

Little by little, Liz pulled the story out of Mia, the whole story: the call from Mrs. Spalding, the flyers at Jacob's apartment, her call to the police, her attempt to go to her parents' house.

"I'm sure everything will be OK," Liz said. "Why don't you call Mrs. Spalding and see what has happened?"

"I can't. Not in the middle of the night."

"OK," Liz said. "But, if they were not OK, Mrs. Spalding would call. And she hasn't. So why don't you lie down right here, and I'll sit with you. Try to get a little sleep."

Liz brought some blankets and a pillow, and Mia fell into a light slumber.

She woke to hear Liz talking on the phone.

"Jacob, I don't know what is going on, but I just got her to sleep." Liz twisted the phone cord as she listened. "No. I don't think you should talk to her. She needs to calm down if she's going to take her exams."

"Is that Jacob?" Mia sat up.

"Yes."

Mia stumbled off the couch and over to the phone. "Hello?"

"What the hell is going on?" Jacob's voice was loud and rasping.

"What?"

"The police are swarming my apartment, asking me all kinds of questions." The fury of his tone jolted Mia awake.

"They've taken Sam into custody, handcuffed him right here, and walked him to a squad car."

Mia exhaled, feeling the menace had been contained.

"It's all your fault!"

"What?"

"Yes. You were here, weren't you?"

Mia didn't know how he knew, but she didn't care. Maybe she dropped something or left something.

"I came looking for you. I wanted to talk to you, wanted to — I was upset about my parents." She paused for a moment, the events of the previous evening rushing through her mind. "My god, are my parents OK?"

"Sure." Jacob's voice was a nasty sing song. "The police broke up the demonstration before it even got up the hill. Tear gas, billy clubs, the whole arsenal."

"Oh." Mia dropped the phone, tears running down her face.

Liz picked up the receiver and placed it in the cradle. She pushed Mia on the couch. "Your dad called earlier to say everything was OK. I told them you had a bad night, but I'd let you know. Do you want to call them?"

Mia considered. She didn't want them to know how upset she was, but she wanted to hear their voices. "Yes," she said, steeling herself. "But what time is it?"

Liz looked at her watch. "It's 7."

Her mother had said one should only call between 10 am and 10 pm. They had probably had a bad night, too. "I'll call them later."

The phone rang, and Liz picked it up. "No, Jacob, I really don't think it's a good idea," she said in hushed tones, but Mia got up and took the receiver from Liz.

"So you've screwed up Sam's life. He's arrested, for god's sake. And they're going through all my papers. My research is scattered. God, it'll take weeks to put it all back together. I'll never get my degree this year. How could you? How could you?"

His diatribe had brought her calm for the first time since she got the call from Mrs. Spalding.

"What did I do?" she asked. "Have parents your friend wants to kill?"

Jacob's voice was low, each word annunciated slowly. "You. You. My work is scattered all over. How will I ever put it all back together?"

"I'm sure you'll manage." Her own coldness and steadiness surprised her. She hung up.

"Is Claire around?"

"Here I am." Claire appeared from the kitchen.

"Can you make me breakfast? Eggs and bacon, if you have them. And some fruit." Mia felt gratitude for Claire, her warmth, her cheerfulness, her support. "Or anything you have."

The exams started at 10. She showered and dressed, ate the breakfast Claire had prepared, and walked to Campbell hall, where the exams were held. She was there by 9:45, just enough time to look up the rooms for each of her exams. Several other students taking prelims that day were talking quietly in twos and threes. She walked to the room for her first exam.

After a few minutes the door opened, and Professor Chou ushered her in. She stood in front of the blackboard and faced the three professors. The panel asked one question after another, algebra questions. She wrote on the blackboard and spoke. It was as if she did not think at all, all the answers spilling out from some dark place she didn't know existed. The hour sped by and she walked out of the room, as if in a dream.

She had half an hour before the next exam, time for a drink of water and a visit to the lady's room.

The second exam, geometry, went just as the first exam did.

Professor Secreti asked a question, Mia wrote on the board, talking as she went, the professor nodding his approval and then asking a follow-up question. "But what happens if you increase the number of dimensions?" Again, the time sped by.

Only one to go, she thought, but she was feeling her fatigue. Another drink of water, another visit to the john.

She walked to the room and was ushered in by Professor Sitar, not an analyst, but on her analysis exam. Professor Sitar was Jacob's adviser, a brilliant fellow, not much older than the students and already a full professor. She didn't know him, never had a conversation with him. Jacob had said he would be a pushover, that he realized how good Mia was because of the paper she and Jacob had published.

Professor Sitar looked at Mia with a smile. He seemed friendly enough. But, she wondered, had Jacob told him about last night? Had Jacob said it was all her fault? Jacob was being unreasonable. No, worse, crazy. But had he talked to Professor Sitar?

Professor Sitar asked the first question, and Mia stared at him and thought about the conversation Jacob might have had with him.

"Mia," Professor Sitar said, "do you want me to repeat the question?"

She shook herself. Now was no time for her mind to wander.

"Yes, please."

He repeated the question and Mia remembered studying it and started writing on the blackboard and talking. But as she talked, she remembered that this was not the right way to approach the problem, that it would lead her to a dead end.

"I'm sorry," she said, "I'd like to start again, because this will be a problem."

"Of course." Professor Sitar nodded with approval.

She started again, writing, talking, writing, and then her

mind went blank. She stopped.

"What if you looked at it another way?" Professor Sitar asked.

She knew he was trying to help, but her mind went back to the conversation he might have had with Jacob. She forced herself to think about the problem, think about the hint. She repeated the hint and tried again.

She got a few lines further with the proof and again stalled. She felt the tears welling. If she stayed she would cry and she didn't want to cry in front of those men.

"I'm sorry," she said, "but I cannot go further with this."

She placed the chalk on the tray and walked out of the room.

She had failed the exam.

She had opted to fail the exam.

Chapter Sixty-Four

"But you got As in both algebra and geometry," Liz said.

"Yes."

"So what happened in analysis?"

"I don't know," Mia said. "I just went blank." She wouldn't tell Liz what really happened.

"Well, never mind. You can take them again in the spring."

"I know," Mia said. "But I'm not sure I want to."

"Of course, you want to. You got top marks in two out of three." Liz shook her head in disgust. "And after your parents were under siege and you broke up with that creep." She snorted. "The best thing about this is you broke up with that creep."

Mia closed her eyes. "I suppose."

"Besides, you've got to pass them. Got to show all those old white males we women make fine mathematicians."

Mia knew a feminist lecture would follow if she disagreed. "Of course. You're right."

At that moment the doorbell rang. Liz, after answering the door, turned to Mia and said, "Speaking of the devil...."

Jacob stood in the doorway. His hair was sticking out at odd angles, his chin shadowed with dark stubble, deep rings under his eyes. "I'm sorry," he said.

Mia looked at him. He didn't look sorry to her.

"I'm sorry I was not more supportive." His voice was mechanical, as if he had memorized a little speech, like a kindergartner at a school play repeating a nursery rhyme.

Mia was silent. She felt tired, exhausted. She didn't want to talk to him. She knew if she opened her mouth she would say angry things, things she could not take back.

"Professor Sitar called me right after the exam. He told me what happened." Jacob was standing at the door, hands in his pockets, slouching. "He's worried about you."

"Interesting that he was worried about Mia," Liz spat the words out, her fists clenched at her sides. "What about you, Jacob? Are you worried about Mia?"

Jacob, not expecting this attack, jerked his head and looked at Liz. "Of course, I'm worried about Mia."

"Well, it's a little late." Liz's vehemence punctuated each syllable. "Maybe you should have shown a little more concern this morning, before the exam." Jacob stared at Liz, unblinking, as if the words had not penetrated his brain. "A few words of support this morning, and Mia would have passed the exam." Liz's eyes were fiery. "Just a couple of words."

Jacob blanched. His lower lip trembled. "Mia, I'm sorry."

Mia nodded, not trusting her voice or her anger.

"Jacob, you've done enough damage." Liz pushed him outside and closed the door after him.

Mia sat motionless on the couch.

"Time for you to get some sleep." Liz straightened the blankets and pillows from the early morning. "Here, if you wish, or in your room?"

***

When Mia woke, the light outside was fading. She was startled. Why was she on the couch? What had happened? She pieced the events of last night and this morning together. Panic settled in her chest.

She went to the phone and called her parents' number. Her mother answered, cheerful, the sturdy soldier.

"Last night was interesting. We stayed with Mrs. Spalding, but we kept our location a secret. We didn't want to cause more trouble for Mrs. Spalding and her husband. The police were very efficient. I came home this morning. Your father isn't home from work yet. Of course."

Mia told her mother the story of her exams, leaving out the details of her going to Jacob's, Sam's involvement with the demonstration, and her attempt to come home. Her mother said nothing about the forbidden visit. Perhaps she didn't know

Her mother laughed. One of her friends, a famous economist in Britain, failed his exams the first time he took them. Of course, Mia would pass them. "Many brilliant people fail the first time, it being more a test of psychology than anything else." Her mom chuckled. "It's a way to make it hard to get a PhD."

Mia felt better. Her mother was such a rock. The danger of one particular demonstration was over. There could be another one. Or something else? Her parents went out in public all the time. But her mother's cheerful voice made Mia's fear dwindle. This particular battle was one of nerves, not might, and her parents had won.

But Sam had profited, too. He had been arrested and would probably be charged with something. Attempted murder? There would be court proceedings and publicity, and Sam would become the martyr he wanted to be.

Chapter Sixty-Five

If one had to have a gate, this wrought iron beauty was perfect, with its simple vertical spindles topped by an arch of twining branches and leaves. But it made Mia sad. The welcoming arms of the stone retaining walls were now imprisoned.

She pressed the buzzer at the side of the gate, as her mother had instructed. A staticky male voice asked, "Yes?"

"Hi. It's Mia."

"Mia?" The voice was gruff.

"Mia Brower."

There was a rustle of papers, and the voice said, "I'll buzz you in. Come to the front door."

That was hardly a warm welcome, and it put Mia off, even though her mom had warned her. She walked up the path, noticing two workmen at the north end of the property putting in posts, which must be for the fence that would secure the house.

Climbing the steps to the front porch, she saw a policeman standing at the door. He was a beefy fellow, with a buzz cut under his hat. His belt was laden with equipment, including a gun. He looked down at the clipboard he held.

"Hi," Mia said as she approached the door.

"Miss, I'll need to see some identification, like your driver's license." He stared at her without a trace of a smile or recognition.

Mia fumbled in her purse, pulled out her license and gave it to him. He looked at it and returned it to her. "Thank you. You may go in."

This was too strange. Too formal. She was angry. It was his job, but she wanted to break through to him, to make her visit something more important than paying a parking ticket. "Thank you for taking care of my parents." She smiled and looked directly at him.

He looked up and his face relaxed into a slight smile. Returning her gaze, he nodded his head. "You're welcome."

Mia found her mother in the living room sitting on the couch, papers spread out on the coffee table. A policeman sat in an armchair, and Bertha was placing coffee cups and a dish of cookies on the coffee table.

"You want some coffee, hon?" Bertha asked.

"Yes! Thanks, Bertha."

A lipstick-stained cigarette was burning in the ashtray beside the papers. Her mom looked flustered. "Oh, Mia. This is Captain Berg. Captain Berg, my daughter, Mia."

Captain Berg stood, and Mia shook his offered hand.

"Captain Berg is helping me plan all the changes that need to be made."

"Mom, you look really busy right now. Maybe I'll go say hi to Dad."

"He's up in the study, working." Her mom's face was pale, her eyes flinty. Mia could see her unspoken complaint, that her father never helped.

Mia looked at Captain Berg. "Thank you for helping my parents."

"Why, of course, Mia."

Mia was relieved to leave her mom. She took the steps two at a time and barged into the study.

Her dad sat at the card table, papers spread in front of him, equations in his thin slanting writing covering half of them. A book lay open on the table. He looked up, his face slack, his eyes dull, the rings under them deep and dark.

Her dad sighed and shook his head. "I am an idiot!"

Mia had to smile. He was still her dad, whining about his stupidity when he was deep into a problem he couldn't understand.

"I followed this when I was 23 and now I can't." He pushed himself back from the table. "Sorry, Mia. How are you?"

"I'm fine." She didn't feel fine. But right now, it seemed her parents needed her to be fine.

"Have you decided to retake your exams?"

"No. Should I?"

"Ha! You'll not catch me giving advice. You get to make your own mistakes."

Mia hugged him. He was impossible, but she loved him.

"Well, given that you aren't busy studying right now, maybe you can help me. Do you know anything about Lie Groups?"

"Dad, you know I wrote my senior thesis on them."

"Oh, yes." He pulled out the chair next to him. "Well, sit and help your senile old father."

Mia wondered why he had decided to work on this problem. Did he really need to know this now? Maybe. Or maybe he didn't want to think. Not about the march on his house. Not about his fuming wife downstairs. Or maybe he wanted to work with his daughter, to convince her to retake her exams. Or maybe all of the above. Or something else.

Chapter Sixty-Six

Mia had spent an hour with her father working on his Lie groups, a happy hour, thinking only about math and enjoying her father's company.

Now she was home, sitting on her couch, doodling on a legal pad, and thinking only about her exams.

"So if you drop out, what are you going to do?" Mia was startled. She had not heard Liz come into the room, but here she was staring down at Mia.

Mia stared back. She had no idea what she would do.

"Maybe you'll run to your new boyfriend." Liz started clearing books and clutter from the coffee table. She looked at Mia with an unpleasant sneer. "The auto designer?"

Where did Liz get that idea? "Chip's not a boyfriend. He's a friend."

"OK. That plan's out." Liz dumped some papers in the wastepaper basket. "What are you going to do? Going to get a job at El Toro with Claire?"

Mia was startled. Was she serious? "No. I have no interest in cooking."

"OK. No boyfriend, no cooking." Liz stacked papers and books. "What are you going to do?"

Mia was silent. What could she do? Certainly, a Harvard degree must be worth something. But she had prepared for nothing but math. She could teach math, she supposed, but that left her cold.

"You'd better find something." Liz collected pencils and pens in a mug. "Because we still need to pay the rent." Liz was such a bitch. "Of course, I could find another roommate."

That stung.

Liz sat on the couch next to Mia, and her tone turned kinder. "You could just take your exams in the spring and continue in math." Liz's face, usually so sour, was softer. "I know you could pass them." She snorted and shook her head. "On no sleep and a family crisis, you aced two out of three and would have done the same on the last one if you hadn't screwed yourself up."

Mia felt like objecting, but she'd already had that conversation with Liz.

"Form a study group."

"Who would want to study with me? I've failed the exams."

"You failed one out of three. The other two you aced. Everyone knows it." Liz looked at her. "Have you even been back on campus?"

Mia shook her head no.

"Well, then, the first thing to do is to go back. Don't you have a class to teach?"

"I got someone to sub for me yesterday."

"And tomorrow? Who's teaching your class tomorrow?"

Mia was silent.

"Look, Mia. Failing an exam is not a communicable disease. Go to campus today. Go teach tomorrow. Then you'll know you must take those exams again."

Chapter Sixty-Seven

Mia didn't want to see people in the department. They all knew she had failed. She was sure they all thought she was a loser, one of the would-be mathematicians, really not up to the standards of this university.

She peeked into her office. The light was not on. No one was there. Thank goodness. She walked over to her desk and dumped her books. There, in the middle of her desk on a scrap of yellow paper, was a note, scrawled in an untidy hand.

Mia,
Please stop by when you have a chance.
John Sitar

She sat and stared at the paper. She did not want people's pity, either. She didn't know Professor Sitar. She didn't want to talk to him. He knew Jacob. She wanted to stay away from Jacob. She laid her head on her desk.

"Mia?"

Mia felt a hand on her shoulder. She looked up into Ray's face. Ray was the office mate who was never there. Mia blinked. "Oh," she asked, "what time is it?"

"About 1:30," Ray said. "I heard what happened. Pissy luck to have all that family stuff happen the night before your exams. Damn shame."

Mia looked out the office window.

"Professor Sitar was looking for you," Ray said. "I think he really wants to talk to you."

"Oh, yes." Mia looked down at the note on her desk.

"C'mon," Ray said, nodding his head in the direction of the math building, "I'm going over there right now anyhow. I'll show you where his office is."

Mia got up, not wanting to refuse, but at the same time not wanting to talk to anyone, especially Professor Sitar.

"Those exams are a bitch," Ray said, holding the door for her. "I failed the first time I took them, too. My son had been born three months before the exam and I wasn't getting enough sleep. At least that's what I tell myself."

"That must have been hard."

"I think it was really just the — what should I call it? — I think they build it up to scare people. Sort of like hazing in a frat."

"That sounds like what my mom says."

Ray smiled. "I'm living proof you can be a mathematician even if you failed your first go at the prelims. I'm finishing my thesis, and I have a job offer. San Jose State. Not a big name, but I'll be a professor, what I always wanted."

"That's great."

"Not like your friend Jacob, mind you." Ray's eyes were kind. "But I'll do what I love."

Mia nodded.

"Here's his office." The tag on the wall beside the door said Professor John Sitar.

Mia nodded to Ray. "Thanks for the encouragement."

Ray bowed his head almost imperceptibly and headed down the hall.

Mia looked at the door. She wanted to leave but Ray might see her. She took a breath, held it, and knocked on the door.

"Come in." The voice was muffled and distracted.

She pushed the door open to find Professor Sitar at his desk, papers and books helter-skelter on the desk, with just enough room for a pad of paper and a pen.

He looked up at her and stood abruptly. "Mia, I'm so happy you came in!"

"Thanks." Her voice quivered.

"Come, come, sit down here." He pushed aside some papers on his visitor's chair.

She sat as directed.

"I know it's been a difficult time for you," He settled back in his chair. "I've talked to other people on your committee." He leaned forward, his eyes directly on hers. "You did very well on your first two exams. Better than very well."

"Thank you."

"So what happened on the last exam?"

"I don't know."

"I know about the problems your dad was having the night before. Jacob told me you were quite upset."

"Yes."

"Well, given all that...." He trailed off. "You have a great deal of talent."

"Oh."

He smiled and nodded. "I'd be disappointed if you let this incident get in your way."

Not knowing what to say, Mia nodded.

"Jacob thinks you are really good."

Mia felt a lump in her throat forming. "Oh."

"Look, Mia. Please don't give up on this. The exams will be given again in the spring. Just take them in the spring."

She mumbled, "I will."

He leaned back in his chair, as if he had accomplished his goal. "Do you know what you want to do your thesis in?"

"No."

"I see." He studied her. "Come see me after the exams. I have a couple of problems that might interest you."

Chapter Sixty-Eight

Her talks with Liz and Professor Sitar whirled in Mia's head. She wandered aimlessly, walking into buildings and out again, until she pushed open the door to Wheeler Hall. The barreled ceiling, the curved sunbeams from the windows streaming into the space, drew her in. She backed up against the wall, staring at the grace of the swooping arches. Sinking to the floor, she sat, her arms wrapped around her knees, her eyes meandering over the cream walls, the honey golden wood. The beauty awed her.

"Mia, what're you doing here?" Mia jumped at the sound of Chip's voice.

She looked up. "Finding solace in a beautiful place." She sighed.

Chip sat beside her. "And you need solace because. . . ?"

Mia shook her head. Of course, Chip knew nothing of the march or her orals. Perhaps there was a god who sent Chip here to give her a sane view of the world. "Stormy seas on the Mia front." Mia told him about the demonstration, her exams, and Jacob.

Chip leaned against the wall and looked up at the ceiling. "I think you're being too hard on him."

Mia stared at Chip. "Me? Too hard?" She had expected sympathy from Chip, and here he was defending Jacob.

"Look. I know he let you down." Chip stood up, stretched his arms and arched his back. "And I can understand you don't trust him now."

Mia ran her hand along the floor tiles. "Yes. That's it for old-what's-his-name. I'm never trusting him again."

Chip ignored her response. "But he went through a trauma, too. His apartment was torn apart, Sam arrested, his work in disarray. Those things are hard. They're not family, but they are hard." Chip stared at Mia, as if he could convince her with his eyes. "Come. Let's find a more comfortable place." He offered his hand and pulled her up.

Chip guided Mia toward the door and down the steps. "Let's go sit at I-House. It's a beautiful space, too." He grinned at her. "And they have chairs."

Mia avoided Chip's eyes, looking down at her feet. "Sam was leading a mob to kill my father." She stared at Chip. "I mean we aren't talking being disrespectful or a pie in the face. We're talking murder."

"I know." Chip looked away. "I didn't say I didn't understand how you felt."

She had hoped for more sympathy. Chip wasn't any better than Jacob.

"Come. Let's go to I-House." Chip took a tentative step forward.

Mia needed to talk. She needed to talk more than she needed to be angry. She followed Chip.

They climbed the hill to I-House. "Your family is OK now, right?" There was concern in his eyes. "That's the most important thing."

"They're OK." He really didn't get it. "But a policeman stays on the front porch, every day, every night. They're going to stay until the fence is in."

"I see." They climbed the I-House steps. "Are these things necessary?"

Mia closed her eyes. He really, really didn't get it. "I guess someone thinks it's necessary, because otherwise police wouldn't be living on the front porch." Mia stumbled on a step and Chip caught her. "And they're getting a dog. A watchdog. They're looking for one now."

Chip led her through the building entrance and onto a patio.

"And my parents — well, they tell me not to worry. But they're worried. I can tell."

"I'll get something to drink. Water? Lemonade? Soda?"

Mia asked for lemonade and settled in a chair. Here and there the brick paving was interrupted by low stone walls surrounding small maple trees, their leaves a sunshine yellow.

Chip returned with glasses and a pitcher of lemonade.

They sat in silence, sipping their drinks, their conversation playing in Mia's mind. She looked at Chip. He had listened to her ruminations.

"Thank you." Mia wiped her hands on her jeans. "Thank you for listening."

She thought about Liz, and Ray, and Claire, how they listened to all her complaints, too. She thought of Nick.

"My friend Nick called, from D.C. He heard about it. McGovern came to talk to him, to try to understand things better. So Nick called, just to see if everything was OK."

Mia took a sip of lemonade. Chip was staring at her.

"McGovern?"

"Yeah, Nick's an intern for McGovern."

"But McGovern is from South Dakota, isn't he?"

"Something like that. I'm not sure."

"Well, not California, right?"

"So?"

"Senators pick their interns from their own state. So how did a high school friend of yours, from California, get an internship with McGovern?"

Mia had never thought of that. "Must've wiggled his way into McGovern's heart." Nick always knew how to please people. "But Nick's passionate about getting out of Vietnam.

He says McGovern can do it. The way it should be done."

Chip refilled their glasses.

"And your exams? What are you going to do about them?" Mia avoided his gaze. "I don't know."

"I think you should take them again, as soon as possible," Chip said. "Sort of like getting back on a horse after you've fallen off."

"But, Chip, I don't even know whether I want to do math. I don't know whether I like math." She looked at him, hoping for some sign of approval. "So why should I torture myself with the exams?"

"Because you love math. You'd miss it." He grinned at her. "Of course, girls probably can't be mathematicians."

Chapter Sixty-Nine

"I can't find one person who thinks I shouldn't take those exams again," Mia said. "Claire, surely you'll be on my side. I shouldn't take those exams again, should I?" Mia dug into the French toast Claire had prepared for her.

"Live in the here and now," Claire said.

The non sequitur didn't surprise Mia. Asking Claire for meaningful advice was like asking Euclid the cat for geometry help. "The French toast is great. You just keep cooking."

After breakfast she drove to Tilden Park.

She had promised herself today she would make up her mind, either full speed ahead with her prelims or quit grad school. This trail through the eucalyptus and bays was her special place. Wisps of fog floated among the leaves, giving it an unearthly feeling, a place away from reality, a place to understand the un-understandable.

She walked rapidly, too fast, so that she was soon panting. She was running away. She wanted to run away, to a place where everything was clear.

She was a follower. She had always been a follower. But now there was nothing to follow.

No. That was not true. Everyone was telling her to take her prelims. Everyone. Except her parents.

She was afraid of making a mistake. Some people knew what to do. Jacob did math. He liked doing math. Math was his destiny. How she envied him. His path was clear.

Or Jamie. She decided what she wanted and then she did it. But how did she know what she wanted? Was Veritas the secret?

All Mia wanted was to be good at something. Good enough so she would be respected. Like her father. He was respected. Was that too much to ask — to work hard, to be good, to be respected?

Was it really respect she wanted? Was it something else? To be included in the group, to be one of the herd? That was it. More than respect, she wanted to be a member of the community.

And given what had happened the last couple of weeks, the encouragement she had gotten from Liz, and Professor Sitar, and even from Ray, who she really didn't know, she was in a community. The math herd was supporting her.

So what was the hesitation? She had told herself that she didn't like math, that she didn't know what it meant to really do math. Was that true?

Maybe. She'd never done anything truly original, except the paper with Jacob. But Jacob had done all the truly innovative things. She wasn't sure she could do something innovative. Everything she had ever done in math was something someone else had already done. Could she do something no one had done before?

Did it matter whether someone had figured something out before? How would one think differently about something that was unsolved? Was doing her problem sets the same as working on an unsolved problem?

Maybe. But in doing problem sets she knew there was an answer. In doing research it was not so clear. What would happen if she spent her life trying to solve something, and she came up with nothing?

Like Einstein and unified field theory. That didn't seem to bother him. But it would bother her. She needed to have some kind of external that-a-girl. Did that make her ineligible as a mathematician?

Maybe not. She liked teaching. She thought of Ray, going to San Jose State. He wouldn't be solving any great problems there. He'd have a heavy teaching load and little time for research. But he was doing something he liked.

Would she like that? Maybe. More than maybe. Probably. Was that such a bad fate? Maybe. Did Ray have the respect of the mathematical hot shots? She didn't know about anyone else, but she, if she were truthful, did not respect him. She'd bet Jacob didn't respect him, either. They had never talked about Ray, so she didn't know for sure. But the fact they hadn't talked about him implied Jacob didn't respect him. His work was not worthy of discussion.

She laughed out loud. She would never admit to anyone she felt this way. How juvenile, she thought, to measure someone purely on his mathematical ability. But — Veritas — that was what was stopping her. She would never be a superstar. She would never be excellent.

And, if she was not excellent, why bother?

She reached the summit, settled on a rock, and looked out over the bay. The sun was high and the fog had lifted. She watched San Francisco shimmering in the distance. She breathed in deeply and allowed herself the animal satisfaction of sitting after a strenuous walk.

She'd brought along an orange. She peeled it, smelling the acidy aroma. She bit into a section, the juice dribbling down her chin. The sweetness filled her mouth.

This was heaven, the view of the bay, the taste of orange, the warmth of the sun on her back. This here-and-now was heaven. She thought of Claire. Perhaps this was Claire's here-and-now.

But Claire's here-and-now was also bussing dishes at El Toro and vacuuming the little house and scrubbing the bath tub. Was each of those here-and-nows as enjoyable as sitting on top of the world in the sunshine?

Maybe it could be. Maybe she could make each problem set, each study session, each prelim exam a here-and-now, a goal in itself.

Maybe she could love math for math.

Chapter Seventy

There had been one little hiccup after another, but now Mia felt her study group was doomed. She walked along Telegraph, the street eerily empty, the rain and gloom having chased the street people away.

Mia thought about the group. Nancy had wanted help, and Mia was happy to have her. Mia had learned teaching helps the teacher learn. George had joined, a real coup. He was bright and personable and had attracted others.

Mia's stomach growled. She hadn't had lunch and it was almost three. She stepped into the next little eatery and plunked herself down at the nearest table. As she picked up the menu, her finger slipped across a greasy spot. She ignored it. She wasn't going out in the cold to look for a more hygienic place.

The group had grown to eight members. She'd been pleased at first, but now wondered whether it wasn't too big. It might be easier finding meeting times if there were fewer people.

"Hey, Mia!" Mia looked up. Claire, clad in black pants, a white shirt, and a gray-blue apron looked down at her. "You came to try our fine cuisine!" Mia looked at the top of the menu, where El Toro was spelled out in garish Mexican colors.

Mia was not in the mood for a Claire conversation right now. She had a problem to solve. But she couldn't run either. "Hi, Claire."

"You look worried." Claire pulled the chair out opposite Mia and sat.

"You OK? I mean, sitting on the job?" Mia smiled to soften

the harsh tone of her comment.

"It's OK. It's the end of my shift anyway. And slow." Claire waved her hand to indicate a deserted restaurant. "Besides, Pedro likes us to be friendly with the customers."

"I'm starving and too tired to read the menu. What should I have?"

"Chili Rellenos." Claire nodded. "A specialty of the house!"

"Great!" Mia looked around for a waiter, but there were none in sight.

"I'll put the order in and be right back. Maria is out back smoking."

Mia went back to pondering her problem. Between all eight of them, there wasn't a time when someone didn't have a class to teach or a class to attend. There were simply no empty slots. They had discussed meeting in smaller groups, but that made scheduling a nightmare.

Her mouth watered as Claire set a plate before her, the aroma of tomatoes and chilies wafting upwards. She blew on a steaming forkful and placed it in her mouth."Mmm!"

"Good, yeah?" Claire's eyes rested on Mia, waiting for a verdict.

"Just what I needed!"

Claire flashed a brief smile, but her eyes softened and again she stared at Mia. "So why the glum face?"

"It's the group."

"I thought the group was great." She scrunched her brows and frowned. "Anyhow, George seems to be really nice." Claire had told Mia all about him. He'd stopped by one day when Mia was out. He'd grown up in downstate Illinois on a hog farm. Claire had a crush!

"George is great. No doubt."

"And everyone was going to impersonate a professor for your mock exams."

Mia was surprised Claire had remembered that. "That's right. George's idea. It's a really good idea." Maybe George had told Claire about it and that's why she remembered. "You get to know how those profs think when you have to pretend to be them."

"So what's wrong?"

Mia swallowed and took a sip of water. "Can't find a time to meet."

"Huh?"

"Too many classes. All the time slots are taken up."

"Bummer!" Claire pulled her ear and gazed past Mia. She looked back at Mia. "Why not meet at night?"

"We talked about that, but everyone worries about getting dinner and it getting too late. Several people have 8 a.m. classes to teach."

"Hmm." Again she pulled her ear and looked into the distance. A smile spread across her face as she turned back at Mia. "I have an idea!"

Chapter Seventy-One

"You ready?" Mia glanced into Chips' room.

"Sure." Chip gripped his Samsonite case in one hand and a briefcase in the other. "Let's roll."

"Your parents must be happy you're coming home for the holidays." Mia guided the car down University.

"It's time." Chip said. "I'm actually looking forward to it."

"Any special plans?"

"My mom always has plans for the holidays. There will be the big New Year's party, of course. And I'll go up to Boston and see Aunt Beverly. Have to see her." He sighed. "And we'll have plenty of time to talk."

Mia glanced at him, but he was looking out the side window so she couldn't see his face.

"I think they understand." He sighed again. "Well, I think my mom understands." His low voice quavered. "My dad? He's really disappointed. Really, really disappointed."

"But he also understands." Mia hoped this was true.

"I don't know." Chip shifted in his seat. "I've always been the perfect son, and now I want to do something that wasn't in his plans."

Mia grimaced. Her parents demanded she find her own way. That was the proper way for parents to act. Chip's parents made her mad. She smoothed her voice. "But he can't think he's allowed to plan your life."

"Theoretically, I'm sure he'd agree with you." Chip chuckled humorlessly. "But in practice, he's still getting used to it."

Mia gritted her teeth. "Practice is what counts."

Chip paused so long Mia glanced at him again. He looked straight ahead, his lips in a tense line. "Sharing a business, like he wanted to do, that's a different relationship from just being a father."

"True, but — "

Chip cut her off. "He said that to me." Chip snorted. "I nearly changed my mind when he said that to me."

"If he feels so strongly about it, maybe he should take up designing cars. You can be the designer and he can be the apprentice."

Chip's laugh was hearty. "Should I suggest that to him?"

"Only if you don't tell him I said it."

They drove in silence over the Bay Bridge. The traffic was light so early on a Sunday morning, and a soft drizzle enveloped the car. Mia put on the wipers.

Chip cleared his throat. "So how's the studying going?"

"Really well." She told Chip about the group, about the impersonation of professors and their mock orals.

She pulled into a parking place at the airport. "You're treating me to breakfast before you take off." She was relieved to see a smile on his face. He would manage his visit with his parents. "Fare for the ride to the airport."

After Chip checked in, they walked up the stairs to the restaurant. It was quiet. Mia ordered an omelet. Chip had eggs Benedict.

"Is your group going to study over the holidays?" Chip asked.

"No, we're taking a break now," Mia said, "but we start up again the day after New Year's." She added cream to her coffee. "All eight of us agreed we needed to break for the holidays."

Chip frowned. "Eight? That's a big group!"

"Yeah," Mia said. "So big we couldn't find a time to meet, what with all the classes we attend and teach. I thought we'd have to split up. But Claire solved the problem."

"Claire?" Mia heard a note of doubt in his voice.

"We meet Monday through Friday at 6 pm. We have half-hour debriefings, as we call them. We talk about anything related to the exams and we have dinner."

"Dinner?"

"That's where Claire comes in. She provides dinner to the group everyday. Everyone pays her, and that also means everyone shows up on time."

"That's a huge amount of cooking." Chip shook his head and pursed his lips. "Can Claire manage that and keep her job?"

"She's taken a leave from El Toro. At least that's what she says. I think she actually quit. Anyhow, she's making more this way."

"You meet at your house?"

"Yup. Meet where the food is." Mia sipped her coffee. "After dinner we have mock prelims."

Chip stared at her, a smile playing in his eyes. "You sound like you're enjoying this." He nodded. "Like it's not really work."

Mia thought about the last meeting. "I do like it." She thought about the others, particularly Nancy. Nervous Nancy. "I'm helping the others. The material seems so much clearer now." But it was more than that. She felt connected to the group. They shared this project. That included Claire. She looked past him, the restaurant a blur. "I didn't think I could do this. Not without Jacob's help."

Chip's eyes caught hers. She bit her lip. She shouldn't have said that. She didn't want to go there.

Chapter Seventy-Two

Nancy took a tissue from the box Mia offered and wiped her tears. "He was such a bastard." She hiccupped and blew her nose. "Like, really, you don't know that? Every high schooler learns that."

"It's not about George." Mia didn't mean to be unkind, but this girl really needed some backbone. "It's about learning the material." Mia gathered some papers on the coffee table. "And if George lets you have it for not knowing something, that may be what actually happens in the exams. I can tell you horror stories...."

"Yes, but really...."

"Yes, really. Do you have a list of everything you didn't know?" Mia looked at Nancy, but saw no response. Never mind. It was time to be tough. "You learn those cold. You'll have the same committee tomorrow."

Nancy looked at Mia wide-eyed. "I couldn't do it all by tomorrow."

"OK." Mia stared at Nancy. "Then day after tomorrow."

Nancy winced, but said nothing.

"Now, off you go." Mia stood. She really wanted to get Nancy to leave. She was tired and had a headache. She longed to lie down in her bed.

Nancy sniffled, gathered her things, and left.

Mia pushed the door shut after her, sighing, only to hear Liz's voice behind her, "You really need to talk to that George."

Mia didn't want to talk about it. Liz had been sitting in on the group meetings and mock exams, making more and more

353

comments. Many were helpful, Liz adding things to the list of questions and information about potential committee members. But tonight Mia was too tired to deal with more trouble.

Liz stood, her hands at her hips. "He tore into Nancy in an extraordinary way."

"He's playing the part of Professor Guthrie," Mia said, "who's known to be difficult."

"He went way beyond difficult. You need to talk to him."

"Maybe I will." Mia looked at Liz. Sour Liz. "Or maybe you could talk to him."

"Oh, I couldn't do that." Liz's smile was icy. "It's your group."

"It's the group's group. And it seems you have become a part of it." It was strange Liz was spending so much time with the group. "Liz, is it OK with you that we meet here every night? I mean, does it get in your way?"

"Oh, no," Liz said. "It's fine."

This didn't ring true, but Mia was so tired she didn't care. It was another month before the exams, and, between classes and group meetings and studying for prelims, it seemed she didn't have time, not for laundry or shopping or managing relations with Liz.

There was a timid knock on the door. Mia sighed. Hopefully it wasn't Nancy back in tears or someone else complaining about who knows what. Hopefully, this was just someone who left his notes or his hat. Mia opened the door.

Jacob was standing there, hands deep in his pockets, his face solemn. "Hi, Mia."

"Hi." Mia was so tired. "Jacob, I don't mean to be rude, but it's late and I am exhausted. I should invite you in, but I really just want to go to sleep."

"Mia, this is important." His brows were pinched.

She hadn't talked to him since her failed exams. She'd seen

him here and there on campus, but they hadn't talked. Still, if he were really in trouble, she felt she owed him a hearing. And now he looked like he was in trouble. She sighed. "OK. Come in."

He shook his head. "No." His eyes drilled into her. "You've got to come out."

She closed her eyes. The quickest route to bed was to agree. "OK. Let me get a coat."

He took her elbow as they walked down the sidewalk. "Come."

He sat on a stone wall in front of one of the houses. "Come. Sit beside me."

She did as he asked.

"Mia, I'm leaving for Switzerland next week."

"Oh?" Mia knew Jacob had planned to get his degree by the end of this school year. Where, she wondered, did Switzerland fit into this plan?

"Yes." She could hear a flurry of pride as he talked. "I defended my thesis today, and I've gotten a postdoc at ETH."

"That's great!" Mia knew ETH, the Swiss Federal Institute of Technology, had a well respected math program. He had met his schedule for getting his degree.

"And John thinks the position would be perfect." John? It must be Professor Sitar. Now he was on a first-name basis with the professors?

The pride vanished from his voice. "Mia, I'm sorry about the way I acted the night of . . . ." He sighed. She waited. She felt the anger rising, but she didn't want a scene. She was finished with scenes.

"I've thought about it a lot . . . ." He took a deep breath. "I was very selfish, not seeing how much all that meant to you."

Mia agreed, but still held her tongue.

"Anyhow, I can't take it back." He sighed again.

The shortest route to rest was to accept the apology gracefully. "That's OK, Jacob. I know it was hard on you, too, having your life disrupted. It's in the past. Don't worry about it."

"Oh." His brows shot up, his eyes were wide. "Thank you!" He took another big breath. "Mia, I promised I'd not leave again without, well...."

She remembered his last departure, and how bereaved she had felt.

"And we haven't seen a lot of each other recently."

As little as possible, Mia thought.

"But I'm leaving now."

Yes, Mia thought, he had already said that.

"And I'd like...." He clasped his hands together and stared at her. "I'd like you to come with me."

It was Mia's turn to take in a breath. "Jacob!"

"Will you marry me?" Jacob asked. "I know that I don't understand people very well. I know that I have not always been good to you." His words ran together. "But I will do my best to be a good husband. I will do my very best." And then he stopped, his eyes glistening.

"Oh, Jacob." Why now? "I don't know." How could she say no to him, who had done so much soul searching? He had laid himself bare before her. How could she possibly say no? "I've got my prelims to take." She thought about her group and how far they'd come. "I've got to take them."

"You don't need to take them. You can come to Switzerland. They have a great program there. You could get your degree there."

Mia was silent. He didn't understand. He had said it himself. He didn't understand she had worked so hard for this. He didn't understand she was determined to get this done. That now, at last, she knew she could do this by herself.

"Jacob, it's important to me to take them. Here. Now."

"Oh." His eyes wandered over her face. "OK." He compressed his lips. "Take them and then we can get married. Or we can get married, tonight, tomorrow, whenever, and you can take them, and then you can come to Switzerland."

"It's important to me to get my degree." Where did that come from?

"Yes, of course."

But Mia thought this had not been in his plans.

"And going to Switzerland would make it more difficult." She had said no without saying no.

"Sure."

They sat in silence. A car drove past, its lights sweeping past them, its tires swishing on the pavement.

"You said you were tired. I'll walk you home."

They walked the few blocks back to Mia's house and she let herself in. He turned without a word. She watched as he walked down the street, his head down, his hands deep in his pockets.

Chapter Seventy-Three

Just her luck, Mia thought, drawing Professor Guthrie for her analysis committee. The scuttlebutt was that Professor Guthrie enjoyed unnerving students in oral exams. He wasn't particularly well known or brilliant. In fact, he never made full professor. Was that why he was such a pill? Maybe he wanted to prove he was better than all those uppity students who might be full professors one day.

Ah, well. She would muddle through. She would make sure she knew everything on the analysis exam. And, of course, she would have the group's trial exam, and George would play the part of Professor Guthrie. George could be a pill, but she found consolation in the fact that George was brilliant and George had studied Professor Guthrie, knew what he liked to ask and how he liked to ask it.

Wednesday evening was the last of the practice exams, and Tom, Nancy and George made up her mock analysis committee. Tom, one of the second-year students, could be counted on for solid questions. Nancy would only ask easy things. And then there was George.

She walked into her bedroom. This was her room, with her bedspread, her curtains, and here were three people who were supposed to test her, sitting at the foot of her bed. The blackboard was set up in front of her closet. Mia smiled at the group. This was not scary. Too bad they didn't hold these pseudo exams in the classrooms on campus. Too late for that.

George began the questioning with the theorem that had flummoxed her on her exam last fall. Well, good for him, making sure she was prepared. She wrote the proof that worked, the one she had missed before.

George considered her equations. "Explain the second equation."

Mia looked at it. She had always done the proof that way, always used what she thought was a well-known fact. "Isn't that clear?"

"No," George said, "I don't think so."

Then he asked her to write down a few equations, which, when she considered them, appeared to lead to a contradiction. Mia looked at the equations. She felt a flutter of concern. What was wrong with this line of reasoning?

"But," Nancy asked, "isn't that third line incorrect?" Nancy was looking at the new set of equations.

"Yes," Mia said. "That is where the problem is." She sent a thank-you look in Nancy's direction. George certainly had Mia worried. And she looked at George, hoping to see agreement. Instead she saw a glint in his eyes, almost glee.

"No." George pointed out the problem with that solution.

Mia considered his logic and then said, "But that is wrong because. . ." and the explanation flowed.

"You would think," George said, "but not true."

Again he found an error in Mia's thinking. The flutter of concern grew. She would not panic, she told herself. There must be a way out of this difficulty. She stared at the equations.

"But this is wrong because," Tom said and started in on an extended explanation, which Mia did not follow.

She could try to follow Tom's logic, but she found her mind stalled and felt tears building. She would not panic. She would not cry.

"Tom," George said, "that will not work, and I will not take the time to explain. This is, after all, Mia's exam, not yours."

Mia swallowed as she looked at Tom, who was shrinking

back on the bed. George had a grim little smile on his face.

Mia hated George, his fucking brilliance, his pride in getting her. He was an arrogant son of a bitch. He liked terrifying people. Nancy was right. He was a Nazi. Again she felt the tears building, and she wanted to run from the room. If she did not leave this minute, she would cry, right here in front of these people.

And what would she do then? Go wash dishes for a living?

No. Now was not a time to cry, like a helpless little girl. Now was not a time to run away.

She took a deep breath. Now and here, she was a mathematician who would find the answer to this problem. It wasn't about her. It wasn't about how good she was. It was about math. There was a problem somewhere and it was her job, at this moment, to resolve the problem. She liked resolving problems. She was good at resolving problems.

"OK," she said. "I am quite sure that the equation in the original proof is correct." George smirked. To hell with his arrogance. She would find his little error. "Let's go through these equations over here one at a time."

She looked at the first one. She talked her way through it and found nothing wrong, looking up at George, hoping to see some glimmer in his eyes to help her uncover the error. She looked at the second equation and then at George, his prideful little smile still there. She found nothing wrong with the second equation.

She stared at the third equation. It was wrong! She was sure it was wrong. She looked up at George, his confident grin unchanged. Maybe she was wrong. But she talked her way through it. It was not correct because — and she listed the reasons, looking at George the entire time.

George raised an objection to her logic. She considered it and wrote a few equations on the board. No, this objection was not valid and she listed her reasons. She looked at him and that smile was still there, but was it malicious? No. Maybe not.

"Good." George said. "I think maybe Tom has some questions for you."

Tom had questions, all out of the known list, and Nancy's questions were not difficult.

At last the hour was over. Mia was exhausted. It wasn't necessary to hold these sessions on campus. It had been scary enough right in her own bedroom.

Tonight was the group's last meeting before the exams. There were hugs and thank-yous and you'll-do-fines as the group departed. Mia was so tired. She just wished them to be out the door so she could have a glass of wine, a hot bath, and bed.

George lingered as the others said good night. He was the last to leave.

"Mia, I did everything I could to unnerve you," he said. "I just couldn't do it."

Mia stared at him.

"You make a fine Professor Guthrie!"

"I'm not sure that's a compliment."

"A little while ago, when you were questioning me, it wasn't. But now it is."

"You'll do great, even with Professor Guthrie. And thanks for organizing the group. It was helpful to all of us."

She blinked. "Even you?"

"Of course."

Chapter Seventy-Four

George's interrogation from last night rolled through her mind. She reviewed every detail, again and again.

Stop!

That was yesterday. Tomorrow would be the exam. Today was a day to get through as pleasantly as possible.

She'd borrowed her parents' car for a trip up to Tilden and a walk to her inspiration point. But first she treated herself to breakfast at the Virginia Bakery: croissants, Brie, and coffee. Not the healthiest meal, but she needed all the spoiling she could get. She exhaled, trying to calm her nerves as she walked into the parking lot.

Her parents' '56 Chevy was one of the few cars parked there, it being barely 8. The chrome detail on the side of the car carried her eye to the rear tire.

It was flat! Not maybe flat, but wheel-on-the-ground flat.

She closed her eyes and exhaled. She should have paid more attention in drivers ed. How do you change a tire?

She riffled through the glove compartment and found the car manual, breathing a thank-you to her mom, who insisted the manual be kept there.

"Got a problem?"

It was a familiar voice, one she didn't want to hear. She looked up at Sam's crooked smile, his wrinkled work shirt, his fraying jeans. Maybe if she ignored him he wouldn't be there. Or at least go away.

She found the section on changing tires in the book. She'd find everything she needed in the trunk.

"I've changed a few tires in my day."

She wondered whether he had slashed her tires. No. That was paranoid. How'd he know it was her car? She pushed past him to get to the trunk.

"Really. I'd be happy to do it for you."

She didn't look at him, but busied herself finding the things she needed.

"Not talking, huh?"

Yup, she thought. Why wasn't he in jail? That was something she'd like to know. But no, she just wanted to change the tire and be on her way.

"You didn't go to Switzerland with your lover."

Why did he care? He just wanted to annoy her. She shoved an umbrella and a raincoat to the side to get at the tire.

"You broke Jacob's heart, you know."

Funny. The last time he'd confronted her about "her lover," he'd accused her of being a whore. This time he only accused her of being a heartbreaker. An improvement, she supposed.

"You're smiling. You like hurting men?"

Her face warmed, but she concentrated on the tire problem. She pulled the tire out of the trunk. She found a heavy metal thing behind it and referred to the pictures in the manual. The jack. Two down, one to go.

"I suppose that's too harsh."

She snorted. She was peeved she'd reacted at all. The lug wrench was in the spare tire well.

"Part of it was my fault."

Really? She was so tempted to ask why, but no. She would not speak with this creep. She set the jack and lug wrench by the flat and stood to get the spare.

"I mean, if you hadn't found my materials, you'd never have called the cops, and...."

She stared at him, gripping the side of the trunk to keep her hands from shaking. She whispered so she wouldn't scream.

"If I hadn't found the materials you used to plan my father's murder?"

"Mia, Mia. I didn't plan that march!"

Sure, he didn't. She must ignore him. She lifted the spare from the trunk, placing it beside the other things on the ground.

"Really, Mia. I didn't plan it. I didn't take part in it."

Right. He had nothing to do with it. That's why he had all the planning materials in Jacob's apartment. She squatted by the flat, placing the manual on the ground face down. Fitting the lug wrench on the first lug, she found she had to lean down on the wrench to loosen the lug.

"It was Harry. Harry Blum."

Harry Blum. That name was familiar. Harry Blum. Harry and Gina. Harry and Gina holding hands, walking through the park next to Berkeley High.

"Harry with the red suspenders?"

Gina and Harry, holding hands, laughing, his red suspenders holding up his loose trousers, his battered copy of *Das Kapital* lying on the ground.

"You know who I mean, I can see you know."

Mia concentrated on the next lug.

"They deported him, you know. Blum was a bad sort."

What kind of sort was Sam? The lug loosened under her weight.

"The Blums of the world make the paranoids of the world think we true patriots are communists."

True patriot? Sure. The next lug gave way.

"We just want to stop this illegal war."

Right. Mia felt her weight pull the last lug loose.

"But the paranoids of the world think we're all the same. Paranoids like you."

Mia felt the smooth metal of the wrench's handle and looked up at Sam. It would be so easy to take a swing.

And it would feel so good.

Chapter Seventy-Five

Mia opened the door. "Chip! Come in, stranger." She hadn't seen him much since she picked him up from the airport after Christmas. He'd been busy with his courses, a full load in subjects that were not comfortable for him. She had been busy herself with the group and her own courses.

"I brought this for you." He handed her a bottle.

"Thanks!" The green glass had a white label and gold foil. Cook's Champagne. Chip was becoming a Californian! "Thanks, but how do you know I deserve it?"

"I knew you'd pass the day you told me about the study group." He grinned.

"How did you know the exams were today?"

His eyes sparkled with mischief. "I have my ways."

Mia didn't care how he knew. She thought she couldn't smile wide enough. "Chip, not only did I pass, everyone in the group passed. A clean sweep!"

"Wow!"

"Come join the celebration!" Mia pulled him into the room. "Let me introduce you to everyone."

After the introductions, Claire found some real glasses.

Chip popped the bottle and poured. He held his glass high. "To Mia, the girl mathematician!"

His eyes danced, and she couldn't help but think about the day she changed her major. She laughed and touched his glass with hers. Their glasses sang delicately.

They settled on the floor in the corner, sipping the wine. "How was the dreaded ordeal?"

"It's a blur now." She could hardly remember anything about today. Yesterday, Sam had finally departed. She had been so angry she didn't dare drive the car even though she had managed to change the tire. Instead she had walked several miles to Tilden. By the time she had reached her inspiration point, she was panting and sweating, but calm. She had carried that calm into the exams today, and they had flown by. "It seemed pretty smooth. Even the evil Professor Guthrie seemed to toss me soft balls."

She noticed Nancy and George in the far corner of the living room. She pointed them out to Chip. "See those two, the tiny girl sitting on that fellow's lap?"

He looked in the direction she indicated. "Sure."

"She was the one I was most worried about, but she passed."

"And the fellow?"

"George?" Mia laughed. "He's a genius. No doubt about him." She took another sip. "But what's funny is I thought Nancy was so mad at him. She thought he was being too hard on her. And now look at them!"

"They seem pretty friendly."

"Look at what success has wrought!"

Mia felt a twinge of regret. Claire had seemed to like George. She scanned the room and saw Claire talking to Tom, laughing. It would be OK.

Mia turned her gaze to Chip. "You know, I'd like to get out of here. Let's go for a walk."

Shouldn't she stay and be the hostess? No, she thought, not tonight. Tonight she deserved to do exactly what she wanted.

Mia walked over to where Claire and Tom were talking. "Claire," Mia asked, "can you handle the party if I leave?"

"Sure."

Mia and Chip slipped out unnoticed. They walked along College, past the crowds on the street.

367

"So what are you going to do now?"

"Look for a thesis topic."

"No rest for the wicked?"

"Oh, I suppose I'll take a couple of days to do the laundry, clean up my room, pay bills," Mia said, "but I want to get a thesis topic. Professor Sitar said he had some problems I might be interested in." She looked at him. "Or maybe I'll do something with computers, like what was being done at MIT."

"So you've launched," Chip said. "You've found your niche."

"It feels pretty good right now," Mia said. "We'll see how it goes."

They walked in silence. They crossed a bridge over a stream that ran through a small grove of redwoods. Mia stopped and looked down into the water. Chip looked, too.

"How about you?" Mia asked. "Have you decided what you're going to do next?"

"Not yet," Chip said. "I got into the design school in L.A., the one with the famous stylist. He designs how the car looks. Got the letter today. And the Berkeley engineering department has accepted me, too. That's the route to being an automotive engineer."

"Wow!" Mia wasn't surprised. She had seen his drawings.

Maybe she should be surprised. He had come so far from the first time she saw him in Walnut Creek. But she was — what was it? Proud? No, that was condescending. Happy for him? More than that. Maybe excited for him.

"So that champagne was for you, too."

"Guess so." Chip captured her gaze. "But I'm having trouble deciding whether I want to design the outside of cars or engineer the guts."

Mia remembered seeing the Avanti and how she teased him about becoming an auto mechanic. She peered into the flowing water, the light of a lamp overhead glinting off the ripples.

Chip was special to her.

Chip might move to L.A.

L.A. was four hundred miles away.

"L.A. You'll be one of those ugly Southern Californians. You know, Beach Blanket Bingo, surfing...." She looked at him.

"Yeah. I think you told me about them." His blue eyes laughed at her. "A long time ago."

"I don't think you'd make a good Southern Californian." He wasn't the type. He was thoughtful. He was serious. "And I don't think you'd be half as happy designing the outside of cars."

"Why?" There was still mirth in his eyes, but he squinted.

"No, engineering the guts would be much more fun."

She could see he was interested.

"And there'd be other benefits to working on the guts."

He was smiling now. He knew where she was going.

"You'd stay here."

He was grinning.

"With me."

Acknowledgements

Thank you to the many people who helped me with this novel.

My critique group, including Alan Balkema, Alisa Alering, Richard Durisen, Carol Edge, Ron Edge, Chas Culp, Dennis McCarty, and Jim Stark, read and commented on various chapters. They helped me understand POV and PTSD, helped me make my scenes more vivid, and encouraged me along the way.

Jim Stark not only critiqued various chapters but also helped me make sure the sailing scene made sense.

Without the various law cases Mark Cutler found for me, the jury scene would not have been.

The blue Avanti and the design school in L.A. would not have appeared without the help of Kenneth Weyand.

My beta readers read an entire draft and commented. Thank you, Carol Edge, Karen Haas, Kathy Halligan, Anita Marsh, and Phyllis Weyand.

The Bancroft Library at University of California, Berkeley, allowed me to read through various archives related to Berkeley in the 1960s.

Ashley Perez read an early draft of the novel and provided input that improved this novel and will improve my next novels.

Ashley was one of the instructors at the excellent Highlights Foundation workshop on the Historical Novel. Kathy Cannon Wiechman, another of the instructors, read my first 15 pages and offered valuable advice, as did Carmine Coco Young, Teddi Ahrens and Karen Haas.

I also took the Odyssey Online Course, *One Brick at a Time*, where I worked on what became the second chapter of

Becoming Mia. Barbara Ashford, the instructor, dissected this chapter with me, helping me understand how to make it work.

Alisa Alering has encouraged me in so many ways, reading my work and commenting, and recommending both the Odyssey course and the Highlights Foundation workshop.

Paul Teller, Gina Moreno, and Janos Kirz discussed their remembrances of 1960s Berkeley, which made the Berkeley scenes more realistic.

The Facebook group Conservative Libertarian Fiction Alliance critiqued my cover, and their input helped make it much more eye-catching.

Last, and most important, thank you to my husband, Rich Weyand, who has put up with all my writing woes, who has tried to teach me how to spell and punctuate, who made sure the train scene was realistic, and who has edited the book, designed the cover, and handled all the publishing work. I would not have a book without him.

Wendy Teller
Bloomington, Indiana
April 3, 2018

If you enjoyed this book visit my website, WendyTeller.com, for interesting background on some of the historical incidents in *Becoming Mia*, to get a glimpse of the next novel, and to read my blog.

About the Author

Wendy Teller received her AB from Harvard University and her MA from the University of California, Berkeley. She was a systems and software engineer in the process control and telecommunications industries.

Now that she is retired she writes fiction, memoir, and history. Her stories have appeared in *Chicken Soup for the Soul*, *The Naperville Sun*, and *Rivulets*. Her story *Dusting the Towels* received the Richard Eastman Prose Award. Wendy's debut novel, *Becoming Mia*, takes place in the 1960s in Cambridge, Massachusetts, and Berkeley, California. Her next project, *Ella*, takes place in the early 1900s in Hungary.

Wendy lives on a cliff in the woods near Bloomington, Indiana, with her husband.

Made in the USA
Lexington, KY
25 April 2018